PRAISE FOR Michael Sinclair
and the 1920s Mystery Series

"The author springs some very good surprises."

—ELIZABETH FERRARS—
veteran author of over fifty novels of mystery and suspense

"It's been a long time since I've enjoyed a mystery as much as this one. The historical background in 1927 was fascinating. The suspense was so effective that I wanted to keep reading and not put it down. The characters were cleverly drawn and believable. Highly recommended."

—GOODREADS.COM—
review of *Murder in Cucumber Alley*

A COFFIN IS WAITING

A 1920s Mystery

MICHAEL SINCLAIR

By Michael Sinclair in the 1920s historical mystery series:

An Unfortunate Coincidence

The Consequences of Murder

Murder in Cucumber Alley

Darker than the Night

Raise Your Glass to Murder

A Coffin is Waiting

A COFFIN IS WAITING

ISBN: 978-1-78324-377-8 (hardback)
ISBN: 978-1-78324-376-1 (ebook)

FIRST EDITION

Published by Wordzworth Publishing

CHAPTER ONE

March 1925

Albany, New York

Just before eight o'clock on Tuesday morning, the tenth of March, Mr. Clement Lewis, a distinguished attorney well known in the local legal community, was found dead at his desk in his prestigious law firm.

An ominous gloom shrouded the morning, threatening rain showers mixed with snow. Trolleys clanged thunderously down State Street, sharing space with cars and trucks. Pedestrians scurried along the sidewalks, dodging each other and the cumbersome raindrops. Slushy pavements from leftover snow and biting winds hastened their footsteps.

Mrs. Rose Castle arrived at the law firm and began her workday as usual. She left her fur trimmed coat on the rack behind the door, placed her cloche hat beside it, secured her purse in her desk drawer and entered a kitchenette to prepare coffee. A routine day, she thought, nothing out of the ordinary. She fixed the coffee and then glanced in a mirror on the wall.

Mrs. Castle fluffed up her grayish-brown hair and straightened her string of pearls. At fifty-six, she was robust and appealing, with a pleasant and optimistic demeanor. Recently, she had purchased new clothes at Whitney's Department Store, keeping up with the latest styles. New dresses, pearls, and a cloche hat suited her fine. She did without the excessive makeup and perfume popular with the younger set.

As she settled into her desk chair, she shivered slightly. Winter still had a grip on the city. Wind hammered at the windows, creating a chilly atmosphere inside. She looked forward to spring but on days like this, she reflected, its arrival seemed an eternity.

Her mind flew to the lawyers and their rather demanding, irritable moodiness. While accustomed to their whims and paroxysms, Mrs. Castle sparkled in her efficiency as the office manager. Her approach oscillated between tyrannical rule and motherly warmth. Few could match her meticulousness. In nearly twenty years, Mrs. Castle had rarely missed a day and took pride in arriving early, her steadfast commitment exemplary. She knew that anything could transpire in a law office, but she managed to persevere. Truly little affected her staunchness and unbending countenance.

She noticed Mr. Lewis's office door closed. She frowned; it was unusual for him to leave it that way. She rose from her chair, her routine momentarily interrupted, and approached the door. After a gentle tap received no answer, she hesitated. Her pulse quickened slightly as she opened the door and saw the elderly man slumped over his desk.

At first, she thought Mr. Lewis was simply asleep. However, as she stepped closer, a cold dread settled in her stomach. Mr. Lewis was dead.

Over the years, Mrs. Castle had dealt with many strange circumstances, but a dead body was another matter altogether. She felt for a pulse, confirming what she already knew. She knew Judge Archie had been at the office yesterday afternoon and had continued working with Mr. Lewis when she left for the day. She looked around, as though seeking assistance, despite knowing she was the only person present. Her mind raced. Nevertheless, she sobered herself from her unique stupor and placed several telephone calls.

Within fifteen minutes, Mr. Clayton Sampson, Attorney at Law, arrived along with his wife, Lucille, both employed at the law firm. Mrs. Sampson, overwrought, sat in the outer office, tearful and visibly upset. As a legal assistant at the firm, Mrs. Sampson was known for occasional bursts of emotional distress. She also was known for an egotistic, opinionated attitude, but at that moment, she attempted a brave composure given the extremely unpleasant circumstances. Mr. Sampson asked Mrs. Castle if she had contacted Judge Archie, who was Mr. Lewis's close friend and colleague. Mrs. Castle shook her head. She told him she did not wish to upset the judge or Mrs. Stafford at home. After all, she pointed out, the Staffords were quite advanced in age, and any undue stress would be detrimental.

Mr. Sampson, a heavy-set, distinguished man of fifty-five with an arrogant tilt of his head and piercing blue eyes, mentioned the importance of contacting the authorities. Mrs. Castle, however, dismissed the idea. It would mean the police at the law firm, and that would never do. Neither Mr. Lewis nor Judge Archie would have tolerated such a thing.

Mr. Sampson disagreed and told her that in cases of uncertain death, the police must be informed. Mrs. Castle was appalled; it certainly was not murder, so what was the purpose of the police? Ignoring Mrs. Castle's pleas, he picked up the Western Electric candlestick telephone on her desk and asked the operator to contact the police. Two policemen arrived within five minutes, having just answered a case of robbery on South Pearl Street.

Mrs. Castle and Mr. Sampson conferred with them in Mr. Lewis's office. Mrs. Castle reiterated that she did not want to contact the judge yet as she did not wish to cause him any undue stress at his age. The policeman told her the judge would need to be informed regardless and made a note in a pad to contact Judge Archie Stafford at his residence this morning.

One of the officers contacted headquarters to send an ambulance to the law firm of Lewis and Stafford, North Pearl Street, along with the photographer. In no time, the office became a scene of chaotic activity. The police photographer took pictures, and the dead body was removed to the city morgue. More questions, probing, inquiries into Mr. Lewis's health and state of mind followed. Mrs. Castle said as far as she knew, Mr. Lewis was in good health and had no undue issues in his life. He was a widower and lived alone in a fashionable apartment on State Street. His only child, a son of uncertain middle age, lived in Olean, New York, but he was estranged from him and had little, if any, contact.

The policeman then questioned the Sampsons. Mr. Clayton Sampson patiently answered the questions put to him. He commented that Mr. Lewis was elderly and perhaps had a bad heart—after all, he was nearly eighty.

Mrs. Sampson looked at the policeman as though in fear for her life. Obviously unused to any sort of turmoil, Lucille Sampson was clearly disturbed by the recent ordeal. She was rather bumptious and brusque at times, precise, frank, demanding in a girlish way, and full of self-importance. Tall and slender, with a pretty face, expressive blue eyes and neat brown hair worn in the bob style, Lucille Sampson, at fifty, could easily be taken for ten years younger. She forced a weak smile and reiterated her husband's comments. Mr. Lewis was an industrious lawyer, almost ready to retire, who most likely had a heart attack and never returned home the last evening. She commented he was a good friend to Archibald Stafford, a well-respected judge in Albany, who began the law firm many years ago. After retiring, he passed the reins to Mr. Lewis but continued assisting him with casework.

The policeman told them he was quite familiar with Judge Archie's fifty-year career in law enforcement and his steadfast reputation. He scribbled notes in a pad and thanked the Sampsons for the information.

Within a few days, Judge Archie scheduled an autopsy and the police continued their arduous investigation despite making little headway and no firm convictions. A shocking turn of events soon altered the circumstances completely. The postmortem and the updated police report confirmed it: a sheer calamity, inconceivable, malevolent, and shocking. The glaring articles in the newspapers instilled fear, distrust, outrage, and suspicion within the community.

After receiving the autopsy results, Judge Archie requested his grandson to contact a private investigator whose office was located in the Albany City Savings Bank Building, an imposing structure that loomed over the bustling streets of the city.

The embodiment of magnificence, the Albany City Savings Bank Building was known locally as an architectural masterpiece. In the center of State Street downtown, its marble floors and vaulted ceilings contributed to its fine reputation, along with the numerous businesses and state agencies that enhanced its eleven floors.

On the fifth floor, private investigator Sloan Sheppard found himself one Monday morning with a relatively empty desk and a silent telephone. The office was quiet, save for the distant hum of traffic and the occasional creak of the old building. Sunlight filtered through the blinds, casting striped shadows across the room.

At the moment, a few cases needed his utmost attention. An urgent report on an assault with a deadly weapon required his review. The victim, a boy delivering the morning newspaper, was listed in stable condition at St. Timothy's Hospital. His assailant had been located at a garage on Green Street in Albany's South End neighborhood. A warrant was issued, and the man was in police custody, much to Sloan's relief. The victim's parents sought his expertise, and through his investigation and work with the police, he ensured the assailant was brought to justice.

His thoughts turned to recently concluded cases and those still needing his attention. One folder contained a divorce proceeding, and another underneath it concerned a custody dispute. He sighed, running a hand through his black hair, contemplating the day ahead.

At only thirty-five, Sloan Sheppard had already established a solid reputation as a competent detective, who had collaborated effectively with the Albany Police on various cases. At six feet two, his strong physical strength and endurance aided him in capturing criminals, although the scar on his chin invoked the calamities he had endured over time. His executive appearance and no-nonsense demeanor cemented his unquestionable status as a true detective, passionately committed to his investigative undertakings, rather exacting and insistent in his approach. Mr. Sheppard's cases nearly always ended in victory, much to his clients' satisfaction.

Sloan lit a cigarette, exhaled smoke slowly, and then leaned back in his swivel chair, looking out the window. It was a cool yet bright early spring day. He read in the *Times Union* that snow showers were due later, although the calendar had already turned to spring. Typical of Albany, he mused. Spring was usually slow in arriving and the fact that it was late March did not preclude more inclement weather. He could see the tops of nearby buildings and a sliver of the sky. He took a drag of his cigarette, the smoke drifting around him like a shroud.

He was about to consider what to order for lunch when the candlestick telephone on the corner of his desk rang. He looked at it, nonplused. He had gotten used to a silent telephone lately. With only a few cases left, he expected a brief reprieve. Nevertheless, he glanced at his desk calendar for today, Monday, March 23, 1925. Seeing there were no expected clients for the afternoon, he picked up the handset, anticipating a new client.

"Sloan Sheppard speaking," he said with his usual professional greeting.

Sloan considered himself an expert in judging character even over the telephone wires. In his private investigations, he had dealt with people from different lifestyles: divorces, child custody, gangsters, loan sharks, drug dealers, bootleggers, kidnappers. His perseverance earned him countless clients, securing his solid reputation and unwavering commitment to integrity.

He heard a young man on the other end of the telephone, rather unsteadily and somewhat nervously, asking him to come to his grandfather's house for dinner. The young man explained that his grandfather, Judge Archie Stafford, did not get out too often and wished to speak to Mr. Sheppard in the privacy of their home.

"I'm his grandson, Preston Hughes," the young male voice added, as though that summed up the purpose of the invitation.

Sloan knew Judge Archie well, although he had not seen him for several years. He figured Judge Archie must be close to eighty. He hesitated about the invitation as he usually kept business appointments to his office, but in this case, he might make an exception. When he asked Preston about the nature of the appointment, he listened carefully to a lengthy discourse about a most troublesome recent event, which he had read about in the newspapers.

As he listened, he estimated Preston to be in his late twenties, possibly nearing thirty. Certainly articulate, intelligent, and resourceful, most likely dedicated to his family, as he explained how he, his widowed mother, widowed aunt, and grandparents lived in the family mansion on the corner of State and South Swan Streets, diagonal to the Capitol Building and across from West Capitol Park. He stressed that his grandfather wished to speak to no one else about this urgent matter but Mr. Sheppard.

Sloan extinguished his cigarette, sat upright, and drew his notepad in front of him. Taking up his fountain pen, he scribbled a few lines, then cleared his throat and addressed his caller. From Preston's account and the newspaper reports, Sloan knew the matter was serious.

He glanced again at his calendar and, except for his weightlifting at the YMCA, his evenings this week were free of obligations. He arranged to meet the family of Judge Archie Stafford at his home at six o'clock on Thursday evening, the twenty-sixth.

Preston Hughes waited with the usual crowd on Broadway for the trolley to take him up State Street, where he would get off at the corner of Washington Avenue and proceed across West Capitol Park to home. It was almost five o'clock and the workday was ending.

Bundled in his jacket, his cap low on his head, he lit a cigarette and puffed rather irritably, as it was colder than he realized. He shivered slightly, wishing it were summer and the cold days were finally over.

The trolley arrived with a clatter, and Preston boarded, finding a window seat. As it trundled up State Street, he watched the familiar sights pass by—the bustling shops, the grand buildings, and the people hurrying home. The rhythmic clanging of the trolley bell and the murmur of conversations filled the air. His thoughts drifted to the upcoming dinner with Mr. Sheppard. He hoped the private investigator would be able to help his grandfather. The death of Mr. Lewis had cast a shadow over their family, and they needed answers.

Arriving at the corner of Washington Avenue, with the ornate columns of the State Education Building brilliantly lit in the encroaching darkness, he got off. He crossed at the stoplight, the cold wind biting at his face, and then hurried through the park, dead leaves crunching underfoot. The gusty winds rustled the bare branches of the trees, adding to the eerie atmosphere. The grass was a dull brown, but he knew that soon enough, the park would be alive with the colors of spring. He took a deep breath, the cold air filling his lungs, and quickened his pace towards the opulent mansion on the corner of State and South Swan Streets, its grand facade standing out against the darkening sky. The sound of the leaves underfoot and the distant howl of the wind heightened his sense of urgency. Despite the cold, a bead of sweat formed on his brow as he neared the mansion. His mind raced with thoughts of what awaited him inside.

At twenty-eight, Preston was rather brusque at times, yet he exhibited a pleasing countenance that often softened the impression. He was handsome in a serious way, with sharp features and a determined expression. Standing six feet tall, with brown hair center-parted and a slim build, his expressive green eyes reflected a mix of intelligence and curiosity. He dressed impeccably, favoring tailored suits that spoke of both his family's wealth and his own sense of style. Despite his polished exterior, there was an air of restlessness about him—a desire to carve out his own path in a world that often seemed predetermined by his family's expectations.

Preston was employed as a salesclerk at the Hudson River Day Cruise Line company on lower Broadway. He graduated from the State Teachers College in 1918 with a degree in English. He then landed a position with the popular cruise line, where he sold tickets and arranged boat trips as well as scenic cruises for hundreds of people up and down the majestic Hudson River between Albany and New York City. Just recently, he scheduled a group tour to the historic sites in Kingston and Newburgh and another to West Point and Yonkers.

Preston often wrestled with a lingering restlessness. The routine of his job, while comfortable, sometimes left him yearning for something more. He found solace in literature, often losing himself in the works of his favorite authors during his free time. His degree had instilled in him a deep appreciation for the written word, and he often dreamed of one day writing a novel of his own. His true ambition lay in the field of law. Inspired by his grandfather, Judge Archie Stafford, Preston harbored a desire to become a lawyer. He had applied to Albany Law School and was anxiously awaiting a response.

Preston lived with his grandparents, widowed mother, and widowed aunt in the family mansion. Like many young people, he had considered renting his own apartment, but the mansion was so big that he had the third floor practically to himself. He got along well with his grandparents, his aunt, and his mother, so why throw money away needlessly on an apartment? Besides, his job was just a short trolley ride away, which was another advantage. As he thought about the dinner, he felt a mix of hope and anxiety, wondering what Mr. Sheppard might uncover.

Shivering as the wind pushed against him, Preston quickened his pace toward home. Most likely Gertrude, the family maid, would be busy in the kitchen preparing dinner. The radio would be on in the living room, with the fireplace blazing comfortably and his grandfather ensconced in his favorite armchair, engrossed in the evening newspaper. The routine never varied and Preston was grateful for his family, who provided him with a nurturing, supportive home life.

Upon entering, he was enveloped by warmth and the comforting presence of cooking filled the air, drifting from the kitchen. He greeted his mother who stood before him in the hallway.

"I thought of taking a walk before dinner," Martha Hughes greeted her son, smiling pleasantly. She glanced at the windows on each side of the large front door. "But the wind is howling something fierce and it looks dreadful out. I'm glad you're home, dear."

Preston took off his coat and cap and left them on the hallway bench. He commented on the brisk winds and the chance of snow showers later in the evening.

"Your grandfather is in the living room," Mrs. Hughes said, her voice slightly unsteady. "He'd like to speak to you, about the telephone call you were to make today." She turned to her son, lowering her voice. "You *did* place the call, didn't you?"

Preston nodded. "Yes, I spoke with Mr. Sheppard this morning. I planned to tell everyone about it this evening." He knew what his mother was thinking, having dealt with his grandfather's whims often enough.

Martha Hughes was relieved. She knew her father, Judge Archie, was archaic to the extreme and exacting, even with his own family. But like her sister Joan and her mother, Martha knew there was a softer side to the judge.

She was a robust middle-aged woman of fifty-five, with pleasing, soft features and a down to earth personality. Her husband fell victim to the flu pandemic eight years ago, leaving Martha to navigate widowhood while continuing to support her son as he stepped into adulthood. She had been employed at the State Capitol almost thirty years and as the commute was a simple five minute walk away, she had no intention yet of retiring.

Preston understood her thoughts—he often reflected on his father and the generosity of his grandparents in taking them in after his death. The house they owned was too large for just the two of them, so in 1918 they moved in with her parents in their mansion on State and South Swan Streets, the house she grew up in. It was an amicable arrangement, keeping Judge Archie, his wife Augusta, and Martha's sister Joan—also a widow—company.

"Hello, Father," Martha said pleasantly, entering the living room. "Preston is here."

Preston went forward and hugged his grandfather, who was comfortably seated in his favorite armchair by the fireplace. An Albany native, Judge Archibald Stafford was a rather large, formidable patriarch, eighty years old, but an active lifestyle and constant mental stimulation had kept him youthful and vigorous. He had a few health issues, including concerns about his heart and high blood pressure, as well as aches and pains in his legs, possibly gout. His dark brown eyes appeared tired, as though the latest ordeal with Mr. Lewis had drained his energy. An experienced lawyer and respected judge in Albany, he had worked side by side with his colleague and friend, Mr. Clement Lewis, for over thirty years. After retiring ten years ago, the judge spent several days a week at his former office, debriefing with his colleague on current cases and other legal issues.

The living room, like the rest of the rooms in the family mansion, was large, ornately furnished and extremely comfortable. A Victorian sofa was against the wall overlooking State Street and two armchairs were on either side of the fireplace. A radio console was in a corner and bookcases lined the other side, with books nearly overflowing from their shelves.

While Preston and his mother lived on the third floor, his Aunt Joan had the top floor to herself. His grandparents lived on the first floor, enabling them to have privacy as needed. The second floor contained the judge's library and study room and an additional bedroom. A close-knit family, Preston was committed to his mother and grandparents as well as caring for his Aunt Joan.

"Sit down, Preston," the judge ordered, placing his cup of tea and the evening newspaper on the end table next to him. "You were to place a telephone call for me today. I assume you were successful at it. I did not hear from you earlier."

Preston and his mother sat on the Victorian sofa across from the judge. He took out his pack of cigarettes from his pants pocket. While lighting one, he told his grandfather, "I spoke with Mr. Sloan Sheppard this morning and included all the necessary information." He took a slow drag from his cigarette, glancing first at his grandfather, then at his mother, who was carefully maintaining her composure. He waited to hear his grandfather's response. From experience, he knew his grandfather's reactions could range from outright anger and harshness to, perhaps, quiet satisfaction.

"We'll discuss it in detail after dinner," the judge said firmly. "Gertrude has prepared a fine meal and I do not want anything to spoil it." He paused, sipping his tea. He then cleared his throat and continued speaking, as though to himself. "Clement and I worked at the law firm for over thirty years. When I retired, the firm became his, and he maintained the dignity and professionalism we worked so hard to establish. Now, that legacy is shattered. My friend died needlessly."

"Grandfather, you really shouldn't put yourself through this," Preston said gently, his voice tinged with concern.

"He was murdered," the judge added harshly, his eyes narrowing with a fierce determination.

Preston and Martha exchanged worried glances when Gertrude entered and announced that dinner was served. The sudden interruption brought an uneasy silence. From the judge's furrowed brow and clenched jaw, Gertrude noticed the tension but said nothing, quietly leading the family to the dining room.

The dining room was grand, with a long mahogany table set with fine dishes and silverware that gleamed under the chandelier's soft light. Portraits of stern ancestors lined the walls, watching over the proceedings with silent judgment.

Preston and Martha took their places at the table, with Judge Archie at the head, as always. To Preston, it was simply the natural order: wherever his grandfather sat became the head of the table. As they settled in, the tension in the room was tangible, each family member lost in thoughts about the murder that had shaken the normalcy of everyday life.

Gertrude soon returned, depositing a bowl of vegetables and another of hot rolls on the table. She began serving, first approaching the judge, as usual. Preston's aunt, Joan Caves, then entered. She managed to have a polite smile, her eyes briefly meeting each of theirs. "Good evening," she greeted them perfunctorily before taking her seat next to her sister, Martha. Joan's presence added a familiar comfort to the room, though a slight strain tugged at her normally composed demeanor.

"Good evening, Joan," Judge Archie addressed his youngest daughter, while helping himself to roast beef from the platter Gertrude held out to him.

Joan smiled at her elderly father. Though only fifty, she carried an air of someone older, worn by life's trials—unlike her sister. The many storms she had weathered over the years had taken their toll. Her husband had died of tuberculosis, and she had suffered two miscarriages during their marriage. The strain had etched lines of sorrow on her face. After her husband's death, her parents had offered her a place in their home, and like Martha and Preston, she had decided to return to the house she grew up in.

As she sat next to Martha, the aroma of the roast beef filled the room, mingling with the scent of freshly baked rolls. The warmth of the dining room contrasted with the chill of her memories, but Joan found comfort in the familiar surroundings and the presence of her family.

She was attractive in a conventional sense, with a fine head of brown hair streaked with wisps of gray and steady blue eyes. Rather demure and soft-spoken, Joan was employed at the State Education Department as a secretary, just across from West Capitol Park. She had spent twenty years there and had considered retirement, but the work did her good, and with several friends in the office, she decided to remain, at least for the time being.

"Hello, everyone," an elderly woman stood in the doorway and greeted them pleasantly. Augusta Stafford entered and sat next to her husband at the head of the table. "I see Gertrude has prepared another delicious meal." She looked appreciatively at the food and at her family, relishing in the comfort they gave her.

"Good evening, Grandmother," Preston said warmly, his voice breaking the brief silence. Martha and Joan echoed his greeting, their faces softening at Augusta's presence.

Mrs. Augusta Stafford was seventy-eight years old and like her husband, an Albany native. After graduating from the state teachers college, she taught elementary school for thirty years. Rather tall, with a fine head of grayish-brown hair, her face was relatively free of wrinkles and her smile was sincere and genuine. She tolerated her husband's frequent moods with good humor, although she would admit to her grandson and daughters that the judge was rather taxing at times. She doted on her daughters as well as her only grandchild and was active in community events and social causes, including the Albany chapter of the League of Women Voters.

"I was in the sewing room," she explained as Gertrude handed her a tray containing warm rolls. "I'm making a sweater for you, Preston. If these cold days continue, you'll need it."

They ate in comparative silence, until everyone had plenty and dessert was eventually served. Gertrude returned with coffee, a jug of cream and a freshly baked chocolate cake. She cut it, dished out servings, and then filled cups with coffee. After she returned to the kitchen, Judge Archie cleared his throat and addressed his family rather seriously.

"I waited until our meal was over to discuss what has been on my mind. I asked Preston to contact Mr. Sloan Sheppard, a private detective here in Albany, someone with whom I have worked before." He paused. "Preston, I would like to hear what you have to tell us."

All eyes turned to Preston as he sipped his coffee and finished his cake. He wiped his mouth on a napkin and turned to his grandfather. "I explained the situation to him, and he told me he read about it in the newspapers. I invited him here for dinner on Thursday, at six o'clock."

Judge Archie nodded. "Perfect, that's exactly what I wanted. What else did Mr. Sheppard tell you? He did remember me, I assume."

"Yes, he knew who you were right away. He'll be here for dinner, as you requested."

Martha's eyes widened slightly, and Joan exchanged a worried glance with her mother. The room, which had been filled with the warmth of family and food, now felt charged with a new, uneasy energy. The rich taste of chocolate lingered on Preston's tongue, contrasting with the seriousness of the conversation. The warmth of the coffee cup in his hands was a small comfort as he met his grandfather's steady gaze.

"I'll tell Gertrude to prepare an extra special dinner," Augusta said, her voice calm but laced with tension.

Judge Archie shook his head. "No need for that. Mr. Sheppard will be here as our guest, but the dinner is secondary. Mr. Sheppard's reputation precedes him. We need someone who can see through the fog of this case and uncover the truth about Clement's murder. The police have no leads and take forever to close a case."

"Father, must you say murder?" Joan said, her voice trembling slightly. "That word upsets me greatly." She put down the delicate porcelain coffee cup, its floral pattern reflecting the chandelier light. She glanced at her father and then at the others around the table, her eyes wide with concern.

Augusta spoke up before the judge had the chance. "There is no reason for alarm, Joan. If Mr. Sheppard finds something out that we should know, then that will clarify any remaining questions. After all, Mr. Lewis's death was rather sudden." She tried to maintain a reassuring tone, but a slight quiver in her voice betrayed her own worries.

"He seemed fine when I saw him recently," Martha commented. "Remember, Father, when I stopped at the office on the way home? He was in such good spirits then."

"That's my point. An autopsy was performed, as you all know. The results were inconclusive, but it showed he ingested a poisonous substance found in berries."

"How dreadful," Joan exclaimed, clearly taken aback.

"What does that prove?" Preston asked, although he feared the answer.

Judge Archie finished his coffee. "There must have been acidic residue in the tea. I made the tea and poured two cups, one for Mr. Lewis and one for myself. Mr. Lewis drank from my cup by mistake. When I left for the day, about five fifteen, he decided to remain and finish the current report. Mrs. Castle, the Sampsons, and the others had already left."

"And you mentioned this to the police, didn't you?" Martha asked.

The judge nodded. "Yes, but the cups were washed that morning, probably by Mrs. Sampson or Mrs. Castle, thinking nothing of it, until the autopsy report. The police have no leads at all. Naturally, they assume Mr. Lewis committed suicide, which is absurd. He had no suicidal inclination." He shrugged, his irritation evident as he rather angrily put down his cup. "When I'm at the office, I always have a cup of tea in the afternoons. I didn't bother to look inside the cups as I poured the water. One usually does not do such a thing." He paused, clearly irritated. "Mrs. Sampson or Mrs. Castle always clean the kitchen area. Miss Blake also makes tea for herself and sometimes Burgess, Thurman, and Quentin."

Preston marveled at the number of employees at the law firm. It had prospered over time, allowing his grandfather to expand the staff. He was acquainted with Quentin Cooper, just a few years older than himself, in his role as law clerk. He knew Mr. Burgess Smith and Mr. Thurman Armstrong, both fastidious lawyers, only through his grandfather's stories.

On a few occasions, he had met Mrs. Rose Castle and Mrs. Lucille Sampson, along with her husband, Mr. Clayton Sampson, while visiting his grandfather at the office. Miss Doris Blake was a busy secretary and rather a flapper. He wondered if there was something in all the speculation that he did not see, at least not at the moment. He turned his attention back to his grandfather as he continued speaking to his family.

"Who discovered Mr. Lewis, Father?" Joan asked, stirring cream into her coffee.

The judge put down his coffee cup. "Mrs. Castle, of course," he replied, as though his daughter should have known that fact already. "Mrs. Castle usually is the first to arrive, setting everything in order for the day ahead. She noticed Clement's office door closed and, upon entering, saw him slumped over his desk. Naturally, at first, she thought he had had a heart attack. She called the Sampsons, and Clayton and Lucille arrived promptly, as did the police." He paused. "The rest is most distressing." He fumbled for words, something uncommon for the judge. Augusta laid a hand on his arm and consoled him compassionately.

"He drank from my teacup." He looked at the faces around the table. "I believe that poisoned cup was meant for me. Clement drank it by mistake."

A chorus of shock and disbelief rippled through the room before the judge silenced them with a raised, wrinkled hand. "That's what I think. We've already spoken to the police, and I conveyed my thoughts to them. That's why I wish for Mr. Sheppard to investigate."

"Most likely it was the type of tea, Father," Joan said sensibly. "Didn't you tell us it was a new aromatic blend? Some teas can be acidic, even toxic. I've read about it in the newspapers."

"Possibly, but I do not wish to discuss this further. We will speak with Mr. Sheppard Thursday evening."

Everyone seemed to accept his rather abrupt termination of the topic. The rest of the conversation revolved around Joan's work at the State Education Department and Martha's duties at the State Capitol. Preston remarked on the increase in ticket sales for Hudson River cruises. Augusta commented on her volunteer work at the community center, in addition to her involvement with the League of Women Voters. She mentioned that the 1926 presidential election would be the third allowing women the opportunity to vote, paramount to the success of the suffrage movement.

"Balderdash," the judge grumbled harshly, his face creased with wrinkles. "Women voting, who ever heard of it? Next they'll be running for office. Stuff and nonsense."

"Now, dear, you're forgetting Nellie Tayloe Ross, the first female governor of Wyoming," Augusta pointed out carefully, aware of her husband's strict opinions. "Since women earned the right to vote less than five years ago, we have made great strides in politics."

"The first female governor of any state," Martha added. "Just this year, too."

"And Mabel Walker Willebrandt, the United States Assistant Attorney General," Joan mentioned. "She's an accomplished attorney. I read about her in *The Saturday Evening Post*."

The judge dismissed their comments with an irritable look and then announced he wanted to hear the evening news. Preston followed his grandparents into the living room. Augusta asked him to turn on the radio and close the curtains—night had fallen, and the room was steeped in deepening shadows. He turned on the radio console to station WGY for the news report. Approaching the tall windows overlooking State Street and about to draw the thick curtains, he looked outside and noticed it had just started to snow.

CHAPTER TWO

Overnight and into the early morning, a fine dusting of snow blanketed the streets and pavements, making for a rather slippery morning commute. While Albany residents hoped for an early spring, the conditions favored winter with its snow flurries, cold winds, and gray skies.

In a large brownstone house on Hamilton Street, Mrs. Philomena Sampson looked out one of the long windows from the living room. The light snow continued to fall, with winds pushing against the house, causing it to creak slightly. She shivered, turned from the window, and slowly returned to her favorite armchair, waiting for her son and daughter-in-law to come downstairs for breakfast. She enjoyed getting up before them as she had the downstairs to herself. She made the coffee already, keeping it warm on the stove. The comforting redolence of it curled in from the kitchen, intertwining with the faint scent of wood.

Mrs. Philomena Sampson, an Albany native, was prestigious in the community. Not as active as in previous years, at eighty, she still possessed vigor and exuberance. Her face held lines from disappointments, but her steadfast determination kept her resilient. A graduate of the state teachers college, she began employment with the New York State Department of Finance and continued there until her retirement. She lived in the home she and her husband bought when first married, although her late husband died nearly thirty years ago. Her son, Clayton, and daughter-in-law, Lucille, moved in with her ten years ago, as they had no children. It was a suitable arrangement, as most times their decorum with each other was pleasant.

Philomena wondered why her son did not wish to have children, but Clayton at fifty-five and Lucille at fifty, were past the childbearing years. Too busy with their own interests and making plenty of money at the law firm, she thought. Of course, her son was a competent and successful lawyer and his salary plus his earnings from the stock market were enviable. And Lucille, too, earned a pretty penny as a legal secretary at the same law firm and didn't she mention she also invested in the stock market?

While sipping her coffee, Philomena cherished these quiet moments, a time to gather her thoughts and enjoy the solitude before the household stirred to life. The fireplace was lit last evening and she would ask her son to start another fire upon returning from the office.

Her eyes wandered around the room, taking in the familiar surroundings. The fireplace was pristine, the mantelpiece adorned with framed photographs, a testament to the family's history. A large, ornate clock ticked steadily, its sound a comforting presence in the otherwise silent room. The furniture, elegant and meticulously maintained, spoke of the family's wealth and refined taste, each piece an indication of their status. The large radio console, a recent addition to their home, sat quietly in the corner, ready to bring news and music from the outside world.

From her armchair, she glanced at herself in the large mirror hanging between the front windows. She did not let age stand in her way.

She still climbed the three flights of stairs to her bedroom and resisted her son's attempt to turn a spare room on the first floor into a bedroom. The exercise, she told him, benefited her greatly. She played bridge with a few ladies in the neighborhood, and they would often go out to lunch. Among them was Mrs. Augusta Stafford, quite pleasant, despite her cranky and domineering husband, Judge Archie. Philomena could only tolerate him for so long, though she had met him often enough.

She enjoyed the newspapers, the *Saturday Evening Post* and *Readers Digest*, as well as current fiction by Mary Roberts Rinehart, Edith Wharton and Scott Fitzgerald. She often visited the new Harmanus Bleecker Library, chatting with the librarians and browsing the book selections.

She put down her coffee cup as her son and daughter-in-law came down the stairs and entered the living room.

"Good morning, Mother," Clayton said, fully dressed for the workday. He hugged her and then walked off to the kitchen.

"Morning, Phil," Lucille greeted her mother-in-law casually as usual, using her shortened first name. "Slept last night? I tossed and turned but finally dozed off. I heard shoveling while I was getting dressed."

Finding her daughter-in-law's usual flippant manner irritating, but hiding her annoyance, Philomena watched as she straightened her bobbed hair in the mirror and smoothed down her dress.

From the kitchen, they heard Clayton humming and open the icebox. Lucille helped her mother-in-law up and together they entered the kitchen, where Clayton had set cups and dishes. He deposited a corn muffin on a plate for his wife and one for himself, then offered one to his mother. Philomena demurred but told him another cup of coffee would be divine.

The Sampsons sat at the breakfast table in relative silence, their thoughts swirling with daily activities. The morning newspaper was on the table from where Philomena left it after collecting it from the front steps when she first came downstairs. Clayton reached for it, unfolding it while he asked his mother if she had plans for the rest of week.

"Tomorrow Agnes and I plan to shop downtown." She paused, glancing at the newspaper. "I see the death of Mr. Clement Lewis is still newsworthy."

Lucille looked up from another section of the newspaper her husband had handed her. "Of course, Mr. Lewis was a reputable lawyer here in Albany. At first, I assumed he had a bad heart."

"It was something in the tea," Clayton said dismissively, turning a page of the newspaper. "Some foreign tea that Judge Archie prepared and it killed him. Must've been really toxic, too."

Lucille glanced at her husband. "The police already looked around the office and questioned all of us. They confiscated the rest of the tea but we don't know anything else."

Philomena was unconvinced. "Poisonous tea? Never heard of it. Poor Mrs. Castle must've been besides herself with fright. The article mentioned Mr. Lewis drank out of the judge's cup."

"That doesn't mean anything, Mother," Clayton told her.

"Suppose that poisonous tea was meant for him?"

"Just because you have an axe to grind with Judge Archie," Clayton said.

Philomena squared her jaw and spoke firmly. "That man ruined my life with your father. He sent him to prison, do you not remember? I don't see how you can even work in his office, Clayton. He drove your father to an early grave while in prison."

Clayton put down the paper. "And now I work for him," he said cheerfully. "Obviously, any issues with you and the judge did not bother him when he hired me. He and I get along and so did Mr. Lewis and I." He paused, noting the serious look on her face. "You must let bygones be bygones."

Lucille agreed. "You don't see the judge too often anyway."

"When I visit Mrs. Stafford he usually is at the house," Philomena said. She paused, thoughtfully. "Maybe someone put the poisonous tea in his cup and Mr. Lewis drank it by mistake."

"Mother, please," Clayton said, knowing his mother insisted on her way in everything.

"It was just bad tea," Lucille said simply. "That's what the police concluded. An article in the newspaper last week mentioned that aromatic teas can be toxic, even fatal."

The eight o'clock hour approached and Clayton and Lucille announced their departure. They got up, hugged Philomena, then made their way to the foyer where, bundled in their winter coats, they went outside and down the steps to wait on Hamilton Street for the trolley.

Philomena got up and slowly returned to the living room. She looked out the front windows just in time to see her son and daughter-in-law board a trolley. She then returned to her armchair, deep in disturbed thoughts.

The judge was an evil man, wicked in his ways, clever, manipulative and spiteful. He drove my poor husband to an early grave. He must have enemies, certainly his work as a lawyer and judge earned him plenty of adversaries. She sat brooding, her mind tangled in the past. Her eyes rested on *Readers Digest*, but her thoughts were far from the printed words.

Judge Archie had ruined so many lives; she knew she was not the only one. He sent her husband to prison where he later died. She would take care of matters for herself. After all, once Philomena decided on a course of action, no one could ever stop her.

The law offices of Lewis and Stafford occupied a large workplace on the tenth floor in an impressive office building on lower North Pearl Street, near Clinton Street. Judge Archie Stafford established his enterprising law practice in that prime location over forty years ago and it remained there ever since. When Mr. Clement Lewis came into the firm, Judge Archie changed the title to illustrate both of their names, as Mr. Lewis was not merely a colleague but also a good friend.

In the busy law firm, Miss Doris Blake was typing a report and working with her customary brisk efficiency. She glanced toward the far side of the room, noticing Mrs. Rose Castle engrossed in writing—though in what, she couldn't say. She bent her head down to the keyboard and the original document and continued typing.

Doris was fifty-five years old and well liked in the law firm, not only for her exceptional work output but also for her pleasant and charming personality. Granted, she flirted at times with men as she kept her eyes open for the perfect suitor, although she enjoyed the single life and was in no rush for marriage, even at her age. She maintained an active social life, frequenting speakeasies and dance halls, keeping late hours and enjoying the company of several eligible men. She paid special attention to her appearance and took pride in the latest fashions, perfumes and cosmetics. Her bobbed hair was fixed tastefully, her slim appearance and pretty face were becoming, especially to the opposite sex.

At that moment, the main doors swung open and in walked Quentin Cooper and Burgess Smith. They greeted Doris and Mrs. Castle pleasantly and then Burgess disappeared into his own office as usual, while Quentin sat at his desk, not far from Doris.

"Did you go to the movies last night?" he asked her. "I went to the Ritz for a Lillian Gish double feature. She's my favorite actress, you know."

Doris lit a cigarette. "Yes, you've told me many times. Personally, I prefer Colleen Moore, but to each his own."

Quentin took a ledger book out from his desk while also lighting a cigarette. Quentin Cooper was employed at the firm as a law clerk, a position he held for five years. At thirty, Quentin was tall and upbeat, an engaging, playful disposition made him appealing to most people. His brown hair, like the style for many young men, was center parted and his dress was professional and his demeanor with clients courteous. He was friends with Preston Hughes, having met him while a student at the state teachers college. They kept in touch and frequently enjoyed Albany's nightlife together.

"Good morning, dears," Mrs. Castle said pleasantly, looking matronly as ever, as she approached the young people. She carried a plate containing slices of banana bread. "I baked this last night." She held out the plate for Doris and Quentin to take a piece, then gave them each a napkin. "I want to save a piece for Mr. Sampson when he arrives. He just loves my baking!"

They thanked her and watched her disappear into Burgess Smith's office, although they knew the reaction she would most likely receive. Before long, Mrs. Castle returned, smiling cheerfully and sat at her desk, depositing the plate with the slices of banana bread on a nearby table. She continued with the work at her desk, humming and seemingly content with the world.

Doris cast a quick glance at Quentin, wondering if Burgess Smith was receptive to her interruption. Although not one to gossip, Quentin got up, winked at Doris and knocked on Burgess Smith's office door. The older man looked up and saw him.

"Do you need me to complete anything this morning before you go to court?" Quentin asked. He was not especially fond of Burgess Smith. He found him arrogant and condescending, full of self-importance. He spotted a slice of banana bread on a napkin atop Burgess's desk—Mrs. Castle had, as usual, managed to charm him.

Burgess Smith removed his glasses and looked at the younger man. Burgess was a tall, commanding figure and a competent lawyer. At forty-five, his career and lucrative dividends on the stock market were of the utmost importance, more fulfilling than a wife and having children. A graduate of Albany Law School, he took his work seriously and had won numerous cases. Of course, bribery and backhanded deals always worked in his favor, too. He puffed at his cigarette and told Quentin to enter. He did not hesitate to say what was foremost on his mind at the moment.

"Quentin, the death of Mr. Lewis has impacted our business here," he said gravely, his eyes scanning the cluttered office. "We still have outstanding cases to complete, but our referrals may dry up." He paused, running a hand through his thinning hair. "When I spoke to Mr. Stafford, he told me he placed Thurman in charge and of course, Mrs. Castle will continue as the office manager. Until he feels well enough to come to the office, that is apparently how Judge Archie wants it here."

Quentin frowned, shifting his weight from one foot to the other. He did not miss the resentment in his tone. Mr. Thurman Armstrong, a more senior attorney on staff at the firm, was now handling business matters as well as his own legal cases since the unexpected death of Mr. Lewis. That should burn him up, Quentin thought looking at the self-absorbed man behind the desk. He remained standing by the chair in front of Burgess's massive desk, never invited to sit. He repeated if there was anything he could do to assist before court. He felt rather foolish standing in front of his desk.

"No, I believe I'm ready for court today." He hesitated. "Has Thurman arrived yet? I looked at the court calendar and noticed he has a few cases this afternoon as well."

"Yesterday, before leaving, Mrs. Castle told me he would be late coming in today," Quentin mentioned. "She reminded me he's the chief operating officer of the firm now, so I guess that means he can arrive later than the rest of us."

Burgess cringed and then glanced at the wall clock, noticing it was almost mid-morning. "Well, thank you, that's all for now. Close the door on your way out."

As Quentin turned to leave, he thought he heard Burgess curse Mr. Thurman Armstrong under his breath, but then decided he must have been mistaken.

Preston arrived at the Hudson River Day Cruise Line offices at his usual nine o'clock.

He settled at his desk and was greeted by his boss, Mr. Stanley Bishop. A good-hearted but irascible older man with a bushy mustache and a penchant for suspenders, Mr. Bishop was impressed with Preston's handling of accounts and praised him for his sales. Fortunately, he had little contact with Mr. Bishop throughout the day. He had his own office, a small but tidy space with a large window overlooking the bustling docks, and the ticket counter to himself.

Preston began work on arranging a guided tour to West Point for a senior citizen group, which included a luncheon at the Thayer Inn at the historic military campus. He enjoyed these tasks, finding satisfaction in the meticulous planning and the thought of providing a memorable experience for the group.

At the moment, he was thinking of the arrival of Mr. Sloan Sheppard on Thursday evening. Of course he contacted Mr. Sheppard for his grandfather's sake, but what exactly did he expect Mr. Sheppard to do? The police were continuing to investigate the death of Mr. Lewis, although Preston admitted it was strange that he drank poisonous tea from his grandfather's cup. Did grandfather really believe the poisonous tea was meant for him? And how did the poisonous tea get in the cup in the first place?

Preston shuddered, recalling his grandfather's words at the dinner table last evening when he proclaimed that Mr. Lewis was indeed murdered. He shook his head, deciding he would read up on poisons during his next visit to the public library.

He had just finished answering a telephone call from a woman requesting tickets for the next ship to New York City, when he looked up and noticed a distinguished gentleman enter.

"Good morning, sir," Preston said pleasantly. "How may I help you today?"

The man was tall and bald, about fifty, with a heavily lined face covered with premature wrinkles, pouches under his eyes, and dark glasses that did not quite fit straight on his rather large nose. With his loose-fitting vest and trench coat, his chin nestling between the wings of a high stiff collar, he looked like a figure from an old, faintly musty illustration—something out of another time. As he looked at him again, Preston realized the man's identity.

"Mr. Armstrong," Preston said, catching his breath.

Thurman Armstrong smiled. "Hello, Preston. Before arriving at the office this morning, I thought I would stop here to inquire about cruises to New York City. A lady friend and I want to make a weekend of it."

"Of course, Mr. Armstrong," Preston said, rather flustered.

He had met Thurman Armstrong while visiting his grandfather's office a few times. He considered him extremely arrogant and self-centered, loaded with money and a high-class attitude. He knew he was divorced with no children and was known as a ladies man about the city, going to speakeasies and dance halls, enjoying the nightlife. He also knew he was a powerful attorney. He remembered Quentin telling him about the rivalry between Mr. Armstrong and Mr. Burgess Smith, two highly competent and competitive lawyers. Preston assumed with his wealth he must invest in the stock market, reaping the benefits of the lucrative bull market. That may have been why so many women gravitated to him, with his power, prestige and money. Nothing seemed to faze Mr. Armstrong—he carried himself as though untouched by worry, the very image of confidence and composure.

Preston consulted a timetable and circled times on Saturdays when the cruises departed Albany for New York City. He handed Mr. Armstrong a brochure with information on the cruises and all the amenities on board, such as a snack bar and café serving light meals. He mentioned the best time to make reservations, as weekend cruises tended to sell out frequently.

Thurman Armstrong nodded in appreciation. "Thank you, Preston, for this information." He paused, about to leave, then addressed him again. "Such a shame about Mr. Lewis, isn't it? I know he was quite close to your grandfather. I never knew tea could be so toxic."

Preston was surprised he would mention Mr. Lewis. But as he stood before him, rather pensively, Preston thought there was more on Mr. Armstrong's mind. He seemed dazed, as though troubled by something secretive that no one else knew about. Of course, Preston knew it was not his place to inquire. He waited to hear if he wanted any further information on the cruises.

Thurman Armstrong continued speaking, making unnecessary small talk rather uneasily, mumbling about the weather, the cruises down the Hudson, and the nasty spring weather. He was silent for a moment or two and then blinked as though just realizing where he was. He apologized, then—almost too quickly—made his way to the exit just as a woman stepped in to inquire about tickets. Preston greeted her, forgot about Mr. Armstrong, and got back to work.

CHAPTER THREE

The next evening, the temperature dropped once again, prompting Preston to kindle the fireplace in the living room, much to his grandfather's delight.

After dinner, the family settled by the fireplace, listening to the radio while sipping after-dinner coffee. A tense silence settled over them—Mr. Lewis's death unspoken but ever-present. Augusta sat at one end of the Victorian sofa, knitting a sweater for Preston, her needles clicking softly. Joan was on the other end, engrossed in the *Albany Evening News*. Judge Archie sat stoically in his armchair near the fireplace, rather subdued and making only desultory remarks. Martha sat in an armchair by the tall windows, thumbing through the latest issue of *True Story*, her brow occasionally furrowing in concentration. Preston was across from his grandfather, smoking and reading the March issue of *Popular Science*, the faint smell of tobacco mingled with the rich scent of coffee.

He glanced up from his magazine, his gaze lingering on his grandfather. "I heard there's a big city council meeting next week," he said, breaking the uncomfortable silence.

The Judge grunted in response, but a glint of interest sparked in his eyes. "Is that so?" he murmured, setting his coffee cup down with a thoughtful air.

The radio was on and the sounds of Ruth Etting and Bessie Smith filled the room agreeably, in contrast to the palpable tension. At that moment, Gertrude appeared in the archway, wiping her hands on her apron. She announced that the kitchen was cleaned for the evening and that if no one required anything else, she would be leaving. Gertrude lived in an apartment further up State Street with her husband, a mere ten-minute walk away.

"Thank you, Gertrude. Everything was delicious as always," Augusta said.

"My pleasure, Mrs. Caves. Good night," Gertrude replied, pleasantly.

Joan walked with her to the front door before returning to the living room.

"I'm going upstairs," she mentioned, yawning, rather tired. She left the *Albany Evening News* on the coffee table in front of the sofa. She heard the grandfather clock in the hallway strike nine. "My favorite drama, *When Love Wakens*, is on WGY, so I'll listen to it in my bedroom."

"You'll miss Eddie Cantor," her father remarked. He glanced at the radio in the far corner, tuned to *The Eveready Hour*, the family's favorite program.

"I know, but I can't resist *When Love Wakens*," she said with a small smile.

"Should be a good program, Joan," Martha said, looking up at her sister. "Why don't you stay and listen to it with us?"

At that moment, the host, Wendell Hall, mentioned that the guests of the hour included vocalists Eddie Cantor, Clara Smith, Martha Copeland, and comedian Arthur "Bugs" Baer. Mr. Hall welcomed Eddie Cantor, and soon the orchestra began, enthralling listeners with the wonderful music and the crooning voice of the popular singer.

Joan shook her head. "I'm too tired to stay up. Good night."

She left the living room, stepped into the hallway, before slowly climbing the stairs to her bedroom. The distant hum of the radio followed her. She couldn't help but feel a slight twinge of unease, as if the night held secrets waiting to be unveiled. As she settled into her room, she glanced at the framed photo of her late husband on her nightstand, finding comfort in its presence.

After a while, Augusta set down her knitting and sighed, mentioning that she was tired. She collected the coffee cups and brought them to the kitchen, then returned to see if her husband was ready to retire for the night. Together they walked slowly to their bedroom, with Preston helping his grandfather out of his armchair. Their bedroom was just down the hallway from the kitchen on the first floor. Preston assured his grandfather he would take care of the fireplace.

Martha got up and sat on the sofa, across from her son. She looked at him, as Preston continued smoking, listening to *The Eveready Hour* and flipping the pages of *Popular Science*.

"I just read an interesting article about air conditioning," he said to his mother. "Can you imagine they anticipate cooling rooms with a machine? That'll be great during the hot summers."

Martha knew her son well enough that an article in *Popular Science* was not of great interest. He continued talking about the new expedient of cooling rooms until he finally stopped when he realized his mother was looking at him rather intently.

Preston puffed at his cigarette, rather solemnly. "Tomorrow evening Mr. Sheppard will be here to have dinner with us." He paused. "I'm surprised grandfather didn't mention it earlier."

Martha put down *True Story*. "He hasn't forgotten, dear. He is very aware of it. He mentioned it to me when I got home from work.

That was why he was so subtle during dinner and while listening to the radio. Usually he enjoys *The Eveready Hour*."

"There's an article here about Mr. Charles Lindbergh," Preston said, as though attempting to change the subject. "He wants to be the first to fly across the Atlantic! That'll put an end to cruises if they start flying people to Europe."

Martha commented that was rightly so, then asked her son what he thought about Mr. Sheppard's visit. Preston stubbed out his cigarette in an ashtray and did not answer her.

Outside, the wind had increased and they could hear it push forcefully in strong gusts against the big house. He got up rather moodily and strode over to the large windows overlooking State Street. Pushing the curtains aside, he looked out the right window, where the wind whipped leaves into a whirlwind as pedestrians scurried along the pavements.

"Seems like we've always been alone, haven't we, Mother?" he said, looking out the window. "After Father died, we've been by ourselves. We've had no one, really."

"Preston, please do not upset yourself," Martha urged her son. "That's why we came here to live with your grandparents. We have each other."

Outside, the wind howled, rattling the windowpanes as Preston spoke.

"Someone must have killed Mr. Lewis," he said bluntly, turning from the window. He returned to the armchair and looked at his mother. "Grandfather thinks so. And the more I think of it, the more I agree with him. There was poison in the cup."

Martha became flustered. "Maybe that was the case, but I don't think it's best to discuss it now." She hesitated. "I'm going to bed too," she remarked abruptly. "Good night, Preston." She got up and left the living room, leaving Preston by himself.

He watched his mother walk out and heard her climb the stairs. He sat in the armchair for a long time, contemplating another cigarette. The crackling fire sent flickering shadows dancing on the walls, and the lingering scent of burnt tobacco hung in the air. He listened to *The Eveready Hour,* the static crackling intermittently as the radio waves traveled from New York City but the music did not occupy his thoughts.

He sat brooding, his mind turning over different possibilities. He did not know Mr. Lewis personally, of course, but had met him on several occasions and heard about him from his grandfather. However hard he tried to accept the poisonous tea theory, he could not rid himself of the conviction that Mr. Lewis's passing was really murder, as Grandfather Archie claimed, and that someone they all knew was responsible for the older man's untimely death.

Mrs. Rose Castle looked carefully at the agenda she typed for Mr. Smith, checking for spelling errors. Meticulous in her endeavors, Mrs. Castle always verified her work. Satisfied it was pristine, she put it in a folder along with a few other documents intended for Mr. Smith.

It was mid-morning on Thursday, the twenty-sixth, and Mrs. Castle, office manager and general busybody, to which she readily admitted to herself, was busy implementing the day's reports. She had already ensured Doris Blake and Quentin Cooper were occupied with their tasks, while she catered to the whims of both Mr. Smith and Mr. Armstrong, whose offices were on opposite sides of the large room. Sometimes she wondered how Mr. Smith and Mr. Armstrong could represent the same firm, given how often they clashed.

Mrs. Rose Castle was a widow, childless, and lived rather simply in a one-bedroom apartment on Dove Street, close to downtown. She dressed conservatively, rather old-fashioned, with little makeup. Instead, her appearance was simple, as she preferred it. She had little interests outside work but managed to keep busy with volunteer endeavors and reading library books. Many saw her as nosy and meddlesome. She was rather matronly and Rose knew she had gained weight once her mid-fifties creeped upon her. Nevertheless, she enjoyed her work at the law firm and enjoyed baking, always delighting her colleagues with cakes, cookies and breads.

The hum of the office surrounded her, punctuated by occasional phone calls and the murmur of distant conversations. Mrs. Castle glanced up briefly, her eyes sweeping the room, ensuring everything was in order. She returned to her documents, her mind ever-alert to the demands of the day. It was a bustling hub of activity, and Mrs. Castle thrived in it. She was dressed in a smart, navy blue dress with a string of pearls, epitomizing the professional woman of her day.

Her mind flew to Burgess Smith and Thurman Armstrong. The tension between Mr. Smith and Mr. Armstrong was noticeable, creating difficulties in the otherwise efficient atmosphere. Their disagreements, rooted in differing business philosophies, often left Mrs. Castle in the middle, trying to maintain harmony.

Doris Blake, the experienced and steady secretary, and Quentin Cooper, the diligent junior clerk, were both under Mrs. Castle's watchful eye. Doris, with her practical attire and no-nonsense attitude, brought a sense of stability to the office, while Quentin, always in a crisp suit, was the picture of ambition. Their interactions with Mrs. Castle were professional yet tinged with the camaraderie of shared daily routines.

Glancing at the court calendar on her desk, she was pleased Mr. Smith was in court for the afternoon, which meant a less stressful environment. Rose shook her head. At least they could try to reach agreements, she thought disdainfully. Certainly, Judge Archie and Mr. Lewis had intervened more than once to create harmony. Of course, they were competitive, as though trying to outdo each other in profits, clients and prestige. She adjusted the string of pearls around her neck, a habitual gesture that brought her comfort amidst the office's hustle and bustle. She looked again at the agenda she finished typing before bringing it to Mr. Smith.

Her mind drifted to Mr. Lewis. Of course, the police questioned her extensively as she was the first to discover the body. She had rinsed out the teacup before they arrived, which irritated the policemen, as though she had destroyed some vital clue. But how was I to know what to do, she thought, frustration creeping up inside her. Sometimes people infuriated her, such as Doris and Quentin, with a quick glance to her right she noticed they were gossiping and laughing, although she anticipated they were completing the assignments due today. Rose took a deep breath, trying to push the lingering doubts from her mind.

She hoped Judge Archie would not make an appearance. Usually, he sauntered in by mid-morning, as if a king arriving at his throne. Always grumbling and miserable, especially since Mr. Lewis died, she did not relish seeing him and she was sure the others shared her misgivings. While she admitted he was a competent lawyer and judge, his attitude and behavior at times were irascible. She kept her distance from him, which did not appear to bother him most likely because he was not too fond of her, either. His presence alone cast a shadow, she thought, shuddering slightly at the memory of his last outburst. The way he slammed his office door, the echo reverberating through the halls, the sound lingering in her mind. Rose took a moment to compose herself, smoothing her dress and straightening her desk. Just another day in the lion's den, she mused, her resolve strengthening.

Discussions often centered about the latest political maneuvers of Governor Al Smith, whose progressive reforms and opposition to Prohibition were widely recognized. The ongoing Prohibition had turned Albany into a hotbed of speakeasies and secret gatherings, often influenced by the city's powerful Democratic political machine, led by Dan O'Connell. Rose had read in the newspapers that the rise of the automobile was also changing the city's landscape, with new roads constructed and the Albany Municipal Airport set to open in a few years, marking it as one of the country's first commercial airports. Indeed, the capital of New York State was growing rapidly, with new businesses and industries emerging, and the fast-paced law office was a testament to this economic expansion. The city's transformation this year, 1925, was outstanding, reflecting the broader changes sweeping across America.

As Mrs. Castle looked out the window onto North Pearl Street, she noticed it was bustling with Model Ts, and the distant sound of construction added to the city's symphony. The office's constant chatter mirrored the city's vibrancy, each phone call and typewriter click echoing the spirit of progress. The changes in Albany were not lost on her colleagues, either. Rose remembered how Doris often mentioned her excitement about the new airport, dreaming of traveling by plane beyond the state's borders, while Quentin eagerly discussed the potential business opportunities arising from the city's growth. The rapid developments fueled the ambitions of everyone in the office, pushing them to keep pace with the city's relentless march forward.

"Mrs. Castle, I finished typing the pile of letters," Doris said, approaching her desk.

Rose sized her up quickly—rather pretty, likely close to her own age, but too much lipstick and rouge for her taste, and an excessive amount of perfume. Fashionably dressed in the latest flapper style, she was a good secretary. Indeed, her typing speed of eighty words a minute was commendable. She knew how to deal professionally with clients when the need arose. Despite her reservations about Doris's appearance, Rose could not deny her efficiency and the ease with which she handled the office's demands.

Quentin then approached her desk. He mentioned his plan to accompany Mr. Smith in court that afternoon. Rose felt a wave of relief: one less person to contend with. Not that she really minded Quentin. She smiled in spite of herself as he told her about the typed deposition he prepared for Mr. Smith, proudly adding that it was quite a big case, involving multiple parties.

"We have a new client coming this afternoon," Rose commented, adjusting the ribbon on her Underwood typewriter. "He's to see Mr. Armstrong about a custody dispute. Doris, you can take down his information and get it ready for Mr. Armstrong before he sees him?"

Doris nodded, her fingers poised over the keys of her typewriter. The office buzzed with the sound of clacking keys and the occasional ring of the telephone. The air was thick with the scent of ink and paper, a testament to the busy day ahead.

Quentin, adjusting his tie and vest, glanced at the clock on the wall. "I'll make sure everything is in order for court this afternoon. It's going to be a long day."

Mrs. Castle appreciated his diligence. "Thank you, Quentin. Good luck in court."

She admitted grudgingly that Quentin was an excellent law clerk. His fastidious attention to detail and invaluable assistance in analyzing cases and managing supporting documents made him indispensable. Though he was younger than Doris, about thirty, his ambition and work ethic were remarkable. And his friendship with Judge Archie's grandson, Preston, certainly didn't hurt his standing here, either.

Of course, she kept her opinion to herself, but she found this friendship a potential conflict of interest. Knowing how young people gossiped, she suspected Quentin fed Preston office news, which no doubt made its way to the judge. Rose had a feeling this had occurred more than once, perhaps explaining why the judge did not particularly care for her.

From her desk, Mrs. Castle heard Mr. Armstrong on the telephone, his voice raised over some case that was in the works. The sharp tone cut through the office's usual hum, making her wince slightly. He must be dealing with another stubborn client, she thought, shaking her head. In the suite next to hers, on the opposite side of the wall, were the Sampsons, whom Mrs. Castle found patronizing and manipulative. She wondered how a husband and wife could work side-by-side five days a week and still see each other in their free time. Obviously, it did not bother them, although she also found it a conflict of interest. What a strange arrangement, she mused, glancing at the wall as if she could see through it. If only they focused on their work instead of scheming over office politics—and their lucrative stock market investments, always chasing the biggest financial dividends.

She found it disconcerting, too, that they were especially close to Judge Archie, despite his archaic viewpoints and downright meanness, which he had displayed to nearly everyone, including them, more than once while in the office. Mrs. Sampson was not particularly friendly, always defending her husband and typing his reports, which was fine with Rose as it meant one less demanding lawyer to please. She was not really aware of the cases Mr. Sampson handled, as he kept his work secret, as though he was above the others. However, Rose easily found out information by checking files and eavesdropping as needed.

It's amazing what people will say when they think no one's listening, she thought, a slight smile creasing her fat face. You'd think after all these years, they'd be more careful about loose lips in an office full of busybodies.

She glanced at Mr. Lewis's office, the door closed as it had been since his death. Nobody had ventured in there, except the police, to poke around and search for whatever evidence they could find. The investigation had stalled and the office was slow to recover, especially with the newspapers having a field day with it. Sensational stories sold newspapers, she thought irritably. The world was moving fast, and so was this office, even Mr. Lewis's premature death was hastily receding into the past.

She toyed with the pearls around her scraggly neck just as she heard Mr. Armstrong call for her, rather loudly. He told her to bring her pad and to take dictation. Without wasting a minute, Mrs. Castle grabbed her steno book and pen and hurriedly made her way to his office.

Mrs. Lucille Sampson removed the sheet of paper from the Underwood typewriter and placed it neatly on a pile on the corner of her desk: a letter needing her husband's signature. One of many successful cases concluded, to his and the client's satisfaction. More to his financial satisfaction, Lucille thought wisely. His growing list of clients plus the lucrative gains from the stock market kept the Sampsons financially secure and satisfied.

She glanced over her large mahogany desk in front of the windows overlooking North Pearl Street. The view was bustling with the sights and sounds of 1925 Albany—Model T Fords honking, the sidewalks crowded as always, and the clang of numerous trolleys. Clayton, a large, imposing figure, rather proud and arrogant, was absorbed in new contracts and had not lifted his head in what seemed at least a half hour. How many more contracts will he pore over before finally looking up? she wondered, frustration mixing with admiration. Lucille's fingers idly traced the edge of her desk, feeling the grain of the wood. The chaotic energy outside contrasted sharply with the heavy silence in the office, broken only by the rustle of papers and the occasional creak of Clayton's chair.

"Clayton," she called softly, not wanting to startle him. "I need your signature."

Flipping through pages, Clayton finally looked up, his eyes momentarily softening as they met hers. "Ah, thank you, Lucille. Just leave the letter on the desk. I'll get to it shortly."

Lucille nodded. "You've been at those contracts for quite a while. Everything all right?"

"Yes, just some new clients with rather complicated demands," Clayton replied.

"It's almost time to leave," Lucille said. "I've finished for the day."

At this, Clayton Sampson looked up, removed his glasses, and rubbed his eyes. Writing contracts and depositions was tiring, but he insisted on doing his work himself, not delegating anything to anyone else. He allowed his wife to type up his papers, but the others remained in the other suite, as Clayton and Lucille preferred. They had little contact with Quentin, Doris, or Rose, although supposedly they worked for the same law firm.

Clayton collaborated with Burgess and Thurman on occasion but only when the lawsuits involved multiple parties and were of a criminal nature. He admitted he did not relish working with Burgess and Thurman, as he knew they did not get along and he never wanted to be in the middle. He tolerated Judge Archie, but the judge had retired ten years ago. Although Clayton respected his firm grasp of the law, he certainly did not miss his tyrannical behavior in the office. He had also worked with Mr. Clement Lewis, someone he greatly respected.

Realizing his wife was still speaking to him, Clayton blinked and came out of his reverie. "Sorry, Lucille. I was just thinking about the old days with Judge Archie and Mr. Lewis."

Lucille smiled gently. "It's good to reminisce sometimes, but don't forget to take care of yourself. Besides, we take care of your mother, too. And our vacation in Florida in a few months."

He put the contracts in his top drawer. He paused, looking at Lucille. She still looked fresh and pleasant as she did at nine this morning. Although prone to occasional emotional outbursts, she had nevertheless remained composed these past few weeks, even regarding Mr. Lewis. Like Clayton, she could be haughty at times. He was surprised she'd mention the Florida vacation amidst the recent turmoil, as though that took precedence over everything else.

Lucille adjusted her pearls, her expression calm yet dismissive. "Mrs. Stafford worries far too much. Honestly, Clayton, Judge Archie is perfectly capable of handling himself. After all, everything is moving along as it should." She crossed her arms lightly. "And as for the tea—bad luck can happen to anyone, can't it? No sense in dwelling on it." She paused. "I understand the Staffords are anticipating a private detective this evening. I called Mrs. Stafford earlier and she told me his name is Mr. Sloan Sheppard, although the name doesn't ring a bell."

Clayton nodded thoughtfully. "Mr. Sheppard, you say? Interesting. I've met Mr. Sheppard. I've also seen him in court. He's a definite asset in resolving issues. Although I don't understand, what more Judge Archie thinks he could unearth. Mr. Lewis died from drinking bad tea. Even the police seemed to accept it. I suppose Judge Archie wants to leave no stone unturned."

Lucille raised an eyebrow, her tone light hearted. "Well, let's hope this Mr. Sheppard doesn't waste time searching for stones that don't exist." She sighed. "Mrs. Stafford mentioned the judge has been restless, pacing around the house. She's worried about his health."

Clayton stood up and walked over to the window, looking out at the dimming lights of North Pearl Street. "Leave it to the judge to dig up old bones—it's as if he hasn't aged a day."

"I wonder if Mr. Lewis really was murdered," Lucille said, rather awkwardly.

He turned and went for his coat and hat. He put a cigarette to his lips and struck a match. "Really, Lucille, such talk is nonsense. We have been through this already. The tea was toxic. It can happen, you know."

Lucille put on her fur coat and cloche hat, checking her appearance in a wall mirror. She adjusted her string of pearls and smoothed her gloves. "Mrs. Castle did well enough, considering the poor woman lacks a certain... poise. But really, Clayton, it's lucky she had the sense to call us first. Things could've gotten messy if left entirely in her hands."

"Doris and Quentin seem to be taking it in stride," Clayton remarked dryly. "I'm sure the younger generation would brush it off, anyway."

"They never worked with Mr. Lewis," Lucille reminded him. She lowered her voice. "You know, Clayton, there is something about them I don't trust. They snoop around the office. I don't know what they're looking for but…"

At that moment, Mrs. Castle entered from the main office. She asked if they needed anything before she left for the day. She mentioned Doris and Quentin completed the contracts for Mr. Armstrong and Mr. Smith, as well as additional typing and filing. New clients were scheduled for later in the week, two for Mr. Sampson regarding real estate.

Lucille thanked her. "We're just about ready to leave. And thanks for the wonderful banana bread. It was simply divine!"

"Always a pleasure, Mrs. Sampson," Mrs. Castle said, then returned to her desk.

Clayton adjusted the lapel of his wool coat, a faint smirk on his face. "The stock report's bound to be good news tonight. And as for the *Waldorf-Astoria Orchestra*—well, I can think of nothing better than listening to elegance while others shuffle home to their crowded boarding houses. And we'll prepare a nice meal for Mother. A glass of port with dinner will be just fine."

Lucille agreed. "That bottle of whisky you bought from Mr. Nichols was the best yet."

They laughed lightheartedly and left the suite, headed for the main office doors. They noticed Burgess busy at his desk and Thurman in his office speaking quite animatedly on the candlestick telephone, obviously embroiled in a heated discussion, most likely with a client.

Quentin observed them leave, self-absorbed and rather snobbish; Mr. Sampson, distinguished in his prestigious wool overcoat, Mrs. Sampson with her luxurious fur coat and stylish cloche hat, her high heels clicking across the floor. He was at the file cabinets near the entrance doors, filing a report under the dim light bulb when they passed, hardly acknowledging him. The scent of Mrs. Sampson's expensive perfume lingered in the air. Looking after them, Quentin's thoughts were filled with hate, envy—and a strange paroxysm of impending doom.

CHAPTER FOUR

Preston sat at the long dining room table, glancing at the windows overlooking State Street. The wind had finally subsided, though it remained cold for the end of March. He turned his attention to the faces assembled around him.

At the head of the table, as always, was his grandfather, a large figure of an elderly man with a perplexed and anticipatory expression on his wrinkled face. At the other end sat Grandmother Augusta, elegant in a navy blue dress and pearls. To his right was his mother, wearing a chiffon dress and pearls. Across from her was Aunt Joan, simply attired in a gray dress of no outstanding features, her expression forlorn and her eyes downcast.

Earlier, his grandfather had mentioned they would discuss nothing of what concerned him with their dinner guest until after dessert, to which the family had concurred. The dining room, adorned with heavy wooden furniture and a large chandelier casting a warm glow over the table, felt both grand and oppressive.

The soft clinking of cutlery and the murmur of polite conversation filled the room, mingling with the savory fragrance of roast beef and potatoes. Preston observed their dinner guest, Mr. Sloan Sheppard, carefully. So this was Mr. Sheppard, he thought, summing him up. He had talked to him on the telephone when he invited him for this evening. He had heard about him from his grandfather and had even seen his name in the newspapers pertaining to numerous cases. But here he was in person.

Preston was curious about his reputation. His grandfather was certainly convinced of his ability. Indeed, Mr. Sheppard seemed a formidable presence. His sharp eyes and composed demeanor suggested a man who had seen much and was not easily rattled. The way he held himself, with a quiet confidence, only added to his imposing aura. Preston noticed the scar on his chin, which hinted at past encounters with the underworld. His solid physique was testament to his enduring strength and perseverance. Handsome in a classic sense, his wavy black hair, worn in an unconventional style, was pushed back from a high forehead and his dark brown eyes caught and held the attention.

Preston's mind wandered to the upcoming discussion. He felt a mix of curiosity and apprehension. He glanced at his grandfather, whose expression remained unreadable, and then back at Sloan, wondering about the investigator's next move. Gertrude entered at that moment, with coffee and chocolate cake.

"Thank you, Mr. Sheppard, for coming this evening," Augusta said pleasantly.

"Thank you for having me, Mrs. Stafford," Sloan replied.

"Father wishes your assistance, Mr. Sheppard," Joan said meekly, sipping her coffee.

"Mr. Sheppard is aware of his visit, Joan," Judge Archie spoke, rather irritably. He turned his attention to his guest. "Mr. Sheppard, my grandson called you because I do wish your help in the death of my friend and colleague, Mr. Clement Lewis. I believe there is more to it than the presumptuous conclusions reached by the police." He took a large gulp of coffee and stopped speaking, as though the circumstances were too overwhelming.

Sloan wiped his mouth on a dinner napkin. "I understand, Judge, that you believe Mr. Lewis did not die a natural death, as first assumed. I've read the newspaper accounts. What is it that you want me to investigate?"

"Father, do you wish to speak to Mr. Sheppard alone?" Martha asked.

Judge Archie shook his head. "No, Martha, I want everyone here. This is a family matter, and I would appreciate your input."

"I'm happy to assist you with your concerns the best I can," Sloan continued. "Have you spoken first to the police?"

Judge Archie nodded. "They came here to speak with us. They also spoke with the rest of the office staff. Useless, and a waste of tax dollars. It's already been two weeks and they've accomplished nothing. They believe Mr. Lewis died by drinking the tea."

"What do you believe, Judge?" Sloan asked carefully.

Judge Archie put down his coffee cup. "I believe the poison was in the cup already and that it was meant for me. Mr. Lewis drank from my cup, which I didn't realize until we started working. I mentioned it but didn't pay much attention as we were finalizing contracts for his clients. I drank my tea from another cup and then left for the day close to five-thirty. He died after I left and apparently after the rest of the staff had gone, too. That was on Monday, the ninth."

"Father, you believe the poison was in the cup already?" Joan exclaimed.

"It was meant for me," her father repeated. "As we've discussed numerous times already, I have no doubt someone is trying to kill me. Clement Lewis, drank from my cup." The judge cleared his throat and continued addressing Sloan.

"My wife and I have experienced mishaps which we at first took as simple occurrences. In hindsight, Augusta and I agree that someone is deliberately trying to do away with me."

There was an uneasy silence while Sloan waited for the judge to continue. He could tell there was anxiety and tension at the table, glancing at Preston, his mother, his aunt, and his grandmother. He looked at the head of the table and listened to what the judge told him.

"In December, my wife and I were shopping on North Pearl Street, just before Christmas. While we were crossing the street, I slipped and almost landed directly in front of a trolley. I would've been killed. Fortunately, my grandson pulled me up just in time."

"Grandfather, what are you implying?" Preston asked.

Judge Archie cast a rather disapproving look at his grandson. "As I mentioned to everyone at that time, I felt a shove in my back, causing me to fall. I did not slip on snow or ice, as first assumed. By the time you helped me up, Preston, the crowd behind us had moved on. North Pearl Street was busy with holiday shoppers and the sidewalks were full. I remember looking around for a policeman, but I didn't see one."

"I looked too, dear," Augusta said from the other end of the table. "I didn't see a policeman, and the crowd behind us had already crossed."

"And you felt it was deliberate?" Sloan asked.

"Most definitely. I didn't bring it to the attention of the police because I believed it was the crowd pressing forward, but I know I felt a shove on my back." He paused. "There was another time in February, when my wife and I were about to cross State Street."

Augusta picked up the narrative as she noticed her husband's agitated state. "It was early evening and my husband, my grandson and I were to meet Martha and Joan at a restaurant on Washington Avenue. My husband was ahead of me and was about to cross at the corner of

State and South Swan at a red light. A car came speeding down State Street and it almost hit him. It continued down State Street past the Capitol. We looked around but didn't see a policeman, although a small crowd had formed, asking if they could help." She paused, deep in thought, looking piteously at her daughters, her grandson, her husband and then at Sloan. "Unfortunately, no one noticed the license plate number of the car or saw the driver."

Preston looked at the faces around him but concentrated more on Mr. Sheppard. He noticed he had taken out a small pad from his jacket and had been scribbling notes. Obviously, he saw the relevance in what he heard. Preston had forgotten about the car incident in February, just attributing it to another speeding car in the city. Apparently, his grandfather thought otherwise.

"Mr. Sheppard, a coffin is waiting for me," Judge Archie said grimly, his wrinkled face creased into tight lines. His tone was serious, even mournful. "It has my name on it. The nails are already in the casket." He looked at the horrified faces of his wife, daughters, and grandson.

"Father, you're overdramatizing," Martha told him. "And causing much worry to us. Why would someone want to kill you? It doesn't make sense."

"It makes every bit of sense," Judge Archie said solemnly. "I've made enemies over the years, on a professional level. As a lawyer and judge, I have made decisions affecting the lives of many people."

"You mean someone in the office?" Preston asked. "How would poison have gotten into the cup if someone from the office didn't put it there?"

"That's exactly my point. Perhaps it is someone in the office. Granted, nearly everyone has had issues with me." He looked at Sloan. "If asked, I'm sure they'd tell you I was far from easy to work with."

"You're the boss, Father," Joan said tenderly. "It's your business, after all."

"Yes, it is my business that I shared with Mr. Lewis," the judge said slowly. "Although now, I'll need to spend more time there, since there is no acting head attorney on staff. I may entrust Mr. Armstrong as the interim president."

"Have you spoken to your staff?" Sloan asked, putting down his pen.

Judge Archie shook his head. "No, I wanted to leave that up to you, Mr. Sheppard. I'd like you to meet the staff while they are present in the office, at your earliest convenience, of course."

Sloan mentioned he would check his calendar book tomorrow and let him know when he would be available. In the meantime, he asked the judge about his staff.

Judge Archie cleared his throat. "Mr. and Mrs. Sampson, who work in the suite next to the main office, have been with the firm for many years. Mr. Clayton Sampson is a fine attorney, and his wife, Mrs. Lucille Sampson is a legal secretary. Mr. Quentin Cooper and Miss Doris Blake maintain their workplace in the outer office. Mrs. Castle is the office manager. Quentin is a law clerk. Doris is a remarkable secretary. The other lawyers on staff are Mr. Burgess Smith and Mr. Thurman Armstrong. Both are exceptional lawyers who have won numerous cases for the firm over the years." He paused. "I've been brusque at times with my staff, I suppose even crude. But I am a businessman as well as a lawyer. I don't allow wasting time in the office." Judge Archie hesitated. "As I said, my staff would not describe me as easy to work with or to get along with. There have been discussions that turned unpleasant. Perhaps that is par for the course. After all, as my daughter Joan mentioned, it was my law firm. I handed the reigns over to my friend Mr. Clement Lewis to take responsibility as I retired ten years ago."

"I know Quentin Cooper," Preston volunteered, addressing Sloan.

"We spend time together some evenings and weekends."

"Mr. Sampson's mother, Philomena, is an acquaintance of mine," Augusta added.

"Her late husband was a criminal here in Albany," Judge Archie said harshly, conjuring up memories of Philomena Sampson's late husband. "He had what was coming to him. As a judge, I enacted the correct sentence as I saw fit."

"His son and daughter-in-law work at the firm?" Sloan asked him, rather surprised.

Judge Archie nodded. "Mr. Sampson is an exceptional attorney. Whatever his father did years ago did not affect his son's ability to administer the law as a member of my staff."

"I've seen Mrs. Castle and Miss Blake while shopping downtown," Martha offered. "I don't know them very well, of course. They seemed pleasant enough."

"Quentin and I have seen Mr. Smith at coffee shops and dance halls," Preston said.

"I understand Mr. Armstrong's divorced but doesn't have children," Martha said. "When I've been to the office, I've found him rather laconic and not especially friendly."

"Most likely tied up in his work, Martha," her father added sensibly.

"Most of the staff lives alone, don't they, dear?" Augusta asked her husband.

Judge Archie frowned. "Yes, I believe so. The Sampsons live with their mother in a brownstone on Hamilton Street, but the others live in apartments scattered around the area. Mrs. Castle lives on Dove Street, not far from here. She is a widow with no children. I believe she spends time at the library and at the Institute of History and Art."

Joan nodded enthusiastically. "I've seen her at the library, really a lovely woman. We like the same literature—Mary Roberts Rinehart, Edith Wharton and Scott Fitzgerald."

Augusta told Sloan she and the judge had lived in the mansion they inherited from her grandparents upon their marriage. She explained their bedroom was on the first floor, while Martha and Preston had rooms on the third floor and Joan had the fourth floor. Gertrude, the daily housekeeper, came five days a week to clean the house and also to prepare lunch and dinner. She had been with them for over twenty years. Augusta added that Gertrude and her husband lived within walking distance on upper State Street.

Preston noticed Sloan had continued writing in his notepad. He then put down his pen and addressed the judge again, speaking determinedly and with some consternation.

"I'll be glad to speak to your staff this week. I'll call you tomorrow to verify."

Judge Archie nodded, mentioning he would be here at the house. He fished in his pocket for his business card, containing the firm address and the telephone number. He took out a pen and jotted down the home telephone number. "The office is an easy walk down State Street and then left on North Pearl," he added, glancing at Sloan. "Is your office still in the Albany Savings Bank Building?"

Sloan tucked his notepad away. "I'm fortunate to be there. It's quite a property with tenants vying for office space." He also produced his business card and handed it to the judge, who accepted it gratefully.

After about twenty minutes of idle conversation and more coffee, Sloan thanked Judge Archie and Mrs. Stafford again for inviting him to dinner. He mentioned it was a pleasure meeting the family. Joan and Martha accompanied him to the door and then returned to the dining room.

Judge Archie seemed satisfied, the evening a success. He then mentioned he wished to retire to the living room, to read the evening newspaper and to listen to the radio, his usual ritual before going to bed. *The Eveready Hour* was on again, and the judge so much enjoyed Duke Ellington's smooth jazz. Augusta helped him up, while Joan and Martha cleared the dessert dishes and coffee cups and retreated to the kitchen.

A strange and uncomfortable silence settled over the dining room, which just a moment ago was full of people. The clinking of dishes in the kitchen and the distant hum of the radio were the only sounds. Preston sat alone at the table, finishing his cold cup of coffee, a puzzled and rather disconcerted look on his face. He could not dismiss the feeling that something was amiss, the lively evening now a stark contrast to the solitude he felt. The shadows cast by the lighting seemed to creep closer, and the air held a tension he could not quite place.

Darkness had settled over the mansion on State and South Swan Streets. Outside, the winds had subsided, but it remained cold. The streetlights cast shadows across the snow-covered ground, creating an eerie stillness.

It was close to eleven o'clock, and the family had gone to bed. Judge Archie limped rather heavily to the hallway in the back of the kitchen, where the bedroom he shared with his wife was located. The old floorboards creaked under his weight, a familiar sound in the quiet house. Augusta, Joan, and Martha turned off the lights and the radio, the last notes of Duke Ellington fading into silence. Augusta followed her husband to their bedroom, her footsteps soft and measured.

Preston, Martha and Joan climbed the stairs, their good nights spoken in hushed tones. The house seemed to exhale as doors closed, each click echoing in the stillness. Martha paused for a moment at her bedroom door, glancing back down the dimly lit hallway toward her son's bedroom, a sense of unease lingering in the back of her mind.

In his bedroom, Preston had changed out of his dress clothes and relaxed in his boxer shorts. He cracked a window; despite the chilly air, he felt warm, and the cool breeze helped to alleviate the misgivings and ruminations he experienced. The distant sounds of the city filtered in, a faint reminder of the world outside.

He tried going to sleep but tossed, turned, and got up fitfully. Sitting up in bed with a cigarette, he picked up the latest issues of *The Saturday Evening Post*, *Vanity Fair*, and *Popular Science*. Usually, he enjoyed reading his favorite magazines, but tonight he merely flipped the pages moodily, unable to concentrate on the printed words. The articles and images blurred together, failing to capture his interest.

He looked up toward the windows overlooking State Street and West Capitol Park, his mind drifting. Grandfather believed someone was trying to kill him. But who and why? What proof did he have, other than the fact Mr. Lewis drank from his cup? Preston's mind raced as he recalled the incidents his grandfather considered attempts on his life. The evening on North Pearl Street before Christmas, when he pulled him just in time before a trolley would have mauled him to death. The speeding car incident was just that; another traffic problem in Albany. He had seen it often enough. But apparently, his grandfather saw it another way.

He put the magazines aside, exhaling smoke irritably. The room filled with the acrid scent of tobacco. Admittedly, he had never heard of poisonous tea, but apparently, it did exist. Unless there was poison already in the cup, but wouldn't his grandfather notice it when filling it with the boiling water?

He stared at the glowing tip of his cigarette, the smoke curling upwards, lost in thought. Could his grandfather be right? Was there truly someone out to get him? The questions gnawed at him, leaving him restless and uneasy.

But who would want to kill Grandfather? There must be a reason, some motive. Grandfather was adamant he had made enemies over the years. In his line of work, there were bound to be resentments. He freely admitted nearly everyone in the firm had issues with him. Preston assumed there wasn't a judge or lawyer in town who didn't have his share of adversaries.

He took a deep drag of his cigarette. How did the poison, if it was poison, get in the teacup? That pointed to someone close to Mr. Lewis. Someone who knew Mr. Lewis drank tea while at the office.

Finishing his cigarette, he crushed it in the ashtray on his bedside table. A sudden chill shook him, so quickly that he sat up, almost shaking. His bare feet were cold, and his heart beat violently. He tried to dismiss the thoughts permeating his mind. No, he told himself, it could not be, it was foolish, preposterous.

Was it possible Grandfather was responsible for these incidents? That he purposely stepped in front of the trolley and the speeding car? Did he want to kill himself but make it seem like accidents? If that were the case, why would he want to kill himself? Why would he elicit the assistance of Mr. Sheppard if he staged these occurrences himself? But then Mr. Lewis died later that day after drinking the tea, from his grandfather's cup.

Preston remembered his grandmother commenting that the judge had not been himself for quite a while. She mentioned he had been under mental strain. Was senility an issue? Or did he mask a darker persona? Would his grandfather actually resort to such drastic measures? He didn't think senility affected his grandfather, but even if it did, would it truly cause him to stage these extreme occurrences—or did the judge have something planned but not yet revealed?

Preston felt confused, almost desolate—and afraid. The room suddenly seemed insufferably claustrophobic, the light casting ominous patterns on the walls as his mind raced with unsettling possibilities.

CHAPTER FIVE

Mr. Burgess Smith sat at his desk at the law firm of Stafford and Lewis, overlooking busy North Pearl Street. It was another cold, blustery March morning, with strong gusty winds and occasional rain, with only a few breaks of sunshine. Upon arriving, he heard the usual complaints about the relentless weather, but the wind and rain were the least of his concerns. 'Another day, another dollar'—a mantra he embraced and indulged in to the fullest.

He glanced at his desk calendar: Friday, March 27, 1925. Three appointments were scheduled for the morning. A new client, regarding a divorce decree; another for a custody battle; and the third for a homicide investigation. Burgess took up his pen and began writing notes on the information he acquired on the cases so far.

Burgess Smith was forty-five and, although never married, he had been involved with several women and had come close to engagements a few times. He was rather indifferent to relationships at this stage in life. He was more concerned with his career and making money. He also maintained an active social life and from time to time dated several eligible women in Albany. He also enjoyed speakeasies, like many others, despite their illegality.

One evening, as he sipped a whiskey sour in a dimly lit speakeasy, he overheard a heated debate about the stock market and a sentiment he could attest to: "It's a goldmine these days," someone said. Burgess's own investments had quadrupled his earnings over the last ten years.

His modest apartment on Hudson Avenue was enough to satisfy him. Granted, he could have afforded something bigger and better, but Burgess did not believe in spending money foolishly. Despite his financial success, he had little interest in the trappings of wealth. He attended college and law school in his native Buffalo and arrived in Albany to make a new start. He traveled by train at times to see his elderly parents, but the ride from Albany was extremely long, so letters and postcards suited him fine.

He puffed at his cigarette and noticed Mrs. Rose Castle in the doorway. He asked her if she needed anything, as she was instrumental in typing his reports and depositions. He saw she hesitated and then asked if something was bothering her. Although he admired her work ethic and demeanor with clients, he found Mrs. Castle difficult at times, and rather nosy.

"Excuse me, Mr. Smith," Rose said, entering the office. She forced a weak smile, her grayish hair somewhat untidy. Her simple brown dress exaggerated her frame, lending an air of dishevelment.

"Yes, Mrs. Castle," Burgess said, patiently, wondering what trivial matter she might bring up this time. With her reputation as a busybody, he expected to hear just about anything.

"I finished filing the previous reports," she told him, her voice steady. "Quentin also finished filing the reports from January and February."

Burgess continued puffing at his cigarette, his eyes narrowing slightly as he leaned back in his swivel chair. The greenish light from the banker's lamp cast shadows across his face. "Is that what you came to tell me?" His tone held a slight annoyance, the smoke surrounding his words.

Rose still hesitated, standing before his large, mahogany desk, the scent of tobacco thick in the air. "I just spoke with Judge Archie on the telephone. He'll arrive by noontime. He mentioned a private investigator will be here this afternoon to speak to us about Mr. Lewis."

Burgess continued smoking, knocking ash into the ashtray. He showed no reaction at all. "Well, that's interesting. I suppose he wants it cleared up. Although I thought the police were satisfied with their findings."

"So did I," Mrs. Castle said, her lips pressed together firmly.

He looked rather intently at Mrs. Castle. She appeared disturbed, as though she dreaded any further contact with the law. Personally, he shared her opinion and found the police annoying and meddlesome, disturbing to his work. She mentioned the police had already interrogated them several times, so what more could a private investigator find out?

"Did you tell the other members of the staff?" he asked her, his tone measured.

Mrs. Castle nodded. "I told Quentin and Doris and I mentioned it to the Sampsons. Quentin and Doris didn't seem to mind but Mr. Sampson appeared rather agitated. Mrs. Sampson mentioned Mrs. Stafford had told her when she spoke with her just yesterday." She hesitated. "But she didn't inform the rest of us."

Burgess tapped ash from his cigarette. "And I assume you told Thurman, too?"

"Oh yes, I went into his office and told him just like I'm telling you."

Burgess shrugged. He was not sure where this conversation was headed. He asked if there was anything else she wished to impart. She still appeared rather preoccupied, even troubled, her eyes darting around the room as if searching for answers.

Mrs. Castle turned as though to return to the main office, then addressed him again. “By the way, Judge Archie informed me he intends to appoint Mr. Armstrong as the interim president of the firm while the death of Mr. Lewis is being investigated.” Without waiting for a comment, Mrs. Rose Castle sailed briskly out of the office.

Burgess kept his cigarette to his lips, which hid the harsh curve to his mouth. Rather stunned at first, he regained his composure. So, Thurman was now president of the firm. He continued smoking, drawing deeply into his lungs with anger and resentment. His mind coiled around dark possibilities.

With Mr. Lewis out of the way and the judge nearly on his deathbed, Burgess decided he would take matters into his own hands. Enough time had been wasted. There must have been some dirt on Thurman Armstrong over the years, he thought maliciously. Under no circumstances would he ever be second best. He returned to the reports in front of him, a distinctive gleam in his eyes.

“Type these reports, Doris,” Thurman Armstrong said, rather brusquely as he handed her a folder full of papers. “And be sure I have them by the end of the day.”

“Of course, Mr. Armstrong,” Doris said, rebuffed by his tone.

Sensing her reaction, Thurman grinned. “You’ll have to forgive my demeanor. I’m too preoccupied with these cases, they’re big money.”

Doris nodded, although she did not believe such positivity could induce someone to act as he did. She struggled to find words, unconvinced that his confidence justified his tone.

"I'll be in court all day on Monday. I talked with Judge Archie earlier this morning. He'll be here shortly with a private investigator named Mr. Sheppard to speak to us about Mr. Lewis."

"Mrs. Castle told me," Doris said. "I think it's a waste of time."

"Mrs. Castle also informed me after I spoke with him earlier," Thurman said. "Once the judge makes up his mind, that's it"

"Perhaps," Doris said doubtfully. "I still think nothing will come of it."

Thurman agreed. He reiterated the importance of the reports by the end of the day and then dismissed her, as he felt an overwhelming need for solitude.

From the main office, he could hear Mrs. Castle speaking on the telephone and Doris conversing with Quentin. He noticed Burgess walk past his office, most likely to confer with Doris or Quentin about some case. Thurman admitted Doris and Quentin were exceptional. He never doubted their efficiency in completing assignments. On the other hand, Judge Archie tended to be critical, but that was the nature of the beast, Thurman thought wryly.

Thurman Armstrong, a graduate of Albany Law School, class of 1899, was proud of his achievements in law. He had established a firm client base and assisted numerous people in winning divorce proceedings, child custody disputes, and real estate cases. One of his most notable cases involved securing a favorable verdict for a mother in a highly publicized custody battle, which earned him significant praise in the local press. He also assisted clients in criminal cases including a high-profile defense that displayed his legal acumen.

Despite facing extenuating circumstances, such as numerous difficult clients and complex cases, Armstrong's perseverance and dedication to his clients' needs never wavered. His reputation grew, with many clients and colleagues admiring his unwavering commitment to justice. Over time, his reputation solidified, earning praise from satisfied clients. "Thurman Armstrong is a beacon of hope for those in need of legal aid," one satisfied client remarked.

At fifty, Thurman remained as slender as he had been twenty years earlier. His brown hair, now sprinkled with gray, framed his blue eyes, which still held a sharp, discerning gaze. Divorced and childless, Thurman focused intently on his law practice. Though he occasionally enjoyed local theater performances at Harmanus Bleecker Hall, he preferred the quiet solitude of his spacious apartment on Lancaster Street, where he had lived for over a decade. The location allowed him to indulge in the culinary delights of nearby Lark Street.

Thurman's relationships with his colleagues were often strained. He had clashed with Burgess on several occasions, their disagreements leaving a lingering tension. Fortunately, they rarely worked on cases together, operating more like independent lawyers within the same firm. Thurman had worked with Mr. Lewis often, which was much more productive and pleasant. Mr. Sampson, on the other hand, was less tenacious but equally problematic. Thurman found his cocky and condescending demeanor grating and often wondered how his clients could tolerate him.

But then I tend to be cocky and condescending, too, Thurman thought, puffing at his cigarette. He turned his attention back to the report in front of him. Over the years, Thurman had learned to take care of himself, prioritizing money, which afforded him the large apartment on Lancaster Street.

His mind wandered to Judge Archie. Like everyone in the office, Thurman had his disputes with the older man. At times, situations became difficult because Judge Archie believed he was always right. Yet, there was no denying his impeccable record as a lawyer and judge.

Thurman recalled their last conversation. "I'm appointing you as the interim president of the firm," Judge Archie had said, his tone leaving no room for argument. "A private investigator is looking into Mr. Lewis's death, and I need someone reliable to hold things together."

His thoughts drifted back to that evening in February, after attending a performance at Harmanus Bleecker Hall. Marion Harris, one of his favorite singers, had been mesmerizing, and Thurman felt fortunate to have secured two tickets for himself and a lady friend.

He cringed as his mind wandered, the document on his desk forgotten. After the concert, he had dropped his date off at her apartment on Upper State Street. Driving home, he had sped through the red light at the corner of State and South Swan Streets, lost in thought. Thurman realized how lucky he was that no other cars were around. He was so deep in thought—a problem he readily admitted—that he did not notice someone at the curb, about to cross.

The memory sent a shiver down his spine. "I should've been more careful," he muttered, taking a deep drag from his cigarette. The near miss was a grave reminder of how easily things could go wrong. I can't afford any more mistakes, he thought, especially with everything at stake, his jaw tightening with resolve.

It was not until Thurman arrived at his apartment that he realized the elderly man at the corner was Judge Archie. The next morning, he kept his mouth shut, fearing that either Judge Archie or Mr. Lewis would fire him on the spot. Both men were notoriously old-fashioned in their viewpoints. A pang of guilt stabbed at him, quickly swallowed by smug self-righteousness. While the judge's near brush with death—the second—was discussed in the office, no shadow of suspicion fell on him.

On the other hand, he wondered if nosy, inquisitive Mrs. Castle could have seen him. Her apartment on Dove Street was close enough, and she spent a lot of time at the Harmanus Bleecker Library. She could easily have spotted a speeding car running a red light, even from a block away. He remembered how she often mentioned her evening strolls down State Street.

His colleagues were well aware of the car he drove. Burgess, with his manipulative and crooked methods, lived nearby on Hudson Avenue. Thurman could easily imagine Burgess reveling in the chaos of revealing the speeding car belonged to him. He puffed at his cigarette, his hatred for his associate simmering.

As he studied the document in front of him, Thurman thought about the secrets everyone in the office seemed to harbor. Even the judge had his own mysteries. Perhaps Mr. Lewis, too

Mrs. Augusta Stafford crossed at the light on the corner of State and South Swan Streets, then continued walking briskly until she reached Hamilton Street. She knew she could have taken the trolley, but it would have gone downtown and then back uptown, which was out of her way and rather far. She much preferred to walk. She breathed in the chilly air and felt replenished.

Before leaving the house, she assured Gertrude she would return for lunch. The morning was hers to enjoy, and she decided it was the perfect chance to call Philomena, a dear friend she hadn't seen in far too long. Philomena's cheerful voice on the other end brightened her mood instantly. "Why not come by for tea this morning?" she offered. She readily agreed, happy to embrace a moment of spontaneity in her day.

Augusta wore her fur coat and cloche hat, although she wished she had put on her scarf. The wind was bitter at times. Finally arriving at Hamilton Street, she turned right and came to the magnificent brownstone the Sampsons called home. Climbing the stone steps, she rang the bell and saw a young woman in the glass. Smiling politely, she welcomed Augusta into the warm home, took her fur coat and hat, and ushered her into the living room, where Philomena sat in an armchair near the fireplace.

Upon seeing her friend, Philomena rose with some difficulty but smiled warmly. Augusta noted the dainty teapot and cups on a coffee table. They were of elegant porcelain, sprinkled with roses. Settling in an armchair, Augusta looked around the comfortable room. After pouring the tea and handing a cup to Augusta, Philomena dismissed Nan, her maid and turned her attention back to her guest.

"Your home is lovely," Augusta said, as though she had never been there before. She admired the exquisite antique lamps and the comfortable Victorian sofa. The plush armchairs near the ornate fireplace, the magnificent dining table in the next room, and the grand staircase in the hallway leading to the bedrooms upstairs all caught her eye.

Looking at her friend, she thought Philomena looked well. Her gray hair was piled neatly, although not stylishly, and she looked fresh and pleasant. She commented on Philomena's beige dress and lovely string of pearls.

"Thank you, dear," Philomena said, her smile as welcoming as the cozy fire crackling in the hearth. "You brighten my day. And look at you—so elegant, as always. I must say, having you here makes this old home feel even more alive."

Augusta chuckled softly, glancing around the room that was infused with Philomena's signature charm. She smoothed down her navy blue dress, taking in the comforting blend of scents—freshly brewed tea and hints of lavender polish. "You're much too kind," she replied.

"Have you given any more thought to Mr. Lewis?" Philomena asked rather bluntly. "It is rather odd, don't you think? I know he was close to your husband."

Augusta kept the teacup to her lips. "Well, I don't really know what to think. Apparently, he drank a bad tea and fell quite ill. I understand he was dead by morning."

"I've never heard of bad tea," Philomena said, her face tightening into lines. "Do you think he was murdered?"

"Why, Philomena," Augusta said, appalled.

Philomena raised her eyebrows. "Stranger things have happened. I'm sure Mr. Lewis, as well as your husband, made enemies over the years."

Augusta hesitated, knowing full well that Philomena's husband had been sentenced by her own husband to state prison, where he later died. Despite their friendship going back to girlhood, it was a subject best left untouched.

"The young people today," Philomena said, changing course. "I just don't understand the loose morals of those flapper girls. I find it repulsive. They go to the speakeasies, where they dance and drink and they smoke in public, too. So disgraceful."

Augusta agreed. "Times have changed, Philomena, dear. I'm afraid today's generation is nothing like ours. I believe our standards were much more appropriate." She then mentioned her activities with the Albany chapter of the League of Women Voters and invited Philomena to attend an upcoming meeting in the evening.

"I'd be glad to attend," Philomena answered, much to Augusta's surprise. "It'll get me out of the house and away from my son and daughter-in-law."

Augusta was rather taken aback. "I thought you got along with them?"

Philomena finished her tea. "My son and his wife are interested in money. I keep silent on what they do so that no arguments ensue."

They were silent for a few minutes until Augusta mentioned how her husband had hired a private investigator to look into the death of

Mr. Lewis. She added that he planned to spend the afternoon at the office while the investigator spoke with the staff.

"A detective?" Philomena said, her eyebrows raised. "Isn't that what the police are for?"

"My husband has his doubts about what happened to Mr. Lewis."

"What is this man's name? Perhaps I know of him."

"Mr. Sloan Sheppard," Augusta told her. "According to my husband, he is quite well known here. He's done business with him in the past."

Philomena's expression sharpened with curiosity. "Mr. Sheppard? That name rings a bell. When my son and daughter-in-law return later today, they might shed some light on this." She paused, choosing her words with deliberate care. "You realize what this could mean, Augusta. Someone might have reason to harm your husband. I wouldn't be surprised if there were multiple people involved."

The air in the room seemed to thicken, as an uneasy silence stretched between them. Augusta set her teacup down with steady hands, though her mind churned. The measured ticking of the grandfather clock in the hallway marked eleven o'clock, its sound heavier than usual. Breaking the tension, Augusta rose and smoothed her dress.

"I should head home now," she said briskly. "Lunch awaits, and there's much to discuss before my husband heads off to the office." She glanced back as she adjusted her hat. "I'll let you know about the League of Women Voters meeting in April."

Philomena's gaze lingered, thoughtful and troubled. "Of course," she replied, escorting Augusta to the door. A crisp swirl of cold air brushed past them as she held it open. Augusta accepted her fur coat and cloche hat from the maid. After ensuring she was safely wrapped against the cold, she waved as the door closed behind her. With quick, purposeful steps, she strode down Hamilton Street, her thoughts racing.

She watched until Augusta vanished from view, the street quiet save for the milkman and mailman making their rounds, and the distant clang of a trolley. She lingered by the doorway, unsettled. Augusta hadn't taken kindly to the mention of danger, but Philomena couldn't help but brood over the possibility. The judge had made enemies—perhaps more than Augusta was willing to acknowledge. Given the chance, Philomena thought darkly, she just might see justice done—on her own terms.

Preston telephoned Quentin at the firm that morning. "Lunch today?" he suggested. "There's the diner on South Pearl Street within walking distance."

Quentin had agreed, and by midday Preston had donned his heavy wool coat, pulling his cap low against the wintry breeze. He reached the diner within minutes after jumping off the trolley on State Street. He loitered briefly, puffing warm breath into gloved hands, until Quentin appeared, weaving through the midday crowd. They exchanged polite smiles before stepping briskly inside to escape the chill.

The diner was modest but bustling, the clink of dishes and hum of conversation creating a lively backdrop. They found a booth near the window, the view offering glimpses of trolley cars trundling past and bundled-up pedestrians hurrying along the street. A waitress approached promptly, her bobbed hair tucked neatly under her cap and took their orders.

The food arrived swiftly: a turkey sandwich and fries for Preston, a hamburger for Quentin. Two bottles of Coca-Cola stood sweating slightly, their condensation catching the light, along with two cups of hot coffee. Preston ate quickly, his cigarette already lit by the time Quentin was halfway through his meal.

Quentin continued eating, pausing to address his friend. "Mr. Sheppard is coming to the firm this afternoon. The judge wants him to meet everyone and see if there's anything else to uncover about Mr. Lewis."

Preston nodded. "Mr. Sheppard came to our house for dinner. Grandfather thinks someone saw or knows something that could help him." He paused. "I saw Mr. Armstrong recently." He told Quentin about his visit to the cruise line office on Tuesday morning to inquire about trips to New York City.

"Well, he has enough money to take whatever cruise he wants," Quentin said, rather in disgust. "They make all the money, Pres. The little people do all the work and don't get any credit."

Preston was surprised his friend would speak so bitterly. On the other hand, he imagined it was true. From what his grandfather had mentioned, the lawyers received a top salary, including Mr. Lewis, and worked hard, putting in many hours, to achieve such a lucrative remuneration.

"Let's go out Saturday night to the new speakeasy off Sheraton Avenue," Quentin said.

Preston agreed. "Provided we don't see Mr. Smith or Mr. Armstrong. They frequent speakeasies, too, you know. Remember when we saw them in January?"

Quentin lit a cigarette. "The hell with them. But doesn't your grandfather disapprove of drinking and speakeasies?"

"I don't have to mention a speakeasy. I'll tell them the dance hall on South Pearl Street."

They were silent while the waitress cleared their dishes and refilled their coffee cups. Preston looked at Quentin through a haze of cigarette smoke and spoke rather seriously.

"Quentin, my grandfather believes someone's trying to kill him. He thinks the poison was in his cup and Mr. Lewis drank it by mistake. That's why he wants Mr. Sheppard to speak to everyone, to get to the bottom of it."

Quentin puffed at his cigarette. "What in the world put that into his head?"

Preston reiterated the time he slipped on North Pearl Street in December and the speeding car last month on State Street.

"I totally forgot about that," Quentin said. He sighed, extinguishing his cigarette. "Pres, if someone is really trying to kill the judge, it has to be the Sampsons. They are the most arrogant people. I wouldn't doubt if Mr. Sampson has his eye on the presidency for the firm now that Mr. Lewis is gone."

"Grandfather made Mr. Armstrong the interim president," Preston mentioned.

Quentin shrugged dismissively. "It's only temporary. I bet Mr. Sampson will pull whatever strings he needs to land the presidency."

Preston looked out the window at the sidewalk full of office workers and shop assistants on their lunch break. Trolleys clanged by and a newsboy shouted the latest headlines about the stock market. He then addressed Quentin again, getting straight to the point. He wondered aloud if his grandfather was behind these events, wanting it to appear that someone was trying to kill him when, in fact, no one was. Quentin stared across the table, momentarily taken aback. Then, he composed himself.

"That's a possibility," he said, seeing it in a different light. "Isn't your grandfather eighty or close to it? Maybe he's senile. Or he could be imagining things. The mind can play tricks on people that age, you know."

Preston was not convinced. He mentioned to Quentin not to say anything about his suspicions and he assured him he never spoke to anyone in the office about such matters. The waitress soon approached with the check and with the cash settled, they put on their jackets and caps and headed outside.

"Good luck this afternoon with Mr. Sheppard," Preston told him, standing on the sidewalk in front of the diner, battling the winds and blocking a trio of businessmen about to enter. He stepped aside and looked at Quentin.

Quentin adjusted his cap against the biting wind. "Thanks, Preston. I'll need it."

As the businessmen hurried inside, their coats flapping in the wind, Quentin glanced at his pocket watch. "I should get going. I don't want Mrs. Castle to tell me I'm late." He had another cigarette to his lips and cupped his hands to light the match, shielding it from the wind.

"No worries, Pres. Even if someone really is trying to kill the judge, we'll find out soon enough." He exhaled a thick plume of smoke, but before it could linger, a sharp gust of wind snatched it away, curling and scattering it into the cold afternoon air until it vanished altogether. His tone turned almost frivolous. "Who knows, maybe the murderer has other victims in mind."

Sloan arrived at the law firm just after one o'clock and was cordially received by Mrs. Castle. She offered him coffee or tea and a piece of her lemon cake, which he declined. She took his hat and coat, then ushered him into Mr. Lewis's office, where Judge Archie sat at the desk, awaiting his arrival. The judge did not smile but merely greeted him perfunctorily.

"Good afternoon, Mr. Sheppard," the judge said, not rising from his chair. "Welcome, and please be seated." He waved him to a chair, his demeanor serious and not especially personable.

Sloan sat in a chair in front of the desk and glanced around the office. It was like many he had visited, although this one was the scene of an unexpected death. The large elderly man remained stoic and unmoved, exuding the weight of years and authority, as though rising would be an unnecessary effort.

Without wasting time, Judge Archie explained that the desk he was at was where Mr. Lewis had died. He pointed to the bookcases on the left, indicating where the teacups had been kept. The teacups were no longer there, as the police had examined them but reached no definite conclusions. He reiterated his dissatisfaction with their investigations and explained why he had hired Sloan to look into Mr. Lewis's death.

"My staff is aware that you were coming today," he told him. "Mrs. Castle, the woman you spoke to as you entered, is the office manager."

Sloan realized he was to make the rounds of the large office on his own rather than being accompanied by the judge. He also realized it was better that way. Perhaps the staff would be more open and forthright in their comments without the domineering and bossy figure of the older man present.

Sloan stood and thanked the judge. "I'll return to the main office, and Mrs. Castle can point me in the right direction."

The judge was seemingly lost in thought. He turned his attention to a few documents in front of him and asked Sloan to return to see him before leaving.

In the main office, Sloan surveyed the faces before him: Mrs. Castle, middle-aged and heavyset; Quentin, young and keen; and Doris, a flapper-type despite her age. As he passed the offices of Burgess and Thurman, he caught their eyes briefly—they seemed to be observing him as much as he was observing them. Sloan could sense the staff's quiet resentment toward law enforcement, a mistrust that lingered in the air. It wasn't directed solely at him, though; it felt as if they were wary of one another. The office was subdued, with little small talk exchanged. Business took priority, and Judge Archie's imposing presence seemed to govern everything.

Sloan found Mrs. Castle both pleasant and overpowering. Her lively demeanor was tinged with an unpredictability that put him slightly on edge. He had learned over the years that such capriciousness often masked layers of complexity beneath the surface. Settling into the chair by her desk, he adjusted his posture to appear at ease. "Mrs. Castle, can you tell me about Mr. Lewis?" he asked, his tone measured.

Her expression shifted, a flicker of melancholy crossing her face. "I discovered poor Mr. Lewis," she said, her voice laden with regret, as though speaking of a dear friend lost too soon. "I arrived early that morning, as I often do, to prepare for the day. His office door was closed, which struck me as odd—he always left it open. When I knocked, there was no response, so I went in." Her hands fidgeted with a paperweight, turning it absently, as if grasping for control over the memory. "That's when I saw him... slumped over his desk."

Sloan's pen hovered above his notepad, waiting. "What did you do next?" he prompted.

"I called the Sampsons right away," she replied, her voice shaking just slightly. "Mr. Sampson is an attorney, and his wife works as his secretary. I thought they'd know what to do." She paused, as if reliving the moment, then straightened her posture and met Sloan's gaze, the mask of composure slipping back into place.

Sloan watched her from his seat, her hands darting between papers, a telephone, and small piles of reports that she clipped with methodical precision. She was robust and matronly, with a nosy streak he recognized instantly—he'd known her type well in his line of work. Dedicated, yes, but always at the forefront when it came to overhearing a whispered conversation or piecing together office gossip.

"Why didn't you call the judge first?"

Mrs. Castle met his eyes. "Because I didn't want to disturb him. Judge Archie is quite elderly and I was afraid the news would upset him terribly."

"Where do you live, Mrs. Castle?" Sloan asked after a moment, his tone casual.

She paused mid-motion, her fingers lingering on a paperclip before she slowly set it down. Turning toward him, she flushed slightly, a sign she wasn't accustomed to such personal inquiries. "I live in an apartment on Dove Street," she said, her voice steady despite her hesitation. "By myself. My husband passed some years ago, and I never had children. I spend my time at the Harmanus Bleecker Library when I can. I belong to a book club there."

Her answer hung in the air, neatly clipped at the end as though to ward off any probing follow-ups. Sloan read her pause like an open book—more details would be deemed improper, and he knew better than to press further. By her demeanor, self-contained and almost Victorian, he suspected she had resigned herself to widowhood as a permanent state of being.

"Do you feel the poisonous tea was meant for the judge? Mr. Lewis drank from his cup." loan aimed to catch her off guard, but she held firm, not so much as blinking an eye.

Mrs. Castle put down a pile of reports. "No, I don't believe that. Judge Archie told us he handed Mr. Lewis a cup without realizing it was his. I left at five o'clock that day, as I do all the time. The judge and Mr. Lewis were still working, but he said he left shortly after I did. So Mr. Lewis was here alone, working by himself." She paused.

"The police said it was bad tea—full of residue. Mr. Lewis had a bad reaction to it." Her tone was superficial as though it was over and forgotten. "He was in good health, as far as I know. Mrs. Sampson and I washed the tea cups, as we do in the mornings without realizing it could've been the tea."

Sloan watched her from his seat, her hands darting between papers, a telephone, and small piles of reports that she clipped with methodical precision. She was robust and matronly, with a nosy streak he recognized instantly—he'd known her type well in his line of work. Dedicated, yes, but always at the forefront when it came to overhearing a whispered conversation or piecing together office gossip.

"Why didn't you call the judge first?"

Mrs. Castle met his eyes. "Because I didn't want to disturb him. Judge Archie is quite elderly and I was afraid the news would upset him terribly."

"Where do you live, Mrs. Castle?" Sloan asked after a moment, his tone casual.

She paused mid-motion, her fingers lingering on a paperclip before she slowly set it down. Turning toward him, she flushed slightly, a sign she wasn't accustomed to such personal inquiries. "I live in an apartment on Dove Street," she said, her voice steady despite her hesitation. "By myself. My husband passed some years ago, and I never had children. I spend my time at the Harmanus Bleecker Library when I can. I belong to a book club there."

Her answer hung in the air, neatly clipped at the end as though to ward off any probing follow-ups. Sloan read her pause like an open book—more details would be deemed improper, and he knew better than to press further. She spoke with an air of finality, as though she was through speaking and did not wish to be bothered any further. She busied herself with papers on her desk, making it clear her work was her first duty. By her demeanor, self-contained and almost Victorian, he suspected she had resigned herself to widowhood as a permanent state of being.

Sloan realized he could not get anything further from her. Possibly, she had nothing else to tell him anyway, although these nosy parkers usually knew more than they told.

He thanked Mrs. Castle for her time. She led him to Thurman's office, the closest to her desk. Upon entering, they noticed he was busy on the telephone. He waved Sloan in, and Mrs. Castle retreated to the main office.

Thurman was rather loud in talking and quite arrogant in speech. Luckily, Sloan was used to the whims of haughty executives and lawyers and prepared for the interview, expecting little if any results. He sat in the only empty chair available, the only other chair piled under stacks of reports. His desk was a chaotic sea of papers, and even the window sills were cluttered with haphazard piles of documents. Looking at him carefully, Sloan sensed a serious and hard-working man of about fifty, certainly well-dressed but visibly impatient. Thurman seemed to prolong his telephone call deliberately, testing Sloan's patience. Finally, he replaced the handset, set the candlestick telephone on a corner of the desk, and asked Sloan impertinently what he wanted.

Sloan leaned back in his chair, observing Thurman's slow movements as he reached for a cigarette. He let the silence linger for a moment before speaking, his tone calm yet purposeful.

"I'm following up on Mr. Lewis's death, as requested by the judge," he said.

Thurman lit his cigarette, the brief flare catching the tired lines etched into his face. He didn't offer one to Sloan—a gesture that spoke volumes. "What do you need to know?" he asked flatly, puffing smoke into the space between them.

"Anything you remember from that day. How did Mr. Lewis seem to you?" Sloan asked, keeping his voice level.

Thurman exhaled, the irritation in his expression barely concealed. "I spoke with him briefly. Nothing out of the ordinary, really. Judge Archie came by after lunch—they were working together in Mr. Lewis's office for the rest of the afternoon."

Sloan nodded, his pen gliding across the page. "What time did you leave?" he asked.

"Same as usual. Five, maybe five-thirty. When I left, the judge was still in there."

Sloan chose his next words carefully, leaning slightly forward. "Do you think the tea Mr. Lewis drank might have been intended for the judge? There's some concern about that possibility, though nothing concrete."

Thurman's cigarette hovered over the ashtray before he crushed it—deliberate, precise. His gaze flicked through the haze of smoke, as it locked onto Sloan's for just a moment. He hesitated long enough for Sloan to register the discomfort.

"I wouldn't know what to tell you about that, Mr. Sheppard," Thurman replied, his voice clipped before bending back to his work.

Sloan asked him about himself. Thurman briefly explained he was divorced and did not have children. His ex-wife had remarried and lived in California. An Albany native, he graduated from Albany Law School at the top of his class. He lived in a pleasant apartment on Lancaster Street and had been with Lewis and Stafford for twenty years. Judge Archie could be difficult at times, he added, but that was only due to his commitment to his work and to seeing justice prevail. He mentioned that Judge Archie had appointed him the interim head of the office in the wake of Mr. Lewis's death. He further commented on Mr. Lewis's rather sedate demeanor, in contrast to the judge.

"I understand there were two incidents where the judge could've been killed," Sloan mentioned, referring to the incident on North Pearl Street and the speeding car on State Street.

Thurman kept his head down, absorbed in his work. He looked up quickly and told Sloan he knew nothing about those events, and then mentioned he needed to return to his work. Sloan took the hint and thanked him, seeing himself out of the office.

Upon entering the main office, he noticed the remaining staff. He approached them and learned their names were Miss Doris Blake and Mr. Quentin Cooper. He introduced himself and found them rather engaging and personable, unlike Mr. Thurman Armstrong. He shook hands with them and asked what they remembered about the day Mr. Lewis died.

"I wish I could help you, Mr. Sheppard," Doris said, finishing a letter and taking the paper out of the typewriter. She looked at him as he stood near her desk. "I left at five as usual that day and don't remember anything. I never made tea or coffee for the judge or Mr. Lewis. Mrs. Castle or Mrs. Sampson usually took care of that."

Quentin agreed. "We were told the judge made the tea that day. Mrs. Sampson offered, but he insisted—he'd started taking on small tasks more often lately."

Sloan thanked him. A likable young man, he thought by his tone and decorum, certainly handsome in an offhanded sense, appearing rather carefree. "Anything else you can tell me about Mr. Lewis in the last couple of weeks? Anything unusual?"

Neither Quentin nor Doris could tell Sloan anything important pertaining to Mr. Lewis. Doris mentioned he seemed fine, although the judge was something entirely different.

"His health hasn't been well recently. I spoke with Mrs. Stafford just last week, and she told me she is concerned about his blood pressure."

Sloan noted Doris's striking features—youthful, self-assured, every inch a modern flapper in the way she carried herself. She told him she graduated from the state teachers college with a degree in English and began working at the law firm close to ten years ago. Quentin was also a state teachers college graduate who intended to be a history teacher but changed focus and entered the law field as a clerk. He had worked for the judge and Mr. Lewis for almost seven years. Doris mentioned she lived in an apartment on Quail Street, and Quentin told Sloan his apartment was on North Allen Street. They took the trolley to and from downtown, as it was convenient for easy access to North Pearl Street.

"I really knew next to nothing about the law," Quentin commented jovially. "But the judge liked my background and hired me. He and Mrs. Castle trained me thoroughly, and he has always been pleased with my work."

Sloan considered his next question carefully, watching Doris and Quentin's reactions. "Have you thought about whether the poisoned tea might have been intended for the judge?" he asked, his voice measured.

Doris and Quentin exchanged a glance, their expressions equal parts surprise and unease. Doris was the first to speak, her words brisk and certain. "The judge has made his share of enemies over the years. People find him... difficult. Even those of us here try to avoid him when we can, though there's no denying his skill in the legal field."

Quentin hesitated before nodding. "That's true," he admitted, his voice quieter. "But making enemies doesn't mean someone would resort to... this." He faltered, his brow furrowed. Sloan caught a flicker of hesitation, as though Quentin was holding something back.

The silence stretched for a beat too long, heavy and awkward. Doris finally broke it by rising from her chair. "Would you like me to take you to the Sampsons?" she offered, her tone polite but clipped.

Sloan inclined his head. "Thank you," he replied, following her out of the room. They passed Mrs. Castle's desk, her typing precise and rhythmic, and continued down a narrow hallway that led to the neighboring suite.

When they entered, Doris gestured toward a tall man standing by a bookshelf. "Mr. Clayton Sampson," she said, and Clayton turned, his handshake firm but perfunctory. Doris motioned toward a woman seated at a desk nearby. "And Mrs. Lucille Sampson." The woman offered only a polite nod, her expression unreadable.

After Doris returned to the main office, Clayton invited Sloan to sit. "Terrible business, isn't it," he remarked, settling into his own chair. "Mr. Lewis dying like that. My wife and I were here that morning after Mrs. Castle called us."

Sloan opened his notebook, his pen poised. "Do you know why she called you first?" he asked evenly.

Clayton leaned back, exuding the air of someone accustomed to control. He spoke with a practiced confidence that bordered on arrogance. "No, not exactly. But my wife and I are close to Judge Archie and his wife. We've been to their home for coffee on several occasions."

Sloan scribbled a note. "And where do you live, Mr. Sampson?"

"On Hamilton Street," Clayton replied. "It's an arrangement that works well for us, given its proximity to North Pearl Street and the conveniences of downtown. My widowed mother lives with us, too."

Turning to Lucille, Sloan asked, "Mrs. Sampson, did you make the tea the day Mr. Lewis died?" He knew the answer but watched her closely for any reaction.

Lucille finally looked up from her desk, her expression calm but her eyes sharp. She took a measured breath before responding. "No," she said simply, her tone giving nothing away.

Sloan's gaze lingered on Lucille Sampson as she sat poised behind her desk. There was an understated elegance about her—her makeup was minimal, her brown hair neatly styled, and her blue eyes carried a quiet timidity. She fit her role effortlessly—meticulous, composed, seamlessly aligned with her husband's ambitions. Yet Sloan detected hints of privilege in her demeanor, a life perhaps accustomed to comfort and ease.

Shifting his attention, Sloan leaned forward slightly. "Judge Archie mentioned incidents where his life might have been at risk. Are you familiar with them?" he asked, his tone steady.

Clayton gave a brief nod, his expression confident yet guarded. "In December, he slipped just before a trolley on North Pearl. Then in February, a car nearly struck him on State Street."

Lucille's voice cut in, softer but deliberate. "The judge and Mr. Lewis certainly had their share of enemies," she said. "It's no surprise, really—judges seldom win affection from everyone they deal with." She hesitated, her gaze flickering toward her husband before continuing. "Clayton, you remember when your life was threatened after you sent that man to prison, don't you?"

Clayton gave a faint smile, nodding just enough to acknowledge the memory. "A lawyer's job is rarely simple," he agreed. Turning to Sloan, his eyes lit with faint recognition. "Your work must be similar, Mr. Sheppard. Haven't I seen you in court before?"

Sloan returned the smile, his professional facade intact. "I believe so, Mr. Sampson. I often find myself at City Hall or the Court of Appeals, working on behalf of my clients."

"Well, it's a pleasure to meet you again," Clayton said pleasantly.

"Perhaps you'd want to meet Mrs. Sampson," Lucille said. "Clayton's mother is a wonderful woman, although I'm afraid she was not on good terms with the judge."

Clayton winced, his expression tightening as though he wished his wife had let that detail remain unspoken. Sloan sensed a certain friction between them. Clayton cleared his throat and explained that many years ago Judge Archie had sentenced his father to prison, where he later died. His mother never forgave the judge—she believed he was wrongly accused.

"What was your father sent to prison for, Mr. Sampson?" Sloan asked, although he knew he could easily find that out himself. He waited to hear if he would tell him the truth.

"Embezzlement, among other things," Clayton admitted reluctantly. "My father was involved with the gangsters here. Apparently, they are still quite active, too."

"Especially with Prohibition," Lucille commented.

"I'm aware of the illegal liquor trade that's rampant in Albany." He asked if they had anything more to offer about Mr. Lewis's death. Both Mr. Sampson and Mrs. Sampson merely looked blank.

"He seemed in good spirits recently," Lucille offered and her husband agreed. "He lived alone but he didn't have any health problems. He came to the office every day and often stayed late. He was rather consumed with his work, despite his age." She paused. "I'm sorry we can't be of any further help, Mr. Sheppard."

"Please let us know if we can be of further assistance," Clayton said, showing Sloan to the door. "And my mother may want to chat with you sometime. She is eighty and rather lonely during the day, at home by herself. She's friends with Mrs. Stafford. They get together occasionally."

Sloan thanked the Sampsons and then returned to the main office. He saw a flutter of activity. Two clients were waiting to speak to Mr. Armstrong, and Judge Archie evidently was unsatisfied with something to which he called somewhat harshly to Mrs. Castle, who scurried into his office.

Upon looking at the nameplate next to his door, Sloan realized he had not yet spoken to Mr. Burgess Smith. He knocked on his door and Burgess, just finishing a call, beckoned him in with a short smile.

Sloan entered Burgess's office, taking in the neat rows of legal volumes lining the shelves. The room was impeccably organized, rather a contrast to that of his colleague Thurman Armstrong, a testament to Burgess's meticulous nature. Burgess sat behind a large oak desk, his appearance as neat and precise as his surroundings.

"Mr. Smith, thank you for meeting with me," Sloan said, extending a hand.

Burgess stood and shook Sloan's hand firmly. "Certainly, Mr. Sheppard." He motioned him to a chair, which surprised Sloan as Thurman Armstrong was not half as welcoming or congenial.

Sloan settled into the chair opposite Burgess, noting the faint smell of polished wood and old paper that permeated the room. "I'm here to discuss Mr. Clement Lewis."

Burgess's expression remained neutral, but there was a flicker of something in his eyes. "Yes, a tragic loss. What would you like to know?"

As Sloan began his questions, he observed Burgess's demeanor closely, looking for any telltale signs of nervousness or deceit.

"I'd like to help, but I really have nothing more to add," he said, his voice tinged with regret. "I didn't speak to Mr. Lewis that day. I was in court for part of the morning. In the afternoon, I returned and saw him and the judge busy in his office. They didn't want to be disturbed. I was tied up with two clients that afternoon and didn't see them again. I left soon after five o'clock. They were both still here, quite busy, it seemed." The answers were precise, but there was a certain guardedness in Burgess's tone. Sloan made a mental note to dig deeper.

Sloan kept his focus on Burgess, letting the man settle into his own rhythm before speaking. "Can you tell me a bit about yourself, Mr.

Smith?" he asked, his tone conversational but with a sharp undertone that hinted at purpose.

Burgess leaned back in his chair, a coy smile playing on his lips. "Well, I'm originally from Buffalo. After law school, I moved to Albany and interviewed with Judge Archie and Mr. Lewis. They hired me almost twenty years ago, and I've had a rewarding career here ever since. I live in an apartment on Hudson Avenue and enjoy spending time at the clubs and restaurants along Lark Street. I'm also a patron of the Albany Institute of History and Art and enjoy performances at Harmanus Bleecker Hall."

Sloan listened carefully, noting the practiced ease in Burgess's words. It painted a familiar picture, rather similar to the others—polished, professional, and socially active—yet he couldn't shake the sense that something was being held back. When Burgess reached for his cigarette and offered one to Sloan, he declined with a polite shake of his head.

"Do you think someone might want to harm the judge?" Sloan asked, his voice steady.

Burgess paused mid-drag, clearly taken aback by the bluntness of the question. He lowered the cigarette slightly, exhaling slowly before answering. "I've never really thought about it," he admitted, the faintest crease appearing on his brow. "I know Judge Archie poured the tea Mr. Lewis drank—he only drank it by mistake. And yes, I've heard about those incidents recently: the near miss with the trolley in December and the car on State Street in February."

Sloan tilted his head slightly, his interest piqued. "The judge is worried for his safety," he said, his tone calm but probing. "He believes someone wants him dead."

His eyes widened slightly. "I can't think of anyone who would want to harm him. He's well-respected, but I suppose anyone in his position could have enemies."

Mrs. Castle stuck her head in the doorway at that moment and mentioned a call was waiting for Mr. Smith. Burgess thanked her, then motioned to Sloan to wait while he took the call. This gave Sloan the opportunity to look around further.

His office was typical of many Sloan had seen, with files neatly stacked on a circular table in the corner. A large window behind the desk allowed a soft stream of daylight to filter into the room, casting a warm glow on the oak furniture. Burgess, somewhere in his mid-forties, was handsome in his three-piece suit. He seemed serious-minded but somewhat personable, clearly dedicated to his profession. Sloan couldn't help but wonder if a man like Burgess had interests beyond the arts and nightclubs—ones he preferred to keep undisclosed. He replaced the handset and looked again at Sloan, thanking him for stopping by, apologizing for not being of much help.

Sloan shook hands with him and made his way to the main office, where Mrs. Castle looked up from her desk with a smile.

"The judge wishes to see you before you leave," she mentioned. She got up and knocked on the older man's door, letting him know Sloan was about to leave.

"Well, what did you find out?" he asked brusquely, impatience evident in his tone.

Sloan summarized what he was told by each of the judge's employees. He watched as the older man shook his head in disgust, a scowl forming on his face. He looked moodily toward the windows before returning his gaze to Sloan.

"I'll be in touch with you soon," Sloan said, deciding to end the meeting on his terms.

Judge Archie nodded, waved him off and irritably called to Mrs. Castle to escort him out. Mrs. Castle entered and accompanied Sloan to the main door.

Upon entering the outside hallway, Sloan could not dismiss the feeling that something was off. The judge's irritation, the employees' vague responses, and the peculiar accidents all pointed to something deeper. Too many unanswered questions.

He paused before the elevator doors, taking a deep breath. He hesitated for just a moment, as though waiting for something—an answer, a realization. The elevator doors groaned open. The attendant, a young man in a crisp uniform, opened the gates, nodding to Sloan. "Going down, sir?"

Sloan stepped into the elevator, his mind racing with questions. The elevator groaned and squeaked, each jolt and shudder echoing the gravity of the case. It was far from over, he realized. He glanced at the people near him: an executive in a Chesterfield coat and a pinstripe blue suit that matched his eyes, and a fashionably dressed woman in a fur coat and cloche hat. The businessman adjusted his fedora hat while the woman whispered something inaudible, her gloved hand clutching a small purse.

Sloan knew the answers he was seeking wouldn't come easily. The staff's ambiguous accounts and concealed motives pointed to truths buried beneath layers of secrecy. As the elevator neared the ground floor, he made a silent vow—no matter how deep the deception ran, he would uncover the truth.

CHAPTER SIX

Saturday morning was another cold and blustery day. The March winds continued creating vexatious conditions for pedestrians who traversed city streets. The howling wind sent chills through anyone daring enough to venture outside, and the threat of rain, as reported by the morning radio broadcast, added to the inclement weather conditions

Upon rising, Martha descended the grand staircase, its steps creaking underneath. As she made her way downstairs, the warmth of the kitchen and the familiar sounds of breakfast being prepared provided a comforting contrast to the bleakness outside. She entered the kitchen, to assist her mother and sister, as Gertrude did not work weekends

After a delicious meal of scrambled eggs, home-fried potatoes cooked in a cast-iron skillet, and plenty of strong coffee brewed in a percolator, the family scattered to their own pursuits. Augusta settled in the sewing room with her treadle sewing machine, working on mending a dress, finding solace in her endeavor. Martha and Joan cleaned the kitchen, with Joan also preparing a grocery list for shopping later. Meanwhile, Preston mentioned he planned to listen to a documentary about aviation on WGY later this afternoon, looking forward to the broadcast.

Judge Archie requested his daughters to tell his wife and grandson to join him in the living room, as he wished to address everyone. The living room, with its rich mahogany furniture and patterned wallpaper, exuded a sense of warmth and tradition. They soon settled in the comfortable room. Joan and Martha sat on the Victorian sofa, their hands clasped tightly in their laps as though fearing the worst. Augusta and Preston took their places in armchairs across from the judge, exchanging uneasy glances, bracing for whatever pronouncement he would make, if any at all.

Judge Archie sipped his coffee, coughed heavily, and stared into the fireplace. "Preston, I would appreciate it if you started a fire this afternoon," he said, his voice rasping.

"You wished to speak to us, Father?" Martha asked him, a trifle impatiently.

"I'd like to get to the market before it gets too busy," Joan commented.

Judge Archie cleared his throat, a bit raspy. He spoke slowly, as though in considerable pain, and Preston wondered if his grandfather was ill. He listened as the older man began to speak.

"Yesterday, Mr. Sheppard came to the office and spoke with the staff. I was under the impression he did not learn anything that could assist in the investigation." He paused, his eyes narrowing. "Therefore, I have decided on a course of action that could produce results."

Preston thought his grandfather knew how to build suspense, leaving them practically on the edge of their seats. They waited in anticipation for him to continue.

"I have made enemies over the years, but most lawyers and judges do not have a favorable impression with criminals and other unsavory characters."

"What is it you want from us, Grandfather?" Preston asked, cautiously.

"I'd like to invite the staff here for a luncheon, informally, of course. The reason for this is to discreetly inquire into Mr. Lewis's death and the attempts on my life. I believe someone knows something but the person isn't saying anything."

"Father, you don't know if they were actual attempts on your life," Joan said, then regretted speaking up. She withdrew, rather sullen, rebuffed by her father's stern expression.

"Think what you will, Joan, but I believe the poisoned tea was meant for me."

"Would you mind if I asked Mrs. Sampson?" Augusta asked, shifting the conversation. Although she knew her husband and Philomena Sampson did not get along, if the Sampsons were to attend, it would be discourteous not to ask the elder Mrs. Sampson too.

Judge Archie acquiesced reluctantly. "I do not especially care for Philomena Sampson. She blamed me for sentencing her husband to jail. Foolish woman, she married a gangster, what in the world did she expect?"

"Perhaps a few of the women from the League of Women Voters could attend, too." Augusta added. "I'm sure they'd love to attend."

Much to her surprise, her husband agreed. "Splendid idea, Augusta. That way the emphasis would not be wholly on me. Outsiders would make a difference."

"You know Mr. Armstrong and Mr. Smith do not get along," Martha reminded him. "From what you tell us, they barely talk in the office. Do you think it's a good idea for them to be here in our house at the same time?"

Judge Archie considered this, his brow furrowing in thought. "True, their rivalry is well-known. However, having them here might provide an opportunity to observe their interactions more closely. Sometimes, tensions reveal truths." He paused, meditatively. "I want to get to the bottom of this soon. I trust Mr. Sheppard, but not the police. They let cases go on and on and never get resolved. That poisonous cup was meant for me!"

His tone was harsh, his family rather taken aback, although they were used to his tantrums. But this was different, Preston thought, watching the reactions of his mother, aunt and grandmother. An informal luncheon with the office staff? Well, there was nothing wrong with that, of course. Perhaps they could learn something, after all. But then he thought, would he really let Mr. Lewis drink from his cup, knowing there was poison in it? He came out of his reverie to hear his grandfather speaking once again.

"Miss Blake, Mrs. Castle and the younger Mrs. Sampson and I have had our share of disagreements." Judge Archie paused again, his expression stern.

"Then would they really want to attend a luncheon here?" Martha asked her father, rather sarcastically. "Most don't get along, which you obviously know." And most don't even like you, much less would want to spend their free time in your company, she wanted to add.

Joan glanced at her sister, as though reading her mind and nodding in agreement.

"I've already addressed that issue, Martha," her father told her. "People give themselves away by mere talking. Outside of the office, they may relate something of importance." He paused, rather irritably. "Doris and Quentin are efficient. Quentin can be difficult and thick-headed. I don't think either would miss me if I weren't there. I'd wager they'd breathe easier in my absence."

"Does Mr. Armstrong like his new title of interim president?" Joan asked.

"Mr. Armstrong is the most reliable and dedicated person in the office to be the interim president, until I can find a replacement."

"You'd look for a replacement?" Preston asked, rather surprised.

"Indeed, Preston, I'm down to only three lawyers. I will take over Clement's work in the meantime, but I cannot go to the office everyday as I used to. With the stock market booming, we have more corporate clients than ever, and their demands are increasing."

"When did you want this informal luncheon, dear?" Augusta asked him.

Judge Archie frowned. "Perhaps next weekend. We could ask Gertrude if she would like to help. We'd pay her for the overtime, of course."

As though concluding the discussion, Joan announced she planned to go to the market on Lark Street. She walked to the hallway for her coat and cloche hat, while Augusta mentioned she wanted to finish her work in the sewing room. Martha told her father she would read upstairs, leaving Preston alone with his grandfather.

He told him he was going for a walk. As though eager to escape, he entered the hallway for his jacket and cap. He opened the front door, letting in the brisk late winter air and walked down the cement steps. The wind whistled softly, and the crunch of snow underfoot echoed in the busy street. Preston crossed State Street, cut through West Capital Park, heading for Washington Avenue. He removed any murderous thoughts from his mind, at least for now.

Mrs. Rose Castle pushed open the doors of the Harmanus Bleecker Library, Albany's new public library, and headed straight for the current fiction selection. The familiar scent of old paper and polished wood greeted her as she walked in, wrapping her in a comfortable embrace. She greeted a few librarians and clerks she knew well, exchanging pleasantries, before becoming absorbed in the titles on the shelf.

Mrs. Castle looked fresh and pleasant, even for an early Saturday morning. Despite being a trifle overweight, which she readily admitted was due to her love of baking, her rather matronly figure looked becoming in a fur trimmed coat. A lovely cloche hat, a recent purchase at Whitney's Department Store, covered her grayish hair.

She gently ran her fingers over the spines of the books, feeling the smooth leather and embossed titles, thinking about the new stories waiting to be discovered. A flicker of nostalgia surfaced as she saw Willa Cather's name—she remembered evenings spent in a comfortable armchair, lost in *My Antonia*, one of her earlier novels. Just last year, she had finished *A Lost Lady*, another of Cather's works. Books had long been her quiet refuge, their pages whispering to her across time.

She glanced over the new fiction titles. She had devoured the recent mystery by Mary Roberts Rinehart, the newest romance by Grace Livingston Hill, and the latest by Frances Parkinson Keyes. She read Scott Fitzgerald's *The Beautiful and Damned* and looked forward to his new novel, *The Great Gatsby*, coming out next month. Finally, she decided on two books: *The Professor's House* by Willa Cather and *Barren Ground* by Ellen Glasgow, recently acquired by the library. A page from *Publishers Weekly*, detailing the latest bestsellers, was posted on the wall next to the shelf. She noted these titles were top sellers for 1925, and Mrs. Castle liked to stay current in her reading. She made her way to the long circulation desk, where the clerk, a pleasant young woman, greeted her.

"Good morning, Mrs. Castle. I see you have some new fiction. The latest by Ellen Glasgow is the best so far. I've already read it and I'm sure you'll enjoy it."

Mrs. Castle smiled warmly. "Thank you, dear, I know I shall."

The clerk finished stamping the dates on the cards for the books and then handed them back to her. Mrs. Castle commented that she was off to shop for a new dress for spring.

"Don't forget your book club meets Monday evening," the amiable young woman reminded her. "You live on Dove Street, don't you? I know they'd be lost without you!"

Mrs. Castle nodded. "Yes, it's so convenient. The book club is wonderful, and the ladies are gracious, too. I enjoy chatting about the books we've read."

She bid farewell to the young woman, then approached the exit and almost ran into Augusta, who had stopped by to return a book. The ladies greeted each other cordially.

"Mrs. Stafford, nice to see you. How's the judge? I know he's had a difficult time recently."

Augusta nodded, but a faint tightness touched her expression. "He needs to rest and spend some time away from the office. He's a tough man and stubborn at times, as I'm sure you know."

Mrs. Castle chuckled. "Indeed, Mrs. Stafford." She paused, adjusting her cloche hat. "You're looking very well today. Lovely fur coat you're wearing."

Augusta caught a note of envy in her tone. Like Rose, she wore a fur coat and cloche hat, but Augusta did not look her age, and her slim figure was certainly in contrast to the matronly appearance of Mrs. Castle. She did not know Mrs. Castle well, but from what her husband had mentioned, it was never anything redeeming. He had commented on Rose's keen attention to detail, though it was clear he merely tolerated her presence. Small talk ensued, centering on neighborhood gossip, Governor Smith, his state politics, and the horrid weather for early spring. As they chatted, Augusta couldn't help but notice the way

Rose's eyes lingered on her fur coat, a silent acknowledgment of envy and perhaps even resentment.

Augusta was rather anxious to escape from her when, at that moment, the doors pushed open and in walked Philomena and Lucille, also clutching books, eager to escape the chilly air. They brought with them a gust of cold air, the crispness of winter lingering on their coats. They smiled upon seeing Augusta and Rose.

"Well, Augusta, nice seeing you," Philomena said warmly. She acknowledged Rose. "Hello, Mrs. Castle. It's nice to see you as well."

Lucille greeted Rose and Augusta pleasantly, commenting on their fine appearances. More idle chatter continued until Augusta mentioned she planned to invite everyone for a luncheon.

Lucille showed surprise. "A luncheon, Mrs. Stafford? How very generous of you."

Philomena wrinkled her brow, not quite sharing her daughter-in-law's opinion. She was dressed in a dark coat, with a cloche hat that complemented her wealth. She asked Augusta, with a hint of curiosity and a tone befitting her status, what the occasion was all about.

"No occasion, dear," Augusta said. "I haven't planned it yet, but I'll call you once we decide the date and time."

Even Mrs. Castle was impressed. She turned to Lucille, commenting on the reports she was finishing at the office, although Lucille found it impertinent to discuss business on their day off, especially in front of Mrs. Stafford and her mother-in-law. She cast a quick glance at Philomena, who nodded briefly as though she shared her thoughts.

"Well, I'm off to the stores," Mrs. Castle said. The faint rustling of books and magazines was a steady hum. "There are sales on ladies' dresses today at Whitney's."

She wished them a good day and then headed for the exit, allowing a cold swirl of air to enter the foyer. Augusta, Lucille, and Philomena approached the shelves against the wall, chatted about books and the most current bestsellers. While Philomena looked at the great selection, Lucille addressed Augusta, her voice low and confidential.

"Excuse me for mentioning this, Mrs. Stafford. Does the judge really believe someone wants to kill him? That private investigator, Mr. Sheppard, was at the office yesterday, questioning us. I don't know what to think."

Augusta glanced around to ensure no one else was listening, shivering slightly. "Yes, he does. Mr. Sheppard is very thorough, but it's all quite unsettling," she said, forcing a polite smile.

Lucille fidgeted with her scarf. "I wonder if Mr. Sheppard will get to the bottom of it."

Augusta looked at her surprisingly, her pulse quickening. She was rather startled that she would question Mr. Sheppard's ability to resolve a case. But then she knew Philomena was not particularly fond of her husband. She assumed it was because the judge had sentenced her criminal husband to state prison, where he later died. Perhaps Philomena harbored a grudge toward the judge, but that had been many years ago. She never let on that she was resentful, although Augusta knew she could be coy and secretive. And Lucille dealt with the judge daily in the office, where animosities and ambivalence at times prevailed.

She mentioned the investigation was continuing into the death of Mr. Lewis, but she did not know anything more. Philomena turned her attention to Augusta and Lucille. She remained tight-lipped, clutching her handbag a bit tighter, shifting her posture, although her morose expression made her feelings on the subject evident. Augusta could sense slight tension in the air and felt a pang of discomfort. She returned her book to the desk, checked out a new one and then rejoined Philomena and Lucille at the shelves containing the newest fiction.

"So you're hosting a luncheon," Lucille commented again. She adjusted her fur coat, dismissively, hesitating slightly. "I'll talk it over with Clayton and see if he wants to attend."

Augusta noted a flicker of doubt and reluctancy. After all, would they really want to spend their free time with the judge? She remembered Martha had already brought up that point. The haughty expression Lucille wore did not escape Augusta's notice. She saw her rather svelte figure and fur coat, much more lavish than her own. Obviously, Lucille's appearance spoke of money, certainly the latest and the best.

"It should be a grand time," Augusta commented, rather nervously, fidgeting with the book she held, nearly dropping it in her distraction.

They continued chatting about the great literature on the shelves. In the back of her mind, Augusta wondered if the idea of a luncheon at the house was really a good idea after all.

Joan walked briskly up State Street, turning right at the corner of Lark Street until she reached her destination. The cool morning air brushed against her cheeks as she moved with purpose, eager to reach the warmth of the indoor market. As she anticipated, the market was busy with a Saturday morning crowd, housewives, maids, and small children cluttering the aisles. The air was filled with the mingling scents of fresh produce, baked goods, and deli meats, creating a pleasing sense within her. The lively chatter of vendors and customers echoed off the walls, blending into a vibrant cacophony within the enclosed space.

Upon entering, she grabbed a basket and squeezed her way through, finding butter, cream, a loaf of *Wonder Bread*, two jars of *Maxwell House Coffee*, a jar of *Hellmann's Mayonnaise*, a box of *Borden's Vanilla Ice Cream*, and a box of *Domino Sugar*. She ordered veal, beef cutlets, and chicken at the deli counter, the butcher's knife rhythmically chopping through the meat. She then selected two tins of *3 Diamonds Tuna Fish*, tubs of potato salad and macaroni salad—her father's favorites—along with a carton of eggs. She chose several packets of *Jell-O* and a few *Baby Ruth* candy bars, another of her father's favorites. Reviewing the items in her basket, Joan felt a sense of satisfaction at having found everything she needed. She was about to enter the cashier line when she spotted a familiar face.

"Well, hello, Mr. Armstrong," she said, catching her breath. "What a surprise to see you!"

Thurman Armstrong was similarly weighed down with a basket full of grocery items, while dodging various women and children in the aisle. He moved to the side along with Joan and they chatted amicably for a few moments.

"You usually shop here?" he asked her, smiling at his own question, although he realized it was rather foolish since the Lark Street market was the closest to their respective houses.

Joan nodded. "Yes, it's convenient. Sometimes my sister Martha goes with me." She looked at the tall, rather striking man in front of her. She knew he was divorced with no children. She had contemplated getting to know him but dismissed it. She knew her father would not approve of her involvement with a divorced man. On the other hand, Joan thought stubbornly, at fifty, she could well make up her own mind, she was no longer under his iron fist. Casting a fleeting glance at his handsome face, she considered asking him to meet for coffee, but hesitated. She could imagine a pleasant conversation over coffee with him. While she continued living in the house she grew up in after her husband's death, she realized she had to tolerate her father's antiquated rules. The conflicting emotions stirred within her, creating an undercurrent of frustration and longing.

"How's everything at the office, Mr. Armstrong?" she asked, wishing to prolong the conversation. "I understand you are now the interim president."

"I appreciate Judge Archie's confidence in me and my work. I don't know how long it'll last. He wishes to hire a new attorney to take Mr. Lewis's place."

Joan nodded solemnly. "Father hasn't quite gotten over his death. So tragic, really. I never knew certain teas could be poisonous," she said, her mind racing with the implications.

"Neither did I," Thurman admitted. He changed the subject. "Do you invest in the stock market, Mrs. Caves?"

Joan blushed. "Oh, please call me by my first name. No, I don't know anything about it. Father doesn't allow my sister and I to take much interest in business affairs."

"And you can please call me Thurman," he said agreeably. "I understand your father's rather old-fashioned sensibilities, but you do have a mind of your own, don't you?"

Joan felt a mix of embarrassment and defiance. "Why do you ask if I invest in the stock market?"

"Because it's advantageous right now," Thurman explained, moving to allow a mother and her two small children to get through the rather cramped aisle. "You can earn quite a lot by wise investments. The stock market has been booming and many people are making fortunes by buying on margin. I have some brochures I can give you if you're interested."

Joan smiled. "I'd like that, Thurman, thank you." She paused. "Father wants to invite everyone to the house for a luncheon sometime soon. Would you be interested in attending?"

Thurman showed surprise. "A luncheon? Well, sure, but what's the occasion?"

"No occasion, really," Joan told him. "He wants to bring everyone together." She hesitated. "Someone may have pushed him on North Pearl Street and then that speeding car last month..." She broke off, as her eyes narrowed, trying to read Thurman's expression.

Thurman looked away, avoiding her eyes, his fingers tapping nervously against his coat pocket. So far, his secret was secure, but there were always suspicions and gossip. It had been well over a month and he had been in the clear. The memories of that evening came flooding back quickly. He did not stop when he ran the red light but nothing bad happened. He wondered if anyone had seen him that night, the fear of being discovered gnawing at him.

"Thurman, is something wrong?" Joan asked him, noticing him stiffening slightly, as several shoppers squeezed past them, the bustling market filled with the sounds of the trolleys clanging along busy Lark Street.

He came out of his reverie, adjusting his coat and swallowing rather hard. "No, I'm fine. Why don't we meet for coffee some evening next week? I'll show you the brochures on the stock market. I think you'll find them interesting. There's a coffee shop here on Lark Street that's good."

Joan lingered on his expression. "I'd like that, Thurman."

They entered the cashier line, Joan content in the company of this tall, good-looking lawyer. He listened as she continued chatting, but Thurman was preoccupied. He could not avoid speculating uneasily if his behavior was safe or if someone in fact did know—but did not divulge that knowledge, at least not yet.

Preston hopped on a southbound trolley on State Street, heading for downtown, where he would meet Quentin and Doris. They planned to dine at Keeler's, an Albany landmark, known for its fine dining and exquisite service.

He got off on the corner of State and Broadway, crossed at the light, looked northward, and in the distance spotted his friends, waiting for him in front of the restaurant. He crossed to the other side of Broadway, catching up with them.

Greetings were exchanged, and Quentin commented he wanted nothing more than to get out of the cold and to eat a good meal as he was starving. Preston and Doris laughed, then entered the opulent restaurant, its grand chandeliers casting a warm glow over the richly decorated interior. The ambience was inviting, an obvious contrast to the chilly streets outside. They were shown to a table with crisp white linens and polished silverware.

Their orders were soon taken, and while waiting for their food, they chatted and lit cigarettes, the smoke curling lazily above their heads. The warmth of friendship and anticipation of dancing at the hall on Sheridan Avenue later added a sparkle to their conversation.

"Grandfather wants to invite everyone to the house for a luncheon," Preston told them. "Honestly, I was rather surprised. He's never wanted anything like that before. He plans to let everyone know about it soon, once we figure out the date."

"Maybe he's getting melancholy at his age," Quentin suggested.

"We spoke to Mr. Sheppard yesterday when he came to the office," Doris said. She looked pleasant in a black dress, with lovely pearls, lipstick, and the scent of Chanel No. 5. "Personally, I don't know what that man thought. I mean, would someone really want to kill Judge Archie?"

Quentin agreed. He appeared more casual with his dress shirt and slacks, tall and slim, his hair center parted. He listened attentively as Preston spoke to them.

"Mr. Sheppard was at the house for dinner." He hesitated. "I think Grandfather really believes someone wants to kill him."

He looked at Quentin across the table, his eyes conveying his earlier suspicions, which he had told him in secret. Quentin assured his friend that his suspicions were safe with him, regardless of their friendship with Doris.

After their meals were served, they continued chatting amicably and then relaxed with after-dinner coffee. Doris took a sip from her cup and then puffed at her cigarette.

Preston always enjoyed her company. Granted, there was an age difference, but Doris looked and acted so much younger than her years and was so modern, too, definitely a flapper. Her bobbed hair, stylish dress, and confident demeanor epitomized the new woman of 1925. He remembered mentioning the age difference to Quentin, but it didn't seem to faze him in the least. Preston rather admired Doris's vibrant spirit and the way she navigated through societal expectations with ease. She had even introduced Quentin and Preston to a few eligible young women, expanding their social circle. The group met on occasion, their outings congenial and rather festive.

"Judge Archie isn't the most pleasant person," Doris said. "It's a challenge to work and get along with him. He's so bossy at times and downright mean, too."

Doris apologized for speaking negatively about his grandfather, but Preston didn't let her comments bother him. He admitted his grandfather was not the easiest person to deal with, to which Quentin heartily concurred. But then he wondered if they would really want to have lunch at their house. They might accept out of loyalty to the judge and maybe even to safeguard their jobs. They continued chatting until a familiar voice suddenly caught their attention.

"Well, hello everyone."

Preston looked up and saw Burgess standing before them, with a young female in tow, obviously his date for the evening. He looked at her quickly, not recognizing her, wondering who she was and where he found her. He did not think Burgess had a steady companion.

Burgess, always the charmer, was dressed in a sharp suit, his hair slicked back in the latest style. His date, a striking young woman with bobbed hair and a fashionable dress, smiled politely.

"Small world in Albany, isn't it?" Burgess said, and it was obvious he had been drinking.

"Certainly is small," Quentin said, not wishing to interact with someone he did not consider a friend. "Did you have dinner here too?"

Preston observed the interaction, his curiosity piqued by Burgess's presence and the unfamiliar young woman. He couldn't help but wonder if Burgess had stumbled upon some new intrigue. The atmosphere felt slightly charged with the unexpected encounter, adding a layer of complexity to their evening.

Burgess's face was rather red but his appearance immaculate, his suit pristine and sharp. His date appeared timid. Preston thought she looked like a high school student, although he could not imagine Burgess would date someone that young.

"We're headed for the dance hall on Sheridan right now," he told them. "Why don't you join us there? Should be the bee's knees, for sure!"

Preston glanced at Doris and Quentin, their unspoken words conveying that they would not want to join Burgess at anything if they could help it. However, since they planned to go there anyway, they were not to be deterred from their plans.

"We might see you there," Preston spoke up, as Quentin and Doris were rather lost for words. "We'll take a look at the scene and see if it's the real McCoy."

Burgess mumbled something incoherent, then with the young woman by his side, they headed for the exit. Preston looked after them as they made their way between tables, then returned his gaze to Doris and Quentin.

Quentin crushed his cigarette in an ashtray frustratingly, and Doris did the same. They were quiet for a few moments until Preston asked them if they were ready to leave.

"I won't let him spoil a fun evening," Quentin said, standing up and putting on his jacket and cap. "I want to make a night of it. Should be a good crowd there, too."

"He's nothing but a cake-eater, anyway," Doris said, also standing, her fur coat wrapped around her slender shape, her pretty cloche hat squarely on her head. "Since when does he go to dance halls? I've never seen him out. That girl looked half his age."

"He thinks he's a big cheese, with all his money," Quentin commented, another cigarette to his lips. "I know if he were knocked off, I wouldn't lose sleep over it."

Doris agreed. "Maybe he'll be the next victim," she joked.

It was close to eight o'clock. Judge Archie and Augusta were settled comfortably in the living room, their after-dinner coffee finished. The radio was turned to a station playing relaxing symphonic music, a popular choice for unwinding in the evenings. Preston had started a fire for his grandfather before going out, and the atmosphere in the living room was warm and tranquil.

Augusta was looking at the latest issues of *Vanity Fair* and *True Story*, magazines that reflected the current fascination with fashion and sensational tales. She pulled the shawl around her shoulders closer. Martha was busy knitting, her needles clicking softly in the background. Joan had finished cleaning up in the kitchen, since it was just the four of them for dinner. She joined them, sitting next to her sister on the Victorian sofa. She picked up the *Albany Evening Journal* on the coffee table. Judge Archie was immersed in *The Wall Street Journal*, a favorite of his, reflecting his keen interest in the stock market and business affairs.

The crackling fire added a soothing backdrop to the peaceful evening. A gusty wind pressed against the windows. Augusta had a wool shawl over her shoulders and she pulled it tighter, feeling the chill. Martha and Joan were drawn to the windows as the wind increased with driving force. Even Judge Archie, usually unflappable, expressed surprise at the wind's velocity.

They were quiet for so long that when the doorbell rang, rather abruptly, it startled them and the judge almost dropped the newspaper. They looked at each other, wondering who would be calling on such a chilly evening. At first, Martha assumed it was Preston, making an early evening of it, but of course, he had his own key, so it was foolish of him to ring the doorbell. Joan, her drop-waist dress swaying as she moved, put down the newspaper and without saying anything, left the living room on her way to the hallway and the front door.

From the living room, Judge Archie, Augusta, and Martha heard Joan speaking and then a rather loud male voice coming down the hallway. Joan returned with Clayton Sampson behind her. She exchanged glances with her sister and mother, the silent communication carrying a flicker of something unspoken—curiosity, perhaps a trace of apprehension. Augusta's gaze lingered an extra second, unreadable but firm, before she smoothed the shawl over her shoulders. Joan, not wanting to seem too hesitant, straightened slightly and gestured toward an empty armchair. Clayton greeted everyone pleasantly, and Augusta asked him to sit near the fire. He complied, stretching his long legs comfortably.

The sudden appearance of Clayton added an unexpected twist to their quiet evening. Judge Archie lowered his newspaper, a rare look of intrigue on his face. The crackling fire cast dancing shadows on the walls as Clayton settled in, and the room's once tranquil atmosphere took on a subtle edge of anticipation.

"What brings you out this evening, Mr. Sampson?" Martha said. "Is Mrs. Sampson with you as well?" Her tone hinged on sarcasm, which Augusta noticed with a quick sideways glance.

Clayton shook his head. He wore a crisp cotton dress shirt and high-waisted trousers, his shoes shined to perfection. "Lucille is home taking care of Mother. Too cold for her to be out this evening. Quite chilly for the end of March."

"Preston's having dinner with Quentin and Doris at Keeler's," Joan said.

"My wife and I were there just last week. Food is exceptional."

"What can I do for you, Clayton?" Judge Archie said, getting straight to the point. "I assume you didn't come here to socialize. Is something wrong?"

"No, Judge, I was out for a walk and decided to stop by. You have such a charming house, Mrs. Stafford."

Augusta thanked him uneasily, wondering where this was headed. Like her husband, she assumed he had an ulterior motive for his visit.

"Actually, I'm concerned about this Mr. Sheppard," he said, looking at the judge. "Personally, I didn't care for his line of questioning yesterday. I noticed it upset my wife as well."

Judge Archie put *The Wall Street Journal* aside, the crisp pages rustling. "I understand completely, but I hired Mr. Sheppard to inquire into the death of Mr. Lewis. Until I'm satisfied with his findings, his investigation will continue."

Clayton lit a cigarette, the tip glowing as he looked at Augusta, Martha, and Joan. He then directed his gaze back to the elderly man in the armchair across from him.

"You really believe Mr. Lewis was murdered?"

Judge Archie cleared his throat. "Should I remind you about the December incident when I was pushed into the street and the speeding car last month that almost hit me?"

Clayton fumbled for words, puffing at his cigarette, feeling rather uncomfortable. "I don't know what to say, Judge."

"There's nothing to say. Mr. Sheppard will get to the bottom of it." He paused. "I have my own suspicions, of course. I have known information for some time, but I've kept quiet. Perhaps someone knows I have certain knowledge and has finally decided to take revenge..." His voice broke off as he stared into the fireplace and the crackling flames.

Martha offered Clayton coffee or tea, but he shook his head. There remained an empty, rather brutal silence, as though they were afraid to speak. Joan was meditative, with the *Albany Evening Journal* on her lap. Martha was still knitting, but missed a stitch, as she could not concentrate. Augusta flipped the pages of *True Story* aimlessly, finally depositing it and *Vanity Fair* on the coffee table, rather exasperated.

"I've decided to invite the staff over for a luncheon," Judge Archie told Clayton. "I understand my wife mentioned it to your wife and mother earlier." He cast a glance at Augusta, who merely nodded. "I haven't decided on the date, but it'll just be the staff and a few friends."

"A luncheon?" Clayton said uneasily, thinking there was an ulterior motive. He did not quite relish spending an afternoon with the rest of the office staff on his day off, but his curiosity was piqued. Given the judge's obstinacy, he'd never forgive anyone who was invited and did not attend. He asked the judge what the occasion was, but the judge merely shrugged.

"No occasion. I've never had the staff here before and perhaps it's time that I do."

"Are you inviting Mr. Sheppard, too?" Clayton asked, appalled.

Judge Archie shook his head. "That's what I don't want to do. I want the atmosphere to be casual. People give themselves away in talking. You must be aware of that, Clayton."

Clayton wondered what the old man had up his sleeve. Certainly a luncheon for the staff was unexpected. He must harbor certain suspicions which he chose not to share with anyone, perhaps not even his family. Desultory conversation continued for almost a half hour until Clayton rose, with the intent to leave.

"It's nice to see you, Mrs. Stafford. Same for you, Mrs. Caves and Mrs. Hughes. Good evening, Judge. I will see you on Monday at the office. Please give Preston my best regards."

Joan got up and showed Clayton to the door, then returned to the living room. She sat next to her sister, but there was an unspoken current of tension and uneasiness.

Augusta sighed. "I'm sure Philomena and Lucille mentioned the luncheon invitation to him earlier in the day. He acted surprised by it."

"Maybe he didn't know," Joan said reasonably. "Both of the Mrs. Sampsons are rather egoists, if you ask me."

Augusta beamed at her youngest daughter. "Philomena does tend toward eccentricity."

The wind rattled the windows again, and the flames in the fireplace caught a quick draught of cold, causing them to dance brilliantly. Martha got up and looked out the windows onto State Street, while Joan picked up *True Story* and *Vanity Fair* from the coffee table.

Augusta listened to the wonderful symphonic music on the radio, her mind enchanted by the soothing melodies.

But Judge Archie was miles away, his mind covered with troubled thoughts. His friend and colleague, Clement Lewis, had died needlessly, drinking from his cup. The judge frowned, deeply disturbed as he stared into the fire. He was very much afraid. Perhaps the next time, he would not be so lucky.

CHAPTER SEVEN

On Monday, Sloan Sheppard left his office and crossed the busy thoroughfare at the corner of South Pearl Street. He hopped on a trolley, heading north on Washington Avenue, past Albany City Hall, the State Capitol and the State Education Building, whose impressive marble columns glittered in the morning sunshine.

The air was crisp, carrying the scent of blooming flowers and the distant hum of factory whistles. He wanted to consult with his contacts at the Albany Police, Inspector John Harris and Lieutenant Frank Taylor. Most likely, they were not aware he was investigating the death of Mr. Clement Lewis. Sloan adjusted his fedora hat, a habit when he was deep in thought, and his brow furrowed. After jumping off the trolley and entering the police station, a policeman who recognized Sloan greeted him cordially.

"You're in luck, Mr. Sheppard," the officer said. "They haven't made the rounds of the streets yet. I'll let them know you're here."

He disappeared behind a partition. Inspector John Harris came out and shook hands with Sloan. Lieutenant Frank Taylor was busy at a table, reviewing photographs and documents. He stood and shook hands with him and invited Sloan to sit at the table.

"What can we do for you, Mr. Sheppard?" the inspector commented, picking up a cigarette he had left in an ashtray.

Inspector Harris, in his fifties, was quite tall, almost matching Sloan's height, with brown hair and fierce, determined brown eyes. Lieutenant Taylor was rather stout, with grayish black hair, also in his fifties, with a no-nonsense manner, who found bluntness worked in speaking with witnesses, criminals, and other law enforcement personnel.

"I've been hired by Judge Archie to investigate the death of Mr. Clement Lewis," Sloan told them. "I understand he died from drinking poisonous tea."

Inspector Harris cast a quick glance at Lieutenant Taylor. "From the autopsy results, the tea itself was poisonous, full of residue, and was toxic. We confiscated the rest of the tea and tested it. We were surprised it would cause death."

Sloan agreed. "Judge Archie believes it was meant for him. Mr. Lewis drank out of his cup. Certainly, he would not have handed his friend a cup of tea laced with poison."

The lieutenant nodded. "The poison came from berries. It was some sort of exotic tea, and many berries contain toxins. Those kinds of teas are gaining in popularity. Apparently, this tea was overloaded, causing certain death."

"Mr. Lewis was alone when he died," Sloan pointed out, shifting in the chair. "Mrs. Rose Castle discovered the body the next morning."

Inspector Harris extinguished his cigarette. "We've questioned the staff several times, as well as Mrs. Philomena Sampson, Mr. Clayton Sampson's mother. Mrs. Sampson had issues with Judge Archie going back many years. I think it's fair to say everyone in that office and many in the legal community have had issues and disagreements with the judge. You know Judge Archie Stafford is an extremely difficult man to deal with. He had a reputation in the courts as a vulture and was merciless when it came to sentencing. He may harbor information on gangsters and bootleggers. Certainly, he dealt with enough of them over the years."

"He may harbor other information, too," Lieutenant Taylor said thoughtfully. "That may be why he thinks someone is out to kill him."

Inspector Harris coughed. "We have nothing concrete except the autopsy report on Mr. Lewis. If the judge has certain information, he hasn't said anything to us." He paused. "Perhaps he may be more open with you, Mr. Sheppard."

Sloan mentioned how he had interviewed the staff, as well as having been invited to dinner at the judge's house, at which time he met his wife, two daughters, and grandson. He mentioned the judge felt two attempts were already made on his life. He told them about the speeding car and the fall on North Pearl Street in December. He waited for the inspector to comment.

"We didn't know about those incidents," Inspector Harris said, casting a sidelong glance at his colleague. "The family didn't report them. Perhaps he just slipped on the snow and ice. There was a lot of snow just before Christmas."

"Speeding cars continue to be a problem in this city," Lieutenant Taylor said. "Did anyone see the driver or get the license plate?" Privately he wondered if these incidents were too coincidental to ignore.

Sloan told them that they didn't see the diver, the license number, or even the make of the car. They were too shaken. Inspector Harris made a few notes, then mentioned they would speak to the judge again.

"Judge Archie retired from the bench only ten years ago," Lieutenant Taylor pointed out.

"So there may be someone whose wounds have not quite healed," Inspector Harris said.

Sloan agreed. "This case may have roots in the past."

"Involving the judge himself, do you mean?" Inspector Harris asked Sloan.

Sloan then stood up to leave. "Judge Archie may have certain knowledge of past occurrences, involving people he knows." He paused. "In that case, the attempts won't stop until the threat has been eliminated."

"I have reached a decision," Judge Archie announced, commanding his family's attention. They were at the kitchen table, having breakfast.

Preston noticed his mother, aunt and grandmother appeared weary, their expressions a strange mixture of anticipation, dread and perhaps fear.

"Yes, Father, please continue," Martha said, not wishing to hear a prolonged discussion.

The sisters were in their housecoats and slippers, preferring to prepare for work later as they always helped their mother in arranging breakfast. Preston preferred to wash, shave and dress in his business attire before coming downstairs, to save himself time. They waited to hear what Judge Archie would tell them.

"Next Saturday, the eleventh of April, is the date I've chosen to invite the staff here for the luncheon," the judge said, getting right to the point. "Since the next day is Easter Sunday, perhaps we could tie in some traditional dishes to celebrate."

Martha suggested ham and sweet potatoes to serve as the main luncheon, while Augusta recommended deviled eggs and tomato salad. Judge Archie nodded in approval.

"I plan to call Mr. Sampson and Mrs. Castle later this morning," he said. "They will relay the message to the rest of the staff, although I assume most already know about it. Saturday is perfect since everyone is off."

"Provided they can come on that date," Augusta said. "And if they want to come here at all." She hesitated, then continued before her husband could interject. "I'll ask some of the women from the League of Women Voters. I'd love to show them around."

"The purpose of the luncheon is to see what they say and how they act while outside of the office. We may learn more about what happened to Mr. Lewis."

"And the attempts on your life," Joan added.

"Joan, we don't know that for sure," Martha said, disagreeing with her sister.

They heard the grandfather clock in the hallway chime an hour. Joan put down her napkin and scurried off upstairs to get dressed for the day. Martha helped her mother clear the breakfast dishes, the clinking of porcelain filling the room, and then also retreated upstairs. Preston announced he would leave to catch the trolley downtown.

Judge Archie continued sitting at the table, alone, drinking his coffee. Augusta was busy at the sink, washing the breakfast dishes. His mind was clouded by thoughts of murder, and he wondered if more violent deaths were to come. He stared into his cup, the bitter taste lingering on his tongue.

Mrs. Philomena Sampson put down her knitting and listened attentively to the radio. At the moment, the latest theatrical performance from WGY, an adaptation of *The Wolf* by playwright Charles Somerville held her attention. An absorbing dramatization and so suspenseful, that her mind, totally enthralled by the searing drama, did not at first hear the telephone ringing from in the hallway. Her maid was off for the day, so she had no choice but to answer it herself. Getting up from her armchair, rather shakily as her arthritis had gotten the better of her lately, she made her way slowly to the hallway. The persistent ringing of the candlestick telephone echoed through the house, grating on her nerves. She answered reluctantly and recognized the rather husky voice of her daughter-in-law.

"Hi, Phil, hope I didn't disturb you."

Her grip tightened on the handset. "Lucille," she replied, her voice betraying a hint of annoyance. "Nice to hear from you," she said, attempting sincerity.

Philomena looked in a hallway mirror and pushed back some gray hair from her forehead. She was hard pressed not to tell her irritating daughter-in-law that yes, she was disturbing her from her favorite radio drama. She enjoyed having the radio to herself during the day, without her son and daughter-in-law in charge. She maintained civility with her as well as with her son, although she found them extremely annoying at times. She asked patiently what she wanted and then almost dropped the handset.

"Judge Archie called here earlier and invited us to his house for a luncheon next Saturday, the day before Easter," Lucille explained. "Remember Mrs. Stafford mentioned it to us at the library recently? The judge spoke to Clayton and to Mrs. Castle and they've informed everyone. I believe you're invited, too, Phil."

Philomena's heart skipped a beat, and she tightened her grip on the handset to steady herself. "Oh, I see," she replied, trying to keep her voice even. Never at a loss for words, she was momentarily speechless.

She gathered her thoughts and asked Lucille the purpose of such a gathering.

"Well, from what I understand, he told Clayton it'll be an Easter brunch. Clayton and I have already discussed it. Of course, you don't have to go with us, Phil."

Philomena had all she could do to keep her patience. So they've already decided they would go to the Stafford house, with or without me. She took a deep breath, feeling the familiar ache in her joints, and then found her voice, speaking calmly.

"Let's talk about it when you and Clayton get home later. I'd like to hear about it from Clayton." Her tone implied she took her son's words at more value.

They ended the call and Philomena hung up the handset, replacing the telephone on the hallway table. Rather tiredly, she returned to the living room and her chair. Her daytime drama was still on the radio, but she could not concentrate. The familiar voices from the radio faded into the background. So Judge Archie wants to invite his staff to the house for an Easter luncheon, as Lucille called it. Since when did that hideous old man want people at his mansion to socialize?

But with a change of heart, Philomena smiled mischievously. I will attend, she thought cleverly. It will be worth it to snoop around that big old house. It will be memorable, indeed.

CHAPTER EIGHT

On Tuesday, Preston worked only half a day, telling Mr. Bishop he needed to attend to items at home. In truth, he planned to see Mr. Sheppard in his office, though he kept his destination to himself. He also decided not to inform his mother or grandparents. He needed space to think.

At his desk, he hesitated before picking up the phone, rolling his pen between his fingers as if weighing his decision. Finally, he called Mr. Sheppard's office, unsure if he would be available. Fortunately, Sloan answered and told Preston to stop by about noon. As Preston hung up, relief mixed with unease. He told himself—again—that Mr. Sheppard would untangle this mystery. And yet, a whisper of doubt lingered.

Outside, the wind had lost its edge, but the sun struggled to burn through thick clouds. Preston tightened his jacket, keeping his cap low against the breeze as he stepped onto a Broadway trolley heading north up State Street. The city hummed around him—footsteps tapping against pavement, exhaust curling from early spring traffic, snippets of conversations slipping past as pedestrians brushed by.

He got off at North Pearl Street, crossed at the light, and made his way toward the Albany City Savings Bank Building. The sight was imposing, its ornate lobby gleaming with polished brass and marbled floors. The air smelled faintly of ink and leather—a mix of contracts and old money. The quiet murmur of businessmen filled the space, blending with the distant chime of typewriters from nearby offices.

Preston approached the elevators. The operator glanced at him before pulling the lever, the gates clanging shut as the lift shuddered upward. He watched the numbers climb. Fifth floor.

He stepped off, his shoes barely making a sound on the thick carpet as he made his way down a long hallway. At the end, Sloan's door stood waiting. Preston knocked, exhaling slowly as he heard a familiar voice.

"Hello, Preston," Sloan said with a smile. "You found me, I see. Come in and take a seat."

Preston removed his jacket and cap, holding them in his hands rather firmly as he sat down in a chair in front of the desk. He looked at the imposing figure before him. He thought Mr. Sheppard could intimidate the most reluctant witness or criminal with his boldness, intelligence, and dark, penetrating eyes. Preston was reminded of his extreme height and muscular physique. He thanked Sloan for seeing him and got straight to the point.

He told Sloan how he believed his grandfather might be behind the recent attack on Mr. Lewis, which led to his death. He also mentioned that he thought his grandfather might have fallen deliberately on North Pearl Street and stepped in front of the speeding car on State Street. He added that he had not shared this with anyone except Quentin Cooper, his best friend, who swore to secrecy. He took a breath and sat back, relieved at getting it off his chest.

Sloan puffed on a cigarette while looking intently at Preston, the glow of the ember flickering in the dim light. He did not say anything but was ruminating on what the younger man had just told him and the possibilities it opened up in the investigation.

"This is quite interesting, Preston," he said slowly, keeping the cigarette to his lips. "This could change the course of the investigation. Have you considered why the judge would hire me if he was responsible himself?"

"I don't know if my grandfather is senile. I don't know what to think anymore. Mr. Lewis drank from my grandfather's cup and died overnight in the office. I can't believe it was poisonous tea, like the police reported."

Sloan saw the confusion on his face. "I spoke to my contacts at the Albany Police. Poisonous tea is unusual, but not unheard of. Right now they're not pursuing other leads." He crushed his cigarette. "I've known your grandfather for over ten years. He can be ruthless in sentencing, and several clients of mine have had unfavorable verdicts administered by Judge Archie. Most are still in prison." He paused. "What I am getting at, Preston, is that your grandfather must have made enemies over the years. In my profession as an investigator, I have had my own life threatened numerous times."

Preston noticed again the scar on his chin and his rugged face which hinted at previous altercations with the underworld. "Honestly, I don't know what to think," he repeated, with frustration. "But please don't tell my family that I came here today."

Sloan assured him that he would not mention his visit today. He asked Preston what he knew of the office staff and if someone held a grudge against the judge.

"My friend, Quentin Cooper, who you met at the law firm, mentioned everyone has had some sort of grudge against my grandfather. Mrs. Castle isn't fond of him and neither are the Sampsons. I heard my mother mention that Mrs. Sampson, Mr. Sampson's elderly mother, resents my grandfather for sending her husband to prison many years ago. Doris has had disputes with him. Mr. Armstrong and Mr. Smith collaborated with my grandfather on numerous cases but, according to Quentin, their opinions were negative." He paused. "Quentin doesn't think too highly of my grandfather, either. He's told me he's been a tyrant in the office, at times."

"Is that enough to try to kill someone?" Sloan asked.

Preston was silent for a few moments until he remembered to tell Sloan about the luncheon planned for next Saturday, the eleventh of April.

"Who is invited to this luncheon?" Sloan asked curiously.

"Apparently, the whole office staff. Grandmother would like to invite a few of her friends from the League of Women Voters. Grandfather decided to have the luncheon to coincide with Easter Sunday, which is the next day."

Sloan nodded. "What does your grandfather hope to accomplish? Has he ever invited the staff to your house for a luncheon in the past?"

"He hopes to find out who may have been responsible for Mr. Lewis's death," Preston explained. "He believes people give themselves away by talking. He's never had the staff over to our house. Grandfather isn't one to socialize much. He's arthritic, and his walking seems to get slower every day."

"Your grandfather is correct when he said people give themselves away by talking. You may learn something you didn't know previously."

"Mr. Sheppard, I'm afraid for my grandfather," Preston said gravely. "Either someone is really trying to kill him, or he's fabricating this himself. If that's the case, then his mental state is really declining." He mentioned how his grandmother worried the judge's mental health was not the best lately and how he had been extremely forgetful and even troubled.

Sloan scribbled a few notes on his pad pertaining to Judge Archie. But then, a knock came on his door. His one o'clock appointment had arrived. He stood and shook hands with Preston, thanking him for stopping by. He mentioned he would be in touch soon.

Sloan opened the door, allowing an elderly couple to enter. Preston thanked him again for his time, then left the office on the way to the elevators. An overwhelming sense of trepidation gripped him, like a tightly knotted rope. He felt even more confused and afraid.

Mrs. Rose Castle sat on the sofa in her comfortable living room, listening to the radio and reading the latest issue of *The Saturday Evening Post*. Her library book was on the coffee table, but she did not feel much like reading. Her one-bedroom apartment on Dove Street, not far from downtown, was suitably furnished. A cup of tea was on the end table. Her beige dress suited her fine, although it was a bit tight around the waist. Mrs. Castle grimaced, knowing she needed to shed a few pounds. She continued flipping the pages of the magazine. It was just after eight o'clock, and evening had settled over the city.

Mrs. Castle sighed and listened to the news broadcast. Usually, WGY was her favorite station, but tonight she turned the dial to a station from Utica to hear a concert by Vaughn De Leath, one of her favorite singers. She finished her tea and then got up to look out a window overlooking Dove Street.

Her usual cheerful countenance was shrouded in dismay. She wondered about this investigator that Judge Archie was foolish enough to hire. Sheppard something or other—now why in the world would he do that? She stared at a woman walking her dog, at the milkman making late deliveries, and at the paperboy delivering the evening newspaper.

Her thoughts turned to the Sampsons, certainly a different kettle of fish altogether. She was glad they were holed up in their own suite and that Mrs. Sampson catered to her eccentric husband's needs. Certainly arrogant to the extreme, money-hungry, and always out for more.

She turned from the window, thinking of the luncheon planned for next Saturday. She could tell the judge she wasn't feeling well and couldn't attend. But she would love to see the inside of the mansion again. Besides, she didn't want to miss anything that was said. She had been to his house only twice over the years.

She wondered if Mr. Smith would attend. She couldn't imagine Burgess Smith and Thurman Armstrong at the same social function. She remembered the constant bickering, backstabbing, and malicious intent from them, causing such an upheaval in the office. She had always acted as peacemaker, even standing between them to simmer the pot before it boiled over.

She returned to the armchair, shaking her head, the plush fabric cool against her skin and tried to lose herself in the concert by Vaughn De Leath. The soft strains of the music filled the room, but irritably, she found it could not hold her attention. Her mind wandered back to Mr. Thurman Armstrong, another narcissist who loved himself and money in equal proportions.

She knew he invested heavily in the stock market, and together with his earnings from the firm, he lived quite comfortably. Always sly, cunning, and secretive. She knew little about his private life, except that he was divorced and childless. However, she did know that he almost caused Judge Archie to be hit by his speeding car after running a red light at the corner of State and South Swan Street in February.

She clicked her tongue, then let a satisfied breath escape. Her inquisitive nature had always served her well. Mr. Armstrong didn't know she had recognized his car that evening. She wondered if he had been drunk, the way he flew down State Street, straight past the red light.

In the distance, she saw Judge Archie, Preston and Mrs. Stafford step back, almost falling onto the pavement. She considered going to their aid but decided against it; she didn't want them to know she had witnessed the incident. She remained in the shadows on State Street, below Dove Street, out of their vision. Foolish of Mr. Armstrong, she thought. She knew she could use that information, but she also knew she had to find the right time. Now was not the opportune moment.

She set her mouth firmly, listening to the crooning voice of Vaughn De Leath. She had information she could use to her advantage. And when the time was right, she intended to do so.

Thurman Armstrong opened a bottle of Scotch and poured himself a generous glass. After a long day at the office, he could think of nothing better than indulging in a bottle of Scotch, female company, and a pack of cigarettes. He put one to his lips and lit it, inhaling deeply with great pleasure and satisfaction. The bootlegger he dealt with had delivered two bottles of liquor just yesterday, and was paid handsomely for it, too.

With his drink in hand and a cigarette between his lips, Thurman Armstrong entered the living room and ensconced himself on the sofa. He had already turned the radio on to *The Eveready Hour*, his favorite evening program. Ruth Etting, Ethel Waters, and Duke Ellington were set to perform, and he didn't want to miss it. He loved jazz and frequently visited speakeasies to enjoy not only the liquor but also the great dance music.

Dressed in casual clothes, his long legs were resting comfortably on top of the coffee table. He was expecting a visit from a young woman he had recently met at a speakeasy.

At fifty, Thurman lived a comfortable, rather easy-going life after his divorce ten years ago. He enjoyed the nightlife, kept himself in fine shape and maintained a youthful vitality. He lived in a spacious apartment on Lancaster Street, valuing its convenience to downtown and the stores, restaurants, and dance halls on Lark Street. He rarely saw his associates after work hours, which was fine by him, so he never even gave it a thought. Until now.

He thought of the near miss with his car in February. Of all times for Judge Archie to cross the street! Not to worry, he told himself, taking a great gulp of the Scotch. No witnesses, no police around. In his rearview mirror, he had seen the judge brushing himself off.

He finished the liquor and was about to get up to refill his glass, but something had been nagging at his mind. He knew Quentin and Doris frequented the area, as they enjoyed the nightlife too, but they lived more uptown. Burgess lived close by, as did nosy Mrs. Castle. The Sampsons catered to the elder Mrs. Sampson in their huge brownstone on Hamilton Street, as though she were disabled and on her deathbed. They weren't too far away either.

Just suppose these interfering busybodies actually *did* see him but decided not to say anything? I could be ruined, Thurman thought angrily, puffing at his cigarette. Judge Archie would never forgive or forget; he knew the old man was not a forgiving person. Granted, the judge wasn't injured. But he did leave the scene, which Thurman knew, was a criminal offence.

And what about this invitation to a luncheon next Saturday at their stately mansion? He didn't know what to make of it. He would attend, realizing that if he didn't, it would look bad for him. Besides, he wanted to see the inside of that huge mansion, which reeked of money.

Thurman shook his head, bewildered. He got up to refill his glass. The liquor fortified him and enabled him to endure whatever trials and turmoil came his way. Of course, no one knew about the flask he kept in his briefcase. He didn't think anyone was foolish enough to rifle through it. But then, he was not the only one in the office with secrets.

Hadn't he seen Quentin opening a flask more than once at his desk when he didn't think anyone was looking? And hadn't he smelled liquor on Doris's breath on occasion when speaking to her after lunch? Perhaps even conservative Mrs. Castle nipped at whisky, and even the staid and upright Sampsons, whose well-heeled life was always kept hush-hush. He knew Burgess was a ladies' man and frequented speakeasies, so he must have a drinking problem no one knew about.

Perhaps, too, the Staffords were not all they claimed. Many times he wondered if the judge was off his rocker. He had caught several mistakes on the judge's part that would have cost the firm a great deal of money and caused embarrassment. Even Mrs. Stafford and her refined daughters, both widows, could have a past. The most well-heeled people seem to hold onto something no one else knows.

He remembered last Saturday at the market on Lark Street, when he bumped into Mrs. Joan Caves. Pleasant enough but dowdy, certainly not up to Thurman's high standards. He had promised her information on the stock market but did not know if her father would approve. He would not jeopardize his stake at the law firm just to appease his daughter.

He did not know the judge's grandson, although he seemed genuine when asked about steamboats to New York City. But did he really enjoy living with his bossy, domineering grandfather? Didn't he and his mother ever crave privacy? He remembered the judge mentioning his daughters and grandson were moving in with them after their husbands passed away, about 1918, less than ten years ago. Well, live and let live, he thought, sipping the Scotch.

Thurman continued smoking and enjoying the liquor. The buzzer at the door was so sudden he jumped perceptibly. His female company for the evening had arrived.

Burgess left the men's clothing store on Lark Street, where he had purchased two suits on credit.

The store's interior was a blend of polished wood and brass fixtures, with the faint scent of cedar and leather lingering in the air. He had opened a credit line at the store and admitted he enjoyed the buy now and pay later way of shopping. He purchased a new pair of oxford shoes, perfect with the new suits. The storeowner, a former client, made sure Mr. Smith received the best service. The suits were meticulously wrapped in garment bags. He handed them and the shoe box to Burgess, even opening the door for him upon leaving. As Burgess stepped onto the bustling street, he felt a surge of satisfaction, the weight of the garment bags a pleasant reminder of his new acquisitions.

It was a chilly evening, typical of early spring in Albany. With his fedora hat on and his coat buttoned, Burgess trudged along, his footsteps crunching on the snowy sidewalk. He was surprised at the crowds for a Tuesday evening. But then, stores were still open, people had money nowadays and wanted to spend it. With the consumer goods available, who could blame them, he thought wisely. He noticed a store selling radios and a box-like contraption, called a television, that apparently was in its infancy. A small crowd looked at the newest radios and at the blank box in the window, marveling at the anticipation of seeing pictures on a screen. He walked past a hat store, a bookstore, a perfume store and a record store, remembering to buy the latest 78 of Rudy Vallee, his favorite singer.

He was about to turn right onto Hudson Avenue, where his apartment was located, when he looked up and much to his chagrin, he met eyes with the Sampsons, coming from Washington Avenue. It would be foolish not to greet them, so he reluctantly stopped, asking them what their plans were for that evening.

"Hello, Clayton," he said pleasantly, as though seeing them filled his cup of happiness to the brim. "And hello Lucille. Fine evening for shopping, I'd say."

"Indeed," Clayton said pleasantly, looking around at the crowds. "We just bought tickets for a show at the Hall."

"We're going to see Marion Harris," Lucille beamed, as she kept her right hand linked through her husband's arm as though afraid to let go. "She's one of our favorite singers."

Burgess agreed Marion Harris was the cat's meow for sure. Her renditions of *Tea for Two* and *It Had to Be You* were sensational. He saw Lucille with her left hand holding onto the newest issues of *Photoplay* and *True Story* magazines. She noticed his glance.

"My favorite reading material," she commented, showing a perfect set of white teeth. "Like the caption says here, *truth is stranger than fiction*. I love reading gossipy stories."

Burgess found that undoubtedly true but was hard-pressed not to say so. He always considered Mrs. Lucille Sampson nothing but a trouble-making gossip. He had seen her whispering with Mrs. Castle and Doris a few times, clandestinely, almost as though they had secrets. And hadn't he seen Lucille spending time in Thurman's office, with the door closed? Was it possible she was carrying on an affair with Thurman Armstrong? If that were the case, apparently her narcissistic husband was blissfully unaware of it. He looked at the handsome middle-aged couple before him. Her elaborate fur coat and matching stylish cloche hat must have cost a pretty penny. And even staid Clayton, ever the self-righteous, moneymaking attorney and self-proclaimed stock market expert, looked authoritative in his fedora hat and winter coat, his two-tone shoes pristine.

They continued with idle small talk until Clayton mentioned the meal planned at the Staffords for next Saturday. It was to be an Easter luncheon, he commented. Burgess had momentarily forgotten about the invitation, not realizing it was almost upon them. Clayton asked him if he planned to attend.

Burgess nodded. "I'll look forward to it." He thought that was a foolish question. Why wouldn't he attend? Obviously as a staff member, he would be invited. He wanted to ask him the same question, to pay him back in the same coin, but decided against it. He trusted no one, especially the arrogant people standing before him. He wondered if Clayton's cantankerous elderly mother would attend and was about to ask but decided against it.

"Perhaps the judge wants to learn more about Mr. Lewis," Clayton said as people brushed past him. "I'm sure that private investigator will return to speak to us again."

"Such a nuisance," Lucille said, tossing her head. "I do feel bad for Mr. Lewis, poor man."

She commented abruptly that it was lovely seeing him, which Clayton reiterated. They swept past him haughtily and mingled with the crowd on Lark Street. Burgess looked after them, shook his head and headed down Hudson Avenue to his apartment. He refused to think of Mr. Lewis and the possibility of murder for now.

In the mansion on State Street, the Stafford family settled in the living room, with the fireplace warming them comfortably. Gertrude served after dinner coffee, while Joan and Martha assisted in cleaning the kitchen. The radio was turned to the *Waldorf Astoria Dance Orchestra*, a family favorite. Augusta sat on the Victorian sofa, knitting and listening to the pleasing sounds of the dance music while Judge Archie was ensconced in his armchair by the fireplace, skimming the *Albany Evening News*. Preston was smoking and listening to the radio. Martha and Joan soon returned, followed by Gertrude. She announced she would be leaving and Judge Archie looked up from the newspaper, thanking her for the delicious meal.

"I haven't finalized plans for next Saturday's luncheon," Gertrude said, putting on her coat. "I should have it by either tomorrow or Thursday. That'll give me enough time to prepare it."

"I'm sure whatever you'll make will be divine, Gertrude," Augusta said thankfully.

Martha showed her to the front door and then joined the others in the living room. A lively concert by the *Waldorf-Astoria Dance Orchestra* was in progress, causing Martha to swirl around the floor before settling on the sofa next to her mother. Augusta looked at her eldest daughter in surprise.

"You should go to the dance halls, dear," her mother encouraged her. "You might meet a fine gentleman there."

Martha shook her head, smoothing down her dress. "Dance halls are for people Preston's age, Mother. I'm afraid I'm rather too old for that crowd. Besides, I don't know the modern dances, like the Charleston."

"Well, I've rather taken a fancy to Mr. Armstrong," Joan said, rather coyly from the armchair across from her father. "He is so good-looking and worldly."

Judge Archie put down the newspaper on the coffee table with a tired sigh. "I assume you mean Mr. Thurman Armstrong, Joan? Under no circumstances will you entertain getting involved with him. He is not the right man for you."

"Father, I believe I'm capable of making my own decisions," Joan said defensively. "After all, I am fifty and a widow. Isn't it about time I find another suitor?"

Martha and Preston looked at each other, shocked that Joan would stand up to her patriarchal father. A side of her they had never witnessed before. Even Augusta looked at her youngest daughter with a mixture of surprise and reflection, glad she was speaking up for herself.

"While you are living in this house, I do not approve of a relationship with a man like Thurman Armstrong," Judge Archie said, quite firmly. "He is divorced, and you know your mother and I, as devout Catholics, do not approve of divorce. Need I remind you of our Catholic values? When you refer to him as worldly, perhaps that is not the right word. I can think of other descriptions for him outside of the office, none of them redeeming."

"Then why did you make him the head of the agency after Mr. Lewis died?" Martha asked, rather boldly, meeting her father's eyes.

"Well, we seem to be outstepping ourselves this evening," the judge said tersely. "I do not feel I need to justify my judgments to my family or to anyone else. While I respect Mr. Armstrong's ability as a lawyer, I do not approve of his social and recreational activities."

That seemed to end the topic of Thurman Armstrong. There settled an uneasy silence, while the *Waldorf Astoria Dance Orchestra* continued its lively broadcast, the uplifting melodies in contrast to the latent tension in the room.

It was almost a half hour later when the doorbell rang. Preston told them he would answer it and soon disappeared into the hallway. He returned shortly with Doris.

"Good evening, Judge Archie," Doris said. "And Mrs. Stafford, Mrs. Caves and Mrs. Hughes. I hope I'm not intruding this evening."

"Please, do be seated," Augusta said warmly "It's nice to see you, dear. You're looking lovely this evening. Would you like coffee or tea?"

Doris glanced briefly at the judge, wondering how he truly fared these days. Despite her irritation with Judge Archie's constant grousing, she still held him in a certain esteem. His steadfast work ethic and commitment to his law practice were, if nothing else, admirable. He had won numerous cases and brought much recognition to the firm. These conflicting thoughts lingered as she accepted Augusta's invitation to sit down. She had taken off her fur coat and cloche hat and kept them with her, while sitting on the Victorian sofa next to Preston and Martha.

"I went shopping for a new hat and scarf," she explained. "I didn't find anything I liked, so on the trolley back, I wanted to stop in to say hello."

"Of course, Doris, you're always welcomed here," Martha said pleasantly. "You're also invited for the luncheon next Saturday. We do hope you'll attend."

"Yes, I plan to attend." She turned to Judge Archie. "Is there anything I should do before the luncheon next Saturday?"

The older man shook his head. "Simply come as you are. It's an informal gathering. Our maid, Gertrude, will prepare the meal for us."

"You live further uptown, don't you, Doris?" Martha asked her.

"On Quail Street. It's on the trolley line, which is convenient."

The sun was setting, casting a warm glow through the living room windows. The scent of blooming flowers from the garden outside mingled with the distant sound of a jazz band emanating from the radio. Joan and Martha commented on Doris's pretty dress and string of pearls, while Preston mentioned the cruise line was already booking tours for the spring and summer.

"Must be beautiful seeing the Hudson River and the historic sites," Doris commented.

"My wife and I used to enjoy the steamboat trips," Judge Archie spoke up. "But with my arthritis, I'm afraid I'm not as active as before."

"Judge, do you *really* believe someone may want to kill you?" Doris asked, rather bluntly, taking them by surprise. She looked at the judge rather intently, awaiting his response.

Joan and Martha exchanged uneasy glances, their smiles faltering. Preston's eyebrows shot up in surprise, while Judge Archie shifted uncomfortably in his seat. Doris felt a pang of guilt for being so direct, but she felt she needed to know the truth.

"Yes, I do believe that," the judge said stonily. "That's why I hired Mr. Sheppard. At the luncheon, perhaps someone will remember something about the days before Mr. Lewis died."

"But we've been through that already with Mr. Sheppard," Doris said, her voice tinged with frustration. "I didn't notice anything out of the ordinary with Mr. Lewis."

"Mr. Sheppard will not be present," the judge told her firmly. "We may learn more about what happened to Mr. Lewis without his presence. People do like to talk and give themselves away." He paused, his gaze steady. "Let the murderer hang himself, is my motto."

"Or herself," Joan put in, her tone sharp.

"Please, dear," Augusta said almost pleadingly to her husband. "Let's not discuss murder, especially since Miss Blake came here on a social call. There are much more pleasant topics than the possibility of murder."

"Excuse me, Mrs. Stafford," Doris said, apologetically. "I didn't mean to cause any unpleasant discussions. I'm simply concerned."

"No reason for concern," Judge Archie said. "The police are investigating as well as Mr. Sheppard, so a definite conclusion will be reached soon enough."

The radio continued with popular dance tunes and Doris commented she enjoyed the great performers too, especially Bessie Smith and Duke Ellington. Another twenty minutes of small talk ensued, until she announced she was ready to leave.

"And tomorrow's April first," she said with a slight laugh. "April Fool's Day! Although I don't really believe in anything so silly, I imagine some people do."

"Preston, why don't you walk Doris across the park to catch the trolley?" Martha suggested. "I don't believe in April's Fool's either but with the recent events, we can't afford anything more happening."

Preston went to the hallway and returned wearing his jacket and cap. Doris put on her fur coat and cloche hat, wished them a good night and followed Preston out of the living room, to the hallway and the front door. Once outside, they crossed State Street, and walked through West Capitol Park, the State Capitol building shimmering in the encroaching darkness. At the corner of Washington Avenue and North Swan Street, they crossed at the light and stood in front of the majestic State Education Building, its massive columns standing as silent sentinels, watching over the bustling city as night fell. The golden glow of street lamps cast prolonged shadows, adding to the building's majestic presence. The air was thick with the scent of distant rain, hinting at an impending storm.

Within five minutes, they saw a trolley round the corner with Albany City Hall, steadily making its way past the State Capitol as it continued northward. Preston asked her if she thought Mr. Lewis drank the tea meant for his grandfather by mistake.

Doris hesitated, her eyes reflecting the confusion she felt. "Honestly, I don't know what to think. But who knows? Maybe there'll be another murder soon."

Her tone was rather flippant, almost irritating to him. He was about to comment further when the trolley came to an abrupt stop and Doris jumped onboard. He watched as it continued up Washington Avenue and out of sight.

As Preston made his way home through West Capitol Park, he wondered if another mysterious death would soon occur. Unbeknownst to him, it would occur much closer to home.

CHAPTER NINE

Preston woke to the sound of rain drumming against the roof and his windowpanes. He glanced at his alarm clock and noticed it was just six o'clock. He turned over and tried to fall back to sleep, but as usual when he awoke first thing, his thoughts revived, making further slumber impossible. He sighed, lay on his back and stared up at the ceiling, a strange feeling in his stomach. Daylight slowly began to fill the room, although by the sound of the rain, he doubted the sun would make an appearance.

For the last week and a half, he had found it difficult to concentrate on practically anything, including his duties at the Hudson River Day Cruise Line. While he carried out his tasks efficiently as always, he struggled through the week, his mind too preoccupied with complex and deeply disturbing thoughts.

He spoke with Quentin and Doris earlier in the week and had dinner with them Wednesday evening at the Ten Eyck Hotel. They did not see Burgess Smith or anyone else from the law firm, much to their relief, so they enjoyed the fine food at the restaurant, discussing their summer vacations and the luncheon planned for this coming Saturday. Quentin mentioned he looked forward to the luncheon, and

Doris added that the Staffords have a charming house, spacious and wonderfully comfortable. Despite a few misgivings, they appreciated the judge's invitation and anticipated the meal on Saturday would be a relaxing and enjoyable time.

And now it's Friday, he thought miserably. He threw back the covers and padded over to the window blinds, lifted one, and saw the rain coming down heavier now, almost in torrents. He looked at himself in his bureau mirror, running his fingers through his brown hair, feeling the stubble on his face and neck. He entered the bathroom next to his bedroom, filled the sink with enough warm water to shave, and prepared for the day.

He selected his shirt, tie, vest and dress slacks, his shoes shined and his tie pin securely in place. Before leaving, he glanced at the wall calendar above his desk and saw today was April 10, 1925, Good Friday, Easter weekend. He imagined downtown would be busier than usual, with stores on North Pearl Street full of customers buying Easter baskets and provisions for the holiday dinner.

Upon opening his bedroom door, he heard a great deal of activity downstairs. He descended the grand staircase and entered the kitchen, where his mother, aunt, grandparents, and, much to his surprise, Gertrude, were already at the kitchen table. Martha looked up and greeted her son warmly.

"Good morning, dear. Gertrude's here to finalize the luncheon for tomorrow."

Preston sat next to his grandfather and accepted a cup of steaming hot coffee from his mother. Augusta placed a tray of corn muffins on the table, while Joan brought the sugar bowl and the jug of cream over to him.

"I've invited ladies from the League of Women Voters," Augusta said as they were preparing the menu for the luncheon. "Mrs. Aldrich and Mrs. Crabtree are also members of the Daughters of the American Revolution. We should have an intelligent group with us tomorrow!"

Her enthusiasm was met with low murmurs, although Preston acknowledged it sounded like an interesting group. Joan, with a slight smile, helped herself to more coffee while Martha buttered a corn muffin.

Judge Archie sat at the head of the breakfast table, apparently eating little and seemingly devoid of expression. As usual, Preston found it difficult to read his grandfather. He wondered if he was sick or just not feeling well. He then turned his attention to Gertrude again.

Gertrude looked at the tablet in which she had written the menu items. "First, we'll start with deviled eggs and potato salad. The main course will be ham, with sweet potatoes, salad, and hot biscuits. For dessert, I prepared a chocolate cake. Of course, there will be coffee, ginger ale, and Coca-Cola."

"That's quite a menu, Gertrude," Judge Archie said, nodding pleasingly.

Augusta commented that most of the food was already finished. "Thank goodness for the new ice box we bought last year," she added. "It holds so many different items. With the office staff and the ladies from the League of Women Voters, we should have about twenty people. Did you invite anyone from your office, Joan and you as well, Martha and Preston?"

"I asked a few associates but they had their own plans for Easter," Joan mentioned, a hint of disappointment in her voice.

Martha nodded. "I asked Mrs. Whitehead and her husband but they're going out of town."

"Mr. Bishop is visiting relatives in Utica for the holiday weekend," Preston added.

"No worries," Gertrude said. "I'll prepare enough for everyone. Guests can help themselves to the deviled eggs and potato salad before the main course."

Augusta was grateful. "Thank you so much, Gertrude. You truly are a blessing!"

"I have 78s of Duke Ellington, Ruth Etting, and Marion Harris that I'll play on the phonograph," Joan commented, her eyes lighting up. "I'm sure our guests will enjoy the music."

"That'll be lovely, Joan," Augusta said. "We can show the guests around, too. I know the ladies from the League of Women Voters would be thrilled to see the house."

"Sounds like a full house," the judge mumbled, sipping his coffee. "Remember, the purpose of this luncheon is to hear what is said about Mr. Lewis. Someone must know something that can shed light on his unexpected death. Perhaps the women from the League of Women Voters can draw information from the others. I'd be interested to know what they have to say afterwards."

Gertrude brought the pot over to the table and poured oatmeal into bowls for Preston, Judge Archie, and Augusta. Joan and Martha declined more, mentioning they needed to prepare for work. They left the kitchen rather hurriedly, their footsteps echoing up the grand staircase.

Preston remained at the table with his grandparents and Gertrude. His grandfather sat stiffly, sipping his coffee, his posture unyielding. As Preston glanced at him, an ominous discomfort crept over him again. The past few days haunted him—shadows lurking at the edge of his mind, refusing to dissipate. His stomach twisted, the familiar knot of unease tightening. He was dreading tomorrow's luncheon and would be only too glad when it was over and done with.

It was an unspoken fact in the Albany business and legal communities that hardly anyone liked Judge Archibald Stafford. Over the years, he had made countless enemies. Yet, his long and distinguished career earned him respect—though not universal admiration.

The old judge was certainly aware of this fact as he sat rather moodily in the living room on Saturday, waiting for the guests to arrive. The room was comfortably lit, with heavy drapes opened to allow the warm afternoon sun to enter, casting silhouettes that seemed to move with his thoughts. The air was thick with the scent of old books, a testament to his years of service and the weight of his responsibilities.

The grandfather clock in the hallway chimed the hour, its deep tones resonating through the room. He mulled over his reasons for hosting the luncheon, hoping—perhaps foolishly—that it wouldn't backfire. He adamantly believed someone was trying to kill him. After years in the courtroom, he had gathered certain information—but he knew how to set a trap, how to lure out a liar. Or, in this case, a murderer. He had just had to wait and see what would happen.

Preston decided to wear slacks, a shirt and vest without his usual tie. He wanted to be comfortable, as he knew it would be a long afternoon. He saw his mother, aunt and grandmother going in and out of the kitchen. They wore pretty dresses, pearls and bracelets, looking refined and very feminine. Upon entering the living room, he saw his grandfather sunk deeply in his armchair, either asleep or in contemplative thoughts. At first, he was hesitant to speak. He sat on the sofa, lit a cigarette and was quiet for a few moments, until his grandfather suddenly addressed him.

"What time is it, Preston? I want our guests assembled here first, of course, then afterwards we can enjoy Gertrude's luncheon."

Preston heard the grandfathers clock in the hallway strike the half hour—it was just twelve thirty. He reminded his grandfather that the guests were scheduled for one o'clock. He saw the consternation emanating from him, his facial expression drawn into tight lines of anticipation. For a moment, he wanted to ask if he was up to having company but then realized that would be foolish. They would soon arrive and Gertrude had already prepared a delicious meal. He could not help notice the tense atmosphere in the living room, wondering if his grandfather would make it through the afternoon.

Joan came in at that moment with a pile of 78 records. She wound up the phonograph and put on a Duke Ellington record, which helped alleviate some of the tension in the room. She opened the curtains further allowing more sunlight to enter and then returned to the kitchen.

Preston heard a scurry of footsteps, back and forth from the kitchen to the dining room as his mother, aunt, grandmother and Gertrude brought in dishes and plates. He joined them in the dining room and saw his mother with bottles of Coca-Cola and ginger ale. Joan carried a tray of deviled eggs while his grandmother deposited a bowl of potato salad on the dining room table. It was just as Gertrude entered with a container of fresh salad that the doorbell rang.

Preston went to the hallway to open the front door. He saw the Sampsons standing before him, looking handsome and rather distinguished, and the elderly Mrs. Sampson, too, in a stylish fur coat. They removed their coats, handed them to him and after hanging them in the hallway closet, he brought them to the living room to greet Judge Archie.

"Well, hello, Archie," Lucille said. Her olive green dress, stockings and high heels were certainly noticeable; the judge did not miss even her makeup and rather strong perfume. He sized her up quickly then his gaze fell upon Mr. Sampson.

"Greetings, judge," Clayton said amicably, ever looking the part of the professional attorney, even on a weekend. His suit was immaculate and his brown hair, parted to the side, made him look younger than his fifty-five years.

Preston's eyes then rested on Philomena, who returned his gaze, coolly. He watched as she strode around the living room, commenting on the comfort, the fireplace and the wonderful Victorian sofa, which he thought was idle chatter. She gave a perfunctory greeting to Judge Archie before continuing to look around. Certainly, the Sampsons lived in a comfortable brownstone on Hamilton Street, one of the best streets in the city, which he assumed was adequately furnished. His grandfather remained sunken in his chair and did not say anything to the Sampsons, except to stare them down as though he waited for the opportunity to spring a trap and catch them unaware.

Preston sighed, questioning whether this luncheon was a mistake. As usual, he could not read his grandfather but knew he was contemplating something.

At that moment, Augusta entered and greeted them, followed by Joan and Martha. Gertrude offered them coffee or ginger ale, and Clayton, Lucille, and Philomena followed her to the dining room, where they helped themselves to the delicious deviled eggs and glasses of ginger ale.

Soon, the doorbell rang several times. Preston returned to the living room with Doris, Quentin, and Burgess, who seemed pleased to see the judge. Doris looked stylish in a simple black dress with pearls, her flapper appeal more dormant than usual. Like Preston, Quentin decided on a casual appearance, wearing slacks, a shirt, and a vest without a tie, as did Burgess, to Preston's surprise. They chatted with Judge Archie, but he remained rather sullen and not too talkative. The room filled with polite conversation, but beneath the surface, there was an undercurrent of distrust and hidden agendas.

"We have drinks and food in the dining room," Preston told them, rather embarrassed by his grandfather's lack of cordiality.

"Oh, how lovely," Doris commented. "I'm sure it's the cat's meow for sure!"

"That's great, Pres," Quentin said. "I'm starving!"

Burgess agreed. "I had a light breakfast so that I could enjoy the meal today. Where's the dining room, Preston?"

As Preston led them into the dining room, Augusta, Joan and Martha greeted them cordially. The Sampsons were enjoying the deviled eggs and ginger ale and standing near the sideboard, chatting amongst themselves. They looked up and greeted Doris, Quentin and Burgess. Philomena began a conversation with Doris and Lucille soon began chatting with Quentin. Burgess and Clayton were discussing the stock market and other business matters, and even occasional outbursts of laughter were heard, especially from Philomena and Doris. Gertrude entered from the kitchen with another tray of deviled eggs.

"Why don't we join Judge Archie in the living room?" Augusta suggested.

They followed her across the wide hallway to the living room, where Joan had put on another 78 record of Duke Ellington. They sat around the comfortable room, admiring the paintings on the wall, the bookcases lined with popular books and the radio console against the far wall. Doris commented that she loved Duke Ellington, and Joan showed her the collection of 78 records. Quentin looked at them, too, and asked her to put on *It Had to Be You* by Isham Jones next.

Burgess sat on the Victorian sofa, ginger ale in one hand and a cigarette in the other, while chatting with Martha. He commented on his cases at the law firm, and his summer vacation plans. He asked her about her work at the State Capitol. Clayton was across from the judge, speaking to him in low tones, although about what Preston could not tell. He saw his Aunt Joan standing near the windows, chatting with

Mrs. Sampson and the elderly Mrs. Sampson, apparently in good spirits, by their laughter and pleasant tones.

The doorbell rang several more times. Augusta went to the door and returned with a few women Preston did not know. He listened as his grandmother introduced them as Mrs. Mary Crabtree, Mrs. Agnes Aldrich, Miss Jane Lodge, Mrs. Lucretia Underhill and Miss Emily Standish. She mentioned they were members of the Albany chapter of the League of Women Voters.

"Mrs. Crabtree and Mrs. Aldrich are also members of the Daughters of the American Revolution," she added proudly. "They are true patriots and lifelong residents of Albany."

Preston glanced at the growing crowd, momentarily overwhelmed. But the ladies were quite friendly, genuine and sincere, all in their seventies or possibly a bit more, certainly well dressed and mannered, with a few wearing white gloves up to their elbows. They had never visited the mansion and commented on the lovely furnishings.

Soon, they were mingling with the others. Mrs. Underhill and Miss Lodge chatted pleasantly with Lucille and her mother-in-law. Mrs. Crabtree managed to strike up a conversation with Judge Archie, who seemed to enjoy her attention. Miss Standish engaged in a lively discussion with Doris, while Mrs. Underhill conversed with Joan and Martha.

The doorbell rang again. This time, Preston went to the hallway and, upon opening the door, saw Mrs. Rose Castle and Mr. Thurman Armstrong on the steps.

"Hello, Preston, dear," Mrs. Castle beamed as she entered the hallway. "Mr. Armstrong and I arrived at the same time!"

Thurman entered, removing his coat and fedora hat and handing them to Preston. Mrs. Castle did the same just as Augusta came to the hallway, greeting Mrs. Castle and Mr. Armstrong cheerfully. She led them into the living room and introduced them to the ladies from the League of Women Voters. Soon, Gertrude appeared, beckoning them to the dining room where the appetizers and drinks were served.

Mrs. Castle and Thurman helped themselves to deviled eggs and potato salad. With their plates in hand, they returned to the living room and soon found themselves in lively discussions with Miss Standish, Mr. Sampson, and Mrs. Underhill.

"My husband and I have tickets to see *The Bat*," Mrs. Crabtree said, standing next to Joan and Martha. "I understand it's quite a production. One of the most popular plays this season. It's been held over at the Ritz Theater, too. I just love Mary Roberts Rinehart!"

"My husband and I saw *The Bat* while in Buffalo last year," Mrs. Aldrich commented, joining them. "It's quite a thriller. I'm sure you'll enjoy it."

Martha mentioned that she also enjoyed books by Mary Roberts Rinehart and might get tickets for the show. Joan excused herself to chat with Mr. Armstrong, who was speaking with Miss Standish and Miss Lodge.

Preston realized that all the guests had arrived. The room buzzed with polite conversation, but beneath the surface, he felt there was a certain tension. He noticed his grandfather scowling in disapproval as his youngest daughter began conversing with Mr. Armstrong. Mrs. Underhill then asked Preston if they could look around the house, after all, it was so lovely and charming.

"Of course, Mrs. Underhill," he replied.

"How many floors does this house have?" Mrs. Crabtree inquired.

"There are four, including an attic," Augusta said. "Please, feel free to wander to your heart's content!"

"I must say, Augusta, your house is just lovely," Philomena said, approaching her. "May I look around a bit, too?"

Preston thought her comment superfluous as he knew she had visited his grandmother at the house many times before and had seen the ground floor in her previous visits.

"Of course, dear," Augusta replied.

"We'd like to see the house, too," Lucille said, with her husband beside her. "It's similar to ours but much bigger and more antique."

"Preston, would you show Doris and me around?" Quentin asked. "I've never been here before, and it's really an amazing place!"

Soon, the living room had all but emptied, except for Judge Archie, who remained in his armchair. Guests were going up and down the stairs, in and out of the rooms on all the floors. The ladies from the League of Women Voters, along with Mrs. Sampson, Mrs. Castle, Burgess, and Thurman, admired the different facades, the ornate banister, the wonderful paintings adorning the walls, and the rich furnishings, including the antique beds and armoires. They were particularly impressed by the judge's bedroom on the first floor, far from the street noise and just behind the kitchen. In the kitchen, they marveled at the most modern conveniences, including a sterling gas stove, an ample icebox, and a circular oak kitchen table.

Lucille commented to her husband that they needed a new icebox, and Philomena, standing next to her, agreed, albeit rather enviously.

Mrs. Crabtree, Mrs. Aldrich, and Miss Lodge, along with the Sampsons and Thurman, went on to investigate the dining room while the others were just coming down the stairs. They uttered gasps of pleasure at the antique table, the crystal chandelier hanging decorously from the ceiling, and the antique sideboard. Mrs. Underhill and Miss Standish entered from the hallway at that moment, commenting on the beautiful house and the lovely furnishings.

Augusta proudly pointed out that her wedding dishes in the sideboard were from 1868, the year she graduated from college. She then added that her duties as a wife and mother were paramount to her.

"You were married in 1868?" Mrs. Aldrich asked pleasantly. "My husband and I recently celebrated our fiftieth anniversary. Fifty-seven years of marriage is just wonderful!"

Augusta nodded, although silently thinking of the judge's occasional moodiness and tyrannical manner. More small talk continued and Preston noted his grandparents appeared pleased. The tour or as he described it to himself, the snooping of the house, soon concluded, much to his relief, as Gertrude brought out the ham and sweet potatoes. Thurman assisted Preston in bringing the dining room chairs into the living room, enabling everyone to eat together.

"A fine meal for Easter," Augusta said, admiring the succulent ham and sweet potatoes.

As the guests began to fill their plates, Preston felt relieved that the house tours had ended. He did not particularly like people walking through all the rooms, though it did not seem to bother his grandparents. He looked around for Quentin and Doris but could not find them. They had been upstairs with him a few minutes ago, but they must have taken the back staircase down to the kitchen. He also did not see Burgess anywhere. He spotted Mrs. Castle helping herself to the ham, sweet potatoes, and warm biscuits. Soon, everyone followed suit, taking a plate and forming a line to enjoy the rich offerings.

Martha brought a plate containing ham, sweet potatoes, and a biscuit to her father in the living room. The judge had gotten up and was looking at Joan's collection of 78 records. He turned as he saw her, thanked her for the plate of food, and then settled back in his armchair. The others sat in different chairs and on the sofa, eating, drinking, and chatting while enjoying Gertrude's wonderful meal.

"The sweet potatoes are delicious," Miss Lodge said, clearly enjoying the food. "The ham is so moist, too. I must say, this is quite a meal, Mrs. Stafford!"

Mrs. Underhill asked the judge about his work at the law firm, while Miss Standish inquired about Thurman's responsibilities. Doris and Quentin were seated on the dining room chairs next to the fireplace, saying little but apparently enjoying the food. Philomena was on the sofa, chatting with Joan, while Lucille and Clayton were talking with Mrs. Aldrich and Mrs. Castle. Burgess sat in an armchair next to Martha, eating ravenously but saying little. Quentin got up and entered the dining room for a second helping of ham and potatoes.

Mrs. Crabtree finished her meal and addressed the judge. "I'm so sorry to hear about Mr. Lewis. I know you were especially close to him. Please accept my sincerest condolences."

"Mr. Sheppard has spoken to us about Mr. Lewis," Thurman commented.

"Mr. Sheppard?" Mrs. Underhill said. "I believe I've heard that name before."

"Mr. Sheppard is a distinguished private investigator," the judge proclaimed. "I hired him to look into Mr. Lewis's unexpected death. I do not believe the tea was poisonous."

"I've read about Mr. Sheppard in the newspapers," Miss Standish said.

"I read in the newspaper about the poisonous tea," Miss Lodge said.

"How very odd," Mrs. Aldrich offered. "Can't say I've heard of such a thing."

Mrs. Crabtree cleared her throat. "Certain exotic teas could cause death, due to the high toxicity and extreme residue, it's rare, but it can happen." Everyone was silent, weighing the reality of Mrs. Crabtree's deduction carefully. "I was a night nurse for forty years here in Albany." She looked around the room, realizing she had an audience. "I started as a nursing student in 1880 and witnessed many disturbing things, some illegal, in the overnight hours."

She stopped talking, realizing she had said too much, and became rather flustered. She continued eating the ham and sweet potatoes left on her plate.

Doris, her curiosity piqued, asked, "What did you mean by illegal?"

Mrs. Crabtree smiled wanly. "Well, dear, the medical profession in those days did not have advanced procedures or medicines. It did not have the legality it does today."

"What sort of disturbing experiences did you have?" Mrs. Underhill asked curiously.

Mrs. Crabtree took a deep breath, her eyes reflecting a mix of pride and sorrow. "There were many nights when I saw things that would chill your bones. Patients brought in under the cover of darkness, some with injuries that were… not from accidents. It was a time when secrets were kept, and not all of them were innocent."

The room grew quiet, the weight of her words hanging in the air.

"I remember that time, too," Philomena spoke up. "My sister died during childbirth in 1885. Her child also died. Their lives could've been saved if that occurred today."

"Please, mother, it's too disturbing to mention," Clayton told her gently.

Mrs. Crabtree turned to Philomena. "I do remember a young woman who died during childbirth around that time. I worked that evening. It was dreadful and so sad." She mentioned her nephews who fought in the Great War; some returned gravely wounded and needed rehabilitation.

"I had a nephew who lost his life in the Great War," Mrs. Aldrich remarked sadly.

Her thoughts running away from her, Mrs. Crabtree commented on how she had witnessed illegal abortions performed and had been threatened to secrecy. Her night duties were precarious, as the hospitals were often scenes of extreme deprivation and even cruelty, during the Civil War and the Great War, particularly in the emergency wards. Infectious diseases were rampant, she added, with tuberculosis, measles, small pox and scarlet fever claiming many lives. She mentioned an abortion she remembered in particular, in the emergency ward.

"Abortions?" Miss Lodge exclaimed. "How dreadful! Who would even think of having an abortion? Were hospitals really so dangerous then?"

Mrs. Crabtree sipped her ginger ale thoughtfully. "Threats to medical personnel were not uncommon. Hospitals had no way to curb violence toward doctors, nurses, and even orderlies." She paused, her expression growing more guarded. "Those were challenging times," she added, her eyes shifting around the room. She stopped speaking, her gaze lingering on the assembled guests, the ginger ale glass hiding her expression as she held it to her lips.

Miss Standish commented on her role as an elementary school teacher and the hardships faced in dealing with young children. Miss Lodge mentioned she was a retired telephone operator, reflecting on the challenges of her own career.

Mrs. Underhill mentioned she had recently retired as a secretary at an insurance company. Mrs. Aldrich, rather demurely, remarked that she had the most difficult job of all: being a wife and mother. This comment brought laughter around the room and seemed to lighten the atmosphere.

Joan got up and put on a new record, this time another Duke Ellington. Gertrude entered at that moment, asking if everyone was ready for the chocolate cake and coffee.

Augusta told her guests that Gertrude's cake and coffee were heavenly. They followed her into the dining room, where the rich cake was beautifully set on the dining room table, along with cups, a sugar bowl, and a jug of cream. Martha and Joan helped Gertrude in cutting and handing out plates of the moist cake. Mrs. Castle joked that it would add to her waistline, which brought laughter to the group. Judge Archie had even gotten up and joined them in the dining room for coffee and cake, but as Preston looked at him, he appeared ill and not too strong. He noticed how the judge leaned against the dining room table for support.

"Why don't we take our coffee and cake into the living room?" Augusta suggested.

They gathered again in the living room, where the Duke Ellington record still played, creating a vibrant atmosphere. Martha assisted her father back to the living room, while Joan and Thurman began talking earnestly about the stock market and shopping in downtown Albany.

The afternoon wore on, with Preston, Quentin, and Doris enjoying seconds on the chocolate cake. Philomena appeared to make friends with Miss Standish and Mrs. Underhill, inviting them to her house for tea. Mrs. Crabtree invited Augusta and the judge to her home on Willett Street for lunch and tea some afternoon this coming week.

After several hours, many cups of coffee and more servings of the delicious chocolate cake, conversations slowly began to wind down. Miss Lodge announced she needed to leave, as did the rest of the ladies. Mrs. Castle thanked the judge and Augusta for such a lovely meal and for their graciousness in hosting the luncheon. Everyone got up rather slowly, feeling gastronomically satisfied from the fine meal, and walked toward the hallway to retrieve hats and coats.

As the guests mingled, getting ready to leave, Miss Underhill remarked, "Mrs. Crabtree, that burgundy coat is simply stunning!"

Mrs. Crabtree laughed softly. “Oh, it’s an old favorite. Perfect for this chilly weather.”

Preston then noticed Mrs. Crabtree lingering in the living room, speaking to Thurman by the windows. Their conversation seemed quite intimate, almost in hushed tones. He also saw his grandfather, now standing and conversing with Mrs. Aldrich.

Burgess thanked Augusta, as did Lucille, Clayton, and Philomena. Quentin and Doris gathered their coats and then departed; with Quentin telling Preston, he would call him tomorrow. Mrs. Aldrich and Mrs. Underhill soon joined them. With their coats buttoned up and their cloche hats on, they braved the chilly air. Mrs. Castle left along with Mrs. Crabtree, Miss Lodge and Miss Standish. Preston saw it was raining lightly, with a chilly breeze, so he quickly closed the door as the last of the guests departed.

He turned and noticed the family had separated. Martha, Joan, and Augusta retreated to the kitchen to assist Gertrude in cleaning up. Judge Archie returned to the living room, where he approached the phonograph player and put on a 78 record of Ruth Etting.

Preston helped the judge set the living room in order and then returned the dining room chairs. In passing through the hallway he saw it was already eight thirty. He had not realized the guests had stayed so long. Augusta, Joan, and Martha finished cleaning in the kitchen, thanked Gertrude immensely, and accompanied her to the door. They returned to the living room and, like Preston, were rather tired after a much longer afternoon than they had anticipated. Martha turned on the radio to a station playing relaxing symphonic music.

“Well, did we learn anything, Father?” Joan asked, sitting next to her sister on the sofa.

“Perhaps,” the judge said, adding nothing more.

"I didn't notice anything out of the ordinary," Augusta said. "Everyone seemed to enjoy the meal and the conversations. They enjoyed wondering the house, too."

Judge Archie sat stoically in his armchair. "People reveal themselves when talking."

"It was nice having everyone here," Martha commented, changing the subject.

"But tiresome," Joan said, putting her right hand to her forehead. "I've developed a headache, but I know I've finished my aspirin."

"There's a bottle in our room, Joan," the judge said. "Should be on my bedside table."

Joan smiled weakly. "I'll just get the aspirin and call it a night."

Within the hour, Judge Archie and Augusta decided they also were tired. Augusta helped her husband up, while Preston and Martha turned off the lights, the radio and secured the front door. Judge Archie and Augusta retreated across the hall, behind the kitchen, while Preston and his mother climbed the stairs to their bedrooms. Soon, the lights were off, and the house was bathed in darkness. All was still in the mansion on State Street.

Easter Sunday dawned sunny but chilly, the temperature dropping just enough to make it brisk yet invigorating for spring. The sun showed promise of a bright day ahead.

Preston glanced at his alarm clock and, seeing it was almost seven thirty, decided to get up. As he opened one of the blinds, the sun warmed him, but his bare feet were chilled in the window alcove, making him shiver slightly. He began the process of preparing for the day, knowing his grandmother intended to attend church services this morning. He assumed his mother and aunt were already up and ready too.

Preston liked the convenience of a door from his bedroom leading to the hallway bathroom. His mother used this bathroom too, but she must already be downstairs. After shaving, bathing, and dressing, he opened his bedroom door and entered the hallway, on the way to the staircase. Upon reaching the hallway, he entered the kitchen and saw his grandparents at the table, drinking coffee and reading the Sunday newspaper.

Augusta greeted him pleasantly. "Good morning, dear."

Preston sat across from his grandfather, who muttered a low good morning. He then accepted a steaming cup of freshly brewed coffee from his grandmother. He noticed his grandparents were dressed for church services, his grandfather in a crisp suit and his grandmother in a modest dress with a lace collar.

"What time is Mass this morning?" he asked his grandmother.

"Ten o'clock," Augusta told him. "This is the special Easter Sunday service, a little longer than the usual Mass. I'm looking forward to it."

Preston took a sip of his coffee. The warmth spread through him, contrasting with the lingering chill of the morning.

"Aren't Joan and Martha going?" Judge Archie asked, his face wrinkled with curiosity.

Augusta nodded. "They were tired from yesterday's luncheon. They'll be down shortly." She paused, and then added, "I'll reheat the ham and sweet potatoes from yesterday for our Easter lunch after we come back from church. And there's chocolate cake left over, too."

Preston helped himself to a blueberry muffin. While buttering it, he could not help but wonder why his mother, usually an early riser, had not gotten up yet. But then they heard footsteps tread down the stairs and cross the hallway. Martha appeared in the kitchen, pretty and pleasant in a navy blue dress and pearls, looking refreshed after a good night's sleep.

"Good morning," Martha said cheerfully. "A beautiful spring morning, just right for Easter services." She poured coffee and sat across from her son. She then looked around the table. "I'm surprised Joan isn't up yet, although she does like to sleep late when she has the chance."

"We plan to go to the ten o'clock service," Augusta reminded her daughter.

She fixed oatmeal and served her daughter and grandson. After returning the pot to the stove, she mentioned someone should check on Joan. Perhaps she was still suffering from the headache last evening.

Martha wiped her mouth on a napkin. "I'm sure she's just oversleeping."

Judge Archie nodded. "She'll be down soon. She isn't one to miss church."

The grandfather clock in the hall chimed the nine o'clock hour, and Augusta looked first at her husband and then at her daughter. Preston could sense something wrong in her expression.

"We'll never make it for the ten o'clock service if Joan isn't up by now," Augusta said.

"I'll go check on her," Martha said, getting up from her chair. Looking back as she left the kitchen, she commented, "Joan is most likely already up and getting ready for the day."

From the kitchen, Preston heard his mother climb the stairs, cracking with the sound of old wood, while his grandmother scoured the pot containing the oatmeal. His grandfather continued reading the newspaper, and it was while Preston was about to light his first morning cigarette that a horrible scream came from above them. It erupted suddenly, taking them by complete surprise. At first, no one moved, until the horrified scream was repeated again and again.

Preston's heart pounded as he dropped the cigarette and dashed out of the kitchen, his grandmother at his heels. Judge Archie carefully made his way to the hallway and joined his wife and grandson at the bottom of the stairs.

"Mother, what is it?" Preston looked up and saw the ghastly expression on his mother's face. She stood at the second-floor landing, looking down at them. She was visibly shaken, her hands trembling, her face covered in tears.

"Martha, what is the problem?" Judge Archie demanded, not one to waste time listening to hysterical females, even if it was his own daughter.

Martha leaned on the banister for support and continued looking down at her son and parents, trying to compose herself. Her voice, when it came, was hoarse and barely audible.

"It's Joan. She won't wake up! There's no pulse and she isn't breathing!"

Preston looked at his grandmother, who sank wearily onto a lower step, speechless and in shock and disbelief. He turned to his grandfather, also shocked but vigilant. Judge Archie held onto the newel post, muttering, rather incoherently, but enough for Preston to catch his words.

"The enemy has struck again, in this very house."

CHAPTER TEN

In less than an hour, the mansion on State Street became a scene of urgent activity. The family physician, Dr. Leonard Stephens, received a frantic telephone call from Mrs. Augusta Stafford. While about to leave his house with his wife to attend Easter services, he hurriedly drove to the Staffords' with his medical bag and a supply of equipment.

Upon arriving, the elderly doctor was greeted by Judge Archie, whom he had known for over forty years. The doctor, rather tall with a fine head of white hair and a steady, serious manner, was well known in Albany for his outstanding medical practice. The scent of pinewood filled the air, mingling with the delicate fragrance of Easter lilies from the downstairs parlor.

"Thank you for coming so quickly," Judge Archie said, his voice tinged with worry. He pointed upstairs, and with Preston and Augusta, Dr. Stephens ascended to the fourth floor to Joan's bedroom. Each step produced a groan from the wooden stairs, a chorus to their hurried pace. Preston's pulse quickened as he exchanged anxious glances with his grandmother, their breaths uneven with rising tension.

As they reached the top, Dr. Stephens felt a pang of concern. He glanced at Preston, whose face was a mask of determination, and

Augusta, who clutched her hands together, her knuckles white. He suggested calling the police, much to the judge's chagrin. Preston quickly descended the grand staircase, entering the hallway to use the candlestick telephone.

Martha was in a near state of collapse, sitting in a hallway chair outside her sister's bedroom, refusing to enter again. She was beside herself, wailing and quite distraught until Dr. Stephens administered a shot of morphine to calm her. He then entered the bedroom to examine Joan's still figure in her bed. From a preliminary examination, he knew there was nothing that could be done. Straightening up, he looked into the startled faces of Augusta, Preston and Judge Archie who managed to climb the stairs, breathing heavily. He stood in the doorway, leaning on the doorknob, his face flushed and out of breath.

Dr. Stephens shook his head. "She's been dead for some time. We had best call an ambulance to bring her to the hospital. How was she last evening?"

Augusta cleared her throat and commented that her youngest daughter was fine yesterday and all week had been in good spirits. She had no medical issues and while she complained of a headache last evening, she was otherwise a picture of health.

"Did she take anything for the headache?" Dr. Stephens inquired.

Augusta nodded. "She finished her aspirin and my husband suggested she take some from the bottle in our bedroom." She pointed to the bedside table. "That's the aspirin my husband uses."

Dr. Stephens picked up the bottle, carefully examined it, and then replaced it on the bedside table. He asked to use the telephone. Preston, who had returned from calling the police, led him down the stairs to the hallway, where he dialed the operator to request an ambulance.

Preston then retreated to the living room, too shocked to speak, fumbling for a cigarette and quickly lighting it. Judge Archie soon joined him, as he needed respite from the recent horrendous discovery. Augusta helped Martha down the stairs and settled her in an armchair near her father. Dr. Stephens entered and addressed the family.

"I suggest an autopsy for Mrs. Caves as soon as possible. I cannot determine what caused her death at this time. I'll plan for the autopsy as soon as possible. She may have had a heart attack or simply died in her sleep."

"Ridiculous," Judge Archie said. "Joan was in excellent health. She didn't have a heart condition or any outstanding medical problems."

"The police should be here soon," Preston managed to say, barely audible.

"The aspirin bottle is nearly full," the doctor continued. "It's unlikely she took her own life. I did a quick search of her bureau drawers and the bathroom next to her room but did not find any medications."

"Of course not," the judge said. "As we stated, Joan was in perfect health."

At that moment, the doorbell rang and Preston, unable to stand the strain, tension and incredulity of what happened to his aunt, quickly rose and entered the hallway to answer the door. He saw three men in white, and on the street, an ambulance parked in front of the house. They mentioned they were from St. Timothy's Hospital. Dr. Stephens instructed them to follow him to the fourth floor.

Preston watched as they climbed the stairs with a stretcher, then returned to the living room, finding temporary solace in the company of his family. A million conflicting beliefs were swirling through his mind, cluttering his thoughts to the point of helplessness. He glanced at his grandfather, as he sat stoic, sullen and unresponsive, deep in apparent grief.

He tried to push the agonizing thought from his mind. Did his grandfather actually know more about Aunt Joan's death? Was he somehow responsible for what happened? A cold shudder went through him, leaving him feeling extremely agitated and very much alone.

Two police officers arrived and questioned the family extensively. After hearing about the incident, they took the aspirin bottle back to headquarters to be tested. Not wishing to cause any further strain on the family, they assured the judge they would be in touch, with more details, as soon as they became available.

"Please call Mr. Sampson and Mr. Armstrong," Judge Archie told the doctor, after the police left. "Their numbers are in the front of the telephone book on the hallway table."

Augusta looked at her husband with concern. "Is that a good idea, dear?"

"Of course," he snapped. "Mr. Armstrong is the interim president. Both he and Mr. Sampson are competent attorneys."

Preston glanced at him incredulously. He found it difficult to believe his grandfather would trust either the Sampsons or Mr. Armstrong, but from a business perspective, perhaps he knew better. He turned his concentration to the situation at hand.

Dr. Stephens disappeared into the hallway and was soon placing calls, speaking in rather low tones. After concluding the conversations, he returned to the living room. He mentioned that the Sampsons and Mr. Armstrong were on their way and that they expressed their extreme shock, disbelief, and sorrow upon learning of the unexpected death of the judge's youngest daughter. The doctor then went back to the fourth floor, where the ambulance crew had finished with Joan, her body on the stretcher and being carried down the stairs, on the way to the ambulance and to St. Timothy's Hospital. Dr. Stephens asked the family if they wanted to go with him to the hospital, but Judge Archie, Augusta, Martha, and Preston were too numb and in shock to go anywhere. The doctor mentioned he would be in touch soon and then left in his own car on the way to the hospital.

At about the same time, Clayton, Lucille, and Philomena Sampson arrived along with Thurman Armstrong. They greeted the doctor, brushed past him, and entered the living room, noting the apparent atmosphere of grieving and sadness. Preston was surprised the elderly Mrs. Sampson would come but then realized she would not want to miss anything. She certainly looked strong and healthy for her age, he thought.

"Augusta, dear, what happened?" Philomena said, approaching her friend. She sat next to her on the sofa and took her hands in hers.

Thurman approached the judge, as did Clayton and Lucille, expressing sincere remorse and wanting to know what they could do to help. The judge motioned them to chairs, and soon they were listening to Augusta's account of what happened to their youngest daughter.

"I discovered her," Martha said weakly from the armchair near her father. "We were getting ready for church and Joan hadn't come downstairs yet. When I went to check on her, she wouldn't wake up. The doctor couldn't tell what her death was attributed to."

"How dreadful," Lucille said, as though unused to any such misfortune.

"Did she have a heart condition or another underlying illness?" Clayton asked.

Judge Archie shook his head. "Dr. Stephens asked us the same question. Joan was in perfect health. We have no idea what caused her sudden death."

"I'm sorry, Judge," Thurman said.

Preston glanced at Thurman and noticed he looked as though he had just gotten up. He was barely shaved, his trousers were baggy, and his whole appearance was rather disheveled. Most likely a late night at a speakeasy, he thought. In contrast, Mr. Sampson appeared pristine as always, and even the younger Mrs. Sampson, sitting comfortably in an armchair as though the world owed her everything, looked immaculate in her fur coat, which she held in her lap, her pretty cloche hat still on her head.

"There must've been something she ate," Philomena said reasonably, still holding onto Augusta's hands, herself almost in tears. "She was so young, only fifty. Perhaps the deviled eggs or the sweet potatoes."

"Mother, please," Clayton said. "That is ridiculous. Deviled eggs, ham, and sweet potatoes are harmless, unless there was poison in them."

"We all ate the deviled eggs, ham, and sweet potatoes," Preston noted. "I didn't get sick. I don't think anyone else did, either."

"Your friends from the League of Women Voters ate them, too," Lucille said to Augusta. "They seemed fine and in good spirits. I found them quite charming and personable."

"We haven't heard if they've been taken ill," Augusta said. "I doubt very much if the food had anything to do with Joan's death."

"I agree with you, Mr. Sampson," Martha said. "That is ridiculous. The food did not cause my sister's premature death."

An uncomfortable silence ensued until the doorbell rang, quite stridently, taking everyone by surprise. Preston got up and told them he would inquire who was calling. He returned with Mrs. Rose Castle and Burgess Smith.

"Well, if this isn't a reunion," Clayton said dryly as they walked in. "What brings the mountain to Mohammed?"

"I was walking along State Street as I usually do," Mrs. Castle said. She glanced at Burgess. "I bumped into Mr. Smith and we decided to come here to express our gratitude for the luncheon."

"I enjoyed myself immensely, Mrs. Stafford. Thank you for having me."

While their appreciation was certainly sincere, Preston remembered they had already expressed their thanks yesterday upon leaving. But then he thought light of it, as their acknowledgment of the luncheon appeared heartfelt and real.

It soon became apparent to Mrs. Castle and Burgess that something was terribly wrong. Burgess apologized if they had stopped by at an inconvenient time, but Judge Archie rather bluntly told them what happened to Joan—that she was found dead in her bed this morning, unresponsive. She was now at St. Timothy's Hospital, where an autopsy would be performed.

Preston saw Mrs. Castle sway and for a moment believed she would faint. Burgess guided her to the sofa, where she sat next to Augusta, speechless and in shock. Burgess was also shocked and confused, offering his condolences to the Staffords for their loss.

Lucille and Philomena said they would make tea and departed for the kitchen, while Mrs. Castle consoled Augusta, who, Preston noticed, needed as much consolation as his grandmother. Burgess ignored Thurman and asked the judge if he could do anything for him.

Thurman once more expressed his sincerest remorse, then mentioned he was due at his country club this afternoon and needed to depart. He told the judge to contact him again if anything was needed. Preston joined him at the front door, while Burgess took his seat and accepted a cup of tea from Lucille. Philomena handed cups to Martha, Mrs. Castle, Augusta, and the judge. No one spoke much, too shocked beyond words to believe what had happened. Augusta sipped the hot tea and commented that it was Easter Sunday and, much to her regret, she would not be attending services.

"I know the priest at St. Mary's," Philomena told her. "I'll call him this afternoon to tell him what happened. Perhaps he'll visit you soon."

About an hour later, the Sampsons, Burgess, and Mrs. Castle got up to leave. They again expressed their extreme remorse over the death of Mrs. Caves and assured the family that if there was anything at all they needed, to please contact them without hesitation.

Burgess helped Mrs. Castle to her feet, still feeling weak from the shock. Her face was covered in tears, but she managed to pull herself together and accompanied him to the front door. Preston saw them out along with the Sampsons, then returned to the living room.

An unexpected Easter holiday, he thought unhappily. His mother and grandparents were in deep sorrow, understandably, but Preston found himself in not only mourning but also confusion. He glanced at his grandfather, sitting sunken in his armchair, staring into space.

Questions swirled in his mind, unanswered. Had his aunt simply died of natural causes? Was his grandfather responsible for his youngest daughter's sudden demise? Or was someone really trying to kill the judge and his aunt ended up the victim?

Preston realized something must have occurred yesterday at the luncheon but exactly what and involving whom, remained unclear.

It was late in the afternoon. Augusta received a telephone call from the priest at the church, expressing his most sincere condolences. He mentioned the parish would be happy to assist in funeral arrangements and Augusta thanked him kindly.

There had been several more telephone calls that afternoon, mostly from friends in the neighborhood and the women from the League of Women Voters, who were contacted by Mrs. Philomena Sampson, who relayed the unfortunate news. Mrs. Crabtree and Mrs. Aldrich conveyed extreme shock and remorse and mentioned they would stop by to see the family during the week. The house felt unusually quiet despite the flurry of calls. Augusta glanced at the family photo on the wall above the telephone stand, her eyes lingering on Joan's smiling face. The weight of the loss pressed heavily on her mind, her temples aching.

In the kitchen, Martha was busy preparing lunch and tea, her movements methodical and precise, a distinct contrast to the chaos of emotions swirling around them. Augusta joined her, grateful for the small comfort of routine.

"How are you holding up, Mother?" Martha asked gently, her voice filled with concern.

Augusta managed to smile. "I'm doing my best. The priest called, and the church is ready to help with the funeral arrangements. It's comforting to know we have so much support."

The telephone calls went on and on and Preston felt stifled, as though he could no longer breathe. He assisted his mother in the kitchen with the leftover ham and sweet potatoes and the meal was soon deposited on the dining room table. Judge Archie was too grief stricken to get up and sit at the table, so Martha brought him a plate in the living room. Augusta joined her daughter and grandson at the dining room table. She managed to eat a little, while Preston and Martha found the food helped them feel somewhat better, as the nourishment appeared to fortify them with newfound strength.

As the afternoon light filtered through the curtains, casting a warm glow over the room, Augusta looked at her daughter and grandson. "It's hard to believe Joan is gone," she said quietly, her voice trembling. She sipped the tea, letting the warmth soothe her.

Preston's thoughts were still a whirlwind of confusion and sorrow. "I keep thinking about yesterday at the luncheon," he said. "Something must have happened."

Martha reached across the table, placing a comforting hand on his arm. "We'll find out, Preston. For now, let's take it one moment at a time."

After cleaning up in the kitchen, they returned to the living room where Augusta announced the church would assist with arrangements for Joan's funeral, but she wished to plan most herself. She took out a writing tablet from a corner table and began writing down details on what she would like for the service, including hymns for the organist and the appropriate gospel readings. Judge Archie said little, absently picking at the food Martha had brought him.

As evening approached, Preston found himself even more restless. He realized he should contact Quentin. He went to the telephone in the hallway and upon picking up the handset, asked the operator to connect him to Mr. Quentin Cooper and gave her the number. After several rings, in which Preston thought of hanging up, Quentin finally answered, rather out of breath. He explained he had just gotten back to his apartment, having spent Easter with an aunt in Schenectady. He asked Preston if something was wrong, as by his tone Quentin could tell he did not sound like his usual self.

Preston explained to Quentin what happened to his Aunt Joan this morning. He told him she was not responsive and despite the doctor's preliminary examination, he was unable to determine the exact cause of death. He planned an autopsy to verify what brought about her unexpected demise.

Quentin was in shock and took a moment to reply. "She seemed fine yesterday, Preston," he said, also holding onto a cigarette. "We enjoyed listening to her records, too, remember?"

Preston agreed. "The doctor said an autopsy might give us some answers, but I can't shake the feeling that something's off."

Quentin took a drag on a cigarette, the sound of his exhalation crackling through the telephone line. "Do you think someone could have done this to her? I mean, who would want to harm your Aunt Joan?"

Preston sighed, rubbing his temple. "I don't know. But I can't ignore the possibility. There were so many people at the luncheon yesterday. Anyone could have had the opportunity."

Quentin's voice grew more determined. "We'll figure this whole thing out together, Pres."

Preston felt a small measure of relief. "Thanks, Quentin." He paused, and then lowered his voice, so his mother and grandparents could not hear him from in the living room. "Quentin, do you remember what I told you about my suspicions regarding my grandfather? I can't help but wonder if there is a pattern here or if someone is really trying to kill him, but Aunt Joan became the victim instead."

Quentin puffed at his cigarette. "That's tough, Pres. Do you really think Judge Archie would kill his own daughter? For what reason? Or has he gone completely mad?"

"We don't know yet if her death was natural or if she ate or drank something that was rotten or sour. Maybe she had a bad reaction to the food."

Quentin expressed doubt. "We all ate and drank the same things." He paused, the sound of his breath heavy through the telephone. "I thought the luncheon was a success and everyone seemed to enjoy it. I don't remember anything unpleasant. Unless whatever happened to your aunt was really meant for your grandfather."

"Or if he was the responsible person," Preston said gravely, the words bitter in his mouth.

Martha entered the hallway at that moment, mentioning she was retiring for the evening. Preston watched as she slowly and tiredly climbed the stairs to the third floor. He then turned his attention back to Quentin.

"Do me a favor, Quentin, would you call Doris and tell her what happened? Maybe she might remember something from yesterday that could throw light on this strange death."

Quentin told his friend he would contact her and would see him soon. After a few more words, Preston ended the call. He looked at the grandfather clock against the wall leading into the kitchen, and realized it was almost nine o'clock. A long day stretching into an even longer night.

He returned to the living room, where his grandparents, still in shock and mourning, were simply staring into space. His grandfather remained sunken in his armchair, and his grandmother was immobile on the sofa, a languid expression on her face. Preston approached them carefully and decided he could not stay there with them, as it was all beginning to affect him. The shock of the death, the doctor and the ambulance crew arriving and removing the body, and then the brief questioning by the police—it was all too much to comprehend. He gently announced he would retire for the evening, said good night to them, and rather swiftly made his way back to the hallway and up the stairs to the third floor.

He noticed the lights on underneath the door of his mother's bedroom. He considered knocking to speak to her, then decided against it. It had been too much for one day, and perhaps she needed to sleep now, rather than rehash the day's events.

He reached his bedroom and, upon closing the door, felt a welcome solace. He removed his clothes, relaxed in his boxers, and opened a window, letting in the cool evening air. As usual, his bare feet were cold, but it was not the cold of winter; it was the refreshing chill of spring, and it helped alleviate his mind a bit.

He then stretched out on his bed, not quite ready for sleep. Lighting a cigarette, he thought about yesterday's luncheon, the guests partaking of the food and seemingly enjoying themselves. He exhaled a large cloud of smoke, deep in thought. He extinguished his cigarette in the ashtray on his bedside table, too exhausted to comprehend the confusion and uncertainty of the entire situation. He would call Mr. Sheppard tomorrow and tell him what happened to Aunt Joan.

Suddenly, Preston felt drowsy and realized he needed to sleep. He would find the underlying cause of this wretched ordeal before it got even worse.

In a fashionable old brownstone house overlooking Washington Park on affluent Willett Street, Mrs. Mary Crabtree was getting ready for bed. Her usual routine, after a cup of tea, was to read her favorite magazines, but tonight Mrs. Crabtree could hardly keep her eyes open. Her husband was downstairs in the living room, listening to a sports program on their new radio console. Her cook and daily house cleaner, Mrs. Davis, had already left, having prepared dinner for them earlier.

However, as she lay in bed, sleep eluded her. She thought of the sudden death of Mrs. Joan Caves, the Stafford's youngest daughter. Certainly kind of Mrs. Sampson to call to relate the news. Her mind then reflected on the luncheon at Mrs. Stafford's lovely home yesterday. Quite a pleasant and rather interesting gathering. Strange, after all these years. Nobody could ever say she did not have a good memory. Certainly, as a night nurse, she remembered. Of course, she remembered…

She turned over and fell asleep.

CHAPTER ELEVEN

Monday morning, Sloan Sheppard arrived at his office at his usual nine o'clock. It was a bright but chilly spring day. Sloan opened a window to allow the fresh air to enter. The office had been closed for the weekend but held onto the musty remnants of cigarette smoke. He took off his jacket and fedora hat, leaving them on an empty chair. He then sat at his desk and settled down for the day ahead.

He took in the familiar sight of his meticulously organized desk. Each item had its place: the neatly stacked case files, the banker's lamp, and the pristine typewriter. The morning sunlight cast shadows across the room, highlighting the dust particles dancing in the air. He made a mental note to remind the cleaning lady to give the place a thorough sweep.

Yesterday, Sloan went to a boxing club, where he participated in amateur fights and grueling weight lifting. Sloan considered maintaining his muscular physique paramount to his job. And with the little free time he had, he enjoyed the physically demanding regimentation. The sound of gloves hitting the heavy bag, the smell of sweat and leather, and the camaraderie among the fighters were a contrast to the solitude of his office. Despite the soreness in his muscles, he felt invigorated.

The physical exertion was a welcomed respite from the arduous strain of his job.

He noted to call Inspector Harris and Judge Archie. Despite his best efforts, Sloan found himself at a dead end. The police had closed the case, citing toxic tea as the cause of death. Judge Archie believed the tea was poisoned, intended for him. His grandson suspected his grandfather's involvement, which Sloan found rather incredulous.

As he was about to review a custody dispute file, the Western Electric candlestick telephone rang. Right on time, he thought, glancing at the clock just past nine. He answered, recognizing Preston Hughes's familiar voice.

"Mr. Sheppard, I'm glad I got hold of you," Preston said, getting straight to the point. "You should know my Aunt Joan died over the weekend. My mother found her still in bed and she wouldn't wake up."

Sloan fumbled for a cigarette, lit it, and exhaled smoke. He waited for Preston to continue, unsure why his aunt's death would concern him.

Preston explained about the luncheon on Saturday, organized by his grandfather to gather information on Mr. Lewis's death. The event was enjoyable, with a sensational meal prepared by their maid Gertrude. About twenty people attended, but no one seemed aggrieved or upset.

"What do you think happened to your aunt, Preston?" Sloan asked.

Preston hesitated, lowering his voice so Mr. Bishop and the others in the office would not hear. "Aunt Joan complained of a headache and didn't have any aspirin. Grandfather told her to take some of his. Our family doctor couldn't determine the cause of death and ordered an autopsy. The police took the bottle for testing." He paused. "I came to work to take my mind off of it. I couldn't take staying in the house with so much sadness."

Sloan tried to reassure him. "I'll call your grandfather as soon as we finish talking. I'll also speak to my police contacts." He was silent for a moment. "I wonder if it wasn't accidental."

Preston was appalled. He glanced up and saw a customer wanting information on steamboats to Yonkers. He spoke quickly. "What do you mean wasn't accidental?"

"I mean it could've been murder," Sloan said gravely.

Clayton reviewed a typed letter his wife had just handed him, shaking his head in disapproval.

"There are several errors here, Lucille," he said. "Unlike you to make typing mistakes. Are you feeling yourself today?"

Lucille looked up at her husband, then glanced toward the windows overlooking North Pearl Street. No, she was not herself since the death of Mrs. Joan Caves and the strange death of Mr. Clement Lewis. The deaths unnerved her and affected her work. She forced a smile as she addressed her husband.

"I'm fine, dear. Just a little preoccupied."

Clayton returned the letter to her. "I assume you're letting the death of the judge's daughter affect you." He returned to his desk, lighting a cigarette. "It's affected me, too. The judge is already in poor health. This unexpected death of his daughter could be the end of him."

Clayton and Lucille sat in silence, their thoughts weighed down by grief. The death of Mrs. Joan Caves had affected everyone in the office and while work continued, there was a latent strain in the atmosphere, a deep sense of sorrow. Clayton leaned forward in his swivel chair, gathered a few papers, and mentioned he would be in court all day tomorrow and Wednesday. A new client was coming into the office soon, which would occupy him for at least an hour.

Doris entered the office, looking preoccupied but composed, her pretty face radiant as usual. "Excuse me, Mr. Sampson; your new client is here to see you."

Clayton got up and entered the main office, returning with a distinguished elder man who sat next to his desk. Soon he was caught up with the particulars of his inquiries, seemingly oblivious to his wife just on the other side of the room.

Lucille was busy at the filing cabinet, but she could not put the death of the judge's daughter out of her mind. She seemed fine at the luncheon. What if her death was not natural and the intended target was actually the judge? Judge Archie claimed, quite vehemently, that someone was out to kill him. If that were the case, his daughter's death would be murder.

After lunch, Sloan picked up the telephone and asked the operator to dial the Albany Police. The operator mentioned circuits were busy but kept Sloan on hold until a line became available. Soon, he heard ringing on the other end. An officer answered promptly and brought Inspector Harris to the telephone.

"Yes, Mr. Sheppard," Inspector Harris said, as though expecting his call. He carried the telephone into the next office. "What can I do for you?"

Sloan explained about the death of Mrs. Joan Caves, the youngest daughter of Judge Archie. He mentioned how Dr. Stephens, the family physician, ordered an autopsy. He waited for the inspector's comments, but surprisingly, he had little to say.

"Dr. Stephens called yesterday. With only a skeleton staff on duty then, I spoke to him earlier. He couldn't determine the cause of death, hence the autopsy."

"Do you think this ties in with Mr. Clement Lewis's death?"

"Mrs. Caves's death could be natural; she might have just died in her sleep. At the moment, there's nothing suspicious."

"Judge Archie believes someone is trying to kill him," Sloan reminded him. "He thinks the poisoned tea was meant for him, but Mr. Lewis drank it instead."

"We've confirmed the tea was toxic," Inspector Harris said.

"Tea that Judge Archie would consume," Sloan pointed out.

"At this point, we're not investigating Mr. Lewis's death further unless something new comes up. Mrs. Caves's death isn't related unless we find otherwise."

Sloan told him about the luncheon at the judge's house on Saturday and the numerous attendees. He mentioned speaking to the judge earlier and arranging to visit the family after work.

"Until we have the autopsy results, there's really nothing more we can do," Inspector Harris said. "I don't see her death as a criminal investigation. We sent officers to the Staffords and did not learn anything from them. The aspirin bottle was clear, so nothing suspicious there."

Sloan mentioned he planned to see the judge later in the day and then ended the call. He replaced the handset on the candlestick telephone and sat back in his chair, deep in thought. Joan had likely taken the tablets before bed. There was the possibility of laced aspirin, likely meant for the judge. But the inspector said the bottle was tested and found nothing incriminating.

Sloan shook his head. Something about this ordeal with Judge Archie was not quite right.

It was just after five o'clock, and the sun was still shining, a clear indication of spring. North Pearl Street glowed in the late afternoon light. Pedestrians thronged the sidewalks, and trolleys and cars dexterously traversed the busy street as the evening rush hour was in full swing.

Mrs. Rose Castle had finished her work and said good night to Quentin and Doris. She noticed Burgess and the Sampsons had also left for the day, but she had been so busy she hadn't noticed their departure.

She stood up, smoothed down her beige dress, and approached Thurman's door. He was absorbed in case files, likely having just returned from court, although she hadn't noticed his arrival. She watched him for a moment, then knocked to get his attention. He looked up and greeted her cordially, then returned to his papers.

"I'm getting ready to leave for the day," Mrs. Castle said, entering his spacious, well-furnished office. "The luncheon was certainly lovely at the Staffords, wasn't it?" She paused. "Did you need my help? I'd be happy to organize your files and type reports. Or perhaps we should discuss how you were driving the car that almost struck Judge Archie in February."

Thurman put down his pen and looked directly at the heavyset middle-aged woman in front of his desk. Nosy, inquisitive, interfering, looking matronly as ever. He compared her to Doris, who was roughly the same age. But Doris looked at least ten years younger, if not more.

"I beg your pardon?" he said, stalling.

She smiled coyly. "You heard me correctly. I happened to be on State Street, where it intersects with Dove Street. I had come out of the library and recognized your car. I saw Judge Archie at the corner, waiting to cross when you flew through the red light, barely missing him." "What's the point?" he asked, trying to maintain his composure.

Mrs. Castle shrugged. "It'd be a pity if the judge learned you were driving that car. I could easily report it to the police. Running red lights is a serious traffic offense. Judge Archie believes someone is trying to kill him. Perhaps it's *you*."

Thurman, never taken off guard, planned to attend an after-hours party at his usual speakeasy. He had no time for this nonsense. After all, he was a prosperous and underhanded attorney, known in the courts for accuracy. He also enjoyed numerous liaisons with women. Therefore, he was not one to be blindsided. He set aside the paperwork and decided to tell Mrs. Rose Castle a few items he knew of interest. She listened without a word, absorbing what he said. Then, without comment, she left demurely, saying she'd see him tomorrow.

He heard her gather her belongings and close the main door. The latch clicked into place, leaving behind only silence—and the distant hum of the city far below. Thurman leaned back, a slow smirk curling at the edges of his mouth. In his illustrious legal career, no one had ever pulled the wool over his eyes. And no one ever would.

CHAPTER TWELVE

Walking through West Capitol Park, Sloan looked up and saw the Stafford's magnificent mansion shimmering in the late afternoon sun. Diagonal to the State Capitol on State Street, it occupied a large portion of the corner with South Swan Street. While on his previous visit, he had noticed its outstanding beauty but now he looked at it in all its grandeur.

An imposing structure, built in the grand Georgian style. Its red brick façade was accented with white limestone and dark brown shutters framed tall narrow windows. A wide, sweeping staircase led to a grand entrance, flanked by beautiful columns that supported a pediment adorned with intricate carvings. The front door, a heavy oak piece with brass fittings, stood as a testament to the house's age and elegance. Above it, large fanlight windows slowed light to filter into the spacious foyer. The roof was steeply pitched with dormer windows peeking out, hinting at the expansive attic space within.

He observed the meticulously maintained grounds, with neatly trimmed hedges and a variety of flowering plants lining the brick pathway that curved around the house. A wrought-iron fence enclosed the property from the sidewalk, adding an extra layer of opulence and security.

Upon ringing the doorbell, Gertrude greeted him cordially, taking his fedora hat and coat with practiced ease. She led him into the living room, where Judge Archie, Augusta, Martha, and Preston sat in somber silence, the radio murmuring softly in the background.

"Tea or coffee?" Gertrude offered, her voice a gentle interruption to the heavy air. Sloan shook his head, opting instead to take a seat on the sofa beside Augusta. The tension in the room was palpable, their faces etched with grief and the weight of yesterday's tragic discovery.

While Sloan lit a cigarette, Preston handed him an ashtray, which he placed on the coffee table. Sloan glanced at Judge Archie, who cleared his throat. Once he had everyone's attention, the judge began to speak, before Sloan had the chance to offer his condolences.

"I understand my grandson spoke to you earlier today. I appreciate your visit this evening, Mr. Sheppard. Yesterday morning, my youngest daughter, Joan, was found dead by my oldest daughter, Martha. We were preparing to attend church services, but Joan had yet to come downstairs. When Martha went to her bedroom, she found her unresponsive."

Sloan nodded. "I'm deeply sorry, Judge Archie, Mrs. Stafford, and Mrs. Hughes." He hesitated, then took a slow drag from his cigarette. "I understand Dr. Stephens ordered an autopsy."

"The cause of death couldn't be determined," Augusta said softly.

"Preston mentioned she took aspirin before going to bed," Sloan said.

"She had a busy day with the luncheon," Martha said, her voice trembling. Seated across from her father, she looked worn and grief-stricken, her eyes still brimming with tears. "She told us she didn't have any aspirin. Father mentioned there was a bottle on his bedside table. Apparently, she took it with her upstairs to her bedroom."

"Mrs. Caves was suffering from a headache," Sloan said, his voice steady, repeating the facts. "She thought nothing of taking pills from the bottle. Perhaps those she took were laced with a narcotic or barbiturate, which induced death."

Augusta let out a horrendous wail, and for a moment, Preston feared his grandmother might faint. Even Judge Archie, always formidable in his armchair, was taken aback, stunned at the possibility of someone deliberately causing Joan's death.

The family remained in shocked silence. Preston, too, was quiet, wondering if the aspirin had been poisoned. He listened as Mr. Sheppard continued to speak.

"I understand you had a full house on Saturday."

Augusta repeated what Preston had told him about the attendees, the women from the League of Women Voters, and the wonderful meal Gertrude had prepared.

"Everyone walked around the house," Preston added.

Sloan raised his eyebrows. "The entire house?"

Judge Archie nodded. "Including the library on the second floor, the bedrooms, and the kitchen. I didn't keep track of who was where, as my legs don't allow me to climb the stairs too often. I suffer from acute arthritis, and at times it is quite painful."

Martha glanced at her father. "I didn't keep track of who was in each room either. I don't believe any of us did. It was very casual, and the guests seemed to enjoy walking around and admiring our furnishings. We didn't think anything of it."

"Perhaps someone took advantage of that," Sloan said thoughtfully.

"If that's the case, then those aspirin were meant for me," Judge Archie said forcefully. "They were not meant for my daughter. I suggested she use the aspirin on my bedside table. I suffer from headaches often, which is why I keep the bottle close by."

Sloan extinguished his cigarette. "I've spoken to Inspector Harris at the Albany Police. The police laboratory tested the remaining aspirin and found nothing wrong with them. We can't make any definite determination until we receive the autopsy results."

Judge Archie insisted the poisoned tea was meant for him. Preston glanced at Sloan, reminding him of his own conclusions about his grandfather.

"The police are satisfied with the poisonous tea," Sloan said. "Exotic teas, although rare, can be toxic, according to my research."

"Mrs. Crabtree mentioned the same thing," Augusta added. "She's a retired night nurse and was here on Saturday. A charming woman, active in the Albany chapter of the League of Women Voters and the Daughters of the American Revolution."

Martha frowned. "Didn't she mention something about an abortion?"

Judge Archie scowled. "Martha, please, such talk is not appropriate in this house."

"But she did mention it, Grandfather," Preston said. "She seemed quite shaken while discussing it, too. Must've conjured up bad memories for her."

Augusta recalled Saturday's luncheon. "Mrs. Crabtree was a night nurse for many years. She told us she witnessed illegal happenings, but she didn't go into much detail."

Sloan asked if they noticed anything unusual during the luncheon. Judge Archie mentioned he did not acquire any information about Mr. Lewis as he had hoped. He had observed his office staff, trying to catch them off guard, but his scheme did not yield the desired outcome.

"I remember something, Mr. Sheppard," Preston said, looking at Sloan. "As the guests were leaving, Mrs. Crabtree was speaking to Mr. Armstrong here in the living room. Most of the other guests were already in the hallway, collecting their hats and coats. It seemed rather secretive."

"I noticed that too," Martha commented.

"What would Mrs. Crabtree say to Thurman Armstrong, of all people?" Judge Archie asked. "He didn't know her from Adam. Could you hear any of what was said, Preston?"

Preston shook his head. "I just found it strange that she'd speak with him after the other guests were almost out the door."

Sloan considered the relevance of this information. He would need to speak to Mrs. Crabtree, who might provide valuable insight into this perplexing case.

Judge Archie cleared his throat and addressed Sloan. "Joan was in fine health, and her sudden death is not acceptable. If the pills she took were poisonous, then they were meant for me."

"Father, please," Martha pleaded.

"Perhaps he has a point," Augusta said slowly. "Maybe someone left poisoned pills in that bottle, knowing your father would eventually take them."

"But who would do such a thing and why?" Martha asked, confused.

"The same person responsible for Mr. Lewis's death," her father mumbled.

"Everyone had free reign of the house during the luncheon," Preston remarked. "It could've been anyone who was here. The guests entered every room, even the bathrooms."

There was noticeable confusion among them as well as unrelenting grief. Sloan realized the family was still in great distress. He reiterated the importance of the autopsy in determining the cause of death. After expressing his sincere condolences again, he rose, with Preston accompanying him to the hallway. Preston handed him his fedora hat and jacket, shook hands with him, and watched as he walked down the steps and outside to catch the trolley.

He returned to the living room, where his mother and grandparents sat in stony silence. He mentioned he would be in his bedroom, needing a respite from the heavy atmosphere.

Bounding up the stairs and entering his bedroom, he felt an unmistakable chill. He remembered his grandfather's unsettling words from yesterday morning. *The enemy had struck again, in this very house.*

Lucille Sampson glanced at Thurman Armstrong, who sat next to her husband's desk, conferring on a recent client. It was a big case, requiring two attorneys. She was surprised her husband would collaborate with Thurman, but since it was Mr. Armstrong's initiative, he preferred working with Clayton to Burgess Smith.

It was early Tuesday morning and a gray, windy day. Glancing at the windows, Lucille doubted the sun would come out, though a few peaks were noticeable. She looked up as Mrs. Castle entered, looking subdued.

"Do you plan to attend the services for Mrs. Caves?" she asked Lucille.

Lucille looked up in surprise. "Of course. Judge Archie needs our support at this time."

Mrs. Castle frowned. "I don't think Judge Archie particularly cares for me. He does have a temper, you know. I've certainly seen it here in the office."

"I've felt the same," Lucille admitted. "He likes us all in his own way; otherwise we wouldn't be employed here. And the luncheon was pleasant enough, too."

"Mrs. Sampson looked wonderful on Saturday," Mrs. Castle said, glancing at Clayton. "She certainly doesn't appear her age. It's nice that you and your husband help her out."

Lucille caught a twinge of envy in her tone. "Yes, my mother-in-law is in good health."

"Perhaps one of these days I'll stop by to see her. I haven't spoken to her in so long. Please give her my best."

Lucille didn't know Mrs. Castle even knew her mother-in-law. She watched her sail out of the office suite, ignoring Thurman and Clayton, who were deep in discussion.

Lucille turned to a new deposition her husband wanted her to type, but her thoughts drifted back to Saturday's luncheon. Something about that afternoon bothered her. It was not the judge's family—Mrs. Stafford was gracious, allowing guests to roam freely around her four-story mansion. Quentin and Doris seemed odd, flabbergasted by the gathering. Burgess appeared charming, though she knew it was just an act.

Doris entered, equally subdued, and handed Lucille the newspaper and the latest issue of *Harvard Law Review*. Before leaving, she surprised Lucille with a question.

"Did you notice anything unusual at the luncheon?"

Lucille hesitated. "Unusual? No, not really. The women talked about their careers. Mrs. Crabtree mentioned her nursing duties. Strange she'd speak to Thurman privately, but about what I have no idea. Certainly seemed rather secretive."

"You're best not to bother with him," Doris whispered.

"As a night nurse, I imagine Mrs. Crabtree witnessed many difficulties," Lucille said thoughtfully. "But why mention abortions? Like she was alluding to a particular time or person."

Doris shrugged. "Perhaps something brought her memory back to her nursing duties."

"Or someone," Lucille said. "Abortions aren't usual topics of conversation."

Doris mentioned she was in the middle of typing reports and returned to the main office. Lucille glanced at her husband and Thurman, engrossed in their discussion. Her mind turned to her meddlesome mother-in-law. She wondered if the old battleax had a few tricks up her sleeve.

I may have married her son, Lucille thought irritably, inserting a fresh sheet of paper into the typewriter, but that does not mean I would ever trust his mother.

At the mansion on State Street, the family sat at the kitchen table, attempting breakfast. Preston looked at his mother and grandparents; nobody felt like eating, and the atmosphere remained somber and quiet.

Augusta's voice was hoarse, as if speaking was an effort in her deep mourning. She sipped her coffee. "Father Chris assured me the service will be on Saturday."

"We're fortunate to have services so soon," Martha said, still in her housecoat and slippers. "Father Chris has known us for years. He's a wonderful man. He baptized us, you know."

Augusta told her daughter she indeed remembered the baptisms. Judge Archie sipped his coffee, looking much worse than he did yesterday. Preston wondered if his grandfather was ill or on the verge of sickness. His face was ghastly, and his whole appearance was disheveled. The death of his youngest daughter had affected him terribly, as it had everyone else.

"I plan to go to work today," Martha said. "Friends at the office have been kind in calling and expressing their condolences."

"I've heard from many of Joan's associates," Augusta said. She paused, then addressed her husband. "Didn't you call the newspaper yesterday morning, dear?"

"Yes, I called it into the *Times Union*," Judge Archie said. "It was the appropriate thing to do. Whenever we had a death in the family, my father would always contact the newspapers. They publish a brief death notice first, and then a more detailed obituary. I gave them the details for the death notice, but they assured me they would write the obituary. I don't know if it'll appear in this morning's edition or the evening paper."

As usual, Preston dressed for work before breakfast. He had skimmed the various sections of the morning newspaper but then handed the rest to his grandmother. Augusta took a section and eagerly turned to the obituaries to see if Mrs. Joan Caves was listed.

"The newspapers do work fast," Augusta said, folding back a page. "There's a death notice here and then the longer obituary in this column." She handed the paper to her husband, who after reading it gave it to Martha. Preston got up and read over his mother's shoulder.

Mrs. Joan Caves, aged 50, passed away suddenly on April 11, 1925. Born in Albany, Mrs. Caves was the beloved wife of the late Arnold Caves. Mrs. Caves worked at the State Education Department for many years and was known for her dedication to her work and her kindness to all who knew her. Her parents, Judge Archibald Stafford and Mrs. Augusta Stafford, her older sister, Mrs. Martha Hughes, and her nephew, Mr. Preston Hughes, survive her. The funeral service will be held on April 18, 1925, at 10:00 am at St. Mary's Church. Her family and friends will sorely miss Joan.

Martha read the obituary, her eyes welling up with tears. She took a deep breath, trying to compose herself. "I need to get ready for work," she said softly, hurrying upstairs.

Preston announced he needed to leave. He said goodbye to his grandparents, then entered the hallway for his jacket and cap, and made his escape outside into the chilly but invigorating air. Crossing West Capitol Park to catch the trolley, Preston felt a strange sense of unforeseen catastrophes ahead.

Mrs. Philomena Sampson finished her afternoon tea and heard the grandfather clock in the hallway strike three. She had eaten little for lunch, lacking appetite. Relaxing symphonic music played on the radio. Her daily maid had left, much to her approval, as she found the young woman her daughter-in-law hired unreliable. Still, the house was clean, so she could not complain.

She had read the morning newspaper and awaited the delivery of the *Albany Evening Journal*. The current issues of *Smart Set*, *McCall's*, *Redbook*, and *True Story* lay on the coffee table. While she found them all entertaining, she especially enjoyed the household hints in *McCall's*. She shook her head, thinking how her daughter-in-law could benefit from *McCall's* practical advice, if only she bothered to read it.

Her mind was preoccupied, not with her son and daughter-in-law, but with other pressing thoughts. She had noticed in the morning paper the funeral services for Mrs. Joan Caves this Saturday. When her son arrived home, she would tell him to take her to the funeral.

She got up from her armchair and crossed the wide living room to the radio console. While she enjoyed symphonic music, she was in the mood for more upbeat tunes. She turned the dial until she found a station broadcasting popular hits. After a bit of static, she adjusted the knob so the station was crystal clear. A smile spread across her face as Eddie Cantor's wonderful voice filled the room. Settling back in her armchair, she began to review what was foremost on her mind.

That Mrs. Crabtree, if she remembered her name right, was somewhat outspoken as were a few others from the League of Women Voters. She had mentioned abortions years ago from her experiences as a night nurse. Philomena shook her head. Of all topics to mention at a luncheon, why would she even remember it? Maybe something brought it back to her. Her own sister had died during childbirth in 1885. Her thoughts returned to that horrific night: the unsanitary, difficult, and dangerous conditions. The maternity ward was squalid, with patients neglected in the hallways, the overpowering antiseptic smell, and staff shortages. She was surprised babies were born under such deprivation.

Philomena leaned her head back, listening to Eddie Cantor crooning his songs, while her mind went back forty years to her sister in agony in the hospital. She remembered frantic nurses and orderlies, but it was not a delivery. Suddenly, she sat upright, realizing what was now so clear in her mind.

She must speak to Mrs. Crabtree. She seemed kind and outgoing enough. She did not think she would mind her calling. She got up, entered the hallway, and grabbed the Albany City Directory from the telephone table. Scanning the listings under C, she found three Crabtree names. Not knowing her husband's first name, she was unsure which one to call. But Mrs. Crabtree had mentioned living on Willett Street, not far from her own house. She spotted the listing with the Willett Street address and, without hesitation, picked up the handset, anxiously waiting for the operator. She gave the number and waited for the call to go through. After several rings, she heard a crisp female voice, which she distinctly remembered from Saturday.

"Hello, Mrs. Crabtree? This is Mrs. Philomena Sampson. We met at the Stafford's on Saturday during the luncheon." A brief pause, menial comments, which Philomena expected. "Yes, it was a pleasure meeting you, too. Mrs. Stafford is a good friend and a lovely woman. Perhaps I can learn more about the League of Women Voters?"

Philomena listened patiently as Mrs. Crabtree talked about various city functions. They discussed Albany and the loose morals of young people today, which Philomena used to lead into her point. Boldly, she asked about Mrs. Crabtree's night nurse duties and the abortions she mentioned at the luncheon.

Philomena held the handset tightly as Mrs. Crabtree briefly recounted witnessing gangsters treated for gunshot wounds, homeless malnourished children, and young girls seeking abortions. Philomena wondered how anyone could have worked under such conditions. Her thoughts flew to her husband, a gangster sentenced by Judge Archie who died in prison. She shook her head bitterly, blaming the judge for her husband's unfair sentence and sudden death. She told Mrs. Crabtree about her sister's death during childbirth in 1885. Mrs. Crabtree remembered the event, recalling how she attended to many women in the emergency ward and assisted midwives, despite many illegalities, which she mentioned with much regret.

Philomena did not pry for more information, at least not on the telephone, deciding to speak to her another time. She mentioned the service for Mrs. Joan Caves would be this Saturday at St. Mary's Church, and Mrs. Crabtree planned to attend. Then she mentioned something unexpected.

"There was a young man who was murdered at that time. I read it in the newspaper, but I don't recall his name. They never found his killer."

"How absolutely dreadful," Philomena said in genuine horror, feeling her whole body twinge in discomfort. Her fingers tightened around the handset. A shadow of unease flickered in her mind. She then chose to brighten the mood. "Perhaps you'd like to visit for afternoon tea?"

Mrs. Crabtree told Philomena she would be delighted to stop by for afternoon tea. Philomena wished her well and replaced the handset on the candlestick telephone. She returned to the living room, where the wonderful voice of Bessie Smith helped calm her nerves and process her emotions, which were running wild.

She ensconced herself comfortably in her armchair and decided to look at her magazines before her son and daughter-in-law returned home. She picked up *True Story* from the coffee table, turning to a page near the middle. The story title leapt out at her: *When the Past Comes Calling.*

She scanned the first few lines with furrowed brows. A memory stirred—a faint echo from long ago. The house seemed unnervingly quiet now, the ticking of the grandfather clock louder than ever. She felt the stillness pressing in, as though it was waiting for her to make the next move.

CHAPTER THIRTEEN

Doris sat in an armchair in the living room of her comfortable one-bedroom apartment on Quail Street, listening to the crackling radio and smoking a cigarette. It had been a long day at the office and she was only too glad when the day was over.

An empty bottle of scotch sat on her kitchen table, an unfortunate reminder of the Prohibition era's challenges. Before settling in the living room, with the latest issue of *Vanity Fair*, she planned for a local bootlegger to supply her with another bottle. She anticipated his arrival later that evening when the city had quieted and the police would not be on the lookout for anything suspicious on residential streets like Quail.

The soft hum of the radio filled the room, mingling with the faint scent of tobacco smoke. Doris leaned back, exhaling slowly, her mind drifting to the bootlegger's visit. The thrill of the illicit transaction added a spark to her otherwise monotonous day. She glanced at the clock, counting down the minutes until the city would fall into its usual nighttime hush. She read in the newspapers that the Albany police were concentrating efforts near the river, especially since it had been used so often for clandestine and illegal liquor exchanges.

As she waited, she ran her fingers over the smooth fabric of her pretty dress, the sensation grounding her in the present. The taste of the cigarette smoke lingered on her tongue, a familiar comfort. Despite the excitement, a small part of her could not help but worry about the risks. She had heard stories of recent police raids and the harsh penalties for those caught in the act. But the allure of the forbidden was too strong to resist.

But what did they expect, Doris thought, rather contemptuously. This ridiculous Prohibition—whose ludicrous idea was it to begin with? She vividly remembered the temperance movement, especially the Women's Christian Temperance Union, which had an office in Albany. They avowed to destroy the liquor trade, enabling the country to go dry. Didn't those foolish women realize liquor could easily be obtained elsewhere? Thank goodness for Canada and the Caribbean, she thought wisely.

Doris puffed at her cigarette, the smoke hanging lazily in the air. She picked up *Vanity Fair*, moodily flipping the pages. She listened to the hit songs on *The Eveready Hour*, certainly one of the most popular radio shows of 1925. She read in *Photoplay* and *Smart Set* that it was projected to continue its popularity into 1926 and beyond. Doris loved modern jazz that was all the rage. Bessie Smith, Duke Ellington and Ruth Etting were among her favorites. She bought a phonograph player and had a sizeable collection of 78 records. The rich, soulful melodies filled her apartment, providing a comforting backdrop to her thoughts.

She had changed into comfortable clothes, a loose dress made her feel much more at ease. Her mind drifted to the last man she had dated; a real loser. How foolish she had been to even waste time with him. But that was her life story. Man after man but no engagement ring, at least not yet. Despite societal expectations, Doris was determined to live life on her own terms. Of course, she was still on the lookout for a suitor, but she knew her childbearing years were behind her. That realization brought a twinge of melancholy, but it did not stop her from enjoying herself and the great nightlife Albany offered. Jazz clubs, the speakeasies, the thrill of the forbidden—all of it made her feel alive and vibrant. She relished the attention she received, the admiring glances from men and the envious looks from women.

However pensive about her love life, Doris admitted at the moment she was preoccupied with the recent deaths, which were too close for comfort. Her thoughts returned to Judge Archie and her visit to his mansion on Saturday.

The luncheon was agreeable, clearly a wonderful house, too. Yet, something about that woman from the voting group discussing her night nurse duties had struck her as odd. She mentioned abortions, of all things. Doris could not help think that something must have triggered the unpleasantness for her to mention it so openly.

She thought of Judge Archie, sitting in his armchair as though the world owed him everything. He insisted the poisoned tea was meant for him. Was it paranoia, or was there something more sinister? She couldn't shake the image of him, looking frail and defeated, yet exuding an air of entitlement.

His daughter died just Sunday but nobody knew what caused it. She was sure an autopsy was planned. The Staffords were a respectable family. She had her share of run-ins with the judge, so she looked at the bright side; having him out of the office was indeed a blessing.

Despite her disdain for his moodiness, she could not help but feel a pang of sympathy for the family. They had been through so much. Mrs. Stafford and Mrs. Hughes had always been kind to her, and Preston, though quiet, had a gentle demeanor. The thought of attending Mrs. Caves's service filled her with a sense of duty and respect, even if it meant facing the judge again.

Doris thought of Mrs. Rose Castle at the luncheon, pleasant and charming, if rather matronly. She was only a year older but looked as though she were on the brink of death, especially with her weight gain. Doris prided herself on her slim figure, her fashionable clothing and her rather provocative perfume.

Without the judge's knowledge, she had dated both Burgess and Thurman on several occasions. While she enjoyed their company and respected their abilities in the legal profession, she did not make the connection she felt was imperative. There was a certain spark missing, a deeper bond she yearned for but could not find with either. She considered Quentin and Preston friends, even though they were much younger, but that didn't bother Doris. Their youthful energy and fresh perspectives were a welcome contrast to the staider company she often kept. She appreciated their camaraderie and the way they made her feel rather vibrant and relevant.

She glanced out her window and considered walking down to Washington Park. The thought of the fresh spring air and the lush greenery was tempting, but the practicalities of her situation took precedence. The bootlegger's supplier would be here soon and she didn't want to miss him. The images of mothers and children in the park brought a fleeting smile to her face. It was a quaint scene; one that sharply contrasted with her own clandestine activities. She even remembered seeing them picking berries in the park.

Doris recalled reading in *Good Housekeeping* how the juice from yew berries was toxic, that only the fleshy part of the berry was edible. The article recommended avoidance of the berries due to their toxicity. For the few yew berry trees in the park, she knew there was a sign posted, warning of the dangers of consumption. Anyone could pick those berries and squeeze the juice from them. Easy enough, venomous and lethal.

The thought sent a shiver down her spine. She could almost see the bright red berries, deceptively harmless in appearance, hanging from the branches. The idea that someone could use them to poison the judge was chilling. She took another breath, trying to calm her racing thoughts. The implications were serious, and she could not shake the feeling that there was more to this than met the eye. She then remembered seeing someone she thought she knew, picking those yew berries in Washington Park.

Doris got up and walked over to the windows overlooking Quail Street. The days were getting longer and people were out walking, many with their dogs. She spotted the milk wagon making its way up the street, stopping at houses and apartment buildings to deposit bottles on the steps. The evening newspaper was soon delivered. She then noticed her bootlegger's supplier, getting off the trolley and carrying a bag, walking casually as though he had not a care in the world.

Doris smiled in spite of herself. She would pay him while in the apartment but decided to meet him downstairs first.

She slipped on her high heels, extinguished her cigarette and locked the apartment door, proceeding down the stairs. Once outside, the fresh air hit her face and she took a deep breath, trying to shake off the lingering unease. The sight of the supplier, so nonchalant and carefree, was oddly reassuring. She put poisonous berries out of her mind as she went forward to greet him.

After breakfast with his mother and grandparents Thursday morning, Preston left earlier than usual, on his way to see Mr. Sheppard. He suggested it to his grandfather, who looked weak and almost disconsolate. He merely appreciated his grandson's commitment to see justice done.

"Do you have an appointment to see him, Preston?" Martha asked him, curiously.

"I already told Mr. Bishop that I'd be late this morning. This'll give me enough time to see Mr. Sheppard. If I learn anything new, I'll call you later, Grandfather."

Judge Archie smiled weakly. He knew once his grandson made up his mind, there was little to stop him. "This has been too much for me. First, the death of my friend Clement Lewis and now the death of my youngest daughter, in this very house." He paused, as Preston, Martha and Augusta looked at him, knowing his deep anguish had not subsided. "See what you can find out, Preston and let me know later."

Preston then got up, said goodbye to his mother and grandparents, then headed for the hallway and his jacket and cap. The morning was sunny and warm so he decided to walk down State Street, past the State Capitol and crossed at the light. He arrived at the Albany City Savings Bank Building and entered an elevator, telling the attendant the floor he wanted.

Upon arriving at the fifth floor, he found it dimly lit and eerily quiet, with no one else around. As he approached Sloan's door, he heard low voices coming from an accounting office and more voices near the offices of a group of stockbrokers. Before knocking, he took off his jacket and cap, as the hallway was warm and rather stuffy. He paused, then knocked and was told rather abruptly to enter.

He saw Sloan seated behind his desk, his dress always professional, exuding power and intimidation as his appearance always commanded. Preston stood in the doorway, twisting the cap in his hands, not sure if he did the right thing by arriving unannounced. But Sloan waved him in, put his cigarette in the ashtray and invited him to sit at the chair before his desk.

"Preston, what brings you here so early? I don't usually get here so early myself, but I have to be in court later this morning on a custody dispute." He hesitated, seeing the anxiousness in the younger man's face. "What can I do for you?"

"My grandfather has been beside himself," Preston said, still twisting the cap in his hands. His face and overall appearance were rather glum, downtrodden. "I don't know if he'll pull through. He's been through a lot and at his age, I don't know how much more he can take."

Sloan knocked ash from his cigarette. "The autopsy results will be the deciding factor. As far as Mr. Lewis is concerned, I'm still investigating his death. Right now, I have no new leads."

Preston told him about the women from the League of Women Voters, who attended the luncheon and in particular Mrs. Crabtree, relating her experiences as a night nurse years ago. Sloan listened but did not see the relevance to either the death of Mr. Lewis or the death of his aunt.

"Mrs. Sampson mentioned her sister died during childbirth," Preston continued, thoughtfully. "She said it was 1885. Mrs. Crabtree was a night nurse then and told us she remembered abortions and gangsters, too."

Sloan mentioned he remembered his parents talking about Jesse and Frank James, along with the Younger brothers, who were notorious for bank and train robberies during that time. Despite this, he still did not quite see the point Preston was making.

"Are you suggesting there are gangsters involved in the death of Mr. Lewis?"

Preston shook his head, irritably. "I don't know what to think."

Sloan tapped a pencil against the desk meditatively. From long experience in dealing with clients and in criminal investigations, he knew someone would not mention something so wretched as abortions or gangsters merely unexpectedly. Certainly, not normal topics of conversation, especially at a luncheon, unless something provoked it. He remained deep in thought, his mind racing through possibilities, until Preston continued speaking, rather excitedly.

"Something has to be done, Mr. Sheppard. I'm really concerned about my grandfather!"

Sloan puffed at his cigarette, turning over different scenarios. He was silent for a few moments, and then spoke reassuringly to Preston, as he could sense his unease and apprehension.

"I'll speak again to my contacts at the police," he told him resolutely. "You've given me a lot to think about."

As soon as his court case concluded, Sloan stopped at a local delicatessen, where he ate lunch and then soon afterwards, he returned to his office. He carried several folders containing court records and no sooner had he opened the door when the telephone started to ring. He closed the door with his foot and almost leaped for the telephone, more so to end its insistent clamoring than to actually answer it. He was surprised at the elderly voice at the other end of the line.

"Good afternoon, Mr. Sheppard. My name is Mrs. Philomena Sampson. I believe you met my son Clayton and daughter-in-law Lucille at the law firm. I hope I am not disturbing you."

Sloan came around his desk to sit at the swivel chair, where he loosened his tie and attempted to light a cigarette, although while holding onto the handset it was rather cumbersome. He greeted Mrs. Sampson pleasantly and asked what he could do for her.

"I'd like to speak to you when you are free. I am most concerned about the recent death of Mr. Clement Lewis and Mrs. Joan Caves. I know Judge Archie considers himself the target that someone is out to kill him. While I cannot say for certain, I do not understand how tea could be poisonous." Philomena paused, catching her breath, realizing she had already said too much. "Perhaps some afternoon when you are free? I'd also like you to meet Mrs. Mary Crabtree."

Sloan remembered Preston mentioning this Mrs. Crabtree at his earlier visit. Obviously, she was someone of importance. Perhaps she had certain knowledge that could shed light on the death of Mr. Lewis.

He listened carefully as Philomena explained about the death of her younger sister and unborn child during childbirth in 1885. She mentioned how Mrs. Mary Crabtree told them at the luncheon she was a night nurse, experiencing the harsh realities of hospital life during that tumultuous time and that she remembered her sister's unfortunate ordeal. She added more details and certain suspicions as Sloan continued writing feverishly in his notepad. Philomena mentioned she met Mrs. Crabtree only once at the luncheon, as did everyone else. She was an intelligent and charming person, very informed about hospitals and medical practices from many years ago.

He realized now that Mrs. Crabtree could have information pertinent to the investigation. He also realized what he heard from Mrs. Sampson was viable and noteworthy, that could potentially break the case of the death of Mr. Clement Lewis and quite possibly explain the sudden death of Mrs. Joan Caves.

After looking at his calendar and realizing he had no other appointments for tomorrow afternoon, he asked her if tomorrow, Friday, later in the day would be convenient. Philomena responded affirmatively, adding her son and daughter-in-law may arrive at that time, as they frequently left the office earlier on Fridays. She would call Mrs. Crabtree to confirm it.

"Mrs. Sampson, before we meet tomorrow, could you tell me a bit more about Mrs. Crabtree? Any information perhaps about her background, anything she might have mentioned about the hospital in 1885 would be incredibly helpful."

"Of course, Mr. Sheppard. She struck me as knowledgeable and experienced. She mentioned she worked as a night nurse during some difficult times. Hospitals then were often under the influence of gangsters and illegal activities like abortions were not uncommon. I could tell Mrs. Crabtree had a sharp mind and keen eye for detail."

"Thank you, Mrs. Sampson. I look forward to meeting you and Mrs. Crabtree."

The call ended and while replacing the handset, Sloan realized he had uncovered a significant lead, but there were several missing pieces. If Mrs. Crabtree had information about abortions and gangster involvement in hospitals, revealing this could somehow threaten someone who was involved in or benefited from these illegal activities. Someone might even go to great lengths to silence her to protect personal interests. Her knowledge of past events, especially if they involved influential figures, could uncover long-buried secrets. This could lead to reputational damage or legal consequences for those involved.

He knew conditions in hospitals during the 1880s were often harsh, with limited resources and high patient loads. He assumed that if there were any unusual circumstances surrounding certain details, Mrs. Crabtree might have developed a sense of suspicion and vigilance and had become more attentive to potential threats or irregularities in the hospital.

He realized the need to establish a good rapport with Mrs. Crabtree was crucial. He needed to approach her with empathy and understanding, acknowledging the emotional toll of her experiences from so many years ago.

Sloan decided to go to the Harmanus Bleecker Library. *The Index to Deaths in Albany, New York 1880-1915* could provide him with more information. He would look through Albany newspapers of that year, too, which could add contexts or leads. He would contact the hospital to inquire about records from 1885, which would be difficult. He knew records during that time were sparse, if kept at all. Hospitals, overwhelmed and understaffed, often were lacking in maintaining accurate and timely information.

He got up rather quickly, put on his fedora hat and headed for the door. He knew he needed to resolve this case soon before Mrs. Mary Crabtree's life could possibly be in danger.

Thurman left his apartment on Lancaster Avenue and strode purposefully south toward South Swan Street. He then turned right, proceeding to State Street and the stately mansion on the corner.

He looked around at the rather deserted area. It was close to six o'clock and the workday was nearing its end. State workers from the education building as well as the Capitol had exited in droves, heading for the trolleys on Washington Avenue or downtown to State Street.

He lit a cigarette and stayed planted on the sidewalk, in front the judge's opulent mansion. He wore his coat and fedora hat, as it was quite chilly, despite the heat of the daytime. It was still only mid-April, and Albany was known for its fickle weather during this month. He puffed on his cigarette, while passersby observed him curiously; perhaps assuming he waited for the trolley to take him downtown.

He contemplated his plan and, after several agonizing decisions, realized he had made the right choice. Determined now, he decided to inform the judge that it was his car that almost hit him in February. With nosy, meddlesome Mrs. Rose Castle armed with that knowledge, he preferred the older man hear it from him. He worried she might have mentioned it to others, especially Burgess or the Sampsons, but their demeanor didn't suggest they harbored such a secret. Of course, Thurman assumed they had other secrets, but he couldn't waste time dwelling on such trivialities. Always one to take care of himself, he took a final puff on his cigarette, ground it on the sidewalk with his shoe, then entered the walkway leading to the front door of the elegant house.

He rang the doorbell without hesitation and was relieved when Preston answered. He wasn't ready to face Mrs. Stafford or Mrs. Hughes, who would undoubtedly bombard him with questions about his visit. Preston stepped back, allowing him to enter, and took his jacket and fedora hat. Much to Thurman's relief, he did not ask the purpose for his visit. Preston mentioned they had just finished dinner and were listening to the radio. He led him into the living room, where the judge, Augusta, and Martha, greeted him pleasantly.

Martha had been reading *The Albany Evening Journal.* She folded it and put it on the coffee table. "We like listening to *The Atwater Kent Hour.* The symphony is just wonderful and so relaxing. Although I do like the jazz hits by Bessie Smith and Ruth Etting, too."

Thurman sat on the sofa next to Martha and noticed Judge Archie remained quiet, staring at him as though he were an alien or someone unknown to him. His penetrating gaze made Thurman feel rather uncomfortable and for a moment, he regretted his decision. But he realized his predicament, as he did not trust Mrs. Castle or anyone else in the law firm, for that matter.

"Gertrude, our maid, has already left for the evening," Martha commented. "Did you want coffee or tea, Mr. Armstrong? I'd be happy to make it for you."

Thurman shook his head, while lighting another cigarette. He found himself perspiring around his temples and he only hoped they did not notice it. Preston sat across from him on an armchair near his grandfather as though supporting him by his presence. Thurman thought that perhaps that was the case, as the judge looked wretched as if on his deathbed. He continued puffing at his cigarette, while once again offering his most sincere condolences for Mrs. Caves.

"Thank you, Mr. Armstrong," Augusta said, maintaining her strength during this difficult time. "The wake is tomorrow evening and the funeral service will be Saturday."

Thurman nodded. "I plan to attend."

Preston wondered what this visit was all about. While Mr. Armstrong was certainly welcomed in their home, he had the distinct impression there was something else that he could not quite determine. He waited for him to speak.

"Judge Archie, I came here this evening to tell you something," Thurman began. He looked at the faces before him, realizing he had their attention. "I want you to hear it from me rather than anyone else." He paused, then continued without hesitation. "Back in February, the car that almost hit you that evening on the corner of State and South Swan was driven by me."

Silence. A strong silence with an undercurrent so thick it made Preston uncomfortable. He looked first at his grandfather, bland and expressionless, his mother rather shocked and his grandmother speechless. Suddenly, the atmosphere was thick with tension and hostility. Before anyone had the chance to speak, Thurman cleared his throat and continued.

He explained what happened, most of which they already knew. As he approached the intersection with South Swan Street, he momentarily lost control of his vehicle. The car swerved dangerously close to the sidewalk, nearly hitting Judge Archie, who was crossing the street at that very moment. Fortunately, the judge, with Preston's help, stepped back just in time, avoiding what could have been a serious accident.

He further explained how he quickly drove away, hoping no one had recognized him. However, the near miss had not gone unnoticed. Mrs. Rose Castle, nosy and meddlesome as was her nature, witnessed the entire event from upper State Street. Thurman knew that if she spread the word, it could cause significant trouble for him, especially given the judge's influential position.

Thurman told them he had been grappling with the decision to come forward and confess to the judge. He feared the repercussions but ultimately decided it was better for the judge to hear the truth from him rather than Mrs. Castle or anyone else. This evening, he finally mustered the courage to reveal the truth, hoping to mitigate any potential fallout from the incident. He told them of his date for the evening, that did not go well and how, feeling upset, he drove hurriedly down State Street, momentarily losing control and passing the red light. He admitted he saw the judge in his rearview mirror but he was too far down State Street to go back and stop. He concluded by expressing his remorse for what happened and offered his apologies.

"My husband was almost struck by your car," Augusta said, regaining her voice. "We are in mourning for our daughter and you came here to tell us this!"

"I am most sorry, Mrs. Stafford," Thurman said. "Mrs. Castle told me she saw it. Before you heard it from her, I wanted to tell you myself. I am deeply sorry it happened."

Judge Archie cleared his throat. Preston again wondered if his grandfather would survive much longer, he looked so incredibly weak and frail.

"Thurman, you've been one of the best lawyers I've ever worked with," the older man said, with respect. "You've won numerous cases and brought the law firm of Lewis and Stafford to much prominence and recognition." He paused, as though in pain. "However, I am rather surprised at this. I agree that it was better hearing it from you rather than Mrs. Castle or anyone else." He sighed, as though he used all his energy. He then forced a tight smile. "I believe in putting the past behind me. Although I have knowledge of incidents of nearly everyone at the law firm, I've learned to keep things to myself. Therefore, I will not mention this to the others, as it does not concern them. I also will not contact the police. You are too worthy an employee."

Preston observed his grandmother, whose expression changed from shock to tranquility and his mother, who was alarmed at first but after listening to her father appreciated not only his words but also his attitude.

At that moment, the Western Electric candlestick telephone in the hallway rang sharply. Preston decided to answer it, as he could not stand the deep emotional turmoil present in the living room at that moment. Upon reaching the hallway, he picked up the handset and heard the deep, firm voice of Dr. Stephens. He called with the autopsy results of his Aunt Joan.

Preston listened, his grip tightening on the handset, then sat heavily in a hallway chair after speaking with him. He heard his mother, grandparents and Mr. Armstrong chatting from in the living room, their voices a distant murmur. He rather wished he had not answered the telephone. The enormity of the news pressed down on him but he knew he had to share what he just learned.

Gathering his strength, he returned to the living room, attempting normalcy. His mother looked up, her eyes immediately sensing something wrong. Judge Archie remained silent, staring at his grandson expectedly.

Preston swallowed hard, his face pale. "That was Dr. Stephens. The autopsy on Aunt Joan was concluded. He called to give us the results."

"Please continue, dear," Augusta said patiently though her voice trembled with concern.

Even Thurman, usually stoic, looked at him worriedly, anticipating something unpleasant. Preston was on the brink of tears, knowing the effect the news would have on his family. He spoke hoarsely, the words barely forthcoming.

"Dr. Stephens told me the autopsy results showed Aunt Joan died of barbiturate poisoning."

CHAPTER FOURTEEN

The family spent a difficult evening. With the autopsy results confirmed, two policemen arrived and once again questioned them extensively about Joan's last activities, her last meal and her behavior at the luncheon. They learned nothing out of the ordinary. They examined the bedroom in more detail but could find nothing amiss and could draw no definite conclusions based on physical evidence. There was no sign of a struggle and a break-in was ruled out as Joan's bedroom was on the fourth floor. The windows were locked and showed no footprints on the ledge. A further examination of the aspirin bottle did not indicate tampering. The policemen assured the family they would be in touch soon and left within the hour.

The wake for Mrs. Joan Caves was set for later in the afternoon at a local funeral parlor on Friday, the seventeenth. The burial was planned for the next day, with a brief gathering at the church hall afterward.

Preston was up early, bypassing breakfast that his grandmother prepared. Entering the kitchen, he was surprised she had the stamina to even make it. But then he knew the fortitude his grandparents had exhibited throughout their lives and this tumultuous day was just another test of their endurance.

"I'm heading out early today, Grandmother. Please let Mother and Grandfather know I'll be back at the usual time after work."

"Leaving so soon?" She looked at her grandson with a mix of concern and curiosity.

"I need to clear my head before work. It's going to be a long day." He took a few sips of coffee, the warmth doing little to ease the cold knot in his stomach. He went forward and affectionately hugged his grandmother. "I called Quentin when I came downstairs. He said he'd meet me downtown. I told him about the autopsy results, so he already knows."

Augusta wiped away a few tears. "Please be careful, dear. It's hard for all of us. Your grandfather and I have seen many hard days, but this one is quite different." She sighed, her hands busying themselves with the dishes.

"You and grandfather are the strongest people I know. I don't know how you do it."

"We do it because we must, dear. Our faith carries us through. Life doesn't give us a choice. But remember, Preston, it's okay to grieve. Your Aunt Joan was special to all of us." She paused. "I'll call Mrs. Castle and Mrs. Sampson later this morning to let them know the autopsy results. They should know, too. Perhaps Mr. Armstrong will mention it to them later."

Preston nodded. "We'll get through this ordeal but I just need to keep moving. It's the only way I can cope right now." He gave another hug before heading for his jacket and cap in the hallway. Once out the door, he decided to bypass the trolley and instead walked down State Street. It was a brisk, cool early spring morning, which Preston found to his liking. Very few cars were about and the trolleys were just starting service. He crossed at the light in front of the State Capitol, the imposing building standing as a silent protector over the quiet streets.

The air carried the faint scent of blooming flowers and freshly baked bread from a nearby bakery. Preston proceeded down State Street, crossing at the main intersection with North Pearl Street.

He dreaded the day ahead, as the thought of the service this evening and then the funeral tomorrow was too overwhelming for him. In the distance, he spotted Quentin near the Albany Savings Bank, where he had told him he would be waiting. Quentin was puffing on a cigarette, the smoke suspended lazily in the morning air. Preston walked past the enormous Ten Eyck Hotel and upon reaching his friend, he smiled; a brief moment of warmth in an otherwise somber day.

Quentin saw the look of worry and even fear in his eyes. Preston told him about the autopsy results earlier on the telephone. Quentin naturally was shocked and dismayed. He promised Preston he would not say anything, as he did not want to be the one breaking the unfortunate news. Preston assured him his grandmother would call Mrs. Castle and Mrs. Sampson. Quentin suggested they walk around a while, as only a few establishments were open. He mentioned a coffee shop near Clinton Avenue and Preston mumbled a few incoherent words. Quentin did not press him into conversation. They began walking north, past the Kenmore Hotel, both deep in troublesome thoughts.

"I can't stop thinking that there's more to Aunt Joan's death," Preston said, as they reached the coffee shop. Quentin opened the door for him. "She was always careful with medication."

"It's hard to believe it was an accident," Quentin agreed. "Do you think someone could have tampered with the pills? Didn't you tell me the bottle was on your grandfather's bedside table? Maybe the bad medicine was meant for him, not your aunt."

He stopped as a pretty waitress, quite the flapper with her makeup and hairstyle, came to their table and they ordered coffee and donuts.

She soon returned, depositing cups of steaming hot coffee and a plate of savory jelly donuts on the table.

"I honestly don't know what to think," Preston lamented, wiping powdered sugar from his mouth. "I spoke to Mr. Sheppard yesterday morning at his office. He doesn't have any new leads on the death of Mr. Lewis. I plan to call him today to tell him about the autopsy results."

As they spoke, more customers entered, enjoying the freshly brewed coffee, the pleasant smell mingling with the sweet scent of the donuts. They took a moment to enjoy the simple pleasure of the warm beverage and the sugary treat, a brief respite from the deep conversation.

"He might know already," Quentin mentioned. "He works hand in hand with the police."

"Then it becomes a criminal investigation," Preston said, horrified. He paused. "I can't believe I'm going to work today. It feels wrong. Maybe I should have called out. I know my mother is taking the day off, to support my grandparents."

Quentin looked at his friend and was rather at a loss for words. It was most likely going to turn into a criminal investigation, since barbiturate pills found in an aspirin bottle were unnatural. He wanted to mention to Preston that anyone could have placed the pills in the aspirin bottle, as during the luncheon, the guests walked around the entire house. When no one was looking, someone could have easily slipped the pills in the bottle. He decided to keep these thoughts to himself, at least for now.

"I've been thinking about your grandfather, Pres. How's he holding up?"

"He's been quieter, more so than usual. I am worried about him. This situation is taking a toll on all of us."

"You need to keep an eye on him. Make sure he's okay. This is a lot for anyone to handle, but especially at his age and condition."

Preston sipped his coffee. "What I confided to you, Quentin, I'd prefer that you keep it to yourself. Initially, I believed my grandfather was behind these occurrences, but with Aunt Joan's death, I don't believe for a minute he would let his own daughter die."

"What about Mr. Lewis?"

Preston was feeling overwhelmed. He mentioned to Quentin how Mr. Armstrong came to their house last evening and confessed it was his car that almost hit the judge in February. He told him how Mrs. Castle witnessed the entire episode. Quentin was about to light a cigarette but stopped in complete surprise.

"Thurman was driving the car? Well, that is interesting to say the least. I suppose he was right in assuming nosy Mrs. Castle could've ruined him by going to your grandfather and spilling the beans. I'm surprised she didn't do it already. This is April and it happened two months ago."

"Do you think there's a connection between Mr. Lewis's death and my aunt's death?"

"In what way?" Quentin asked. "Let's review what we know so far about your grandfather. First, the push in front of the trolley, but now we know it was Thurman driving the car, so that can be eliminated. The second time was the poisonous tea that Mr. Lewis drank, which your grandfather believed was meant for him. And the third was the barbiturate poisoning of your aunt, which your grandfather also must believe was meant for him, as it was his aspirin bottle."

"He may believe that's the case," Preston said slowly.

"He *does* believe it," Quentin continued. "Mr. Sheppard will figure this whole mess out before someone else gets killed."

Preston looked at him with raised eyebrows. "Someone else gets killed?"

Quentin looked at his watch and mentioned he needed to leave. He slurped his coffee, and they gathered their jackets and caps and once outside, he told him, "I'll call you later." Preston watched as he crossed North Pearl Street heading for the law firm.

Feeling alone and extremely confused, Preston walked along the almost empty sidewalk at this early hour, his hands deep in his coat pockets, his cap pulled low over his eyes.

A nagging sense of unease lingered in his mind. He replayed Quentin's words in his head: "Someone else gets killed?" A shiver went through him. He boarded a trolley to take him along Broadway. Finally reaching the office of the Hudson River Day Cruise Line, and with a deep breath, he entered the building, the weight of the unknown pressed heavily on him, unyielding and unsettling.

Doris collected the morning newspaper from the hallway and entered the office. As usual, she knew Mrs. Castle was already there. She left the newspaper on the hallway table, then entered the main office.

Mrs. Castle, impeccably alert and appearing fresh and pleasant, greeted her warmly and then spoke rather bluntly, "Doris, do you plan to attend Mrs. Caves's wake tonight?"

She doesn't beat around the bush, Doris thought, hardly settled at her desk. She took the cover off of her typewriter and prepared her desk for the workday ahead. "Yes, I think it's important to pay my respects. The funeral tomorrow, too."

"Mrs. Caves was the judge's daughter," Mrs. Castle lamented. "It's only right we honor her memory. Such a sad time for the family. I should stop by to see how they are coping."

"It's the least we can do. Despite my past disagreements with the judge, I wouldn't want anyone to think I don't care." Doris hesitated, glancing at Mrs. Castle's pleasantly plump face and rather oversized shape. "You must be quite an early bird, arriving before the rest of us."

Rose smiled. "I'm not one to sleep late. I'd rather arrive early to beat the crowded trolley."

Doris agreed. "Yes, I suppose that's true."

Such an inane conversation, she mused, watching as Mrs. Castle began typing and then afterward started to sort the contents of a pile of folders, although Doris noticed a faint shadow to her semblance. She listened as Rose made small talk about the death of Mr. Lewis and Mrs. Joan Caves that were platitudinous. Her rather clichéd comments were repetitive and unnecessary and Doris was glad when Quentin entered, greeting them and heading for his desk.

Quentin, with his usual brisk stride, brought a sense of energy into the room. "Good morning, ladies," he said, flashing a quick smile. Doris could not help but feel a bit of relief at his arrival, hoping it would steer the conversation away from the mundane.

He appeared in a cheerful mood, despite the obvious aura of sadness in the office. "I plan to attend the wake this evening and the funeral tomorrow to support the family." He did not mention what he had just learned from Preston about the cause of his aunt's death. He did not want to be the bearer of bad news, especially in such a toxic office environment.

Quentin took a deep drag from his cigarette. He glanced around the room, noting the restrained expressions of his colleagues. The rather dim ceiling lights and the steady clatter of Doris's typewriter added to the apparent melancholy.

Mrs. Castle offered a plate of sugar cookies, her face a mask of polite concern. "It's good of you to support the family, Quentin. They need all the comfort they can get."

Quentin forced a smile. "Yes, it's the least I can do." Inside, he felt a pang of guilt for keeping the news to himself, but he knew this was not the time or place to share it.

The morning continued, with Thurman arriving a half hour later, his usual gruff demeanor softened by the somber atmosphere. He looked slightly disheveled but offered a respectful nod to his colleagues. He buried himself with his caseload, only briefly entering the main office before returning to his desk, absorbed in his work.

At that moment, Lucille made her grand entrance like the queen of the Nile, a strong scent of Chanel No. 5 wafting after her as she glided to her office suite. Doris could not help but admire her confidence, though she wondered if Lucille's dramatic flair was entirely appropriate given the circumstances. Surely, she must feel sadness for Judge Archie and the rest of the family.

"My husband's in court this morning," Lucille told them, taking off her fur coat with a graceful flourish. "I don't expect him back till after lunchtime."

"Mr. Smith's in court this morning, too," Mrs. Castle echoed, hesitating slightly. "Do you and Mr. Sampson plan to attend the service for the judge's daughter?"

Lucille removed her stylish cloche hat, revealing perfectly coiffed hair. "Well, of course, Mrs. Castle. My husband and I feel deep remorse for the judge and the family. My mother-in-law as well." Her tone implied it was really none of Mrs. Castle's business if they did or did not attend, but she managed to convey a polite, if not entirely friendly, tone.

Doris observed the exchange, noting the subtle tension in Lucille's voice. She glanced around the office, the morning light filtering through the windows. The sound of footsteps echoed in the outside hallway, testament to the beginning workday.

Several new clients came for their morning appointments. The first was a woman seeking custody of her two children. The second was an insurance man who was swindled out of quite a bit of money. Thurman interviewed them, wrote up drafts of his notes and then entered the main office, handing the papers to Mrs. Castle and to Doris for typing,

After the last appointment left, Thurman turned to go back to his office when the main office telephone rang. The sharp sound cut through the quiet, making everyone pause. Mrs. Castle answered it promptly, her face growing alarmed as she heard the voice of Mrs. Augusta Stafford. She listened, her expression shifting from confusion to fear. Ending the call, she looked up, her face pale. She was at first speechless and deeply afraid.

Thurman and Doris exchanged worried glances, their curiosity piqued. "What's wrong, Mrs. Castle?" Thurman asked his voice tense.

Mrs. Castle hesitated, glancing at Quentin, who remained silent but visibly alarmed. He knew what she had just learned, and the burden of that knowledge hung uncomfortably in the air.

He carefully observed Doris and Thurman while Mrs. Castle told them the results of Mrs. Caves's autopsy revealed her death was due to barbiturate poisoning, possibly something in the aspirin bottle. Thurman registered complete shock, incredulity, and even a little anger, his fists clenching at his sides. Doris turned extremely pale, looking as though she might faint, her hands trembling as she gripped the edge of her desk.

"Mrs. Stafford mentioned she wanted us to know," Mrs. Castle said, choking up. "Before the services, she didn't want us kept in the dark about the real cause of Mrs. Caves's death." Her voice wavered, and she too exhibited an overwhelming sense of dread, remorse, and pity.

An unsettling silence filled the room, broken only by the distant ticking of the wall clock. Doris felt her breath quicken, her mind racing with the implications of the news. Thurman's jaw tightened, his eyes narrowing as he processed the information. Quentin remained silent, his gaze shifting between his colleagues. He watched and waited, ready to step in if needed.

Lucille entered, visibly upset. "I heard what you were telling them, Mrs. Castle," she said, her voice trembling with alarm. "Is what you were saying true? The judge's daughter died from barbiturate poisoning? How could that happen? I don't understand!"

Her face paled, and she swayed for a moment in front of Mrs. Castle's desk. The room seemed to hold its breath as she began to pitch forward. Thurman, reacting swiftly, caught her just before she hit the floor in a dead faint.

Doris gasped, her hand flying to her mouth. Mrs. Castle stood up, her face frozen, her eyes wide with shock. Quentin, still silent, stepped forward, ready to assist. The tension in the room was clear, the startling realization of the news settling heavily on everyone present.

Thurman gently lowered Lucille into a chair, his face a mask of concern. "Someone get some water," he barked, his voice breaking the silence. Doris hurried to the small kitchenette, her hands shaking as she filled a glass.

Quentin watched the scene unfold, his mind racing. He knew he should say something, do something, but the words caught in his throat.

Doris returned with the water, handing it to Thurman, who carefully helped Lucille take a sip. She blinked, slowly coming back to consciousness, her eyes filled with confusion and fear. She mumbled a few words, assuring them she was feeling better, although she was obviously still rather distraught by the latest news. She continued sipping the water, color returning to her face.

"What are we going to do?" Doris whispered her voice barely audible. "This changes everything! Mrs. Caves didn't die a natural death, she was murdered!"

Mrs. Castle's expression was resolute despite the tears in her eyes. "We'll support the family and find out how this happened. We owe them that much."

Quentin took a deep breath. He glanced at his colleagues, seeing the same determination mirrored in their faces. Rather selfishly, he was glad he did not break the news to them, especially since Mrs. Stafford had called to tell them herself.

The room fell silent again, each person lost in disturbing and chaotic thoughts. The magnitude of the situation weighed heavily on them and they knew the days ahead would be filled with difficult questions and even harder answers. As the clock on the wall ticked away the seconds, the office seemed to hold its breath, waiting for the next ominous chapter to unfold.

Sloan arrived at Mrs. Sampson's stately brownstone house on Hamilton Street and rang the bell. While waiting for the door to open, he cast a quick glance at the overcast sky, which emitted a gloomy pall, matching the somber mood of the upcoming wake and funeral tomorrow.

Earlier in the day, Sloan conducted much research. First, at the Harmanus Bleecker Library and then at the hospital. Both proved highly effective and worth his time. In his notepad, which he carried with him, he had made copious notes of the information which he intended to share with Mrs. Sampson and Mrs. Crabtree.

It was close to four o'clock and he assumed he was not too early. He saw the door slowly open and a pleasant faced older woman stood before him, smiling and welcoming him in. She introduced herself as

Mrs. Mary Crabtree, her voice warm and inviting yet tinged with a hint of weariness. She took his hat and coat, leaving them on a hallway chair. Sloan then followed her inside, noting the opulent grandeur of the house, the rich furnishings, a vase with what looked like wax flowers on a hallway table, the grand staircase, the crystal chandelier in the spacious living room, and the elaborate fireplace in the center of the far wall. The faint scent of lavender lingered in the air, mingling with the scent of freshly polished wood. A chintz covered Victorian sofa stood before the large windows overlooking Hamilton Street. He looked with interest at the other woman in the room.

Philomena sat in a high-backed chair, her frail frame wrapped in a shawl. Despite her age, her eyes were sharp and observant; following Sloan's every move as he entered. She thought him a handsome man, quite courteous and certainly his appearance exuded confidence and strength. She gestured to a nearby chair. "Please, Mr. Sheppard, have a seat. Perhaps you have some important information to share with us?"

Mrs. Sampson's maid appeared, a young woman of no more than twenty, looking competent and committed, carrying a tea tray. With practiced grace, she set the tray down on the coffee table and poured the tea into three delicate porcelain cups. She handed one first to her mistress, then to Mrs. Crabtree and finally to Sloan, her movements precise and efficient.

"Thank you, Mr. Sheppard, for coming here today," Philomena said, sipping her tea. "And thank you, also, Mrs. Crabtree for not only coming here but for answering the door. Usually Nan answers to see who's calling, but I insisted she have the tea ready for us." She sighed, looking at her company. "This evening is the wake for Mrs. Caves. My son and daughter-in-law will bring me and to the service tomorrow, too."

"I plan to attend," Mrs. Crabtree said, turning to Sloan. "I didn't know Mrs. Caves, but Mrs. Stafford is a lovely woman and so active in the League of Women Voters. For Augusta and her family, I will pay my respects."

Sloan appreciated their willingness to talk and to listen. "Thank you both for your time. What I have to share is quite significant and may shed light on recent events." He sipped his tea, admiring the dainty cup, decorated with tulips. He put it on the coffee table and realized the ladies were expecting him to continue. Once the maid left the room, he opened his notepad and looked at the two women.

Sloan explained how he spent a busy morning. He called the hospital and spoke at length to a woman in the personnel department, his mind racing with questions and possibilities.

"She told me records from the 1880s are sparse," he continued. "She managed to locate a file from that time and there was a notation about an abortion in the emergency room on the evening of March 15, 1885, but it didn't give the name of the woman or anyone else. It didn't state who wrote the note, either."

Upon calling the police and after a policeman found the right records, he learned that later in March 1885, a gangster named Mr. Philip Mavity was stabbed in his apartment on Jay Street with a kitchen knife. His killer was never found. Sloan mentioned that while at the library, he consulted several newspapers and also *The Index to Deaths in Albany, New York 1880-1915,* which confirmed the death of Philip Mavity.

At the Albany Police station, Sloan told them how he met and spoke to a retired policeman who remembered the death of Mr. Mavity. The officer, now assisting with clerical duties a few days a week, managed to locate a file in the police archives. It mentioned that Mavity was involved in organized crime and illegal contraband. His arrest record prior to 1885 was extensive, but there was nothing more Sloan could glean from that information. Frustration plagued him as he realized the dead ends he was facing.

He added that he spoke to his contacts at the Albany police again, Inspector Harris and Lieutenant Taylor, regarding the deaths of Mr. Lewis and Mrs. Caves, both by poisoning. The connections between these cases and the historical records were becoming more tangled, and Sloan felt the pressure of uncovering the truth. He didn't add anything more yet, as he did not want to overwhelm them at this point.

Philomena's face grew pale as she listened, her hands trembling slightly as she set her teacup down on an end table. "I had no idea these events were connected," she whispered.

Mrs. Crabtree leaned forward, her expression a mix of shock and recognition. "I remember that might vividly. The hospital was in chaos, and the young woman was determined to have the abortion. She may have used an alias. Many gangsters and their molls used different names in hospitals as they were afraid of being caught."

Sloan paused, letting the enormity of Mrs. Crabtree's words sink in. "I believe these events are connected, and that they point to a larger conspiracy that we have yet to fully uncover."

Philomena's brow furrowed, her eyes narrowing with concern. "A larger conspiracy? What do you mean, Mr. Sheppard?"

Sloan took a deep breath. "The timing of these events is too coincidental to ignore. The gangster's murder and the illegal abortion happened within a short span. Although Mr. Mavity's death appeared in the index, I didn't find an obituary in newspapers from March and April 1885."

Mrs. Crabtree cleared her throat. "I remember hearing about that young man's murder. There were rumors about certain doctors and nurses in cahoots with gangsters. They'd perform illegal procedures and keep quiet about it. If this young woman was connected to the gangsters, it would explain a lot." She paused, thoughtfully. "I wish I could remember her name, or the name she gave. She was a young girl, but dangerous looking and ill kept. Abortions were performed in the emergency room, undercover of the normal procedures, of course, and sworn to secrecy."

Sloan understood the limitations of memory after so many years. "Thank you, Mrs. Crabtree. Your recollections are invaluable."

Philomena's eyes filled with a mix of curiosity and concern. "How can we uncover the identity of this young woman and her connection to the gangster?"

Sloan's mind raced with possibilities. "I believe the key lies in finding more about Philip Mavity's connections."

"As a night nurse, I witnessed the horrid conditions of emergency rooms," Mrs. Crabtree continued. "Many women who had abortions then died themselves because it was such a risky procedure. Whoever she was, I remember she survived."

Philomena's eyes brightened with a glimmer of hope. "That could be a lead worth pursuing. And what about the police records? Is there anything more you can find there?"

Sloan nodded. "I'll revisit the police archives and see if there's anything more. Sometimes, the smallest detail can break a case wide open."

The conversation continued, the burden of the unknown remained suspended in the air, but there was also a sense of determination.

"Would this have to do with Mr. Lewis's death and the death of Mrs. Caves?" Philomena asked, rather confusedly. "She died from barbiturate poisoning. Mrs. Stafford called to tell me."

"Yes, I got a call from her as well," Sloan said gravely. "I also spoke to the police earlier today. They intend to handle it as a criminal investigation."

Philomena's eyes widened with concern. "A criminal investigation?"

Sloan's look was serious. "Yes, the police believe there may be a connection between Mr. Lewis's death and Mrs. Caves's poisoning.

The fact that both deaths involved substances, toxic tea and barbiturate poisoning, suggests a deliberate act."

Mrs. Crabtree's face grew pale. "This is more sinister than I imagined. Do you think the same person is responsible for both deaths?"

"It's possible," Sloan replied. "We need to find out who had access to these substances and what the motives might be. The connections between the events are becoming clearer, but we still have many questions to answer."

Philomena took a deep breath, her resolve strengthening. "Whatever you need from us, we are here to help. We must uncover the truth and bring justice to those who have suffered."

Sloan smiled. "Thank you, Mrs. Sampson and Mrs. Crabtree. Your cooperation is much appreciated. I'll continue to dig into the police records and see what more I can learn from the hospital archives."

"My goodness," Mrs. Crabtree said. "I don't usually become frightened, as my nursing duties hardened me to the harsher realities of life, but this is most unsettling."

Sloan could tell he had learned as much as he could from Mrs. Crabtree as well as Mrs. Sampson. They were both strong willed women, who had experienced much in their years. Philomena mentioned her son and daughter-in-law were due home relatively soon, but Sloan, having already spoken with Mr. and Mrs. Sampson, felt now was not the ideal time to speak with them again. He did not want anything to impede on his rapport with the two women. However, he made a mental note, sensing there was more to uncover.

Philomena rose from her chair, rather shakily as her arthritis flared up, making her wince slightly. She shook hands with Sloan, thanking him for his visit. Mrs. Crabtree saw him to the door, handed him his fedora hat and coat, and assured him he was welcome to call on her again.

He hesitated briefly, looking back at Mrs. Crabtree with interest and respect. He stepped outside, the late afternoon air crisp and invigorating. With renewed focus, he strode purposefully down Hamilton Street.

The mysterious deaths, the illegal abortion, the unsolved murder from 1885—the gravity of these events lingered in his mind, refusing to loosen its grip. The truth was out there—and he was determined to find it.

CHAPTER FIFTEEN

Preston sat in the living room, sipping a cup of coffee. He held the cup to his lips, more to hide his facial expression of extreme remorse than for the actual drinking of the hot liquid. He glanced over at his mother and grandmother, both solemn and silent, their hands resting motionless in their laps. His grandfather, speechless and in deep mourning, in his usual armchair, accepted a cup of coffee from Gertrude but hardly touched it, his eyes fixed on a distant point.

The air was heavy and difficult, as Preston had expected. He could hear the clock ticking loudly in the hallway, each second dragging on. He wondered if anyone else felt the same crushing weight of guilt and sorrow.

"We should have done more," his mother finally whispered her voice barely audible.

His grandmother sighed, a sound filled with years of unspoken pain. "We all should have," she said, her eyes glistening with unshed tears.

It was close to five o'clock on Saturday, and the funeral for Joan was over. The church service and burial had been well attended by many of Joan's colleagues from the office, as well as friends of the Staffords. Mrs.

Crabtree and Mrs. Aldrich attended and returned to the house along with the office staff, creating another uncomfortable conglomerate in the living room.

Mrs. Castle assisted Gertrude in the kitchen, while Doris and Quentin chatted with Preston and Martha. Burgess had spoken with Judge Archie, again expressing his sincerest condolences, as did Thurman and the Sampsons. Philomena sat beside Augusta, speaking to her in a soothing way to help calm her.

Within an hour, the house was nearly empty, except for Gertrude and Mrs. Castle, who stayed to clean up in the kitchen. They too shortly departed, leaving the family in the living room to sort through their grief.

Preston put his cup on the coffee table and asked his mother if she needed anything. She merely looked his way but did not respond. Augusta and Judge Archie were also incommunicative, so Preston decided to remain silent. It was obvious their mourning was far from over. He rather wished Quentin had stayed. At least he would have had someone to talk to.

To his surprise, his grandfather cleared his throat and addressed them, quite clearly and forcefully. "Joan's death has affected me deeply. She did not deserve to die as she did. Those barbiturates were meant for me. Someone put them in the bottle, thinking I would take them, since it was my aspirin on my bedside table."

Preston felt a chill run down his spine. He looked at his grandfather, trying to process the revelation. His mother gasped, her hand flying to her mouth. Augusta's eyes widened in shock, and Judge Archie leaned forward, his expression turning grim.

His grandfather shook his head slowly. "Someone wanted me dead."

Augusta agreed. "Someone put the pills in that bottle while we were busy, getting the food ready and chatting with our guests."

"We couldn't be everywhere at once," Preston commented, rather frustrated.

"Exactly my point," Judge Archie said. "The enemy struck again, right here but did not succeed. Perhaps next time, I won't be so lucky."

"Father, please," Martha implored, her voice trembling. "We don't know yet for sure."

"Mr. Sheppard will find out," her father told her, his tone resolute. "Preston, if you would be so kind to contact him again on Monday morning. I want to know what more he has discovered."

Preston felt the immense pressure of responsibility. He glanced around the room, noting the tension etched on everyone's faces. His mind raced with questions and fears.

An uneasy silence settled over the room, each of them trapped in their own thoughts. Preston knew that contacting Mr. Sheppard was the right step, but the uncertainty troubled him. He took a deep breath, steeling himself for the challenges ahead.

"You should rest, Grandfather," Preston said with concern.

Judge Archie shook his head. "Not yet, Preston. I'd like to listen to the radio and then I'll retire to our bedroom, where there are papers and notebooks I wish to review."

He did not elaborate further, so Preston just accepted his grandfather's wishes. Augusta got up and turned on the radio, turning the dial until she found *The Atwater Kent Hour*, always a relaxing program of hit songs and wonderful symphonic music. The familiar melodies filled the room, providing a brief respite from their heavy thoughts.

Preston admired his grandfather's resolve, even as worry weighed heavily on him. The mystery surrounding Joan's death was far from over, and the stakes seemed higher than ever. The hourly news report soon began. The announcer's voice crackled through the radio.

"Welcome to the evening news report. Our top story; the death of Mr. Clement Lewis remains unresolved, and now, another tragedy has struck. Mrs. Joan Caves, daughter of Judge Archibald Stafford of Albany, has been found dead under mysterious circumstances. Authorities are investigating a possible connection between the two deaths…"

Augusta's eyes filled with tears. "Archie, what are we going to do?" she asked, her voice breaking. "We can't just sit here and wait for something else to happen!"

Unable to stand the tension any further, Preston got up and approached the radio. His hand trembled slightly as he adjusted the volume, trying to mask his unease. Questions crowded his mind. Answers had to come—before another life was claimed.

Quentin arrived at his apartment on North Allen Street. It was several hours after the funeral for Mrs. Caves and he was glad to be home. He kicked off his shoes, made a cup of tea with a splash of bourbon, and headed to the living room.

He turned on the radio to listen to *The Atwater Kent Hour* but found the music rather stilted, so he played with the knob until he found a station broadcasting popular tunes by Bessie Smith and Duke Ellington, more to his liking. He then sat down, put his feet up on the coffee table and with a cigarette to his lips, lit it and exhaled a fine cloud of smoke. His thoughts returned to the service earlier today for Mrs. Caves.

Like the others, he had returned to the mansion but unlike the others, he did not stay exceptionally long. He found the funereal atmosphere stifling and even though he spoke with Preston, he was glad to leave. He approached Judge Archie and Mrs. Stafford, who were clearly alarmed but composed. He not only offered them condolences, but he also gave them a brief hug. He felt bad for Preston and his family and only worried about what would come next.

He looked toward the living room windows, sipping his tea, enjoying the bourbon burning his throat and then puffed at his cigarette. He did not know what to think of the situation. Mr. Lewis drank poisoned tea and now Mrs. Caves died from barbiturate poisoning. Something was happening and Quentin admitted, he felt afraid. He could not shake the feeling that he was missing something crucial. The deaths of Mr. Lewis and Mrs. Caves were too coincidental to be unrelated.

He then picked up the telephone on his end table and asked the operator to dial the Stafford's number. Within a few moments, a tired but familiar voice answered.

"Preston, it's Quentin. I want to ask you a few questions about your aunt."

There was a pause, then Preston's voice came back, more alert. "Quentin, this isn't the best time. Can it wait until tomorrow? We can meet since it's Sunday."

"I think there's more to her death than we realize."

Preston sighed, the stress of the day's events evident in his voice. "I agree. Come here tomorrow afternoon. We'll talk then."

While speaking to Preston, he thought of asking him if he wanted to go to a few speakeasies, as on Saturday nights the crowds were full of eligible ladies, but he decided against it. He did not think it appropriate if he went drinking and dancing on the evening of the same day as his aunt's funeral. He concluded the call, exhaling a large cloud of smoke as he hung up.

He finished the tea, the bourbon now a comforting warmth in his chest. The soft, crackling sound of jazz tunes by Bessie Smith and Duke

Ellington played on the radio, blending with the distant hum of traffic outside. A single lamp, casting dark outlines on the walls and creating a cozy yet slightly melancholic atmosphere, dimly lit the room. He took another drag from his cigarette, the lingering scent of tobacco smoke mixing with the faint smell of burnt matches.

He noticed Thurman acting strangely at the service, avoiding Mrs. Castle and even the younger Mrs. Sampson, as though he was afraid of them. Even Burgess was complacent, as if by his presence he was doing the Staffords a favor by attending. He saw Doris weeping into a handkerchief, but he could not tell if she was mourning or possibly involved with something else. The elder Mrs. Sampson looked as though she would collapse and Quentin had considered assisting her but knew her narcissist son and daughter-in-law would cater to her every whim.

The warm tones of jazz wrapped around him, soothing but unable to quiet his nagging thoughts. He wondered about that Mrs. Crabtree or whatever her name was. She certainly struck him as a Budinski. Why did she talk about abortions and illegal hospital activities at the luncheon? Although she reminisced about her hospital days, something must've conjured up those unpleasant memories for her to mention them.

Preston confided in him that he suspected his grandfather was doing this himself. But would he kill his own daughter? He dismissed that idea and he believed Preston did as well. He could not help but wonder who hated the judge enough to want him dead.

His thoughts drifted to the judge's history with the others—Doris, Mrs. Castle, Burgess, Thurman and the Sampsons. The memory of the older Mrs. Sampson's husband, who had died in jail after being sentenced by Judge Archie, was a dark shadow that loomed over them all. Certainly, the elder Mrs. Sampson would not hold a grudge after so many years. Or would she?

A chill crawled up Quentin's spine as he pieced together fragments of guarded words and fleeting glances from the luncheon. Something tied them all together in a web of deceit and hidden motives. Burgess had been unusually tense lately, and the Sampsons had been avoiding the judge altogether.

The silence of the apartment seemed to grow heavier and an uneasy feeling settled over him. As he extinguished his final cigarette and prepared for bed, he knew one thing was certain: the judge's fate was intertwined with secrets that ran deeper than he imagined.

The soft glow of the early evening sun entered the living room of Mrs. Castle's apartment on Dove Street, creating a comfortable atmosphere. She sipped her tea, its warmth offering a small comfort against the somber mood of the day. The faint scent of Earl Grey mingled with the crispness of the pages she turned while skimming the latest issue of *Reader's Digest*, one of her favorite magazines. The soft hum of the radio in the corner played a jazz tune, adding a layer of sophistication to the room. Mrs. Castle's fingers, adorned with a few rings, paused occasionally to sip from the porcelain teacup, the bitter fragrance of the tea a reminder of the day's melancholy.

Her thoughts turned to the service for Mrs. Caves earlier. The funeral had been a somber affair, filled with whispered condolences and veiled glances. Mrs. Castle felt a pang of sorrow, not just for the loss of Mrs. Caves, but for the palpable tension that seemed to hang in the air. She noticed the judge's stern face; Preston's expression, rather awkward and even fearful, which suggested he may know more than he let on. Mrs. Stafford, poised but upset, clutched her rosary beads and a handkerchief tightly, her knuckles white, and Mrs. Hughes, tearful and overwrought, dabbed at her eyes incessantly.

So many people attended, too. Even those ladies from the League of Women Voters, there out of respect for Mrs. Stafford, understandably. Mrs. Crabtree, more subdued than at the luncheon, her face hidden behind a veil, seemed lost in thought. The others appeared deep in mourning, although Mrs. Castle wondered if it was just an act. Doris, Quentin, Burgess, Thurman, and of course the arrogant Sampsons and that hideous old Mrs. Sampson, who looked like she could barely walk, were all present. The old woman wouldn't miss a moment—she was there, of course. Mr. Sampson seemed oblivious to it all but did offer his condolences again to the family, although rather stiffly. The younger Mrs. Stafford put on airs as always, but she too appeared genuinely moved by the service. But what secrets were they all hiding? Mrs. Castle wondered if beneath the surface of their polite expressions lay a web of deceit and hidden motives.

She sighed deeply, flipping through *Reader's Digest*, seeking solace in its pages. Judge Archibald Stafford was a man of many secrets. Like most people, there were parts of her past she wanted to remain hidden. Didn't everyone have something to hide, she mused, her eyes lingering on an advertisement for *Borden's Ice Cream*, the image of an ice cream sundae making her mouth water. An article on the historic district in Schenectady kept her focused for several minutes, the black-and-white photographs evoking a sense of nostalgia.

She finished her tea and put the delicate porcelain teacup down with a steady hand, though her mind was anything but calm. She had always maintained her composure, but the judge's perceptive nature unnerved her. He seemed too aware of the undercurrents that flowed beneath the surface. A shiver ran down her spine, as she knew Judge Archie was not to be trusted.

Now that his youngest daughter was dead, what would become of him? Would he linger at the office occasionally, or retreat into grief entirely? The thought of Thurman as interim president unsettled her. She had believed she held the upper hand when she confronted him, certain that revealing she knew it was his car that nearly struck the judge would shake him. She hadn't expected what he said in return—his words had dismantled her carefully laid plans. He couldn't prove anything, of course. But was he lying?

Certainly, Thurman was aware that Doris was involved with bootleggers and that the Sampsons played the stock market quite heavily. Mrs. Castle suspected that Thurman dealt with bootleggers, too. She knew he liked his liquor as much as Doris. Burgess boozed it up often and likely had contacts with bootleggers. He was an underhanded lawyer who finagled his way through the court system, just like Thurman. She had not realized until recently the extent of corruption among some lawyers, but then she assumed corruption was everywhere, including law.

She couldn't quite put her finger on exactly what had occurred at the luncheon. The startled faces, the quick glances—something she had yet to grasp. A faint unease stirred within her. Something lurked just out of grasp—too subtle to name, yet impossible to ignore.

She glanced around the living room, the ticking of the mantel clock adding to the oppressive atmosphere. The faint, staleness of the finished tea filled the room, a blatant contrast to the crisp spring air outside. She sighed, knowing that navigating these treacherous waters would require all her cunning and composure. The sense of foreboding grew stronger. Whatever lay ahead, she knew it was only the beginning.

Burgess closed the door to his apartment, the click of the lock echoing in the silence. The dim light from the streetlamp outside cast dark shadows across the room. He turned on some lights, shrugged off his coat and tossed it onto an armchair, feeling the anxieties of the day settle on his shoulders. He glanced around his apartment. While not luxurious, he considered it comfortable and kept it pristine. Its location on Hudson Avenue was ideal, especially since he regularly frequented a speakeasy on Lark Street.

He had just arrived back from the Staffords, as he felt it only appropriate to return to the house after the funeral. He poured himself a drink, the amber liquid swirling in the glass as he stared at it, lost in thought. He placed a cigarette between his lips and flicked the match to life, inhaling deeply. He was glad tomorrow was Sunday as he could sleep late and not have to report to the office. It was still early and he considered attending the speakeasy on Lark Street but decided against it for tonight. He settled comfortably on the sofa in the spacious living room, puffing at his cigarette, the smoke moving slowly toward the ceiling.

He was in shock when he learned that Mrs. Caves died from barbiturate poisoning. When he arrived back to the office yesterday afternoon, Mrs. Castle told him. He knew something was definitely wrong just by her expression but it just did not make sense. The funeral had been a blur of faces and condolences, but certain moments stood out with sparkling clarity. He remembered how Thurman avoided his gaze, his eyes red-rimmed and distant. Burgess could not shake the feeling he was hiding something. And even Doris, acting rather coy, as though a guest at the funeral. The Sampsons behaved as though they were the king and queen as usual and Mrs. Castle seemed filled with genuine grief but with her, it was always hard to tell. Those ladies from the women's voting group were there, too. Mrs. Aldrich was pleasant and so was Mrs. Crabtree but she acted reticent as if she harbored certain secrets. He did not quite understand why the woman mentioned abortions and illegal medical practices at the luncheon. But then he did not feel it his place to say anything, so he decided to keep quiet.

Certainly, the family was overcome with emotion, which Burgess understood. He observed Preston supporting his grandfather. Preston's mother, Mrs. Hughes, was overcome and was supported by Miss Lodge, from the women's voting group.

He took a sip of his drink, the warmth spreading through him, but it did little to ease the chill that had settled in his bones. He wandered over to the mantelpiece, where a collection of photographs stood. One picture, in particular, caught his eye—a group photo from a summer picnic years ago. The judge was there, smiling, surrounded by his family and associates. Burgess traced the edge of the frame with his finger, lost in memories.

As he continued to mull over the events of the day, his thoughts turned to the judge's many enemies. He had a history with the old man, too. He knew he was not the only one with a grudge. The judge's harsh sentences and unyielding demeanor had earned him plenty of foes.

He returned to the sofa, deep in contemplative thoughts, his drink in hand, a cigarette to his lips. The shadows in the room seemed to grow longer and an anxious feeling settled over him. A creeping dread settled over him—his own secrets felt perilously close to the surface.

It was not unusual for Sloan to spend an inordinate amount of time on his work. Therefore, Saturday evening found him at the police station, sitting in a conference room with Inspector Harris and Lieutenant Taylor. There were ashtrays on the table, with plenty of blue smoke, swirling and eddying out of the window that the inspector had opened. Sloan put down his cigarette and addressed the policemen.

"You've been informed of the death of Mrs. Joan Caves by barbiturate poisoning. This is the second death to follow the same pattern. Mr. Clement Lewis was also poisoned." He paused. "The possibility that the intended target of these attacks was the judge is a harsh reality."

Inspector Harris nodded. "There seems no uncertainty now to believe the judge was indeed targeted for murder. The aspirin bottle has been tested and the remaining pills showed no signs of barbiturates. Mrs. Caves took the pills from the bottle that were not aspirin but barbiturates."

Sloan's eyes narrowed as he absorbed the information. "The judge was the intended target, but Mrs. Caves and Mr. Lewis were collateral damage. This changes everything. I believe someone put those pills in the aspirin bottle during the afternoon of the luncheon. According to the family, the guests had free reign of the house, looking into all the rooms. It would've been easy for someone to slip pills into an aspirin bottle on the judge's bed stand. With the guests moving from room to room, most likely no one noticed a thing."

"What suspects do we have and the motives?" Lieutenant Taylor asked.

Sloan related his conversation with Mrs. Sampson and Mrs. Crabtree. He mentioned how Mrs. Crabtree explained her duties as a night nurse, in which she witnessed firsthand the enormities and depravations of hospital work during the 1880s. She had mentioned abortions and gangsters at the hospital were common. He told them how Mrs. Sampson's sister died during childbirth at around the same time an illegal abortion was performed. When he called the hospital, records during that time were sparse and provided no further leads as to the identity of gangsters or anyone involved with abortions.

"But what would that have to do with the judge?" the inspector questioned.

Sloan knocked ash from his cigarette. "Judge Archie knows more than he lets on. I believe he knows information about these abortions and may know who the woman was and even the identity of the gangsters. There was a murder around that time, Mr. Philip Mavity."

"We've searched in the archives for information on him," Inspector Harris said. "He had quite an arrest record. However, he was murdered at his apartment, stabbed with a kitchen knife, but his killer was never found. That was also in March 1885."

"Forty years is a long time to fear exposure," the lieutenant added.

"There is never a timeline for murder," Sloan said grimly. "I want to check if the judge kept records on his discoveries. Possibly the killer knows about it and wants to find it. Certainly, it could easily implicate someone."

"Then why doesn't the judge just tell us what he knows?"

"Possibly he may not be quite sure himself. It may be recent information he unearthed during his research. As a judge, he's used to scouring through old files at city hall and the hall of records to acquire information on certain cases. Perhaps he came upon information that he realized was detrimental to someone's livelihood and could ultimately cause ruin."

"Ruin?"

Sloan nodded. "Of the person's character. Judge Archie has been a powerful figure here in Albany for over fifty years. He could easily have access to medical records, although such files are not usually open unless by a court order."

"He'd know how to work the system."

"He may have learned something he was not intending to uncover. Perhaps he wrote it in a notebook and the person or persons discovered it, which provides an ample motive for murder."

Inspector Harris leaned forward, his expression grim. "We'll speak to the family again and examine the crime scene. We had officers there on Thursday evening to speak to them and investigate the bedroom where Mrs. Caves was found. There might be a connection we missed."

He then cleared his throat, addressing Sloan steadily. "We recently received a call from Mrs. Martha Hughes, the judge's oldest daughter." He related how Mr. Thurman Armstrong visited the family recently, admitting that it was he who drove the car that almost hit the judge in February. She told him her father did not want to press charges, as he considered Mr. Armstrong a valuable employee. His admittance was forthright and meaningful to her father. She mentioned Mr. Armstrong told the family Mrs. Rose Castle witnessed it but did not report it to the authorities. She added her father did not know of her calling the police and appreciated if they kept silent about it.

Sloan let out a low whistle, slicing through the thick tension in the room. "Such secrecy in this case. Now we know Mr. Armstrong drove the car that night, but it doesn't mean he wanted to kill the judge. We can eliminate that as a murder attempt."

Inspector Harris drummed his fingers lightly on the table, his brow furrowing—a clear sign of mounting impatience. "Right now, the most important thing is to safeguard Judge Archie. He's dismissed the car episode with Mr. Armstrong. But another murder attempt has been made. Whoever's responsible won't stop until the judge is eliminated. We're racing against the clock."

As they left the conference room, Sloan felt they were missing something crucial. Something in plain sight. The pieces were all there—scattered, disconnected. But something refused to fall into place. His foot hesitated slightly before stepping forward, as if his body mirrored the uncertainty in his mind. Perhaps Judge Archie did have pertinent information to the case. Perhaps it was the right time to pay him another visit, too

CHAPTER SIXTEEN

Mrs. Mary Crabtree stood in front of her vanity, adjusting the delicate lace collar of her Sunday dress. The rain pattered softly against the window, a steady rhythm that matched her calm demeanor. She was preparing for church, a ritual she never missed, regardless of the weather. The familiar routine brought her a sense of peace, a respite from the chaos that had recently enveloped her. She sighed, pleased with her appearance and then descended the staircase to the hallway.

At almost the same time, Mrs. Justine Davis, her cook and house keeper, arrived promptly as always, her rather shabby coat wet with rainwater, an umbrella in hand. "Good morning, Mrs. Crabtree," she greeted her, smiling, her voice warm despite the chill in the air. She was a fresh faced woman in her fifties, personable and hardworking, with a pleasing disposition and a commitment to her work. Her brown hair was neat and while she wore no makeup, her appearance was agreeable. Her hands and fingers showed the results of strenuous manual labor.

"I'll start lunch for you and Mr. Crabtree," she said, hanging up her coat in the hallway closet. "It'll be ready when you return from church." She scurried off to the kitchen to begin preparing the meal.

Mr. Walter Crabtree, a distinguished man in his early eighties, with a pleasant smile and rather wrinkly forehead, greeted Mrs. Davis warmly on her way to the kitchen and then joined his wife in the hallway. He mentioned he was about ready to attend church.

"Almost time, dear," Mrs. Crabtree told him. "We'll walk over to State Street to catch the trolley. It's raining and I'm not up to walking in this weather."

They settled in the living room, listening to the pleasant Sunday sermon by Sister Aimee McPherson, the famous evangelist, on the radio. While relaxing with the Sunday newspaper, and realizing the time was fast approaching, Mrs. Crabtree told her husband it was time they leave. She turned off the radio, and as they stepped into the hallway, she gathered their coats, noticing Mrs. Davis also preparing to leave. Mr. Crabtree looked at her curiously and asked where she was going in the rain.

"To the market," Mrs. Davis explained. "We're running low on a few things."

"You mean the market on Madison Avenue?" Mr. Crabtree asked. "We're lucky it's open for a few hours on Sundays. All the other markets are closed."

"Along with everything else," Mrs. Crabtree commented. "It is Sunday, after all."

She then turned to face Mrs. Davis, her eyes narrowing at the sight of the worn coat. "You can't go out in this weather wearing that old thing, dear. You'll catch your death of cold." She remembered Mrs. Davis struggling in harsh weather before. She then walked over to the closet and pulled out a burgundy coat, rich and thick. "Here, wear this. It will keep you dry and warm."

As she handed the garment to her, Mrs. Davis was awed. "But Mrs. Crabtree, this is such a fine coat. I couldn't possibly wear it. It belongs to you, anyway."

"Nonsense," Mrs. Crabtree said, with a wave of her hand. "We'll walk out with you, dear."

Mrs. Davis hesitated, her hands trembling slightly as she took the elegant coat. "Thank you, Mrs. Crabtree. It's truly kind of you."

Mrs. Crabtree watched as Justine slipped into the warm and fashionable coat, feeling its warmth envelop her, the burgundy color suiting her agreeably. "Be careful, Justine," she added softly, her voice barely above a whisper.

Mrs. Davis stepped out into the rain, opening her umbrella, the burgundy fabric of the elegant coat standing out against the gray morning. The Crabtrees soon followed, noting the rain had let up making their umbrella rather cumbersome. They turned right onto Willett Street toward State Street while Mrs. Davis turned left on Willett Street toward Madison Avenue.

The market was just a few blocks away, and Mrs. Davis moved rather quickly, her mind focused on the errands ahead. Mrs. Crabtree was such a nice woman, she thought, and so kind to let her wear her expensive coat. She was fortunate to work for such good people.

Mrs. Davis looked up at the rain, which had lightened but it continued raw and cold. As she approached the intersection, the sound of a trolley clanging down the tracks grew louder. She waited for it to pass, the drizzling rain blurring her vision slightly. Suddenly, she felt a hard shove from behind. Her feet slipped on the wet pavement, and she stumbled forward, directly into the path of the oncoming trolley. The last thing she saw was the bright light of the trolley's headlamp, heard an ear-piercing scream and then everything went dark.

Mr. and Mrs. Crabtree heard the hideous scream and turned instinctively. In the distance, they saw a commotion near the intersection. They hurried up Willett Street, toward the scene, their hearts pounding with a mixture of fear and curiosity. As they approached, the sight of the burgundy coat on the ground made Mrs. Crabtree gasp.

She recognized it and the lifeless form of Mrs. Davis beneath it. The Crabtrees looked at each other, the realization hitting them like a physical blow, leaving them stunned, grief-stricken and frightened.

Later in the day, Quentin stopped by to see Preston. The weather had improved, although a sharp wind had picked up, creating a vexatious atmosphere. As he walked up the pathway to the imposing mansion, the gate rattled in the wind, adding to his unease. The cold air bit at his cheeks, and he pulled his coat tighter around him. He rang the bell and anxiously waited for the door to open, eager to escape the blustery conditions. The wind howled through the trees, and he could hear the distant sound of a branch snapping. His heart pounded as he strained to hear footsteps approaching from inside. After what felt like an eternity, the heavy door creaked open, revealing a shadowy figure in the dim light.

Martha answered the door and greeted him solemnly. Quentin realized her sister's death was still affecting her. She took his jacket and cap, her hands trembling slightly, and then directed him to the living room. Preston was there, engrossed in the Sunday edition of *The Times Union.* Augusta and Judge Archie appeared distracted, their thoughts filled with grief. Augusta had *The Saturday Evening Post* open on her lap, but her eyes were unfocused, staring blankly at the pages. Judge Archie was flipping through the latest issue of *Popular Science*, more to occupy his mind than to read. The radio played softly in the background, a symphonic melody that added to the somber and reflective atmosphere.

Augusta and Judge Archie greeted Quentin, but their minds were elsewhere. They had returned from the morning church service, a solemn affair that did little to lift their spirits. Lunch had been served, but neither felt up to eating. Augusta's plate remained untouched, and Judge Archie had merely picked at his food. Preston looked up from his newspaper, greeted Quentin with a nod, and placed the newspaper on the coffee table.

Quentin sat on the Victorian sofa, but Preston noticed he seemed ill at ease. Perhaps it was the presence of his grandparents, making it difficult for him to discuss what was on his mind.

Just then, Judge Archie turned to his grandson. "Preston, would you retrieve my copy of *Blackstone's Commentaries* from the library on the second floor?"

Preston seized the opportunity. "Of course, Grandfather," he replied, standing up. He glanced at Quentin, giving him a subtle nod to follow. This was the perfect excuse to speak with Quentin privately.

"You can look at some of my books, if you wish," the judge said to Quentin.

Quentin thanked him and then joined Preston in the hallway, following him up the stairs to the second floor. The library was indeed a beautiful room, with bookcases built into the walls, filled with an impressive collection of books. A mahogany desk stood in the corner, and two comfortable armchairs were positioned in front of the tall windows, with reading lamps casting a warm glow beside them. Preston ushered his friend to sit in one of the armchairs while he took the other. He looked at Quentin expectantly, urging him to share what was on his mind.

Quentin cleared his throat and then spoke rather seriously. His voice held conviction as though he wanted to arrive at a conclusion to the unanswered questions. "Like I told you, I remember something from the luncheon," He kept his voice low. "A conversation between that woman who was a night nurse and Mr. Armstrong. Something about abortions and gangsters."

"Maybe that's why she spoke to Mr. Armstrong," Preston mused. "Sometimes I wonder if he isn't a gangster himself. Certainly seems sly enough to belong to that social group."

"I couldn't hear everything she told him, but I think she may have recognized someone or knew information tied to someone."

"Someone at the luncheon?" Preston gasped, his eyes widening in shock.

Quentin's face showed signs of anguish. "I'm curious to find out just what she told him." He hesitated. "Of course, I'm not on close terms with him."

"I didn't understand why she mentioned them at all," Preston said his confusion evident.

"Possibly someone or something triggered her memory," Quentin said thoughtfully.

"But if it was in 1885, that's forty years ago," Preston commented. "Could it really have anything to do with Mr. Armstrong? Isn't he around fifty? He would have been ten years old!"

"Maybe gangsters started young back then," Quentin reflected, though he realized how unlikely it sounded. "Honestly, I don't know what to think."

"You seem to have certain suspicions about Mr. Armstrong," Preston observed.

"Just what I've seen in the office. That's why I don't trust him. He's sneaky and devious. He'd blackmail someone in a heartbeat. After all, he was driving the car that almost hit your grandfather, you know."

They were silent a few moments before Quentin spoke again, his voice even more agitated.

"I wonder if your grandfather knows more than he tells. Maybe he found information about somebody or something. Even approached the person or persons involved, too."

"You mean blackmail?" Preston asked, more horrified at the thought.

"He's old enough to remember things from 1885. So is your grandmother. Sometimes people don't speak about issues such as abortions and gangsters because they are so unpleasant."

Preston's mind raced. "I know Grandfather would spend a lot of time researching at city hall and the hall of records for certain cases."

"A sort of quiet blackmail," Quentin said logically. "The person or persons may know but realize the judge isn't saying anything, at least not yet."

They lapsed into silence again for several moments. Then Preston got up fitfully, strode over to a bookcase, and located the law book his grandfather wanted. He returned to the chair but continued sitting in silence, his agitation evident.

"Mr. Sheppard should be able to help, Pres," Quentin told him. "Your grandfather is paying him to investigate the death of Mr. Lewis. Now there are two murders with poison. He should solve this to your satisfaction."

"Mrs. Crabtree may have information," Preston said. His thoughts returned to the luncheon and the myriad of faces; most pleasant, some shaken, others defiant. But exactly what had occurred that caused a possible uncertainty amongst the guests? Had someone felt threatened? If that were the case, by what or whom?

Preston and Quentin were silent for a few more minutes. Then the sound of hurried footsteps echoed up the stairs. Both men looked up to see Martha standing in the doorway. She looked first at her son and then at Quentin, her face pale and her eyes wide with fear.

"Preston, you need to come quickly," she said gravely, her voice trembling. "There's been another incident."

An uneasy silence prevailed as the family gathered. Judge Archie sat in his usual chair, his stern expression betraying a hint of concern. Augusta stood by the window, her back to the room, gripping her hands tightly. Martha hovered near the doorway anxiously, her face still pale.

Preston and Quentin entered, their expressions a mix of confusion and apprehension. Augusta turned to face them, her eyes filled with worry.

"Mrs. Crabtree just called," Augusta began, her voice trembling. "Her maid, Mrs. Davis, was found dead this morning."

Judge Archie's brow furrowed deeper, but he remained silent, letting Augusta continue.

"Dead? How?" Preston asked, his voice strained with the weight of the news.

Augusta shook her head, struggling to find the words. "She didn't say much, only that it looked… unnatural." Her voice wavered, eyes wide with fear.

"Another strange death?" Preston said, tension in his voice, his eyes darting between his grandmother and the judge. "How many more people will die before we learn the truth?"

An unsettling hush, filled with unspoken tension and remorse, fell over the room, inexorably. Martha mentioned her father should rest. Judge Archie agreed and got up from his armchair. Suddenly and without warning he gave a short, horrid gasp, clutching his chest. He collapsed heavily onto the floor, his face contorted in pain, struggling to breathe. The sound of his labored breaths filled the room, echoing the shock and fear of those present.

"Call Dr. Stephens, quickly!" Augusta cried her voice breaking.

Martha dashed out into the hallway and picked up the telephone. The operator came on the line immediately. "Operator, I need Dr. Stephens right away. It's an emergency."

"Connecting you now, ma'am. Please hold," the operator replied.

Preston knelt beside his grandfather, his hands shaking as he tried to comfort him. "Stay with us, Grandfather," he whispered, his voice choked with emotion. "Help is on the way."

Judge Archie's breathing was labored, his face pale and clammy. He reached out, gripping Preston's hand with surprising strength. "I believe I know," he managed to say. "From the past…"

"Try not to talk now, Grandfather," Preston assured him. "Just try to stay calm. Dr. Stephens will be here soon."

Martha's voice echoed from the hallway. "Dr. Stephens, it's an emergency. Judge Archie… he's collapsed and is in severe pain. Please come right away."

Within minutes, Dr. Stephens arrived, his medical bag in hand. He hurried to Judge Archie's side, checking his pulse and giving instructions to the family. "We need to get him to his bed. Carefully now."

Preston and Quentin helped lift Judge Archie, guiding him to his bedroom and laying him gently on the bed. Dr. Stephens worked swiftly, monitoring his condition.

"Will he be alright?" Martha said her voice barely above a whisper.

Dr. Stephens looked up, serious but calm. "He's stable for now, but we need to keep a close watch on him. The next few hours are critical." He placed his stethoscope on the judge's chest, listening intently. "His heartbeat is steady, but we must remain vigilant."

Preston stood by his grandfather's bedside, full of fear and uncertainty. The faint ticking of the grandfather clock in the hallway seemed to echo his distressed thoughts. He observed Quentin next to him. His jaw was clenched as he stared at the judge in deep sorrow. He looked up at his mother, her eyes red-rimmed and filled with worry. His grandmother stood stiffly, her hands clasped tightly, a mask of stoic determination on her face.

Preston's heart pounded as he returned his gaze to his grandfather, lying so still. Outside, the wind was harsh, rattling the windows, a distinct chill in the air. The sense of impending turmoil hung oppressively in the room, and he could not shake the feeling that they were on the brink of descending into further chaos.

CHAPTER SEVENTEEN

On Monday morning, the storm that plagued the area moved out and a rather weak but persistent sun broke through the clouds. Glancing skyward, pedestrians were hopeful the bright skies would last and bring much needed sunshine.

Downtown Albany was busy as always, the morning rush hour in full swing. Stepping off a trolley on the corner of State Street and South Pearl Street along with a sizeable crowd, Sloan walked up State until he reached the Albany Savings Bank Building. As he anticipated, the lobby was rather congested and the elevators were just as full, but the morning operator, known to Sloan, managed to include him before he closed the gates and the car shot upward.

He glanced around the elevator car, noting the mix of businessmen, clerks, and women in fashionable cloche hats. The operator, a young man with a crisp uniform and a friendly smile, expertly maneuvered the controls. The elevator ascended smoothly, the soft hum of the machinery a constant backdrop to the murmur of conversations.

As the car reached Sloan's floor, the operator pulled the lever to a stop and opened the gates. Sloan, grateful to exit the rather claustrophobic lift, stepped out into a corridor lined with polished wood paneling and brass fixtures. He took a moment to adjust his hat and straighten his tie before heading towards his office.

He inserted the key into the heavy oak door and had not even reached his desk before the candlestick telephone rang sharply. Depositing his coat and hat on a nearby chair, he hastily came around the back of his desk and picked up the handset to still the insistent clamor. He heard the firm, slightly strained voice of Inspector Harris on the other line.

"Mr. Sheppard, Inspector Harris from Albany Police. We have another death, which may tie in with Mr. Lewis and Mrs. Caves."

Sloan turned the banker's lamp on and sat down on the swivel chair slowly, trying to comprehend what he just heard. He asked the inspector for more details.

"Seems Mrs. Mary Crabtree's maid, a Mrs. Justine Davis, was out yesterday morning to pick up items at the market on Madison Avenue. She was crushed by an approaching trolley."

Sloan waited for more details, as he did not see how this death related to the other two. He heard the inspector take a deep breath before continuing.

"There are two things that make me think this was not an accident. First, there was a witness, a Miss Laura Johnson, a young woman on her way to her visit her elderly aunt, claims she saw someone push Mrs. Davis in front of the trolley. Second, the coat Mrs. Davis wore belonged to Mrs. Crabtree."

Sloan nearly dropped the handset. His knuckles whitened as he gripped it tighter, the weight of the inspector's words sinking in. He could hear the distant murmur of voices and the clatter of typewriters from inside the police station, a dark contrast to the storm brewing in his mind. He hung onto the handset, knowing what the inspector implied. He listened as Inspector Harris continued talking.

"Mrs. Davis was a widow who lived alone. She was a maid for Mrs. Crabtree. When we spoke to the Crabtrees yesterday, Mrs. Crabtree mentioned she loaned her coat to Mrs. Davis as it was rainy and chilly out."

"Perhaps Mrs. Crabtree was the intended victim," Sloan added thoughtfully.

Inspector Harris agreed. "Mrs. Crabtree told us she has two coats for the chilly weather. She wore her burgundy coat at the Stafford's luncheon and to the services for Mrs. Caves."

"Which means everyone saw her with it," Sloan said, his grip on the handset still tightening. His tone held a mixture of regret and anger. "Someone wants to silence Mrs. Crabtree."

"She also mentioned a member of the League of Women Voters, a friend of hers, casually mentioned her burgundy coat at the luncheon," Inspector Harris continued.

"That would draw attention to it," Sloan added. "Burgundy is a color that would stand out."

The inspector agreed. "We spoke with Miss Johnson. She is adamant she observed someone push Mrs. Davis in front of the trolley. She couldn't make out who it was but she insists it couldn't have been an accident. She came into the station last night and signed a statement." He paused. "She seems reliable and intelligent. I believe what she says."

Sloan was silent for a few moments, contemplating the serious situation. He realized that Mrs. Crabtree might be in imminent danger and mentioned this to the inspector.

"We'll send an officer to see her today," the inspector said. "Have you spoken with her?"

Sloan related the conversation he had with Mrs. Philomena Sampson and Mrs. Crabtree at Mrs. Sampson's house on Friday in the refined neighborhood of Hamilton Street, known for its elegant brownstones. He mentioned they planned to attend the wake that evening for Mrs. Caves at St. Mary's Church. He added he had established a respectful rapport with both women and was welcomed to Mrs. Sampson's house again and to Mrs. Crabtree's home on Willett Street for afternoon tea.

"Perhaps another talk with Mrs. Crabtree should be necessary," the inspector suggested. "You've established a rapport with her. Some elderly residents are reluctant to speak to law enforcement."

Sloan knew that fact well, which is why the tea at Mrs. Sampson's house and the meeting she arranged with Mrs. Crabtree was extremely beneficial. He mentioned he had no further leads on the death of Mr. Lewis but was continuing his investigation along with the death of Mrs. Caves.

"A definite connection," the inspector said. "But at the moment, that link has eluded us."

"Maybe not for long," Sloan told him determinedly. He thanked him for the call, replaced the handset, and then moved the candlestick telephone to the other side of his mahogany desk. The steady glow from the green shaded banker's lamp illuminated the room.

Sloan sat brooding rather angrily, his jaw tightening. His mind turned over numerous possibilities, each more troubling than the last. The clock on the wall ticked loudly, a reminder that time was slipping away. He would contact Mrs. Crabtree and arrange to see her at once.

Sloan reached for the Albany city directory on a bookcase behind his desk. A search for the telephone number yielded several people with the same last name, but he remembered she lived on Willett Street. He glanced at the clock on the wall and noticed it was still early, almost nine thirty, so with luck he would find her home. He grabbed the telephone, picked up the handset and waited for the operator to come on the line.

"Please connect me to Mrs. Mary Crabtree on Willett Street. Number AL-5728."

It rang several times, and he contemplated hanging up when finally it was answered. From her voice, Sloan could tell Mrs. Crabtree was preoccupied and upset. She seemed glad to hear from him, although her voice was strained as though she had been crying.

"Good morning, Mr. Sheppard. My husband and I were just visited by two policemen. They asked us about Mrs. Davis and what happened yesterday morning. I assume you're calling about the same incident?"

Sloan knew he was speaking to an intelligent and insightful woman, who, as a night nurse, had been used to reckoning with the harsher realities of life.

"Yes, Mrs. Crabtree, I would appreciate some of your time today if that's fine with you. My afternoon is open, and I can stop by after lunch." He mentioned he found her address and number in the city directory.

Mrs. Crabtree told Sloan she and her husband planned to arrange Mrs. Davis's wake and funeral, then shop on North Pearl Street, and have lunch at Keeler's. She invited him for tea and mentioned she would look forward to seeing him again later in the afternoon.

Somewhat reluctantly, Sloan ended the call and then stared out the window overlooking State Street, deep in contemplative thoughts. He had to wait almost the entire day to speak to her but decided to revise his notes on the case for more clarity. The morning wore on with telephone calls, letters, invoices sent, and two appointments from new clients.

With his work caught up and no new clients scheduled, he decided to walk to Willett Street. Once outside, he found the brisk air invigorating. The sounds of the city enveloped him—trolleys clattering, the occasional honk of an automobile, and the distant hum of conversations. He passed the opulent State Capitol building, its grand architecture rather indifferent to the more modest surroundings. The fresh air and exercise helped clear his mind, and he mentally prepared himself for the conversation with Mrs. Crabtree. He knew that every detail she provided could be crucial to solving the case.

Approaching the intersection with Lark Street and then seeing the broad expanse of Washington Park in front of him, he crossed State Street and turned left onto Willett Street. He found the number he wanted. Before climbing the stone steps, he stood back and admired the beauty of the house; a handsome brownstone, well maintained and opulent with its high windows, brick façade and ornate outdoor lighting. He assumed the Crabtrees had a daytime maid at most, as he knew Willett Street was an address of much prestige. He would inquire if Mrs. Davis had been their part time helper and cook. Wealthy families often employed several servants and he further assumed the Crabtrees would delve in that area.

He climbed the steps and rang the bell. Within a few seconds, a young girl, perhaps no more than twenty, who looked as though she had been crying, answered the door. She welcomed Sloan inside, taking his fedora hat and coat and then showing him into the living room, where Mrs. Crabtree was sitting in an armchair, knitting. She looked up at Sloan.

"Good afternoon, Mr. Sheppard," Mrs. Crabtree greeted him warmly. "Please, have a seat. Carol will bring us some tea shortly."

Sloan assumed Carol was the young woman who answered the door. As he settled into the armchair opposite Mrs. Crabtree, he could not help but feel a sense that he was close to uncovering the information he needed. If only the woman before him could remember pertinent details from so long ago. Mrs. Crabtree continued knitting, her needles clicking rhythmically.

"I don't really know what more to tell you, Mr. Sheppard," she began. "My husband and I are still quite upset. Our daytime maid is also very disturbed. Mrs. Davis died yesterday, wearing my burgundy coat. My husband and I believe she was mistaken for me and that someone intentionally pushed her."

The elderly woman before him put down her knitting and looked out the window, her mind going back to many years ago. Sloan was quiet, as it seemed as though she was thinking of events from her years as a night nurse. He waited for her to speak.

"I remember she was a troubled girl back in '85," Mrs. Crabtree said suddenly, almost to herself. She paused, reflectively. "Had an abortion, you know, and then that dreadful business with her boyfriend, the gangster. There was talk she killed him." She paused, a sour expression on her face. "So disgraceful, the young people, even back then. She could have been in her teens, no older."

Sloan's interest piqued. He leaned forward slightly, his detective instincts kicking in. "What happened to her?"

Mrs. Crabtree looked up, her eyes meeting Sloan's with a knowing look. "Well, when I was at Mrs. Stafford's luncheon, I was taken by surprise. I have a good memory, even if I am getting on in years. Forty years is a long time and I suppose people change, but I don't forget too many things." She paused. "I didn't know Judge Archie at that time or his wife, but I did know he was quite unscrupulous, even back then. He may know more than I do."

"I intend to speak to the judge again," Sloan told her, as he accepted a cup of tea from the maid who entered carrying a tray. His anticipation was almost unbearable as he realized Mrs. Crabtree was on the point of revealing important facts. To hide his latent impatience, he sipped the tea, an excellent English brand and listened to her as she continued speaking.

"I'm afraid my details may not be too accurate. But as a night nurse, I got used to the whims of patients and their burdens, their hardships and the depravations they endured." She paused. "I was not sure at first, of course. But I believe I remember who the young girl was who had the abortion then."

Sloan was almost on the edge of the chair. He finished the tea and then asked Mrs. Crabtree if he could smoke, to which she nodded, still deep in thought. She motioned to an ashtray on the end table next to him. He did not want to rush her as he realized she was replaying memories from the past, details coming back to her, seemingly quite vividly.

Then without hesitation she told him what she remembered, what he needed to know. Sloan's eyes widened as the connections became clearer. The lush living room seemed to enclose him as the meaning of her words settled. He took a deep drag from his cigarette, the tendrils of smoke weaving through the room like the mysteries he was unraveling.

At the mansion on the corner of State Street and South Swan, breakfast was in progress. At around eight o'clock, Preston, his mother, and grandmother sat down at the kitchen table, eating oatmeal, which

Augusta had prepared. Their appetites were slowly returning, and Preston admitted he was famished. He devoured two helpings of oatmeal, a slice of toast, and two cups of coffee brewed in the percolator.

Augusta cleared her throat and addressed her daughter and grandson. "I believe the best we can do is hire a nurse. I have already contacted the hospital and spoken with the private duty-nursing supervisor. She promised she would see who was available."

"That's an excellent idea, Mother," Martha told her.

"First, I need to hear back from the nursing supervisor. She will recommend someone, and we'll take it from there. I fear your father may not be strong enough even to get out of bed."

"Is Dr. Stephens returning today?" Preston asked, finishing his coffee.

Augusta nodded. "This morning. He wishes to check his vital signs." She paused, her expression somber. "I feel terrible for Mrs. Crabtree. Her maid was killed yesterday morning while going to the market on Madison Avenue. She fell in front of a streetcar."

"The streetcars in this city are rather reckless at times," Martha said.

"Mrs. Crabtree told me her maid was wearing her burgundy coat," Augusta mentioned.

"I remember that coat," Preston said. "I thought it was a really nice color."

Martha agreed. "She wore it when she came to the luncheon and at the services for Joan. I admired the color, too. It was stunning." A cold realization hit her, almost as though a force struck her between the shoulder blades. She looked at her mother and then her son, whose expressions mirrored her own.

At that moment, the doorbell rang, echoing rather loudly throughout the old house. Augusta heard the grandfather clock strike the half an hour, its chime resonating through the halls. Preston and Martha mentioned they needed to leave for work. They kissed Augusta goodbye, and then Preston went to the hallway to see who was at the door. Upon opening it, he was surprised to see Sloan standing before him.

"Mr. Sheppard, please come in," he said, stepping back to allow Sloan to enter.

"Hello, Preston," Sloan said, handing him his fedora hat and overcoat.

He noticed Preston was about to leave as he put on his jacket and cap. Martha entered at that moment, greeting Sloan perfunctorily and asked if he wanted something. She also went for her fur coat and cloche hat.

Sloan mentioned he wished to speak to Judge Archie. He apologized for not calling but it was imperative he speak with the judge. Preston and Martha look at each other, realizing Sloan was unaware of the judge's recent condition.

"Mr. Sheppard, you should know my grandfather had a slight heart attack yesterday morning after hearing about Mrs. Crabtree's maid," Preston told him. "He didn't take it well and got really upset. He's been in bed and he's very weak."

Augusta joined them in the hallway. "Oh, good morning, Mr. Sheppard. I hear my grandson told you about my husband. He's in bed resting and I'm not sure if he's up to visitors."

"I apologize, Mrs. Stafford," Sloan told her. "If it isn't a good moment to speak with the judge, I can return later." The urgency in his voice made them realize the situation was precarious.

"I'm just on my way to the office," Martha said as she shrugged into her coat.

"I'm leaving, too," Preston said.

Sloan wished them a good day and then with the heavy door closed behind them, he turned his attention to Augusta. She looked at him anxiously, not sure what to expect.

"I'll check on him again," she said, her voice tinged with concern. "He was sitting up in bed and sipping some coffee."

She disappeared down the hallway and to the passageway behind the kitchen, where their bedroom was located. Within a few moments, she returned, telling Sloan he could see her husband.

Sloan followed her down the hallway and along the passageway and entered the bedroom. He saw Judge Archie, sitting up in bed, a cup of morning coffee on his bedside table. He smiled wanly at Sloan and motioned for him to pull up a chair so they could talk. He thanked his wife, which she took as a dismissal and then turned his attention to Sloan.

He looked at him carefully, noting his fine, distinctive features. "Handsome young guy like you, why are you chasing criminals and bootleggers? You should be a lawyer or a statesman."

Sloan thanked the judge for his astuteness. "I recently spoke with Mrs. Mary Crabtree. She told me some interesting things about events in 1885."

The old man winced, as though in pain. Sloan paused, not sure whether to continue. But the judge turned his face toward him, although he appeared in some discomfort.

"Mrs. Crabtree told me you might remember more details," Sloan mentioned.

To his surprise, Judge Archie merely pointed with an arthritic finger to his mahogany desk in the corner. He told Sloan to open the bottom drawer and to extract a notebook. Sloan did exactly what he told him and returned with a rather old and well-worn leather notebook, with several loose pages. He handed it to the judge but the old man shook his head.

"Look through it," he whispered. "You may find what you what."

Sloan flipped open the worn leather notebook, its pages filled with surprisingly neat, legible script. In reading some of the notes, he could tell it was written when Judge Archie was a lawyer, having graduated from Albany Law School in 1869. He did not see anything of interest, but fortunately, most of the pages were dated. He continued reading while the judge spoke, weakly.

"I used to keep that notebook in my desk at the office," he told Sloan "Someone may have gotten hold of it. I could tell someone had ruffled through it, because it wasn't returned to the drawer where I kept it."

Sloan flipped through the pages thoughtfully, absorbing details about life in Albany during the 1860s and 1870s, the judge's marriage to Miss Augusta Miller, and the birth of their two daughters. As he reached the last few pages, he noticed notes from recent years, 1923 and 1924. Intrigued, he turned back to earlier pages and continued reading, his interest piqued by the entries dated 1885. He observed that several pages were filled with hastily written notations, as if the judge had been eager to record the information before it slipped from his memory.

"Have you found anything?" he asked Sloan.

Sloan continued reading notes from 1885. He saw several pages dated March 1885. He read how Mrs. Sampson's sister died during childbirth, the woman whose husband he had sent away to prison and who later died while still incarcerated. But then something else caught his eye.

He read about the illegal abortion at the hospital, the same night of Mrs. Sampson's sister's death. He noticed the name of a local gangster, Mr. Philip Mavity, who was later murdered. He scanned details about the judge's suspicions as to who murdered Mr. Mavity—and the possible identity of the woman who had the illegal abortion in the emergency ward at the hospital. This also concurred with the information supplied to him by Mrs. Crabtree. He sighed somewhat irritably, his jaw tightening, as he realized how deep and tangled this case actually was.

"Why didn't you voice your suspicions earlier?" Sloan asked him.

Judge Archie spoke weakly. "I wasn't sure, just what I heard and read in the newspapers. She must've run around with gangsters. She seemed reliable but then they all do, until you get to see their true side."

"But you have no proof that she killed Philip Mavity?"

"I believe she did kill him."

"How did you find this out? And why would you make a note of it?"

Judge Archie sighed softly. "I always wrote down information back then. I still do, but not as often. As a lawyer, I kept in touch with policemen who became informers and a few became friends. Most have passed away, sadly." He paused, his eyes reflecting a distant sorrow. "Mr. Lewis and I considered contacting the police about the illegal abortion at that time, but that would've involved the doctor, nurses, and midwives who were there, assisting the procedure. Illegal abortions were common then and, sadly, still are. We decided to let it go."

Sloan looked down at the notebook again and noted where the judge had written about the bloody knife. He asked him why the police did not make an arrest then.

Judge Archie let out a long, weary breath. "There was no proof who murdered Mr. Mavity," he said, his voice laden with old secrets. "I remember the police found the kitchen knife, but there were no fingerprints. Without evidence, it was impossible for a conviction." He paused. "I hoped at the luncheon someone might have noticed or said something."

"It worked in your favor," Sloan told him. "Mrs. Crabtree remembered."

The judge nodded, then looked away. Sloan realized it had taken a lot of his energy to speak to him just now and he knew when to conclude it.

Sloan thanked the judge immensely for help. "May I keep this notebook and show it to the police, Judge? I will return it to you, of course."

Judge Archie nodded. "Be careful, Mr. Sheppard."

"Your wife told me a nurse may be here to help you," he told him.

Judge Archie scowled. "Waste of time." He looked at Sloan carefully as though he would never see him again. "Such a handsome man. I wish I was as debonair."

Sloan smiled again and then with the old leather notebook in hand, he left the room to meet Augusta in the kitchen, where she was preparing lunch with Gertrude. She turned when she heard someone enter. The kitchen was warm and filled with the smell of freshly baked bread. Augusta and Gertrude moved with practiced ease, their faces etched with concern. Outside, the spring breezes rustled the tree branches pleasingly, a glaring disparity to the tension inside.

"Thank you, Mrs. Stafford, for letting me speak to the judge," Sloan told her.

Augusta showed him to the door, anxiety evident in her expression. Her hands trembled slightly as she handed Sloan his coat and fedora hat.

"Thank you, Mr. Sheppard for coming," she said, her voice barely above a whisper.

Sloan felt a mixture of determination and trepidation as he stepped out of the judge's house. The leather notebook felt heavier with each step, as if it meant carrying the truth itself—and all the danger that came with it. He could not shake off the judge's ominous words. "Be careful, Mr. Sheppard," as though they were a warning of the perils ahead. He waved goodbye to Augusta and walked down the stone steps, the crucial evidence he needed securely in his hands.

Sloan arrived back at his office, the old notebook clutched tightly. He avoided taking the trolley, fearing the loose pages of the delicate notebook might come apart by the insistent jarring. The weight of its contents seemed to grow heavier with each step. Upon opening his office, he placed it gently on his desk, the worn leather cover a marked difference to the polished wood beneath it.

It had been a long morning, the revelations now apparent. He put his feet up on the desk, reached for the telephone, intending to call Inspector Harris and share the judge's revelations. As he was about to lift the handset and speak to the operator, it rang. He hesitated a moment before answering, not wanting to waste crucial moments when so much was at stake. With a practiced motion, he grabbed his pack of Lucky Strikes and lit a cigarette, keeping it between his lips as he picked up the handset.

"Sheppard here," he said, exhaling a fine trail of smoke.

"Mr. Sheppard, this is Nurse Collins from St. Timothy's Hospital," a firm female voice said on the other end. "We've found more records from 1885. They include the names of the people involved with the abortion from March of that year." She paused. "I believe you inquired about this previously." Her tone was strictly business and matter of fact.

Sloan took his feet off the desk and leaned forward, keeping the cigarette to his lips. To his astonishment, she provided several interesting facts. He made notes as she continued talking, his grip tightening on the handset. He thanked Nurse Collins and replaced the handset, his mind racing with the implications. Judge Archie and Mrs. Crabtree corroborated what he just heard. The pieces of the puzzle were starting to come together, but the picture they formed was more disturbing than he anticipated. The notebook sat before him, heavy as a coffin. Despite the unsettling revelations, Sloan's resolve hardened, ready to face whatever came next.

CHAPTER EIGHTEEN

Toward lunchtime, Preston made his way to the law firm to see Quentin and inform the rest of the staff about his grandfather's prognosis. Earlier, Quentin had called him at the cruise line office, asking him to meet for lunch and to inquiry about his grandfather. Preston told his friend that his grandfather was still weak and needed rest.

Stepping off the elevator, Preston approached the distinguished metal plate next to the glass door that read *Lewis & Stafford, Attorneys at Law*. He opened the door and was immediately greeted pleasantly by Mrs. Castle, the firm's ever-efficient receptionist. Quentin and Doris looked up from their desks and greeted him warmly.

"Preston, dear," Mrs. Castle said kindly. "Please come in. Are you here to see Quentin?"

He nodded, then decided without hesitation to make his announcement. He told Mrs. Castle and Doris about his grandfather's heart attack yesterday morning and how the doctor insisted he stay in bed until he got stronger. He noticed the startled expressions on their faces. A sharp intake of breath from both women signaled their distress. Quentin mentioned he already knew as he was there when it occurred and even assisted in getting Judge Archie to bed, but he did not want to worry everyone with the news. He told them it was too disturbing and felt they should hear it from the family rather than him.

"Regardless, you should've told us this morning, Quentin," Doris said, rather irritably.

"He did what he thought was right," Mrs. Castle said, in Quentin's defense.

Lucille and Clayton entered at that moment, having overheard the conversation. Lucille was visibly upset, and Clayton shook his head, wondering what had happened to the judge to cause such a calamity. Clayton offered his sympathy and told Preston if there was anything they could do to help the judge, simply to call them right away. Doris and Mrs. Castle also reiterated their sentiment, extreme concern apparent in their voices.

Thurman entered the main office as well, having finished writing a deposition which he intended to hand to Mrs. Castle. He saw the grave expressions on their faces and asked what was wrong. Preston told him about his grandfather and how, at that moment, he was bedridden.

"Preston, I'm sorry to hear this," Thurman said, holding onto the papers.

The silence in the main office was overwhelming. The clock on the far wall clicked loudly in the still room, as though reminding them of the seriousness of the situation. Preston addressed Thurman, realizing he was deeply concerned.

"He needs bed rest," he told him, then turned to look at everyone. "We're in the process of obtaining a private duty nurse to look after him. We feel it'll be best for him."

Burgess opened the front doors and entered, carrying his briefcase. He removed his hat and coat with a moment's hesitation, hanging them in the closet. Upon entering the main office, he stopped as he realized everyone was there, including Preston. From their expressions, he could tell something was wrong.

"Preston, what brings you here today?" Burgess asked, rather afraid of the answer.

"I'm having lunch with Quentin," Preston told him. "But I wanted to let everyone know my grandfather suffered a heart attack yesterday morning and, on the doctor's recommendation, he needs to remain in bed." He paused. "There's something else I want to tell all of you. Mrs. Crabtree, who you met at the luncheon, experienced the death of her maid, Mrs. Davis. She was wearing Mrs. Crabtree's burgundy coat and was struck by a trolley."

"I remember that coat," Doris commented, recalling the luncheon.

"I do, too," Lucille said. "It was beautiful."

"How terrible for Mrs. Crabtree," Mrs. Castle said respectfully.

Silence ensued, as though the inhabitants of the room were too dumbstruck to articulate words at such devastation. Burgess started to say something, then changed his mind, his thoughts too cluttered. Preston observed how he appeared peaked and morose. Only Mrs. Castle was brave enough to speak.

"Please tell your grandparents I wish them well," she said.

Doris agreed. "There isn't much to hold down Judge Archie!"

That comment appeared to lighten the atmosphere a bit. Thurman excused himself and returned to his office, while Burgess found solace in his own office. Lucille and Clayton exchanged concerned glances but remained silent, clearly affected by the news. Quentin gathered his coat and cap and joined Preston in the outer hallway, on their way to the elevator.

"How do you think that went?" Preston asked him.

Quentin had a cigarette to his lips. "Hard to tell. Mrs. Castle and Mr. Armstrong were upset. So were the Sampsons. Doris always hides her feelings."

Preston agreed. "With the nurse's care, he should improve, but he's really weak right now."

The elevator arrived, the gates opened, and the young men stepped in. It was full of the lunchtime crowd. Preston could not help but notice the difference between the rather jovial faces and the turmoil of his thoughts.

Once outside on North Pearl Street, despite the sun, a brisk wind stirred up. The sunlight cast shadows on the buildings, highlighting the intricate details of brickwork and the occasional glint of glass. They walked in relative silence, brushing past the crowds. Preston pushed his cap lower on his head and also reached for his cigarettes from his jacket pocket, cupping his hands to light the match. He took a slow drag from the cigarette, but even the familiar burn did little to ease his mind. The sharp scent of tobacco mingled with the crisp air, creating a momentary distraction from his swirling thoughts.

His mind drifted to Mrs. Crabtree's burgundy coat—the same coat Mrs. Davis wore when she was killed by the trolley. The memory added to his growing suspicion. He could not rid himself of the feeling that something more ominous was looming, a sense of unease that tormented him.

Augusta walked steadily toward St. Mary's Church. It was past one o'clock, and the judge had eaten half a sandwich and drank some coffee. His appetite was slowly returning. She told Gertrude and her husband she was going to church and would return shortly.

Despite the chill, she chose to walk. She donned her cherished fur coat and low-heeled lace-up boots. Clutching her pocketbook and an umbrella as the dark clouds threatened rain and with her cloche hat perched firmly on her head, she crossed State Street and passed through West Capitol Park. The opulent neoclassical State Capitol building loomed ahead, its grand columns standing tall against the sky. She continued down Washington Avenue, crossing at Albany City Hall with its stately façade, until she walked down Pine Street and reached her beloved church. Her steps were steady and deliberate, each one a testament to her resilience and determination.

Upon entering, Augusta took off her cloche hat and replaced it with a white shawl. She blessed herself with holy water from the marble font, then walked solemnly down the aisle. The stained glass windows cast colorful patterns on the floor as she genuflected before a pew and then sat immediately, praying fervently for her husband and the soul of her beloved daughter. Tears sprang to her eyes, as she struggled to understand the turmoil she and her family had been through. She got up and genuflected again, then approached the candles. Her hands trembled slightly as she lit one, depositing a nickel in the slot for offerings. She looked up at the beautiful statue of the Blessed Mother, the flickering candlelight casting gentle shadows on its serene face. Praying again, more deeply, she pleaded for the recovery of her husband and for peace for her youngest daughter, who had died much too soon.

She turned and realized there were other parishioners, although midday Mass had already concluded. She spotted a few people she knew and greeted them briefly with a nod and a gentle smile, not wishing to endure long conversations. The scent of the candles lingered as she admired the Stations of the Cross, pausing before each, praying as she made her way to the end.

She took a church bulletin and folded it, putting it in her pocketbook. Upon exiting, she almost collided with a short, stout woman who seemed to come out of nowhere. She recognized Mrs. Rose Castle, apparently just entering.

"Oh, Mrs. Stafford, I'm so sorry," Mrs. Castle exclaimed, her round face flushed. "I've been so overwhelmed by all that has happened recently. I want to offer some prayers."

Augusta smiled wearily, her eyes reflecting a deep-seated fatigue. "That's very kind of you, Mrs. Castle."

"I just missed the rain," Mrs. Castle remarked, attempting a lighthearted tone.

Augusta nodded politely, her mind elsewhere, as Mrs. Castle made desultory comments about the office, the workload increasing, and the influx of new clients.

A light drizzle continued in earnest, and with the brisk winds, it created a harsh afternoon feel. The cold droplets stung Augusta's cheeks, matching the unease she felt inside. She exchanged her shawl for her cloche hat, pulling it firmly onto her head to shield herself from the rain. She folded the shawl carefully and tucked it away in her pocketbook.

"Do you always wear a shawl on your head in church?" Mrs. Castle asked, her tone curious.

Augusta was rather taken aback. Of course, she always wore a shawl in church. It was customary for women to wear head coverings. Certainly as a practicing Catholic, Mrs. Castle would know that. She must have noticed it at Joan's funeral. But then Augusta did not remember ever seeing her attend Mass. She looked at her bare head and spotted the stylish cloche hat in her right hand. Such hats were not encouraged in church.

Mrs. Castle commented on the prayer books she noticed in the doorway. "I'm afraid I don't understand much Latin. Is everything in Latin?"

Augusta maintained a sense of decorum, although it was difficult. "Yes, the prayer books and the Mass are in Latin." Privately, she thought Mrs. Castle would know that too, if she attended services. And again, Augusta was reminded of Joan's funeral, where the organist evocatively rendered the famous *Dies Irae,* a solemn hymn reflecting on discernment and the afterlife.

The silence between them grew heavy, filled with unspoken judgments and the weight of tradition. Augusta tightened her grip on her umbrella, her lips pressing into a thin line. Mrs. Castle, seemingly oblivious, adjusted her hat with a satisfied smile, totally unaware of the silent rebuke.

A few more moments of idle talk ensued, rather awkwardly, while the light rain continued, the wind increasing. Augusta mentioned she needed to return home.

"It was nice seeing you, Mrs. Stafford," Mrs. Castle said pleasantly, as she continued standing in the doorway to the beautiful church. "Please give Judge Archie my best regards."

"Thank you, Mrs. Castle," Augusta said warmly. "Good day to you, dear."

Opening her umbrella to shield herself from the raindrops, she walked back up Pine Street, Albany City Hall to her left and the Court of Appeals to her right. While crossing to Washington Avenue, Augusta could not help but wonder if Mrs. Castle was at church to pray or for any other religious reason. The thought lingered, unsettling her as she continued her journey home.

Martha stepped out of the State Education Department building at five o'clock, the heavy wooden doors closing behind her with a soft thud. The late afternoon air was cool, and the sky was beginning to transition from the bright light of day to the soft hues of dusk. After crossing at the light and instead of heading straight home, she found herself drawn to a nearby bench. She sat down, rather tiredly, her mind swirling with the recent devastating events, including the death of her younger sister. Memories of her sister lingered, unsettling her.

The sounds of the city began to fade into the background. The distant hum of traffic, the clanging of the persistent trolleys going up and down Washington Avenue and State Street, the occasional chirp of a bird, and the rustling of leaves in the breeze created a soothing symphony. Martha pulled her fur coat tighter around her, seeking comfort in its warmth.

Lost in her thoughts, she almost did not notice a figure walking up Washington Avenue, carrying a briefcase, obviously coming from his place of work. She recognized Burgess Smith, his tall frame unmistakable even from a distance. He walked with purpose, his eyes focused straight ahead. He shifted his gaze in her direction and smiled in recognition. He stopped and made brief conversation, much to her surprise.

"Hello, Mrs. Hughes. Nice to see you again. Are you off from work now?"

Martha nodded, holding onto her cloche hat as a gust of wind swooped down. Burgess sat next to her on the bench, not asking if she minded company. Oddly, she found his presence rather reassuring, even welcomed. Looking at him sideways, she thought him a handsome man in his own style, tall, distinguished, certainly professional, in his mid-forties to her fifty. But she remembered her father mentioned Mr. Smith's devious ways in the field of law. Of course, she knew her father had his own deviousness and temperament. She assumed

Burgess Smith invested in the stock market like nearly everyone else. And enjoyed his share of liquor, too.

She knew Joan had been interested in him although her father would not have approved. She listened while he talked about work at the office, his new clients, his apartment on Hudson Avenue and his vacation plans for the summer. He realized he was talking practically nonstop.

"I guess once I get talking, I can't stop," he joked. "That's just the lawyer in me."

Martha lips curved weakly. "I'm sorry I'm not good company. I still have a lot on my mind. My sister's death, the death of Mr. Lewis, the death of Mrs. Crabtree's maid and now my father's heart attack. It's really been too much for us."

Burgess offered apologies. "How is the judge?"

Martha shrugged, indifferently. "He's holding his own, for now. We're getting a nurse for him. It's been an awful strain, especially for my mother. The nurse will help alleviate some of the pressure. My father can be rather demanding, as I'm sure you already know."

Burgess smiled slightly, his fedora hat sliding a half inch down his forehead. "How are you holding up? And Preston?"

Martha turned to look at him. She was surprised he would show concern about herself and her son unless he was just being polite. But something told her he was sincere, in contrast to some of the others in the law office.

"I'm holding my own, too," she managed to tell him. "Preston is patient and persevering. We support each other. And my mother is also a tower of strength."

Burgess continued sitting next to her on the bench, overlooking Washington Avenue in front of the State Education Building, with its tall and opulent white pillars. Trolleys, cars and pedestrians were caught in the evening rush hour, making for quite a congested scene.

"My father believes someone pushed him on North Pearl Street in December," Martha said. "Mr. Armstrong admitted it was his car that almost ran Father down that night in February."

For a second, Burgess did not say anything, and then he turned his attention to her. "Thurman was responsible for almost hitting your father that night?"

"He came to the house and admitted it. He told us Mrs. Castle knows. He wanted Father to hear it from him rather than her, or anyone else for that matter."

"That's news to me," Burgess said, his gaze at a trolley as it passed. "But that does sound like Thurman. Reckless, irresponsible, arrogant." He paused. "Perhaps I will see you again, Mrs. Hughes. It's been nice chatting with you. I must be going. I plan to attend a poker game later."

Martha nodded. "You like poker, Mr. Smith?"

He stood, looking down at her on the bench. "Please call me Burgess. I like a good card game and the guys and I have a great time." He did not mention the liquor they consumed.

Martha guessed as much but did not say anything. "And please call me Martha," she told him, offering a smile.

He tipped his hat, nodding at her. She watched as he walked up Washington Avenue, turning left on South Swan Street, until he disappeared out of sight.

Martha continued sitting on the park bench, the trolleys and cars a faint murmur in her already overcrowded and troubled mind. She could not dismiss the feeling that there was more to Burgess Smith than met the eye.

As the shadows lengthened and evening approached, she wondered if he could even be trusted—or if he was hiding something no one else knew.

CHAPTER NINETEEN

Mrs. Philomena Sampson stood on State Street, waiting for the trolley to take her downtown to North Pearl Street. The late morning sun bathed the cobblestone streets in golden light, and the air was filled with the clanging of the trolley bell and the chatter of well-dressed pedestrians. It was a typical Tuesday, and she, her son, and daughter-in-law planned to have lunch. They had decided on the lunchroom at Whitney's Department Store, as Philomena expressed her desire to shop for a new hat and dress afterward.

At breakfast, Clayton had voiced his concern about her traveling alone. Nonsense, she had told him, waving off his worries with a dismissive hand. She was perfectly capable of traversing the city herself. Albany was her hometown, and she knew the streets well. Even her daughter-in-law had told her to take care, but Philomena was determined to maintain her independence.

She sighed impatiently, more from the impertinence of her daughter-in-law than the gusty winds tearing at her fur-trimmed coat. In her hand, she clutched a book, the latest novel by Frances Parkinson Keyes, one of her favorite authors. At least she could read it on the trolley or if her son was held up at the law firm, which she knew from experience was highly likely.

It was refreshing to get out of the house. While her daughter-in-law may have considered her advanced in years, at eighty, Philomena did not yet consider herself old. She had her bad days, of course, and her arthritis often played tricks on her, but lately, the spring weather had been most agreeable, adding to her buoyant mood. She had suggested lunch today, and surprisingly, her son and daughter-in-law had agreed.

A few others waited with her, a mother and her small son, tugging at her sleeve, a businessman smoking a pipe and a nurse perhaps on her way to work. Looking ahead, she spotted a trolley steadily making its way down State Street. A man allowed her to enter first, and she grabbed a seat near the front. With the others on board, the trolley clanged onward, past the State Capitol, stopping for a red light at the top of State Street hill before proceeding further. It arrived at the corner with South Pearl Street.

Philomena joined a crowd crossing at the light and then walked carefully along North Pearl Street toward the office building where her son and daughter-in-law worked. She enjoyed the lovely spring weather, despite the gusty winds. The daytime crowds, the shops, restaurants, and theaters all were blooming with life after a harsh and cold winter.

Upon reaching her destination, she entered the grandiose lobby and headed for an empty elevator. She told the attendant the floor she wished, and with the gates closed, it shot upward. Philomena put her hand to her head, as she had not taken an elevator in some time. It finally arrived, and upon opening the gates, the doors slid open, much to her relief. The office was almost in front of her, but it had been several months since her last visit. She pushed open the door and was warmly greeted by Mrs. Castle in the front office.

"Good morning, Mrs. Sampson. So lovely to see you. Were you wishing to see your son?"

Philomena was cordial. "Yes, we're having lunch today."

Doris and Quentin looked up and greeted Philomena. She smiled at them in return, internally hating idle small talk with people she barely knew. Of course, she knew she would see them here, so she was ready for it.

At that moment, Lucille emerged from the other suite and seemed surprised to see her mother-in-law, as though she did not know about lunch. She then remembered and appeared glad to see her, although Philomena knew her daughter-in-law too well. Lucille's stiff smile and overly cheerful greeting did little to mask her true feelings. Philomena caught the brief hesitation in her step before she composed a brighter expression.

Clayton also joined his wife in welcoming his mother to the office. A brief silence ensued, filled with more idle chatter between them, Mrs. Castle, Doris, and Quentin. Just then, Burgess stepped out of his office and greeted Philomena pleasantly. Thurman also appeared, as though on cue, to see the main office full of people, much to his chagrin. He met eyes with Burgess, something he instinctively avoided.

Thurman greeted Philomena pleasantly, listening to their plans for lunch and her intention to shop later. Doris commented that there were sales at Whitney's, and Quentin mentioned a new Italian restaurant on Lodge Street. Clayton noted they would eat at the lunchroom at the department store and were about to take their leave when Burgess stopped them in their tracks. In fact, he rather stopped all activity from that point on.

"You've got a lot of nerve working here after almost killing the judge," Burgess said to Thurman menacingly, his voice low and dangerous. "Why don't you tell everyone it was your car that almost hit Judge Archie that night in February?"

Thurman smirked, crossing his arms over his chest. Never at a loss for words or rebuffed in any way, he countered what was thrown at him. He let out a short, disdainful chuckle. "Really, Burgess? If we're dredging up history, perhaps we should also discuss your own secrets. But I suppose that would make things… inconvenient." His tone was laced with mockery, his smirk unwavering.

Philomena exhaled shakily, feeling the weight of the exchange settle in her chest. Mrs. Castle was clearly alarmed at the scene unfolding before her. Doris sat at her desk, anticipating the worst, while Quentin merely looked at the two men, assuming another disagreement between them was about to unfold. Of all times for this to come out, he thought, shaking his head. The conversation had taken on a dangerous edge—one that was far from over.

"You drove the car that almost hit the judge?" Doris spoke from her desk, her face a mix of surprise and fear. Her voice trembled slightly, betraying the shock.

Burgess, still seething from the revelation Martha had shared with him in the park just yesterday afternoon, glared at Thurman. "Yes, Doris, he did. He's been hiding it ever since," he growled, the anger in his voice burning bright.

Mrs. Castle, unaware that Quentin already knew, exchanged a shocked glance with him. Quentin's jaw tightened, but he remained silent, his eyes dark with unspoken thoughts. The Sampsons, however, were taken aback, their expressions a mix of confusion and concern. Clayton's brow furrowed, while Lucille clutched her pearls, eyes wide.

Thurman contained his anger directed at Burgess, then looked at Doris. "Yes, it was me. I told the family about it, and the judge wants to put it behind him." He looked at Burgess, then surveyed the room, and the myriad of expressions, deciding how to play his hand before launching his retort. "I don't see why you'd mention that in front of everyone. It isn't important now." He paused, a jeering smile playing on his lips.

Philomena, Clayton, and Lucille first looked at Burgess, who remained firmly planted near them, his fists clenched as he struggled to control his anger. Their gaze then traveled to Thurman, who stood near his office door, arrogant and proud, not one to be undermined.

"I think it's a good idea for the judge to put it behind him," Quentin spoke up, his voice steady. "Since Mr. Armstrong admitted it, that spoke well of him. It's in the past."

Thurman glanced at Quentin and thanked him. Mrs. Castle, almost on the brink of tears, spoke rather hoarsely. "But didn't the judge say someone pushed him before Christmas on North Pearl Street?"

"We don't know that for sure," Clayton said, glancing at her with frustration.

"Or the poisonous tea that killed Mr. Lewis," Philomena added, her voice trembling.

"Or Mrs. Caves' sudden death," Lucille chimed in, her eyes wide with worry.

By now, Thurman had heard enough. He straightened his posture, his expression hardening. "I am the president of this law firm, and I do not appreciate the conduct nor the topic of apathetic conversation. Now, I insist everyone return to work and let's not waste time, unless we want to lose business and then we'll have to seek employment elsewhere."

"You mean you're the *interim* president," Burgess clarified, with a smirk. He then stormed back to his office, his footsteps echoing down the hallway. Clayton and Lucille fetched their hats and coats. Before leaving, Philomena bid a subdued goodbye to Mrs. Castle, Doris, and Quentin, then joined her son and daughter-in-law. They left the law firm and headed for the elevator, the apprehension between them thick and rather uncomfortable.

Philomena shivered slightly, pulling her fur-trimmed coat tighter around her shoulders. The clang of the elevator arriving echoed through the corridor, followed by the attendant opening the gates with a metallic scrape. They stepped inside, the cold, polished walls amplifying their uneasy expressions. Conflicting thoughts raced through their minds; Mr. Lewis' and Mrs. Caves' unexplained deaths and now Thurman's daring revelation of almost hitting the judge with his car.

Suddenly, snapped back to the present, the elevator doors slid shut, enclosing them in a tense, oppressive silence.

Augusta sat at the kitchen table with Gertrude, who had just arrived to prepare lunch. The comforting scent of the coffee filled the kitchen, mingling with the savoring smell of turkey and crisp lettuce. The clinking of cups and the soft murmur of their conversation created a warm, hopeful atmosphere. Augusta's mind raced with cautious optimism. The judge had shown slight improvement this morning, lifting her spirits. She prayed the nurse would bring changes that were positive.

Their conversation was light, but both were preoccupied with the judge's fragile condition. Earlier in the morning, she had received a call from the head of the private duty nurses unit at the hospital. A nurse had been selected based on the judge's symptoms and Augusta was anxiously awaiting her arrival.

She heard the grandfather clock strike eleven, its chimes resonating through the quiet house. At the same moment, the doorbell rang, its sharp sound cutting through the stillness. Gertrude started to get up to answer it, but Augusta told her she would get it herself. She felt a mix of worry and hope as she entered the hallway, glancing at herself briefly in the hallway mirror. She smoothed her hair and took a deep breath before approaching the door.

Upon opening it, she saw a pleasant-faced woman in her mid-forties, with kind eyes, dressed in a starched white uniform beneath her fur-trimmed coat. On her head was a nurse's white cap. Her smile was warm and reassuring. Augusta felt a small wave of relief wash over her.

"Mrs. Stafford? I am Miss Eloise Bennett, the private duty nurse. I know you spoke to my supervisor about your husband," the nurse said, her voice gentle and professional.

Augusta stepped aside, allowing her to enter. Nurse Bennett took off her coat, handing it to her. Augusta closed the door and looked approvingly at the woman in front of her.

"Pleased to meet you, Miss Bennett. Please come in and meet our maid," Augusta said, leading her down the hallway, her heart pounding slightly.

Miss Bennett followed her to the kitchen, where she was introduced to Gertrude. They sat at the kitchen table, and although offered lunch, Miss Bennett politely declined, clearly focused on her duties first and foremost, which impressed Augusta. She did accept a cup of coffee, which Gertrude brought over to her, along with the sugar and cream.

Augusta cleared her throat, trying to steady her voice. "My husband suffered a heart attack on Sunday evening. While his condition has stabilized, Dr. Stephens does not want him to suffer any undue stress. He's still quite weak."

Nurse Bennett took out a notebook from her pocketbook, her movements precise and efficient. "I understand, Mrs. Stafford. I will spend the day with your husband and into the evening as needed. I will give you my telephone number for after hours." She wrote the number on a piece of notebook paper, tore it out, and handed it to Augusta. "May I meet Mr. Stafford?"

Augusta took the piece of notebook paper, feeling a sense of relief at having a direct line to the nurse. She hesitated for a moment, glancing towards the hallway.

Nurse Bennett sensed the hesitation and instead began writing notes. She asked questions about medications, sleeping times, eating habits and other family members living in the house.

"My daughter, Martha, lives here with her son, my grandson, Preston," Augusta explained. "They're both at work at the moment. My youngest daughter, Joan, recently passed away, which contributed to my husband's stress. We also learned that an acquaintance's maid died when she fell in front of a trolley."

Nurse Bennett made appropriate comments, shaking her head. "The city really needs to conduct thorough investigations into the trolleys. There have been far too many accidents lately." She paused, noticing Gertrude stiffen slightly. "Is there something wrong, other than your husband's medical condition, Mrs. Stafford?"

Augusta hesitated, her voice trembling slightly. Her fingers tightened around her coffee cup. "Well, my husband believes someone is trying to kill him. He feels the poisoned tea that Mr. Lewis drank was meant for him and the barbiturate pills in the aspirin bottle that my daughter Joan took were also meant for him." She elaborated on the two deaths, causing the nurse to write notes.

Nurse Bennett's eyes narrowed with concern. "That's quite alarming, Mrs. Stafford. We must take extra precautions to ensure his safety," she said, her tone firm yet reassuring. Her pen moved swiftly as she took further notes, her expression remaining calm and focused. She mentioned she had read about the recent deaths in the newspapers. She then looked up and repeated her request to meet the judge, her no-nonsense demeanor evident.

Augusta was impressed by Nurse Bennett's professionalism.

Together, they walked out of the kitchen, down the back hallway, and to the bedroom. Upon opening the door, Augusta was pleased to see her husband sitting up in bed, apparently resting peacefully and looking at his favorite magazine, *Popular Science*. He looked over the top of the magazine with suspicion at the person next to his wife.

"And who is this woman?" he demanded, his voice somewhat harsh.

Augusta managed a smile. "Dear, this is Miss Eloise Bennett from the hospital's private duty nursing unit. She will be here weekdays to care for you. Dr. Stephens believes it's best."

"Bah," he grumbled, his eyes peering slightly before he returned to the magazine.

Augusta cast a quick glance at Nurse Bennett. Obviously, she was used to the whims of patients. She appeared neither fazed nor alarmed at her husband's impertinent remark, maintaining a calm and appropriate demeanor.

"Pleased to meet you, sir," she said pleasantly. "I have a lot of experience in private duty nursing and I'll be happy to help you as needed."

Augusta appreciated her adding "as needed," so that he would not feel overwhelmed by constant supervision.

He put the magazine on his lap and then smiled slightly. Augusta was rather surprised that Nurse Bennett appeared to win him over, at least for the moment. She noticed her husband observe her in more detail, then a small smile spread across his face.

"Pleased to meet you as well, Nurse Bennett. Please call me Judge Archie; everyone refers to me that way. I'm sure we'll get along fine."

Gertrude appeared in the doorway just then, announcing that lunch was ready. Nurse Bennett offered to bring him a tray, but Judge Archie insisted on eating at the kitchen table. He also managed to convince her to have lunch with them. Augusta watched as Nurse

Bennett assisted him carefully out of the bed, slowly guiding him down the hallway to the kitchen. She heard them chatting softly, much to her further surprise.

Before joining them, she took a moment to compose herself, feeling a slight tightness in her chest. She leaned on the bedpost to steady herself. Now, perhaps, her husband would not have to suffer such anguish. Returning to the kitchen, she could not help but think that despite the reassurance of the private nurse and her husband's stabilized condition, the worst was yet to come.

Sloan glanced at the clock on the wall. Almost noon. The room was dimly lit, with the banker's lamp on his desk casting a warm, greenish glow over the scattered papers. He looked at the worn, leather-bound notebook belonging to Judge Archie, its pages yellowed with age and ink slightly faded. As he read several entries from 1885, a sense of unease crept over him. The handwriting was old-fashioned, the language peculiar, an obvious reminder of the past.

He ran his fingers over the cover before turning to his notes from *The Index to Deaths in Albany, New York 1880-1915,* which he had meticulously copied during his visit to the library. The notes confirmed Mr. Philip Mavity's death, but surprisingly, there was no obituary in the local newspapers, almost as if someone wanted to erase his existence.

As Sloan read further, he noticed cryptic references to "business deals" and "meetings" that seemed out of place for a judge's notebook. Despite knowing Mavity's long criminal history, these entries hinted at something more far-reaching. His heart raced as he realized these were coded entries about Mavity's most secretive and dangerous activities. Philip Mavity was not just any gangster; he was involved in a web of corruption that extended far beyond what Sloan had imagined. His discovery was more dangerous than he had anticipated.

He then looked at the notes from his conversation with Nurse Collins yesterday. She had verified the abortion that occurred at the hospital in the emergency ward, but mentioned it was most likely performed clandestinely, as illegal procedures were usually not administered within the hospital. She provided the names of the doctor and the midwife, both long deceased. There was nothing else in the records explaining why the procedure was performed in the hospital, except that the girl was experiencing extreme pains and the abortion needed to be done as soon as possible.

While at the library, Sloan had also reviewed newspapers from 1885. He learned that Mr. Philip Mavity was indeed murdered in his apartment in Albany, by a person or persons unknown, with a kitchen knife. The picture showed a rather bloody mess, with a white sheet covering the corpse. The article mentioned the investigation was ongoing but no further leads were forthcoming.

Sloan frowned, his mind racing. The secretive nature of the procedure and the urgency suggested something more sinister. The notebook entries hinted at a young woman involved in Mavity's world and someone who had been desperate enough to seek an illegal procedure. These revelations added another layer of complexity to the already tangled web of secrets he was uncovering.

Sloan puffed at his cigarette, realizing he held the answer to this case in front of him but was not quite sure how to proceed. There was little evidence to indict someone from the 1885 murder. As far as the deaths of Mr. Lewis and Mrs. Caves, anyone could have tampered with the tea and the aspirin. He drummed his fingers frustratingly on the desk. He sat in comparative silence until the telephone at his side rang. He anticipated a woman seeking information about a custody dispute but instead he heard a familiar voice, although he did not quite place it.

"Mr. Sheppard, oh, I'm so glad I caught you. I didn't know if you would be in your office. I have some information that may be of interest to you."

It was a woman, with a rather husky voice, who sounded middle-aged and quite pleasant. He was waiting for her to identify herself. When she continued rattling on, he interrupted her.

"Who is this?" he asked, a hint of impatience in his tone.

"Oh, forgive me, Mr. Sheppard. This is Miss Doris Blake; I work at the law firm."

"Yes, Miss Blake. How can I help you?"

In the background, Sloan could hear traffic, trolleys and a low murmur of distant conversations. It sounded as though she was at a pay telephone.

"I remembered something that might help you," Doris continued. "I think Mr. Lewis died from poisonous yew berry juice that must've been in the teacup intended for the judge!"

"What makes you think that, Miss Blake?"

Doris paused, taking a rather deep breath. "Because not long ago I saw someone picking berries from a yew berry tree in Washington Park. I thought it was strange at first, since there was a sign posted that the berries were toxic, but then I put it all together!"

Sloan knocked ash into the ashtray. "Please continue, Miss Blake."

"I know who picked those yew berries!" Her voice was rather loud and almost hysterical as she spoke up, due to the street noise. "Someone we all know!"

Sloan extinguished his cigarette, as he realized the pieces of the puzzle were coming together. Judge Archie's suspicions were reiterated. There was now ample evidence and an arrest was imminent. He thanked Doris and as he was about to replace the handset, he heard a rather loud commotion, several shattering screams and the distant roar of traffic. He then listened as people frantically called to a woman whose body lay motionless on North Pearl Street.

Preston arrived home after work to find Mrs. Rose Castle and Mrs. Philomena Sampson having tea with his grandmother in the living room. The soft clinking of cups and saucers and the faint scent of lavender from the freshly cut flowers on the coffee table filled the room. The gramophone in the corner played a gentle tune, adding to the serene atmosphere. It was still light out, but the day was slowly ending, and the cool evening breezes would soon grip the city.

"Preston, dear," Augusta said, as he entered, her voice warm but with a hint of weariness. "Mrs. Castle and Mrs. Sampson have been so kind to assist us with your grandfather. They will be here to help Nurse Bennett and Gertrude with food, cleaning up, and spending time with him."

Preston looked at Mrs. Castle and Mrs. Sampson, feeling a mix of gratitude and unease. While he appreciated their help, the situation with his grandfather was still a distinct burden. He also wondered why they would volunteer to help someone they did not particularly like. He had yet to meet the nurse who he assumed was still in the house. As though reading his mind, Augusta got up and proceeded to the bedroom, returning shortly with Nurse Bennett.

"Your grandfather is certainly tough," Nurse Bennett said with a reassuring smile, shaking hands with Preston. "But he seems to be doing well, and his heart rate is much better."

Augusta introduced Nurse Bennett to Mrs. Castle and Mrs. Sampson. Nurse Bennett commented that she would appreciate a break during the day at certain times. Mrs. Castle commented she would help in the late afternoons and evenings, and Mrs. Sampson assured her she was free most weekdays, including mornings.

As he stood in the living room, listening to Mrs. Castle and Mrs. Sampson chat pleasantly with Nurse Bennett, Preston felt something was amiss. The cheerful conversation seemed almost too perfect, masking a strange undercurrent. The extra help was certainly commendable, and he was appreciative of it, but a nagging sense of dread lingered. He decided he would call Quentin later to discuss his concerns. As he was about to retreat upstairs before dinner, the rich essence of Gertrude's roast beef and potatoes curled in from the kitchen. The comforting scent momentarily distracted him from his worries. The candlestick telephone on the hallway table rang shrilly, breaking the moment. Since he was closest, he told his grandmother he would answer it.

From the living room, Augusta heard a low cry coming from the hallway. Philomena looked at her with concern, and Mrs. Castle put down her teacup in fear and confusion. They waited for Preston to return, and when he did, his face was flushed and pale.

"Preston, dear, is there something wrong?" his grandmother asked, her voice tinged with worry. She gripped her teacup tighter. Certainly, it had nothing to do with the judge, as he was resting comfortably in bed with Nurse Bennett at his side. She waited for him to speak, the room falling into a tense silence.

Preston had turned ashen white, swallowing with difficulty. "That was Quentin. He got a call from Burgess, who told him Doris was found on North Pearl Street with a head injury. She's at the hospital with a concussion. Her condition is critical."

CHAPTER TWENTY

Sloan tightened his coat around him, his fedora hat secured on his head as he jumped on a trolley headed uptown, toward the police station, the leather-bound notebook clutched tightly in his hand. The streets were still busy, with shopkeepers opening their doors, trolleys gliding down State Street and the occasional Model T rumbling by.

Wednesday morning dawned with a crisp chill in the air, the kind that hinted at the lingering touch of winter, regardless of the date of April twenty-second. The scent of fresh bread wafted from a nearby bakery, mingling with the faint smell of coal smoke. Sloan had attended to a client earlier, and then with time this morning, he decided to see the police again. His mind raced with the possibilities contained within the notebook, his fingers curling around the worn leather, the weight of its secrets pressing against his palm.

The police station loomed ahead, a sturdy brick building that seemed to exude authority. Sloan got off at the corner of Central Avenue and Quail Street. He took a deep breath before stepping inside, the warmth of the interior contrasting sharply with the cool morning air. The faint smell of ink and tobacco greeted him as he walked across the tiled floor. He approached the front desk, where a stern-looking officer glanced up from his paperwork, the sound of typewriters clacking in the background.

"Good morning," Sloan said, his voice steady and composed. "I need to speak with Inspector Harris. It's urgent."

The officer raised an eyebrow but nodded, picking up the phone to make the call. Sloan stood tall, his expression unreadable, waiting with the patience of someone used to high-stakes situations. Moments later, Inspector Harris appeared, his expression a mix of curiosity and concern, his uniform crisp and his demeanor authoritative.

"Mr. Sheppard, what brings you here so early?" Inspector Harris asked, motioning for him to follow. Once settled in the office, Sloan mentioned the valuable notebook.

"This belongs to the judge. I told him I'd return it. It contains information we need to crack this case." He paused, then continued, "Miss Doris Blake called me late yesterday afternoon. She mentioned seeing someone picking yew berries in Washington Park not long ago. After ending the call, I heard a commotion and screams. I later received a call from Mr. Burgess Smith before I left my office yesterday. He was contacted by the hospital and he told me that she either fell or was pushed onto North Pearl Street."

"Is Miss Blake all right?" the inspector asked, concern evident in his voice.

"I called the hospital last night," Sloan replied. "She suffered a concussion and is stable. I haven't called this morning yet."

"Perhaps the person she saw picking the yew berries was onto her and overheard her telephone call," Harris suggested, his irritation evident.

Sloan nodded. "She called from a pay telephone. I heard traffic and people talking in the background. Maybe she didn't want someone from the law office to hear her."

"Apparently, the person did overhear," the inspector remarked dryly.

Inspector Harris took the notebook back to his desk, flipping through the pages with a furrowed brow. He took his time thumbing through the notebook, noting the brittle pages and the handwriting that at times was difficult to decipher. He came to the pages dated 1885. Sloan pointed out the information on the illegal abortion, the murder of Mr. Philip Mavity, and the girl who was suspected of the murder.

He paused mid-page, his brow tightening as his gaze lingered over a familiar name—one he hadn't expected to see in this context. His fingers ran over the brittle paper, the faded ink barely legible in places, but the weight of its meaning was undeniable. He exhaled slowly, tapping the edge of the notebook against his desk as a thought took shape.

"If what's written here is true," the inspector murmured, barely above a whisper, "then we're looking at…a cunning and cold-blooded murderer."

Sloan pointed out the information on the illegal abortion, the murder of Mr. Philip Mavity, and the girl who was suspected of the murder.

Inspector Harris's eyes narrowed as he read. "This is quite the revelation," he muttered, tracing a finger over the faded ink. "An illegal abortion and a murder. So the judge told you his suspicions? And he feels the person uncovered this notebook?"

"Yes, he mentioned who he suspects. He told me he used to keep the notebook in his desk drawer but after realizing someone had gone through it, he brought it home."

Inspector Harris closed the notebook gently; as if afraid it might crumble in his hands. "This case just got a lot more complicated. We'll need to tread carefully. If someone was willing to kill to keep this secret back then, the person might still be dangerous now." He puffed at a cigarette. "Many gangsters have molls, even incredibly young ones. Most likely she killed him because he wouldn't support her, so she had the abortion and then killed him in a fit of rage."

Sloan's black hair fell crisply over his forehead, his expression calmer and more composed. "I believe an arrest is forthcoming. We have enough circumstantial evidence and a witness to Mrs. Justine Davis's death. Someone wanted to silence Mrs. Crabtree, because she recognized a guest at the luncheon at the judge's house. Even without further evidence, we can move forward."

The inspector agreed. "Where is Judge Archie at the moment?" He stubbed out his cigarette with a deliberate motion, exhaling slowly as he processed Sloan's words. The tension hung thick between them, neither man speaking for a long beat.

Sloan cleared his throat. "I spoke to him on Monday. He suffered a heart attack Sunday, after hearing about Mrs. Crabtree's maid. The death of Mr. Lewis and his youngest daughter have taken a toll on him." He hesitated, almost as though he could barely continue sitting in the chair. "We have to act quickly, before someone succeeds in killing him." His voice was resolute and unwavering. "I won't let that happen."

Preston's mind was a whirlwind of worry and unresolved questions. Despite the steady flow of customers at the cruise line office, his thoughts were fixated on Doris. Her accident had deeply unsettled him, and he could not shake the concern for her well-being.

When he called the hospital, the nurse reassured him that Doris was in stable condition, which brought a small measure of relief. Still, he felt the need to see her, to confirm with his own eyes that she was all right. He picked up the telephone again and called Quentin, hoping his friend would join him on the visit.

"That sounds like a good idea, Pres," Quentin told him. He was in the middle of proofreading a deposition intended for Thurman. He had a cigarette in his hands, the smoke swirling through his fingers. "How about just before lunch?"

Preston suggested they meet at the corner of State and North Pearl Streets to take the trolley together. They ended the call and then Quentin entered Thurman's office, to inform him of their visit to Doris in the hospital. Thurman told him to take the rest of the afternoon off, giving them enough time to see her and have lunch. Quentin thanked him and called Preston back to make similar arrangements. Upon hearing his friend's voice again, Preston eagerly concurred. He spoke to his boss, Mr. Bishop, to ask for the afternoon free. Much to his delight, Mr. Bishop granted him as much time as needed to visit Miss Blake in the hospital, to which Preston exhaled in great relief, a slow release of tension escaping his shoulders.

Back at the law firm, Mrs. Castle expressed her sincere wishes for Doris's speedy recovery.

"Poor Doris," she said, almost on the brink of tears. "Just what is happening in this city? Too many accidents! I'm even afraid to walk around now."

Burgess came out of his office at the same time that Lucille and Clayton emerged from their suite. Quentin mentioned that he and Preston intended to visit Doris at the hospital soon.

Clayton reiterated his sentiments. "There's a new client coming this afternoon, so please give Doris our best wishes for a quick recovery."

Burgess announced his departure for the Court of Appeals, briefcase in hand. He conferred with Mrs. Castle on upcoming documents, reports, and letters that needed to be typed. Then, he headed for the main doors and out of the office.

As the noon hour approached, Quentin gathered his coat and cap. He mentioned his visit to see Doris again to Mrs. Castle. He then entered the Sampson's office, addressing Lucille, who practically ignored him, standing in front of her desk. She told him she needed to assist her husband with the new client this afternoon and would be too busy to concentrate on anything else. Quentin told her rather bluntly she need not concern herself. She looked up at his surprising response, stiffening slightly, her lips parting as if to respond—then, after a brief pause, she decided against it. Shaking his head in frustration, he headed for the exit doors. Once in the hallway, he waited for the elevator. He took out a cigarette, lighting it with extreme precision, watching the flame flicker as if lost in thought.

As the elevator arrived and the attendant opened the gates, he decided not to give it another thought. He trusted Mr. and Mrs. Clayton Sampson as much as he trusted none of the people in the office, including Judge Archie. He wondered if the old man had secrets even time could not erase.

Preston stood at the corner of State and North Pearl Streets, his eyes scanning the bustling street for signs of Quentin. The trolley tracks gleamed in the midday sun, and the sound of clanging bells filled the air. He checked his watch, noting that it was almost time for their meeting. Just then, he spotted Quentin approaching, his jacket flapping in the breeze and his cap pulled low over his eyes. Quentin waved as he drew near, a cigarette dangling from his lips.

They soon boarded a trolley, finding seats near the back. The ride was bumpy, and the cityscape blurred past the windows. Preston's mind was racing with thoughts of Doris and the strange events unfolding. The trolley rattled on, each bump and jolt adding to the tension.

Arriving within twenty minutes, they jumped off the trolley and entered the massive concrete structure. Upon inquiring at the information desk for Miss Doris Blake, they were directed to her floor. There were three elevators, and Preston chose one that was already in the lobby. The attendant closed the gates, and the car shot upward, arriving at their desired floor in no time.

There was a distinct chill in the air as they approached the nurses' station. Preston bundled his jacket around him to keep warm. He asked for Miss Doris Blake, and with the correct room number, they proceeded down the hall. Entering the room, they saw Doris lying still, conscious but weak, her forehead wrapped in a large white bandage. She looked up at them and smiled weakly in recognition. A nurse had just finished attending to her but warned them that she was still fragile and should not become excited for any reason. Preston assured her they would not stay long.

"Doris, what happened?" Quentin said, pulling up a chair alongside the bed.

Preston sat in another chair, eagerly anticipating her response.

Doris spoke weakly but her words were coherent. Her fingers twitched slightly against the bedsheet. "I called Mr. Sheppard from a payphone on North Pearl Street." She stopped there as though she had told them everything.

"Why would you go to a payphone when you could have called from the office?" Quentin asked her in some confusion. "Was this during your lunch hour? You could've used my phone."

Doris moistened her dry lips. "I didn't want anyone to overhear me. I thought I was safe there. It was crowded and the traffic and trolleys made it hard to hear him on the other end, but I told him my suspicions."

"Doris, can you be more specific?" Preston pressed her, catching his breath. He struggled to stay composed. "Do you know something that can help Mr. Sheppard?"

"I thought I did," she admitted. "I told him I saw someone picking yew berries from a yew berry tree in Washington Park not long ago. And then Mr. Lewis drank the poisoned tea. It had to be yew berry juice in the teacup, the tea wasn't poisonous."

Quentin leaned in closer. "Did you tell Mr. Sheppard your suspicions?"

"Yes," Doris replied, her eyes closing briefly. "I told him I was scared and that I didn't know who to trust. He said he would look into it, but then… the accident happened."

Preston looked at Quentin. "Did someone approach you on the sidewalk?"

Doris mentioned she was pushed from behind and hit her head on the street, almost directly in front of a trolley. The next thing she remembered was waking up in the hospital. She remembered feeling a shove on her back, causing her to fall.

The sterile smell of antiseptic filled the room, mingling with the faint scent of flowers from a nearby bouquet. Preston looked at the whitewashed walls and the metal bedframe, feeling a chill run down his spine. Preston and Quentin exchanged worried glances. The threat was real, and time was running out. They needed to uncover the truth before it was too late.

The room seemed to grow colder, the strain of anticipation hanging in the air like a dark cloud. Preston's eyes widened and he exchanged a startled glance with Quentin. Quentin inhaled sharply, the sound barely audible, as if bracing for what was coming. With renewed strength, Doris drew in a slow breath, as if steeling herself, her tone dropping slightly, before she voiced her suspicions.

After leaving the hospital, they made their way to the trolley stop, the clanging of the trolley bell echoing through the bustling streets. The ride was quiet, each man lost in his thoughts. The trolley took them across the city, enabling Quentin to arrive at his apartment on North Allen Street. He told Preston he would contact Mr. Sheppard with the discovery, provided he was still in his office. Glancing at his watch, Preston saw it was just four o'clock, so chances were good he was still in.

After Quentin got off at the corner of Western Avenue and North Allen, Preston noticed he was not sure where he was. Although he knew Albany, he realized he should have gotten off and taken another trolley toward State Street. Preston cursed under his breath, realizing his mistake too late. Now, with precious time lost, he had to endure a seemingly slow and endless ride through parts of Albany he would not ordinarily traverse. As the trolley reached Lark Street, after making numerous stops to pick up and let off passengers, he decided to get off and walk down Washington Avenue. However, the trolley started up again before he could jump off.

He remained on it as it slowly continued its journey, picking up more people and dropping off others, stretching the journey into an agonizing test of patience, turning minutes into hours in his mind. The trolley's wheels screeched against the tracks, his foot tapping against the trolley floor as if trying to will it to move faster. The faint smell of coal smoke mixed with the city's air of baked bread and gasoline, which stung his nose. His impatience and anticipation were insufferable, causing little beads of sweat on his forehead. He gritted his teeth, watching the city crawl by through smudged glass, every turn of the trolley's wheels dragging him further from where he needed to be.

Finally, it turned left onto Hamilton Street but quickly became entangled in traffic congestion as rush hour began to take shape. The ringing of the trolley bell echoed through the narrow street, blending with the distant honking of car horns. He noticed the Sampson's elegant brownstone house as the trolley clanged laboriously down Hamilton. But by now, he had had enough of sitting still. The hard wooden seat felt like a prison and the heat of the crowded car was stifling. Restlessly, he looked at his watch in frustration and could not believe it was just after five o'clock. Time was slipping through his fingers, and with each ticking second, dread twisted tighter in his chest.

He stepped off at Dove and Hamilton, dodging the trolley as he hurried down Dove toward State Street. He had no sooner crossed Lancaster Street than he recognized Mrs. Philomena Sampson walking slowly but steadily toward him. She stopped and greeted him pleasantly.

"Preston, dear, what brings you to Dove Street at this time of day? Rather chilly, isn't it now that evening is approaching?"

Preston listened to Philomena's comments but could barely maintain his composure. Sensing his urgency, Philomena asked if there was a difficulty or issue. She offered her assistance and that of her son and daughter-in-law if he wanted it.

Preston explained that he and Quentin had just come from the hospital to see Doris. She was in stable condition following her accident on North Pearl Street yesterday. Philomena clicked her tongue and expressed sadness, mentioning that her son and daughter-in-law had told her after receiving a call from Mr. Smith late yesterday. She mentioned she had been visiting his grandparents and had spent time with Judge Archie and the nurse.

"How is Grandfather?" Preston asked eagerly.

Philomena smiled. "He has an excellent nurse to care for him. Mrs. Castle is there now, at least for a while, to help as needed. So kind of her, too." She clutched her fur coat a little tighter against the evening chill.

Preston managed to maintain a semblance of stability, although he was bursting inside. "Mrs. Sampson, when you get home, would you please call the police and Mr. Sheppard? Tell them to come to our house at once. It's urgent!"

"What is wrong, Preston?" Philomena asked, confused and rather alarmed.

But Preston had taken off at a brisk pace toward Dove and State Street, his heart pounding with each step. The sharp chill bit his skin, and the shuffle of hurried pedestrians grew louder as he approached. He had to reach the family mansion quickly—before the worst could unfold. The fear of what might happen drove him forward with relentless haste.

Arriving at the mansion, somewhat out of breath, Preston hurriedly walked up the pathway, fumbled for his key in his pocket, and then quickly opened the front door. The comforting redolence of Gertrude's cooking filled the air, mingling with the warm, lingering presence of freshly brewed tea. He took off his jacket and cap, tossing them uncaringly on a chair, and then entered the living room.

Augusta was sitting on the Victorian sofa, sipping her afternoon tea with Martha, who had recently arrived home from work. They sensed the anxiety in his manner.

"I'll ask Gertrude to bring you a nice cup of tea, dear," Augusta said pleasantly.

"No, not now, Grandmother. Where's Grandfather?"

"He's resting comfortably, Preston," his mother told him. "Nurse Bennett is conferring with Gertrude on dinner for your grandfather. Mrs. Castle just brought him a cup of tea."

Preston turned white, his stomach twisted, his pulse hammering in his ears. Without explanation, he bolted from the living room, his mother and grandmother's voices calling after him. He sprinted down the main hallway, his footsteps echoing off the walls and almost stumbled as he came to a halt at the back hallway. With a trembling hand, he flung open the door to his grandparent's bedroom.

Mrs. Castle, startled by the unexpected sound, turned her head to see who had entered. Before she had time to react, Preston was by the bedside, his breath catching in horror, gripping both her hands tightly, releasing the pillow that a moment before had been suffocating his grandfather.

A silent, intense battle erupted. Mrs. Castle launched herself at him—reckless, furious, her eyes burning with rage. He held on tighter, determined not to release her. Losing any self-restraint, she scratched at him, her nails leaving painful, fiery marks on his skin. The bedframe rattled, violently, amplifying the turmoil. The judge let out a faint, startled moan. The room seemed to close in around them. Preston felt a surge of adrenaline, driving him to hold on. The air thickened, heavy with tension and unspoken wrath. He could feel it pressing down, tightening around him as Mrs. Castle fought with wild desperation.

The struggle intensified, her wrath consuming her. She twisted his hands with ferocity and then stepped down painfully on his foot, throwing him off balance. But soon the nurse came in, and together she and Preston subdued her with ease, their combined strength rendering her frenzied attempts futile, as she was no match for them, despite her extreme fury. The conflict ended as abruptly as it began, leaving an oppressive silence in its wake.

At that moment, the doorway filled with people, among them Sloan, Inspector Harris, and two policemen. Mrs. Castle, restrained by Preston and Nurse Bennett, was placed in handcuffs by the inspector. Sloan spoke for him in his authoritative tone, decisively and firmly.

"Mrs. Rose Castle, you are arrested for the attempted murder of Judge Archibald Stafford, for the murders of Mr. Clement Lewis, Mrs. Joan Caves, and for the assault on Miss Doris Blake. There is also sufficient evidence to implicate you in the murder of Mr. Philip Mavity."

Mrs. Castle tried furiously to untangle the policeman's grip, her hair escaping recklessly from its pins, her appearance disheveled. Her nails dug into his skin as she strained to reach Sloan, wanting desperately to claw his face. The cold metal bit into her wrists, a stark reminder of her captivity. She was led out of the bedroom and through the hallway, her voice spewing bitter vituperation that echoed through the house, her words cutting through the air, ricocheting off the walls and high ceilings. Sloan watched her go, his face a mask of calm, his eyes a semblance of satisfaction. Inside, he felt a quiet triumph.

Augusta stood against the doorway, trembling lightly, with Martha and Gertrude supporting her. She noticed the pillow on the floor Mrs. Castle used to try to kill her husband. Her eyes then darted around the room, her utmost concern for her husband and grandson. Preston took a deep breath and assured his grandmother he was fine, thanking

Sloan and Nurse Bennett for their help. From the pillows, Judge Archie looked at the assembled company and smiled wryly.

"Well," he said with a slight chuckle, "looks like I know how to throw a party, don't I?"

CHAPTER TWENTY-ONE

It was several hours later. After the climactic turmoil in the judge's bedroom, an uneasy calm settled over the mansion on State Street. Inspector Harris had departed with Mrs. Castle in tow, the policemen's footsteps echoing down the marble hallway.

Judge Archie sat in his armchair near the fireplace, the flickering flames casting long shadows across his weary face. Nurse Bennett, ever vigilant, occupied the armchair opposite, her eyes never leaving him. The silence between them was thick, filled with unspoken questions and lingering doubts. She too had questions and waited to hear what would be told to them.

Augusta requested her grandson call the others to inform them of the recent events, including the Crabtrees. Preston spent several tense minutes on the telephone in the dimly lit hallway, his voice low and urgent. He first contacted the Sampsons, then Quentin, Thurman, Burgess and Mrs. Crabtree. Each call was met with gasps and hurried promises to come at once.

After finishing the calls, Preston returned to his grandmother, assuring her that they would arrive soon. The Crabtrees had just finished dinner and were appalled at the news. Mrs. Crabtree's voice trembled as she promised they would be there within half an hour.

By the time the Crabtrees arrived, the living room was filled with a mix of family, friends, and staff. Gertrude brewed a fresh pot of coffee, the bold scent curling into the charged atmosphere. She carefully balanced a tray with several cups, her hands steady despite the turmoil. Martha followed, carrying a jug of cream, a sugar bowl, and a tray of sugar cookies.

Everyone gratefully accepted the coffee, but the cookies remained untouched, a silent testament to the confusion and seriousness of the situation. Preston and Martha brought in several chairs from the dining room, arranging them in a semi-circle around the fireplace. The guests sat down, their faces etched with concern, a distinct chill in the air, despite the warmth of the fireplace. As Sloan looked at the assembled faces in the living room, he realized they wanted answers. The low murmur of conversation filled the room, punctuated by the occasional clink of a coffee cup. An undeniable air of relief and confusion hung over the gathering.

Sloan noticed Burgess and Thurman, though not sitting near each other; both wore expressions of shock and incredulity. The elderly Mrs. Sampson was at a loss for words, her hands trembling slightly as she found consolation in speaking with her son, Clayton, who remained steadfast and unshakeable.

Quentin sat next to Preston on an extra chair, still overcome but with an expression of relief flooding his face. The younger Mrs. Sampson, her eyes wide with shock, seemed rather taken aback by the revelations, as though nothing in her dainty life could ever impinge on it.

Mrs. Crabtree sat next to her husband on the sofa, their hands intertwined. They seemed glad the ordeal was over, although they too waited for further explanations, their eyes fixed on Sloan with a mixture of curiosity and apprehension.

Sloan stood by the windows overlooking State Street, his silhouette framed by the light filtering through the heavy drapes. He took a deep breath, the troubles of the moment pressing down on him, before turning to face the room.

"Thank you all for your patience," he began his voice steady. "I know the past few hours have been overwhelming, and I owe you an explanation."

He paused, glancing at Judge Archie, who nodded encouragingly, his eyes reflecting a shared understanding. Sloan continued, "It started with a series of strange occurrences. At first, they seemed like mere coincidences, but as they piled up, it became clear that something more sinister was at play."

"Mr. Sheppard, please tell us more about your investigation," Philomena interrupted. "I find this extremely disturbing. That murderous woman was in this house!"

Her tone was disquieting and seemed to shake everyone in the room. Judge Archie winced and Nurse Bennett placed a hand on his arm, to alleviate any undue stress. She asked if he wanted to return to his bed but he insisted he wanted to remain to hear what Mr. Sheppard would tell them.

At that moment, the room fell silent, the crackling of the fireplace the only sound. Faces turned towards Sloan, eyes wide with anticipation and unease. The air was oppressive with tension, each person bracing for the revelation that was about to unfold.

Sloan had lit a cigarette and was seated in one of the extra chairs Martha and Preston brought in from the dining room. A cup of coffee was on the end table at his side. He realized the unsettledness of the people before him. He cleared his throat and explained what he knew.

Mrs. Rose Castle, or according to the few hospital records kept from 1885, Miss Rose Linden, as she was then known, was only sixteen years old and in dire straits when she paid for an illegal abortion at the hospital, performed under extreme secrecy. She had been involved in a local gang and apparently was the moll of Mr. Philip Mavity. She murdered Mr. Mavity because he would not support her or claim to be the baby's father, which is why she decided on the abortion. Rose Linden got away with the murder and continued living her life into her adult years, acting the perfect matron, while holding a variety of office positions. While marriage records had yet to be verified, Miss Rose Linden became Mrs. Rose Castle.

"She told us her husband died years ago," Burgess added.

Sloan's eyes narrowed. "From then on, her cover was under wraps—until she discovered the judge's notebook in his desk drawer."

"Foolish woman," Judge Archie grumbled, his voice dripping with disdain. "Should've never hired her in the first place."

"Mrs. Castle realized her secrets were known and that despite the passing years, her reputation would be ruined," Sloan explained. "She was a patron at the library and the Institute of History and Art. Such news, if revealed, would cause her much shame and disgrace."

"That's an understatement," Martha said dryly, raising an eyebrow.

"Doris Blake mentioned she saw someone picking yew berries in Washington Park not long ago. Yew berry juice is quite toxic and deadly if consumed. She realized it was Mrs. Castle. She called to tell me her discovery, and unfortunately, for her, Mrs. Castle was on the street at the same time. She must've overheard her speaking to me because after the call ended, she pushed Miss Blake despite a sizeable crowd on the sidewalk."

"Nobody saw anything?" Mrs. Crabtree asked her voice tinged with disbelief.

"Apparently not," Sloan replied, puffing at his cigarette. "Mrs. Castle was very clever. She knew how to blend in and avoid suspicion.

After pushing Miss Blake, she quickly disappeared into the crowd. It wasn't until later that we realized what happened."

"Poor Miss Blake," Mrs. Crabtree murmured. "She didn't deserve that."

"No, she didn't," Sloan agreed. "But her discovery was crucial. It led us to investigate Mrs. Castle more thoroughly and uncover her sordid past. The judge's notebook was the final piece of the puzzle. It contained detailed notes about his suspicions and the evidence he had gathered. Mrs. Castle discovered it in the judge's desk. She realized the threat the judge posed to her."

"So she tried to destroy it," Quentin said.

"She didn't count on the judge taking it home and out of her reach."

"How did she kill Mr. Lewis?" Philomena asked. "Did she really mean to kill him?"

Sloan shook his head. "No, the target had always been Judge Archie. She took the yew berry juice and easily poured it into the judge's cup. She did not reckon Mr. Lewis would drink from it instead."

"That explains why she got to the office so early that morning," Lucille said, reliving that morning in her memory. "She always arrived early, but especially early that day."

"She wanted to be sure the judge was dead," Sloan said. "She was surprised when she found Mr. Lewis dead instead."

"Her shock was genuine," Clayton said.

"Certainly, it was genuine," Philomena spoke up, slight anger in her voice. "She realized her plan didn't work and that Mr. Lewis died instead."

"Perhaps her arrival at the house on Easter Sunday morning was also part of her plan," Martha said, rather bitterly. "She wanted to be sure Father was dead. When she learned it was Joan who died instead, she realized another attempt to kill Father had been ruined."

"She stopped by to thank us for the luncheon," Preston remembered. "She put on a good show that morning."

"Of course," Martha continued. "She was upset because Father wasn't dead!" She paused and then turned to her father. "If you knew these terrible things about Mrs. Castle's past, why didn't you say something earlier?"

Judge Archie shrugged slowly. "I didn't realize who she was until recently. Clement hired her and I was impressed with her work. She hadn't caused any problems while employed with us."

Mrs. Crabtree cleared her throat, then paused, having everyone's attention. "I recognized her at the luncheon. Forty years can change a person but certain things don't change. Her mannerisms, her facial features. I remember the night of her abortion very well. It was the same night your sister died during childbirth." She spoke to Philomena who fought back tears, her fingers trembling as she pressed a handkerchief to her lips.

"How did she place the barbiturates in the aspirin bottle?" Thurman asked, his brow furrowed in confusion. "I remember being in the judge's bedroom with her at the same time."

"Mrs. Castle was cunning," Sloan replied, his voice edged with contempt. "She waited for the perfect moment. When no one was looking, she emptied the barbiturates into the aspirin bottle on the judge's bedside table, thinking he would take them. It was another foiled attempt at murder."

"She must've thought Mrs. Davis wearing my coat was actually me," Mrs. Crabtree said, her voice filled with pain and remorse. "Perhaps she recognized me at the luncheon, too."

"She never imagined being recognized all these years later. When she saw the opportunity, she acted swiftly, but her plans kept unraveling."

"After the judge's heart attack, she offered to help care for him," Philomena said. "We had tea and she was so charming. She saw it as another opportunity to kill the judge."

Her gaze shifted to the older man in the armchair, who remained unmoved, though inside he was deeply troubled by these revelations.

"Mrs. Crabtree, you shared with me your suspicions at the luncheon," Thurman said, looking sympathetically at her. "I mentioned it to Mrs. Castle. She witnessed when I drove through a red light and almost ran the judge down with my car. She brushed me off, but she didn't admit to killing Mr. Mavity or to the abortion. I didn't trust her, thinking she might blackmail me."

Mrs. Crabtree nodded. "I didn't know anything about Mr. Mavity, except what I read in the newspapers at the time."

Preston cleared his throat and spoke rather unsteadily. "Grandfather, I admit, I considered you might be doing these things yourself."

Augusta and Martha looked at him, aghast and speechless. Even Nurse Bennett, the Crabtrees, and the Sampsons were surprised. Finally, the judge addressed his grandson.

"I may be old, Preston, but I'm not senile. I never contemplated murder at any time in my life. Clement and I were associates and good friends. I would never harm him or my lovely daughter, Joan." He paused. "I can understand your inclination. But I assure you, I never once thought of conjuring up such incidences to draw attention to myself. I had no reason to do so."

An unsettling silence ensued while Sloan sipped his coffee. Clayton then addressed him.

"What will happen to Mrs. Castle now?"

"She'll be booked, processed and most likely stand trial, although she may be declared incompetent. Depending on the court's recommendation, she could end up in a mental institution."

The room became quiet again as everyone absorbed the significance of the situation. The judge, still seated in the armchair, finally spoke, his voice steady but laced with underlying tension. He glanced at Nurse Bennett, who gave him a reassuring smile.

"Justice must be served, not just for me, but for everyone she's harmed."

Quentin agreed. Preston watched him, feeling a surge of resolve.

"We will, Your Honor," Quentin told him. "We'll see this through to the end."

The respect the younger man felt for the judge was inherent, a reminder that despite the judge's arduous ways and temperament, he was still appreciated and perhaps even admired.

As the group began to prepare to leave, lost in their own thoughts, the gravity of the revelations hung in the air. Outside, the sun dipped below the horizon, casting shadows across the room—a reminder that the darkness of the past was not so easily dispelled.

CHAPTER TWENTY-TWO

Preston blinked his eyes, adjusting to the early morning sun. The warm blaze of the sunlight slanted through the slats of the blinds, casting gentle patterns on the walls. Glancing at his alarm clock, he saw it was almost eight o'clock. For a lazy Saturday morning, he relished the luxury of sleeping in. He stretched pleasantly, savoring the comfort of his bed. After a few more minutes of relaxing slumber, he decided to get up. He padded over to the bathroom, the cool floor tiles on his bare feet in contrast to the warmth of the bed and began to prepare for the day ahead.

It was two weeks since the arrest of Mrs. Castle. In a revealing telephone call from Sloan earlier in the week, the family learned that while in custody, Mrs. Castle broke down and admitted it all: the attempts on the judge's life and how Mr. Lewis and Joan were killed by mistake, as the target had always been Judge Archie. She confessed to putting the yew berry juice in the teacup and the barbiturates in the aspirin bottle.

Sloan also informed them that Mrs. Castle confessed to pushing the judge on North Pearl Street in December and Mrs. Davis in front of the trolley, mistaking her for Mrs. Crabtree because of the burgundy coat. She attempted to kill Doris by pushing her into traffic on North Pearl Street, as she overheard her conversation on the telephone while out shopping during her lunch hour. She admitted to having the abortion in 1885 and to the murder of Mr. Philip Mavity. While even a teenager she had been involved with the underworld in Albany as his moll. He was also the father of her unborn child. She told the police that Mr. Mavity wanted nothing to do with her, so in retaliation she stabbed him in his apartment with a kitchen knife. Sloan concluded he would be available to speak to them at any time for further clarification.

Just yesterday, Preston called the hospital to inquire on Doris's condition. While listening to the nurse, he exhaled deeply, rubbing his temple, anticipating the worst. However, the family was relieved to learn that she had improved significantly. While her doctor insisted she rest, she had already made plans to return to the office as soon as she could. She looked forward to getting back to work and seeing her colleagues again.

Preston wrapped himself in his robe and thrust his feet into slippers, then made his way still rather sleepily toward the door. The rich fragrance of fresh coffee greeted him, always a pleasing scent. Descending the stairs, he heard his grandparents and mother in the living room, conversing and listening to the radio.

Upon entering and greeting them, he noticed they were dressed and must have been up for some time. It was a beautiful Saturday morning in early May, the windows were open, allowing the fresh air in and the scent of blooming flowers wafted in from the garden. A warm, golden light radiated the room, as the sun streamed through the long windows. Judge Archie, Augusta, and Martha sat comfortably, enjoying the peaceful morning.

"Good morning, dear," Augusta said, smiling. "You're certainly a sleepy head today!"

Preston stifled a yawn and then sat on the sofa next to his mother. He ran his fingers through his hair and felt the stubble on his face and neck. "I guess I needed the extra rest."

"I can reheat the oatmeal for you," Martha said as she turned a page of the *Times Union*.

Preston shook his head. "I'm not hungry at the moment," he told her.

They were silent for some time, Augusta knitting, Judge Archie reading a law book, and Martha engrossed in the morning newspaper. The sound of footsteps on the veranda broke the tranquility. Preston went to the hallway, opened the front door and then returned to the living room with the morning mail delivery. He stood by the sofa, sorting through the envelopes. Suddenly, he gasped in surprise, his eyes widening as he saw an envelope addressed to him.

"What is it, dear?" Augusta asked, rather concerned. She put her knitting aside, concern flickering across her face.

Preston's heart raced as he opened the envelope, revealing an acceptance letter for the fall semester at Albany Law School. He practically broke down as he read it aloud.

Martha, Augusta, and Judge Archie erupted in cheers and congratulations. The judge smiled broadly at his grandson, beckoning him to his armchair. He gave Preston a big hug, his eyes shining with pride. "You've earned this, Preston. I'm proud of you."

The burdens of the past seemed to lift, replaced by the bright promise of the future. The gentle rustle of leaves in the breeze drifted through the open windows, adding to the serene atmosphere. Clutching the acceptance letter with deep gratitude, he felt a sense of peace he had not known in months. The house, recently filled with sorrow, now felt like a sanctuary, bathed in the soft, golden light of the mid-morning sun. Preston felt the warmth and compassion from his mother and grandparents. New beginnings were always possible.

THE END

www.ingramcontent.com/pod-product-compliance
Lightning Source LLC
Chambersburg PA
CBHW070543310726
48982CB00010B/1456/J
* 9 7 8 1 7 8 3 2 4 3 7 7 8 *